BROKEN CODE

THE GENESIS OF REBELLION

THE HELIX CHRONICLES
BOOK 1

BROKEN CODE

THE GENESIS OF REBELLION

MONICA CHASE

Publishing Services provided by Paper Raven Books LLC
Printed in the United States of America
First Printing, 2024

ISBN 979-8-9904469-0-8

To the hearts that beat with mine—my family, my unwavering lighthouse; to Memphis, the rhythm to my words; and to the endless wonders of science, sparking the fire of my imagination. All of you are the music in the story of my life.

This book sings for you.

ONE

The Bluff City Standard Newspaper, Memphis, TN

Present Day

On the Brink of Revolution: The Double-Edged Sword of Genetic Enhancement, by Adam Burke

A single drop of blood—so small, yet with the power to alter the course of human history. The once theoretical marvels of CRISPR technology now loomed at the edge of reality, promising cures for diseases like sickle cell and the potential eradication of muscular dystrophy. But beneath these bright advancements, shadows were stirring.

Adam Burke's fingers flew over the keyboard in his cluttered office, piecing together the first lines of his latest exposé. Night had settled outside, but inside, his desk lamp cast a steady glow, fighting off the fatigue that threatened his focus. His determination as an investigative journalist didn't waver, driven by a hunger to unearth the truths hidden within scientific breakthroughs.

Dr. Anika Patel's warning resonated as he typed:

```
'CRISPR's power is monumental—akin to
a genetic Swiss Army knife. It allows
scientists to precisely alter DNA
sequences and modify gene function. Yet
such power demands extreme caution. Its
capabilities are boundless, but so too are
the potential risks it harbors.'
```

Adam paused, his thoughts veering towards the ominous interest shown by the Department of Defense. The potential of genetic technologies being weaponized was a chilling thought, one he couldn't ignore.

Leaning back, Adam massaged his weary eyes before delving deeper into his narrative. He envisioned a future fractured by genetic disparity, where access to CRISPR could become a luxury for the elite, deepening societal rifts. His article painted a vivid picture of looming conflicts—social upheaval, the crumbling of merit-based achievement, the emergence of a genetically enhanced elite.

This piece was more than an informative article; it was a wake-up call to the masses. Finishing his draft, he murmured, "Let's hope this gets people talking."

With a final scan, Adam pressed "send." His words, a fusion of caution and insight, disappeared into the digital ether, set to reach the citizens of Memphis and perhaps ignite a broader dialogue.

Adam Burke's fingers halted as Ben's voice echoed down the hall. "Adam, are you still here?" The concern in Ben's voice was clear. Glancing at the clock, Adam realized the late hour.

"Who else?" replied Adam, his fatigue obvious.

Ben appeared, worry etched on his face. "You need a break, Adam. This isn't healthy."

Adam's gaze stayed on his screen. "I can't, Ben. There's too much at stake. People need to be aware of the dangers of CRISPR."

"But at what cost to you?" Ben countered.

Adam's resolve was firm. "If I don't expose these truths, who will?" His focus returned to his article, driven by the immense implications of genetic editing.

The next morning, amidst a storm of negative feedback on his article, Adam's frustration mounted. Despite extensive research and expert consultations, his cautionary tale was met with skepticism.

He refocused on the heart of the issue: the lag in legal and ethical frameworks surrounding CRISPR. "If only they grasped the seriousness," he thought, disheartened by the dismissive reactions.

Ben's voice cut through his reverie. "We need to talk about the article's backlash," he said, stepping into the office.

Adam braced himself. "Is it that bad?"

"Mahogany Row isn't happy," Ben disclosed. "You've struck a nerve."

Adam sighed, his mind racing. "I just wanted to highlight the real issues, Ben. The science is advancing without adequate checks and balances."

Ben nodded, understanding his intent. "I get it, Adam, but there's a delicate balance here."

Adam leaned back, his thoughts turning to the co-inventor of CRISPR. "The creator feared her invention's potential weaponization after a literal nightmare involving Hitler. She's pushing for gene editing to be a force for good. But then, there's the Department of Defense," Adam continued, a hint of concern in his voice. "They're eyeing CRISPR too, hinting at countermeasures against misuse while also exploring... other possibilities."

Ben listened, his expression thoughtful. "It's a tricky road, Adam. Highlighting potential dangers is one thing, but sparking undue fear is another."

Adam nodded slowly, feeling the gravity of his role. "I know. And that's why we need to keep the conversation going. We can't let the potential dangers of CRISPR be swept under the rug."

With Ben's words echoing in his mind, Adam's commitment to revealing the complexities of genetic advancements remained firm. Despite the backlash, he knew his mission to inform and caution the public was more important than ever.

Ben Mitchell, a stalwart of journalism with his long, gray hair and newsroom-etched face, began his illustrious career in the 1970s at the *Memphis Press-Scimitar*. Navigating Memphis's crime-laden streets, he found himself captivated by the city's journalistic spirit and made it his home after graduating from Memphis State University. Despite a career that could have led to an early retirement, his wife Caroline's belief in his ongoing contribution to journalism kept him in the game.

One of Ben's protégés was Adam Burke. Unlike others who doubted Adam's unconventional story ideas, Ben saw their hidden potential and offered him both freedom and guidance.

With Ben having stepped out, Adam refocused on his computer screen. The echoes of past criticism spurred him to balance compelling storytelling with factual integrity. His previous exposé on PenCore had already shown his knack for unmasking corruption and power abuse.

Adam's own story was one of resilience. Raised in poverty and hardened by his father's battle with cancer, he was propelled by his parents' firm belief in education's transformative power. His journalistic zeal, sparked at the University of Tennessee, was noticed by Ben, who spotted his work in *The Daily Beacon* and brought him into the fold at *The Standard*. Under Ben's tutelage, Adam's raw talent and relentless drive flourished, pushing him to illuminate the darker corners of society.

The desk lamp's dim glow struggled to light the cramped, shadowy room filled with clutter. Adam's fingers drummed a restless rhythm on the desktop, echoing the blink of the taunting cursor on his screen.

Memories flooded back to him—sitting beside his father's hospital bed, watching the man he revered slowly succumb to cancer. His mother, burdened with the need to work three jobs due to lack of insurance and funds, only added to the painful recollection. These memories, too harrowing to dwell on, fueled a deep-seated suspicion about CRISPR and its potential for misuse. He had a gut feeling about the dangers, one he couldn't ignore.

Despite Ben's cautions, Adam couldn't pull himself away from the investigation. He was certain that something was amiss in the world of gene editing. His days and nights became a whirlwind of sifting through confidential documents and deciphering cryptic messages. His life now centered around uncovering what lay hidden in the industry.

"Hey, Adam," Lila, a colleague, greeted as she entered his cluttered office. "How's it going?"

"Slow but steady," he replied, his eyes betraying weariness. "I think I'm on the verge of a major breakthrough."

Lila's eyes flickered with concern. She took his hand in hers, saying softly, "Be careful, Adam. The people in Mahogany Row wield significant power. Their reach could be farther than we imagine." Her touch was tender as she let go of his hand.

"I have to expose them. If not me, then who will?" Adam asserted.

Lila nodded in agreement. "Just make sure this investigation doesn't consume you."

Adam paused, giving her a warm, reassuring smile before turning back to his work with renewed focus.

One night, following an intense interview with a whistleblower, Adam found himself at Wolf River Harbor. The Hernando de Soto Bridge's lights cast an otherworldly glow over the scene. Walking along the river's edge, he felt a deep connection to its dual nature of nurturing and destruction.

Many had underestimated Big Muddy's treacherous currents, often with fatal consequences.

"Is this the essence of having power over creation and destruction?" he wondered aloud.

Observing a lone piece of driftwood caught in the river's unyielding current, Adam saw a stark reminder of his role in a larger narrative, a point of no return.

Leaving the riverbank, his determination only hardened. Each step reinforced his commitment to truth, his constant in a world shrouded in ambiguity.

With a firm set of his jaw, Adam readied himself for the challenges ahead. Uncovering the hidden dangers of gene editing would be daunting, but he was prepared to confront any obstacle in his quest for the truth.

TWO

Downtown Law Firm, Memphis, TN
Present Day

Harper Brasfield, or 'Brass' to the bold few, entered the Chapman, Whitfield, & Gold Law Group office, her urgency almost desperate. Her normally sleek, dark waves were now unruly, barely held together by an elastic band. The fatigue deepened the lines on her face, and her movements—a slumped shoulder, a faint tremor in her hands—revealed the strain she was under.

Benched for six weeks, she was still seething with rage from her last encounter with the Assistant District Attorney. Back now, she couldn't dismiss the dread as she observed her colleagues' routine bustle.

Trying to shake off a hangover and anxiety, Harper hardly noticed her assistant at first.

Melanie's voice wavered slightly. "Glad you're back, Ms. Brasfield. I've missed you."

Harper responded curtly, "Thanks, I guess," her words

sharper than she intended. She felt the weight of regret almost immediately, wishing she could pull the words back as soon as they were out.

The office air felt oppressively thick, charged with the electric current of whispered gossip and silent judgments. In a burst of frustration, Harper's hand swiped at a precariously stacked pile of files, sending them cascading across the floor. As she knelt to retrieve the papers, muttering curses, Melanie stepped forward to help.

Their hands briefly met amid the chaos of scattered documents, a fleeting touch that brought Harper face-to-face with the concern etched deep in Melanie's eyes. This unintended intimacy only deepened Harper's discomfort, enveloping her more fully. She murmured a terse 'thank-you,' her eyes carefully averted from Melanie's sincere look.

"You know, maybe easing back into things " Melanie started.

"No," Harper interjected sharply, her gaze firm. "I'm fine. Just keep the coffee coming."

Melanie left, casting a worried glance back. Alone, Harper sank into her chair, exhaling loudly and massaging her temples. She needed the work, craved the immersion to escape the turmoil of her life. Focusing on the first file in the now tidy stack, she braced for the day's challenges.

Harper stumbled into her home downtown in South Bluffs after a grueling day, the whispers of her colleagues still echoing in her mind. The dimly lit house, cluttered with unopened mail, scattered clothes, and wine bottles, mirrored her internal chaos.

Memories of happier times—Charlotte dancing with her father, Lucas's toys strewn on the floor, the aroma of baking cakes—now only intensified her sense of loss. Trapped between the pain of the past and the longing for a fresh start, Harper felt the weight of her shattered dreams.

Rob, her estranged husband, lingered in her thoughts. She had affectionately shortened his name from Robert, a playful claim on him, while he had lovingly nicknamed her 'Brass.' Their relationship, facilitated by her best friend Deandra, had once seemed unbreakable. Yet, somewhere along the way, their perfect life—his engineering career, her law practice, their two children—had crumbled. Harper blamed herself, recognizing her role in pushing Rob away, yet she couldn't find the words to apologize.

Frustrated, she kicked a damp towel aside and noticed Rob's belongings piled in a corner, a stark reminder of their failed marriage. As a surge of anger and grief overwhelmed her, her lips moved in a silent reproach, her voice caught in the raw turbulence of her emotions.

Collapsing onto the couch, Harper grappled with feelings of inadequacy. She had always been the strong one, but now she felt like an imposter, struggling to keep her life together. The internal criticism was relentless, berating her for failing her children, her colleagues, and her clients.

"Enough!" she shouted, the word echoing in the silent house. She paused, seeking stillness to quell the inner turmoil.

Determined to reclaim some control, Harper focused on packing Rob's belongings. With every item she meticulously placed into the box, it felt as though a weight was being lifted from her shoulders. As each object found its place, her determination deepened: she wouldn't let her life unravel. Rising from the couch with renewed hope, Harper committed to facing whatever challenges lay ahead. Packing Rob's things was a small but significant step towards rebuilding her life and silencing her doubts.

The morning sun filtered through the blinds, casting shadows across Harper's cluttered office. She sat at her desk, surrounded by stacks of legal documents and case files, her eyes bloodshot from hours of relentless research. The ringing phone cut through the silence like a knife, jolting her back to reality.

She responded abruptly, using her fingers to pinch the top of her nose as if it could ease the pain in her head that had been there for days. "Brasfield," she said.

"Ms. Brasfield, it's George Nelson, your client. I've been trying to reach you for a while now. What's going on with my case?"

"George, I promise you I'm doing everything in my power to make sure you get the best outcome."

"Alright, Brass."

The moniker brought a slight grin to her lips. "Thanks," she said.

She hung up before he could speak and returned to her growing pile of work. George's case was merely one of many that called upon the legendary Brass. She needed to dig deep to find her.

As the day progressed, Harper noticed the increase in whispers and concerned looks among her colleagues. Their attempts to engage her were met with nothing more than a curt nod or a brief, sharp reply, her attention fixed on the documents before her. Once a beacon of strength and stability in the office, Harper had gradually become withdrawn, her interactions growing distant and mechanical. In her mind, she was building a protective barrier around herself, a necessary defense even if it meant sacrificing the warmth and camaraderie she once cherished with her team.

A tentative knock interrupted Harper's focus. Through the slightly ajar door, a concerned coworker peeked in. "Harper, everything alright? You've been at this nonstop."

Without lifting her gaze, she responded abruptly, "I have a lot on my plate."

The coworker hesitated, then nodded, slowly retreating. "Just... take care, okay?"

Harper's internal struggle showed no signs of easing. She threw herself into her work, trying to find some sense of achievement in her professional skills. Yet she couldn't shake the nagging doubts. *They see right through you. You're falling apart.*

She forced herself to focus on the legal documents again, seeking comfort in the familiar work routine that used to bring order to her life.

As the evening turned to night and the office building grew calm, Harper's office was still lit up. She was determined to accomplish something meaningful before leaving.

When the clock ushered in a new day, Harper finally stopped. Leaning back, she surveyed the sea of papers and notes around her. It wasn't ideal, but it felt like a small step in the right direction.

Harper's eyes fell on the photograph of her, Rob, Lucas, and Charlotte, taken years ago when they had been a happier family. The silver frame caught the morning light, casting a soft glow around their smiling faces. She traced the contours of her son's face with her fingertips, the glass cool against her skin.

"Ms. Brasfield." Melanie knocked gently on the door before entering. "I have the updated case files you requested."

Harper mumbled a thank-you, quickly turning her attention back to the mountain of work on her desk. She adjusted in her chair, arms crossed as if to guard against the fear she was struggling to hide.

"Can I assist you with anything else?" Melanie inquired, hesitating in the doorway.

"Actually, yes," Harper said, straightening her posture. "Can you please schedule a meeting with George Nelson? I'd like to discuss our strategy in person."

"Of course." Melanie nodded and paused for a moment. "And Ms. Brasfield, if you ever need to talk, I'm here."

"Thank you, Melanie." Harper managed a small smile, touched by her assistant's concern.

Melanie left with a nod, closing the door behind her. Alone, Harper's façade momentarily slipped, and she confronted the weight of her strained relationships with her children. She glanced at her phone, the screen showing missed calls from Lucas. Each missed call was a sharp pang of guilt. Lucas's message played. "Hey, Mom. Guess we missed each other again. Wanted to know how you're doing. Call me back when you can."

She knew she should return his call, but the words eluded her. How could she bridge the growing gap between them? Anger mixed with guilt; she was so engulfed in her own struggles that reaching out seemed impossible. The divorce had taken its toll on everyone, and while she hoped time would heal, the fear of lasting scars lingered.

A silent curse slipped out as tears threatened to fall. Harper fiercely held them back, refusing to surrender to her emotions.

She picked up her phone and dialed Lucas's number, her heart pounding with each ring. After a few seconds, his voicemail greeting filled her ear.

"Lucas, it's me," she began, her voice trembling. "I'm sorry I haven't been able to talk lately. Work has been… overwhelming. But I miss you, and I want us to reconnect. Let's try to meet up soon, alright? I love you."

Harper ended the call, feeling a mixture of relief and sadness wash over her. At least she made contact, even if it was just a message. It was a start.

Harper threw herself back into her cases with renewed determination, her mind a tightrope walk between her son's needs and her clients' quest for justice. She wouldn't allow the turmoil of her personal life to seep into her professional one. The stakes were simply too high. She owed it to her clients, her colleagues, and, above all, to her children, to not falter.

Hunched over her desk, Harper felt a hot flash sear through her, beads of sweat forming despite the whir of the air conditioning in her outdated Adams Avenue office. She gripped the legal briefs tightly, knuckles blanching, as she willed herself to focus, pushing through the oppressive heat that seemed to mirror her internal struggle.

In the doorway, Deandra Jackson's voice carried a hint of hesitation, woven with concern. "Brass, are you alright? Is there something going on you want to talk about?" She scanned the surroundings, alert for eavesdroppers. Deandra, Harper's lifelong best friend and fellow attorney, pressed her with questions, but Harper wasn't prepared to face them yet.

Harper's walls shot up, her voice sharp. "I'm managing, Dee. Let's not do this here." The bond that once felt unbreakable now seemed fragile, strained to its limits.

But Deandra's gaze held a weary understanding, a departure from her usual confidence. "I've known you forever, Harper. This isn't you. You've changed... Talk to me."

Harper felt cornered, her voice quivering. "Dee, it's all just... too much. The menopause, the mood swings... I don't even recognize myself."

Deandra sighed loudly, her words deliberate. "We all face tough times, Harper. But it impacts everyone, the whole team. We're all feeling it."

Tears welled up in Harper's eyes. "I know, Dee. I've felt the distance, and it hurts. We've been through so much..."

Deandra's expression softened, conveying a mix of compassion and caution. "Harper, it's about rebuilding trust, not just with the team, but with me too. We need time and space to heal and reconnect. It won't happen overnight."

As Harper gazed at the fading light over Memphis, reality sank in. She faced Deandra, resolute. "I'll fix this. They deserve an explanation. And I need to cope better."

Deandra hesitated, then offered, "There's someone who can help. They're discreet. Think about it, okay? We're here for you, always."

Harper's tears flowed freely. "Thanks, Dee. Rawls Hall girls, right?" A weak smile flickered.

Harper was swept up in memories, recalling her bond with Deandra from their carefree school days to now. She felt a pang of guilt over their growing distance and yearned for those simpler times.

With a reassuring squeeze on Harper's arm, Deandra left her in solitude. Harper steadied herself. It was time to mend fences and find her way back.

THREE

A heavy silence hung over the negotiation room, punctuated by the rustle of papers and the occasional cough. Harper's gaze, steady and accusing, was locked on ADA Marcus Turner, who lounged in his chair with a smirk that oozed condescension.

He leaned forward, his voice slick with a patronizing tone. "Ms. Brasfield, in light of your recent... shall we say, colorful criticisms of the justice system, this offer is more than generous. I'd take it if I were you."

Harper's jaw tightened, her anger a live wire beneath her skin. "Your 'evidence' is about as solid as your integrity. This isn't about justice for you, is it, Turner?"

Waving her off, Turner sneered. "Relax, Ms. Brasfield. Don't let your emotions overrule your better judgment—again."

Her voice, sharp as a blade, cut him off. "Demanding

justice for my client is emotional? Or is it too much to expect you to understand that?"

His smirk widened. "If that's how you want to spin it, Brass. Seems your reputation for being unhinged is well-earned."

She leaned in, her voice a low growl. "I'll show you unhinged if you keep mistaking my passion for justice as weakness."

Turner's retort was smug, taunting. "Oh, I see plenty of passion, but I'm still waiting on the substance."

Harper's scoff was derisive. "You underestimate me at your own peril."

Turner's laughter was abrasive, riling her further. "All fire and bluster. It's predictable."

"I am justice," she hissed, the words slicing through the tension.

He stood, the smirk never leaving his face. "Prove it in court. Your call, Ms. Brasfield."

Her face turned scarlet, a testament to her contained fury, as the room seemed to tilt around her. "Enough!" The sound of her palms hitting the table sent papers scattering like startled birds. "You have no right!"

The room fell silent, Turner's confident veneer cracking for a moment before snapping back into place.

"Someone's hormonal," he sniggered, just loud enough to carry.

Harper surged to her feet, her voice venomous. "Who the hell do you think you are?" Turner recoiled, his arrogance faltering.

"Do your damn job!" she bellowed, her arm sweeping the table and sending a glass of water crashing to the floor.

Silence reigned. Harper, breathless with righteous indignation, stormed out with her client in tow. Outside, she leaned heavily against the corridor wall, gasping for air as the threat of sanctions loomed.

"Are you sure you're okay?" her client asked, concern edging her voice.

Harper straightened, steel in her spine. "I'm fine. Let's go."

Her resolve was ironclad, a stark contrast to the chaos inside. The trust her client placed in her was the beacon she'd follow into the coming storm.

As Harper sat in her office, surrounded by the familiar scent of worn leather and stale coffee, she couldn't escape the weight of her tumultuous past year. Her impulsive media interview accusing the system of corruption had teetered her career on the edge. Challenging a judge's verdict publicly and her fiery encounter with the ADA weeks before, splashed across newspapers, only darkened her already tarnished reputation.

In this room, surrounded by case files and enveloped in silence, Harper often felt adrift, caught between her own determination and a sense of disconnection. The aftermath of her confrontation with the ADA lingered in her mind, unsettling her. She envisioned hushed conversations among the senior partners and felt their disapproval. Her six-week suspension now appeared almost lenient. Driven to reassert her value, she immersed herself in work, clocking in billable hours long into the night.

Harper sighed, her mind wandering to brighter days. Once, she'd been at the top of her game, unraveling complex cases, basking in her colleagues' respect. She reminisced about the times when her relationship with Rob was solid, and their children, Lucas and Charlotte, were the heart of their life together.

But now, the thought of Charlotte, who had chosen to live with Rob, pained her. Harper knew it wasn't about proximity to her private school; it was a direct rebuke against her prioritizing work over family, a choice that had cost her dearly.

Holding her phone tightly, she was on the brink of dialing when it suddenly rang. It was Charlotte. Wiping her sweaty palms on her shirt, Harper eagerly answered.

"Mom?"

"Hey, sweetie. How are you?"

"Fine."

"Are you excited about graduation?"

"Yeah, I guess... It's not for, like, months, Mom."

"Charlie, I know things haven't been great between us... but I want you to understand why I've worked so hard," Harper began, reaching out to her daughter.

"It's Charlotte, Mom," she corrected sharply, her tone laced with frustration. "And I don't need another speech about your career..."

"Please, just listen. I did it for you and Lucas, too. I wanted to show you that women can be just as strong and successful as men."

"Maybe you're right. But sometimes I wish you could've been there for us more."

"I know, and I'm sorry."

"Mom, I have to go. Can we talk about this later?"

"Of course, I love you, Charlotte."

"Love you too, Mom."

Harper felt a glimmer of hope as she hung up the phone.

"Harper? Still working?" a voice called out, startling her from her reverie.

"Of course, Sam." She forced a smile as her boss entered the room. "Burning the midnight oil."

"Listen, about the incident with the ADA... I've been getting some heat from the other senior partners," Sam admitted, rubbing the back of his neck nervously.

"Really?" Harper feigned surprise, her heart sinking as she realized her situation was worse than she'd thought. "I didn't think it was that big of a deal."

"Unfortunately, it is. They're not happy, Harper. They want you to apologize publicly to the rest of the firm. I really went to bat for you, Harper, but I'm afraid this is nonnegotiable. It took a lot of groveling and ego stroking with the DA's office to avoid formal sanctions."

Her gaze intensified, a swell of indignation and bitterness surging within her. Despite her years of unwavering dedication and numerous triumphs for the firm, they still demanded her subservience. Wasn't her six-week hiatus supposed to have wiped the slate clean?

"Fine," she conceded, folding her arms tightly. "I'll do it."

"Thank you, Harper. Sometimes we have to swallow our pride for the greater good," Sam said with a sympathetic smile before leaving.

In the midst of her struggles, Harper could still feel a spark of her former self. The once-formidable lawyer, known for turning the tide in the most hopeless cases, was still there, under the scrutiny of her colleagues and the burden of her own pride.

Standing before the mirror on her office door, she straightened her pristine white blouse and made a silent vow to reaffirm her unmatched legal prowess.

The conference room buzzed with subdued chatter as Harper entered. Associates and partners, some familiar for years, filled the seats. A wave of tension washed over the room, their eyes a mix of curiosity and judgment. Dee's empty chair stood out, a stark reminder of the rifts yet to be mended.

Taking a deep breath, Harper faced them at the podium. "Thank you for gathering," she began, her voice betraying no hint of the storm within. "I'll be direct. My recent actions have not reflected well on our firm, and for that, I am sincerely sorry."

Harper scanned the room, making eye contact with many familiar faces. "For almost thirty years, I've been part of this legal community, alongside many of you. Together, we've celebrated victories and learned from our losses. My commitment to this firm and to all of you is unwavering. I take full responsibility and will ensure we don't face a situation like this again."

She paused, her voice strengthening. "We've all faced challenges, both professionally and personally. It's not about never faltering; it's about how we recover when we do."

Harper took a deep breath, then shared a personal story. "I remember, early in my career here, I was working on a particularly tough case. The night before the trial, I was here, alone, burning the midnight oil. Jim, our late-night security guard, brought me a cup of coffee. He said, 'Harper, you've got this. Nobody sorts out a mess like you do. Keep on pushing.' That simple act of kindness, his belief in me, it's stayed with me. This firm is more than just a workplace; it's a family. And like a family, we support each other, through triumphs and mistakes."

She then challenged the room. "If anyone here can claim they've never erred, please stand up." The room stayed still.

"That's what I thought," Harper said, a soft smile appearing. "We're all human. We make mistakes, and we grow from them. I'm asking for your support, as equals, as partners on this journey."

As Harper concluded, a contemplative silence fell over the room. Then, gradually, figures rose from their seats. It wasn't a sweeping gesture of forgiveness, but rather a cautious acknowledgment of her earnest effort. Harper could see in their hesitant movements a budding willingness to rebuild, a fragile yet hopeful first step towards mending the bonds within the firm.

"Thank you," she said, her voice a fusion of relief and determination. "Together, let's begin the journey of moving forward, continuing our pursuit of legal excellence for Memphis."

As Harper stepped back, the room's atmosphere subtly shifted. Despite Dee's absence, she felt a renewed sense of purpose. There were bridges to rebuild and challenges to face, but Harper was determined, fueled by the same resolve that had always defined her.

As her colleagues dispersed or resorted to checking their phones, a familiar face stood out.

"Brass!" Sam Chapman called out, his voice cutting through the lingering echoes of clapping hands. "A moment, please."

Harper felt uncertain as they made eye contact in the crowded conference room. She had faced far more daunting adversaries in her time, and she squared her shoulders, striding confidently toward her boss.

"Sam," she greeted him, offering a tight-lipped smile. "What can I do for you?"

"That was quite a speech," he acknowledged, a hint of warmth in his expression. "Your message seems to be resonating with everyone here. Now, let's get back to work."

Harper's stomach twisted as she nodded, bracing herself for whatever the senior partner had in store. Sam handed her a thick manila folder and warned her it was a challenging case.

With quick, practiced eyes, Harper scanned the summary

pages inside, feeling anticipation building within her. She was eager to prove her capabilities and show she was back.

"Thank you, Sam," she breathed as she closed the folder. "I won't let you down."

"See that you don't. It's a slim chance, to be honest. Our client is facing his third strike, which means a life sentence, and the prosecution won't budge an inch on the charges."

The thrill of the courtroom was beckoning, and Harper was determined to rise to the challenge. Harper's heart sank as she realized how bleak their chances were. A three-strikes case was notoriously difficult to win, especially in a city where the law was so mercilessly enforced.

"Every defendant deserves the best defense possible," she said, clutching the folder tightly. "And I intend to provide just that."

"Good," Sam repeated, his eyes searching hers for any hint of doubt or weakness. "I know you can do it, Harper. Just remember, we're all counting on you."

As she stood there, Harper knew that this case would be the ultimate test. A way to prove she was still a formidable attorney to herself and colleagues.

She mouthed a silent thank-you, her voice muffled by the clatter of the conference room. Sam nodded in response. "I won't let you—or our client—down."

FOUR

Years ago, it was Judge Isaac Jackson's glowing recommendation that led Sam Chapman to offer Harper a position at the firm. She had always respected Sam for his unwavering integrity, which made her current unease even more disconcerting.

Even during her suspension, Sam had shown faith in her, maintaining contact and offering support. But now, as she sat at her desk, fingers tensely gripping the edge, Harper couldn't escape an awful feeling. The case file before her seemed like an intricate maze, and she couldn't shake the suspicion that it was a setup, a test designed to lead her to failure.

"Brass, you alright?" Sam Chapman's voice broke the silence as he leaned against the door frame, his face etched with concern.

She glanced up at him, forcing a tight smile. "Yeah, just going over this case you assigned me. Seems like a real winner."

"Harper, I know it's not an easy one, but I trust you. You're the best we've got," he said.

She suspected the other senior partners had coerced Sam into giving her this hopeless case as humiliation. Despite her rousing apology, their faith in her remained tenuous.

"Thanks, Sam." Her voice betrayed none of her doubts. "With the new three-strikes law in Tennessee, it's gonna be tough. The DA's office might treat me poorly after my encounter with ADA Turner."

"Look, Brass, you can handle it. You always do," Sam assured her, his gaze steady. "Just give it your all, like you always do."

Harper's jaw relaxed as she nodded vigorously, signaling her understanding that everyone deserved a proper defense, regardless of their past.

Sam nodded, his face softening at her determination. "I'll leave you to it then. Remember, if you need anything, I'm here."

Harper paused; her gaze momentarily lost in thought. Then, clearing her throat, she managed a meek response before her attention shifted back to the documents on her desk.

Just as Sam was about to leave, he hesitated. "Oh, and Harper, there's one more thing. I've been in touch with ADA Turner and his office, and…"

Harper let out an exasperated sigh, her posture suddenly rigid in the chair. "Out with it, Sam."

"Brass, please call the man and apologize."

"Copy that, boss. On it."

"This isn't an order, Brass. It's a firm suggestion you may

want to consider for your future success within the Criminal Court system."

Harper's face twisted into a wry smile. "You're right, as usual, Sam."

"I'm relieved we've gotten that out of the way. Go ahead and kick some butt. Just make sure it's not from the prosecutor's office."

Harper sighed and pinched the bridge of her nose. She knew an apology was necessary, but even thinking about it filled her with dread. Today wasn't about her discomfort; it was about giving her client undivided attention.

As she delved into the details of the case, a knot formed in her stomach. The crime was horrific. An elderly woman was brutally assaulted during a robbery. She couldn't back down from the case despite her waning enthusiasm.

Harper sifted through the evidence, searching for any glimmer of hope to cling to. She would not let this case break her; she would fight for her client until the very end, no matter how hopeless it seemed.

Harper looked up from her mound of paperwork as she entered the Glamor Slammer, Memphis's city jail known for its stark 1980s architecture. Ethan Cook, the firm's seasoned investigator, stood out with his sharp suit and neatly tied tie, a stark contrast to the drab surroundings. His military haircut hinted at a disciplined past.

Harper had immense trust in Ethan; his experience

in law enforcement provided him with a deep insight into the city's gang dynamics. His intelligence was equally impressive, allowing him to assimilate complex information with remarkable speed.

"Hey, Brass," Ethan greeted her warmly, his eyes crinkling at the corners. "You ready for this?"

Harper tucked a strand of dark hair behind her ear and took a deep breath. "As ready as I'll ever be."

Ethan opened the door for her and offered her a warm smile.

"I'm glad you're here, Ethan."

"Wouldn't miss it for the world."

Deep inside the building, in a compact room with stale air, they waited to meet Harper's new client. Finally, the door opened, and Darrius Robinson sauntered in, flanked by a guard. The young man barely looked twenty, but his hardened expression and the tattoos snaking up his arms told a different story. He was surly and reeked of defiance.

Darrius slunk into the chair, his eyes narrowing as he sized up Harper. His lips twisted into a sneer as he spat out the question. "Yo, you my lawyer?"

"Harper Brasfield," she introduced herself, extending her hand. Darrius ignored it, his eyes flicking between her and Ethan with suspicion.

Harper raised her chin and gestured towards Ethan. "This is the investigator who will help me with your case."

She took a step back, but kept her hand extended. "We're here to discuss your defense strategy."

Darrius scoffed and slouched in his chair. His voice was

full of disbelief. "Defense? Ain't no defense. They got me, right?"

Harper's throat tightened as she tried to quell her nerves. Darrius's hostility was unambiguous, and his voice dripped with disdain. She resisted the urge to lean back and glanced at Ethan instead, grateful for his presence.

"Everyone deserves a proper defense, Mr. Robinson."

Darrius slammed his fist on the table. Anger filled his eyes, and he shook his head, "Man, I ain't talkin' 'bout nothin'. You think you gonna save me or somethin'? Lady, I'm done."

Harper leaned in and fixed him with a steely gaze. She had momentarily forgotten her fear. "I'm not here to play games. Your life is on the line, so I suggest you take this seriously."

"Or what?" Darrius leaned closer. "You gon' lock me up for life? Oh, wait, they already tryna do that."

Ethan snapped his fingers, and both of their attention shifted to him. "Harper is trying to help you, man. You need to work with her."

Darrius glared at Ethan before turning to Harper again. His expression changed from hostile to something more lascivious as he grinned. "A'ight, baby girl," he drawled. "Let's see what you got."

Her heart pounded as Harper straightened and spoke sternly. "Mr. Robinson, I will not tolerate any disrespect. We're going to work together on your defense, whether you like it or not."

"Fine," Darrius spat, slouching back in his chair.

Harper was acutely aware of the risks involved in

dealing with Darrius. His unpredictable behavior, swinging between overt aggression and aloof withdrawal, presented a formidable challenge. This didn't just unsettle Harper; it also complicated her approach, forcing her to constantly adjust to his unpredictable shifts from confrontational to disengaged.

Harper remained steadfast, her focus unwavering as she delved into the case, committed to delivering the strongest defense possible. As she sifted through Darrius's extensive criminal history, her attention was drawn to a reference to Tall Trees, a juvenile facility notorious for its brutal abuse allegations. Noting that Darrius had spent time there, she pondered the impact of such an experience on him, deepening her resolve to understand and effectively represent him.

"Darrius," she began gently. "I see you spent time in Tall Trees."

He clenched his fists, and the veins in his neck bulged. "Damn right I did!" His eyes lit up with fury. "That hellhole ain't no place for kids." He spat out the words like venom. "They don't give a damn 'bout us, only 'bout the money they makin' off our misery."

"Tell me more about your experiences there," Harper pressed, despite her unease. She needed to understand his past if she was going to build a solid defense.

"Those so-called guards be some real gangstas, yo," Darrius spat angrily, his voice rising higher with each passing moment. "They'd jump on you for the slightest thing, laughin' cuz they ain't got no fear of nothin'. An' that Warden? That mothafucka close his eye to all a' that, as long as the money keep comin' in. They wanted us to know dat place belonged to somebody else, not the city so dey could do whateva dey wanted."

As Darrius spoke, Harper felt her stomach churn, both from his words and the furious passion behind them. She pushed herself to stay focused, making mental notes of every detail he provided. Whatever remnants of innocence may have once existed in Darrius had been crushed beneath the boot of Tall Trees.

Darrius opened his mouth to continue his rant, but she brought her hand up. "Don't.

"I get it. You've been through a lot. But focus on what's in front of you now: life without parole. If you want help, then ditch the attitude and work with me."

"Fine," Darrius spat, the fire in his eyes momentarily dimmed. "I'll do what I gotta do."

"Good." Harper nodded, her heart pounding as she faced down the young man who seemed to embody the worst of humanity. She couldn't back down now, despite knowing it would be an uphill battle.

She kept her voice steady, although turmoil swirled within her. "We should start by discussing the case's facts. Knowing more helps me represent you better."

As they dove into the details, Harper felt the old Brass coming to life within her. She would fight for Darrius's defense with every ounce of her skill—even if it meant facing demons from both their pasts.

She noticed the way his eyes gleamed when she recounted the facts of the case, his smile widening as if to confirm his guilt without actually saying the words. It was a dangerous game he was playing—one that would likely cost him his freedom.

Harper studied Darrius's face as he leaned back, hands clasped behind his head, a smug grin spreading across his lips. "My gang is my family," he bragged, the gold glinting from his teeth clashing with the cold fluorescent lights of the room. "We got each other's backs, no matter what. This charge ain't nothin'."

"Alright, Darrius," Harper began, placing the case file down on the table and clasping her hands. "Looking at the evidence we're up against, we need to weigh our options carefully." She felt a pang of hopelessness as the conversation progressed, despite her best efforts to find a viable angle for his defense.

"First, we can attempt to suppress some of the evidence," she began, watching his expression for any sign of comprehension or interest. "If they got it illegally or violated your rights, we might convince the judge to exclude it."

Darrius's gaze dropped to the floor, his words barely audible. "Whatever works."

A chill ran through Harper at the thought of her client admitting guilt for a plea bargain, but she pushed it down and cleared her throat.

"If you have credible information about other criminal activities, the DA may work with you on a plea bargain…"

"Snitchin' ain't my style, lady," Darrius spat with contempt emanating from him like a force field. "I ain't gonna turn on my family for some deal."

"Understood," Harper nodded, her pulse quickening as

she steeled herself for the inevitable conflict.

"Finally, we can take this case to trial and fight for your acquittal," she said, her voice firm. Harper wrung her hands, her expression grave. "The three-strikes law has stacked the odds against us," she began, her voice firm yet empathetic. "Under this law, because of your past offenses, the state sees you as a 'persistent offender.' It means they're coming at you harder this time. A third felony conviction could lead to a significantly harsher sentence, potentially life imprisonment. It's a heavy-handed approach, and it's put us in a tough spot."

Darrius remained defiant. "They ain't gon' break me."

Harper nodded, understanding his resilience. "I know you're tough, but we need to approach this with strategy and caution. It's not just about proving innocence or guilt now; it's about navigating a system that's already biased against you. We're going to fight this, but you need to be prepared for every angle they might use."

As she laid out the stark reality, the client's tough exterior showed a crack, the enormity of his situation sinking in. Harper's words had not only outlined the legal battle ahead, but had also underlined the personal struggle that came with it.

A profound sadness washed over Harper as she regarded Darrius. Behind his tough exterior, she saw a young man lost in the harshness of life, a soul adrift in a sea of adversity.

Witnessing the defiance flickering in his eyes, his apparent denial of the severity of his predicament, Harper's resolve deepened. She felt a compelling need to steer him away from the destructive course his life had taken.

She scribbled on a piece of paper and gave him an intense look. "We're in this together," she said, her voice heavy with determination. She fixed him with a gaze that asked for his loyalty and trust. "Can you do that?"

He met her gaze, the fire in his eyes burning brighter than ever, and nodded. "Yeah. I got you."

After the door clicked shut behind Darrius, Harper leaned against the table, her shoulders sagging with the weight of the case before her. Ethan stood and paced the tiny room, his arms crossed over his chest as he studied her.

"Brass," he began, his voice a mix of sympathy and pragmatism. "You might just try sweet-talking the DA's office. See if they're open to reducing the charges."

Harper let out a sardonic chuckle, her eyes narrowing as she considered the idea. She knew Ethan meant well, but the prospect seemed laughably impossible. The three-strikes law had no wiggle room. And she was still in the DA's doghouse. Still, she rubbed her temples and sighed, mulling it over. "I suppose it couldn't hurt to try, though I doubt they'll budge."

Ethan nodded, understanding the futility of the suggestion, but their options were limited. Harper straightened up and changed the subject, her mind still turning over every angle.

"Tell me, Ethan, do you know anything about Tall Trees? The juvenile facility Darrius mentioned?"

Ethan's expression darkened, and he shifted his weight, looking uncomfortable. "Yeah, I've heard some horror stories. It's run by a private company called PenCore Limited. They take over when government entities want out of the incarceration business. Thing is they're driven by profits, so corners are cut—conditions are bad, real bad."

Harper felt a shiver of disgust crawl up her spine as she absorbed this new information. She pictured the young, hardened Darrius trapped in such a place, subjected to the worst kind of treatment. Her determination to help him only grew stronger.

Her lips twisted in a sneer. "Profits over people."

The sadness in Ethan's eyes had aged him beyond his years as he nodded. "Unfortunately, yeah."

"Well, we'll do what we can for Darrius. Somehow, we'll find a way to help him."

"I'm with you, Brass. Whatever it takes."

"Let's get out of here. I have work to do."

In the quiet of the next morning, Harper's thoughts lingered on her recent meeting with Darrius. It wasn't just his case that weighed on her; she felt a deeper calling to challenge the system that ensnared so many like him. Steeling herself for the battle ahead, she drew strength from Ethan's unwavering support. Together, they stood a chance to make a meaningful difference.

As she watched the rain slide down her office window, a mirror to her tumultuous thoughts, Harper felt a profound sense of injustice stir within her. The more she delved into PenCore's actions and their impact on young inmates like Darrius, the more her determination solidified. She couldn't—wouldn't—let them get away with their corrupt deeds. Harper was ready to fight back, to peel back the layers of deceit and bring the truth to light.

"Hey, Ethan," she said, "you mentioned earlier that there have been rumors about PenCore. Any specific stories come to mind?"

Ethan's brow furrowed as he recalled what he'd heard. "Well, I remember reading about some investigative journalist who dug into the company. They cited anonymous sources, but nothing concrete ever came out of it. Years ago, there was a wrongful death lawsuit. I think PenCore paid a trivial amount to settle it."

A sudden determination flared in Harper's eyes. "Locate the journalist who wrote about PenCore. I need to talk to them."

Ethan's fingers flew over the phone as he launched into a search. "Sure thing, Brass."

Each click of Harper's heels on the polished office floor echoed her racing thoughts, dominated by Darrius and the dark cloud of his past. This case was more than just a fight for justice for her client; it was also a quest for her own redemption. Harper aimed to reveal how a flawed system shaped Darrius, hoping to mitigate his sentence by highlighting these injustices in court.

Her heart pounded at the thought of uncovering deep-seated corruption and amplifying the voices of those silenced. Visions of young, faceless victims haunted her, their pain unmistakable. While confronting systemic abuse wasn't typically the role of a defense attorney, Harper was adamant about bringing these critical issues to the attention of those capable of enacting change.

"Got something here," Ethan announced, breaking through her thoughts. "An investigative journalist by the name of Adam Burke wrote a piece in *The Bluff City Standard* last year. It seems to be the most in-depth report I've found so far. He interviewed me once for background information and seemed like a decent guy."

Harper's eyes sparkled with anticipation as she clapped her hands together. "Good work! Let's set up a meeting."

"Consider it done." Ethan's fingers flew across his phone's screen as he typed out a message to the reporter.

FIVE

Harper stood by the brick exterior of Front Street Deli, where the aroma of freshly baked bread spilled out from the open door. A Memphis favorite, it had been her preferred spot ever since she first savored their sumptuous salads. The anticipation of their taste made her mouth water. Glancing at her watch, she felt a twinge of frustration at Adam Burke's tardiness. Eager for the meeting, Harper hoped the investigative reporter from *The Bluff City Standard* would offer the crucial insights she desperately needed.

As Harper waited, her mind wandered to Deandra. Their friendship had been strained lately, and the recent confrontation with ADA Turner had only exacerbated the tension. Harper let out a deep sigh, burdened by their troubled relationship. Seeking a moment of comfort, she took out her phone and dialed Deandra's number.

"Hey, Dee!"

"Harper."

Harper's heart sank as she heard Deandra's voice, now infused with a defensive edge instead of its usual warmth.

"Listen, I just wanted to talk about what happened… I'm really sorry about everything. I guess you heard about my apology to the firm. I didn't see you—"

"Can't talk now."

"Dee, please. I can't handle us being like this."

"Harper, we'll work it out… someday. I need some time, okay?"

"Okay."

Deandra murmured back a distant goodbye before ending the call, leaving Harper to stare at her phone in disbelief.

Harper steadied herself. She couldn't afford to fall apart now, not with her meeting with Adam Burke looming. She was determined to get the answers she needed and wouldn't let personal issues, including the strain in her relationships, derail her quest for justice. Resolutely, she entered the deli, prepared for whatever challenges awaited.

Inside, Harper scanned the lively scene of laughter and the clatter of dishes. She hoped for Deandra's presence at Sunday dinner, but knew not to count on it. As she pondered this, Harper's half-smile curved her lips as she dialed the number of the Jacksons, familiar and warm like home.

"Hey there, Harper sweetie. What can I do for you, dear?" Mama Dee's Southern drawl coated the words like sweet molasses.

"Hi, Mama Dee." Harper bit her lip. "Do you need me to bring anything for Sunday dinner?"

Mama Dee's response was gentle but firm. "Now, you know I never ask my guests to bring anything, honey. But you're always welcome to surprise us."

Harper's sigh of relief was audible as she ended the call. "Alright, Mama Dee, thank you. I'll see you Sunday," she said with gratitude. At least one relationship had survived the storm.

Harper put away her phone as the door of Front Street Deli opened. Adam Burke, instantly recognizable from his newspaper profile, entered in a rush. His unkempt hair and crooked glasses gave off an air of disarray. Spotting Harper, he scanned the room briefly before heading towards her table, a flustered look on his face. She greeted him with a nod.

"Sorry I'm late," he huffed, sliding into the booth across from Harper. "Got caught up with some leads on another case."

Harper studied the journalist as he tried to catch his breath. "Understandable," she said finally. "Let's begin."

She paused, her gaze fixed on Adam's face. "Ethan Cook mentioned that you've crossed paths before?"

Adam rubbed his chin thoughtfully. "Who? Oh, Ethan! Right, yeah, I remember him now. Good guy. Helped me with some research once."

Harper leaned forward, her eyes ablaze with purpose. Her hands shook as they grasped the table's edge. "It's Ethan who set up this meeting so I could ask you about PenCore Limited, the for-profit prison company that ran Tall Trees." She watched him closely, searching for any sign of recognition.

"PenCore." Adam's eyes widened as the connection clicked into place. "Right, that exposé I did last year. What do you want to know?"

Harper's fingers beat out a rhythm on the tabletop as her thoughts raced. She needed information from Adam, but she couldn't afford to reveal too much and lose his trust. When she spoke, her voice was steady and determined.

"I believe there are still some unresolved issues surrounding PenCore and its connections to our city's justice system. I'm hoping you can help me uncover the truth."

Adam's gaze shifted away from Harper, his attention divided. He adjusted his glasses and fiddled impatiently with the edge of a napkin.

Harper watched as he scratched the back of his neck, the tension in his shoulders a clear sign of how he felt.

"I'm pretty swamped with my current assignment, so if you could just tell me what you need—"

But before he could finish, Harper leaned in slightly and lowered her voice to a conspiratorial whisper. "It's not just about an old exposé or legal case, Adam. It's about the lives of those caught in a corrupt justice system."

As she gazed into his eyes, her voice erupted with determination. "I fight for clients chewed up and spit out by the system. The same injustices happen repeatedly. If we don't hold people accountable—judges, lawyers, prison officials— then the system will keep failing."

Adam paused, taking a deep breath as he weighed her words. His eyes, once unfocused and distant, now held a new spark of understanding. "Alright," he conceded, offering a small nod. "Tell me more about what you're hoping to uncover."

Harper practically exhaled with relief. Not wasting a moment, she dove into her suspicions, the details of her research spilling out in a passionate yet factual onslaught.

"I have a client," she began, careful not to reveal any identifying details. "He was treated horribly at Tall Trees. Horrific living conditions, abuse… you name it." She watched Adam's eyes narrow, his interest piqued despite his initial reluctance.

Harper asked slowly, "PenCore Limited, right? The corporation that runs this place?" She paused, allowing the information to sink in.

Adam's shoulders sagged. "Yeah, that's the one. The first part of the exposé came out and then…nothing." Frustration simmered beneath his words, and Harper could see the fire that drove him as a journalist.

Harper's voice brimmed with enthusiasm as she offered, "Maybe we can pick up where you left off. Advocates for the little guy like us must hold those in power accountable. We can't allow this to happen."

As their conversation progressed, Harper observed Adam's tension easing, giving way to a budding camaraderie fostered by their mutual quest for justice.

Adam pushed his glasses up the bridge of his nose. "Look, I'd have to dig through my old notes, but I'm willing to share whatever isn't tied to a confidential source with you. The article already contained most of what I found."

Harper's gaze softened, and she gave him a gentle smile.

"Thank you. I appreciate your help. This means a lot to me."

Adam glanced at his watch, his impatience beginning to show. He paused, clearly trying to remain composed. "It's not a problem, Harper. We both want the same outcome."

As Harper listened to him, her pulse quickened, her thoughts racing towards the possibilities that lay ahead. She might not save Darrius from going to prison, but she could expose the brutalities within the prison system. It was a minor comfort, but she couldn't stand idly by while injustice prevailed.

"Adam," she said, determination lacing her words. "I want to pull on this thread. Uncovering the truth behind those walls could make a difference. We owe it to people like my client and all the others who've suffered at their hands."

A flicker of admiration sparked in Adam's eyes as he studied her face. "You're a real crusader, aren't you, Brass? Isn't that what they call you around town?"

The nickname made her smile inwardly. "Someone has to be. Even a small impact is worth it."

"Alright," Adam conceded, his tone softening. "I'll get you what I can. I need time to retrieve those notes."

"Thank you."

Adam flicked his wrist, impatiently examining his watch. "Harper, I have to leave," he said with a sense of urgency in his voice, eyes darting away from the menu. "I promise I'll look into my old notes and get back to you soon."

She watched as he gathered his belongings, preparing to leave. A nagging thought tugged at her mind, urging her to ask for one last reassurance. "You will call me when you find something, right?"

Adam nodded, his annoyance scarcely concealed under a veneer of professionalism. Shifting his bag on his shoulder, he spoke with an earnest intensity. "I think my exposé on PenCore's kickback scheme got buried because it threatened city officials, judges, politicians. I was close to having sources go on record when they suddenly killed the series, just before I could reveal the damning evidence."

Harper's eyes widened as she considered his words. The implications were enormous.

Adam sighed, running a hand through his hair. "You know, after I started digging deeper into the PenCore story, the pushback was intense. I was warned about potential legal threats from some big players, and I could feel the editorial pressure mounting. There were whispers about losing major advertisers if we continued. It felt like the walls were closing in, and then, just like that, they pulled the plug on the series. I just didn't expect them to cave so easily." Adam's tone became serious as he warned, "Be careful, Harper. If you pull on this thread too hard, you might face some powerful enemies."

She straightened her spine, a hint of trepidation in her voice. "Someone has to stand up to them. If nobody else will, I'll do it."

As she watched him walk away, the bustling deli seemed to fade into the background, replaced by a maelstrom of thoughts and worries swirling in her mind. The abuse of inmates was damning enough. Allegations of a coordinated conspiracy implicating city officials meant the stakes had never been higher, but neither was her determination.

SIX

Summer 1985, Memphis, TN

The old grandfather clock in the corner of Judge Isaac Jackson's study ticked away, its rhythmic beat adding to the tension in the room. The solemn face of the Shelby County Judge, a tall, distinguished African American man, surveyed the girls standing before him. His dark eyes bore into them, assessing their guilt.

His dark face's stern lines softened momentarily at the sight of two scared teenage girls still in their party attire.

Harper and Deandra shifted uncomfortably under the weight of his gaze. His voice, heavy with disappointment, echoed in the room. "Harper Brasfield. Deandra Jackson," he said. "I expected better from both of you."

Harper's cheeks burned with a mix of embarrassment and defiance, her green eyes sparking with indignation. While she was unaccustomed to such admonishment—her own parents were often absent and, when present, largely indifferent—she was well-aware of Judge Jackson's reputation. A revered legal authority in Shelby County, he had climbed his way out of poverty and was known for his unwavering dedication to the law, order, and his family. Deep down, Harper appreciated the structure he provided, though she'd never dare voice it.

Deandra's eyes darted away, avoiding any direct contact. She fidgeted with the hem of her shirt.

"I'm sorry," she muttered, almost inaudibly.

Judge Jackson, without breaking eye contact with Harper, addressed Deandra sternly, "Deandra, go to your room."

She nodded, taking a hesitant step back before turning to leave.

Harper remained silent, her body language radiating hostility. Yet, beneath this front, she harbored a secret relief, envious of the stability found in the Jackson household, a stark contrast to her own tumultuous home life.

"Harper Brasfield, I will speak to your parents about this. You may go upstairs now," the judge said.

Once in Deandra's bedroom, the tension between them dissipated as quickly as it had arrived. They collapsed onto her bed, giggling, and blushing as they recalled the wild party they'd just attended. Their laughter filled the room, a testament to their unwavering bond.

Deandra and Harper shared a look filled with mischievous glee, laughing.

"Totally worth getting caught!" Harper exclaimed, her grin stretching from ear to ear.

After the girls left, his wife, Della—affectionately known as Mama Dee—met the judge in the kitchen, her warm presence filling the room. Isaac glanced at his wife and couldn't help but smile. She was wise and comforting, a strong maternal force in their family.

Mama Dee prepared some food, her hands moving in practiced motions as she whispered, "Isaac, you know teenagers will test the limits." She glanced at him with a twinkle in her eye, and a private shared laugh seemed to pass between them, a reminder of their own youthful escapades when they were dating.

"Did you smell any alcohol on their breath?" Mama Dee asked, her voice hushed but concerned.

Isaac sighed, his voice filled with disappointment. "Of course."

Alone in her house, Harper's thoughts drifted back to that distant teenage summer night, sharply contrasting with her current estrangement from her children, Lucas and Charlotte. She reached for her phone, sending a tentative text to Lucas, an attempt to close the growing gap between them. As she pressed send, a wave of worry washed over her, his recent aloofness weighing heavily on her mind.

Her heart ached as she reflected on her past decisions regarding Lucas. His childhood need for attention and bouts of tantrums were memories that lingered painfully. Harper now recognized that convincing her husband to send Lucas to a military academy, under the pretext of discipline, was a misguided effort to compensate for her own parental failings.

The familiar buzz of her phone brought Lucas's reply: "Hey, Mom, can't talk right now. On the new high-speed rail to DC for a job interview."

As she stared at her phone, Harper remembered how grateful she had been for the boundaries set by Judge Jackson all those years ago. Reminiscing about her past, she could still hear his deep, resonant voice in her head guiding her through every challenge she faced.

He had leaned closer to her, his face furrowed with a grave expression. "Harper," he spoke with emphasis, "your future is as bright as the sun itself, but it all hinges on your dedication to education."

He had looked down with the weight of his experiences clouding his gaze. "Memphis may have its struggles, but we can't let that hold us back. Remember, the day you're born is just another sunrise. Death is just another sunset. Life is about making your daylight matter. I expect you to shine. Make a difference where you can. Make the best of the time you have between sunrises and sunsets."

He'd been there when she got sidetracked in college, making sure she had a tutor to keep her focused. He played a significant role in her acceptance into law school alongside his daughter, Deandra. The judge's unwavering support had been a constant beacon of light in her life.

Harper was haunted by a sense of regret, feeling she

hadn't been the guiding figure for Lucas and Charlotte that she had hoped to be. As Lucas contemplated a job on the East Coast, she found herself torn. While she recognized his need for independence, she couldn't help but mourn the widening physical distance that could make reconciling with him more challenging.

As Harper waited for Sunday dinner at the Jacksons', she immersed herself in online research about PenCore and its activities. Her search led her to an old post about a tragedy at Tall Trees, the juvenile facility that had come under fire following the suicide of a young inmate.

The deeper she dug, the darker it became. Numerous posts decried PenCore, branding them malevolent and alleging judicial collusion, given the high number of convicts sent to PenCore-owned facilities. A comment listing city officials purportedly in cahoots with the corporation made her blood run cold—Judge Isaac Jackson's name stood out starkly.

"Is this even possible?" Harper wondered, her mind spinning with possibilities. Her efforts to track down the source of these claims led only to a series of dead ends and inactive accounts, fueling her frustration. Reminding herself that the real truth might be uncovered through more official routes, she set her phone down, mentally preparing for the challenges ahead.

She hissed under her breath a cynical, "Social media."

Shaking her head, she muttered, "Can't trust anything you read anymore."

She forced herself to think about the upcoming dinner. Mama Dee's warm hospitality and delicious Southern cooking would be a welcome respite from her troubled thoughts.

The sun was setting as Harper pulled up to the Jackson home, casting a warm glow on the stately Southern house. It stood proudly in the upscale Midtown Memphis neighborhood, surrounded by neatly trimmed hedges and ancient oak trees that whispered stories of the past. The grand porch stretched across the front, adorned with white pillars and elegant rocking chairs where Isaac and Mama Dee would often sit, watching the world go by.

Harper's heart clenched as memories of playing in the spacious backyard with Deandra as children flooded her heart. The Jackson home and family were her sanctuary from the world, offering love, laughter, and solace.

As she stepped through the door, the familiar scent of Mama Dee's cooking enveloped her, and she instantly felt embraced by the warmth and comfort of the home. The rich aroma of fried chicken, okra, and corn tickled her senses, filling her with anticipation for the meal ahead.

"Harper, my dear!" Mama Dee called out from the kitchen, her voice melodic and filled with affection. As Harper entered, Mama Dee enveloped her in a warm embrace that seemed to melt away the tension she had been carrying. Harper breathed in the heavenly scent that clung to Mama Dee—a mix of sweet perfume, spices, and a hint of vanilla.

Her voice was a near-silent murmur as the reverence and gratitude filled her. Mama Dee held Harper's gaze, her expression a tumultuous mix of worry and love.

"Child," she began, her deep voice full of tenderness, "you are always welcome here. You were almost a daughter to me, and I'm so proud of the woman Deandra has become because of your influence." Her dark eyes shimmered with unsaid emotion.

Harper smiled, feeling a wave of gratitude wash over her. Mama Dee had always been there, offering support and wisdom when she needed it most. She wondered how much Mama Dee knew about her recent struggles, but she couldn't bring herself to burden the woman with her concerns.

Harper's lip quivered, a single tear rolling down her cheek. She swallowed hard, the emotion swelling in her throat. "Thank you. It means more than you'll ever know."

Mama Dee brushed away the tear with gentle fingers, giving Harper another reassuring hug. "Now, let's not get all misty-eyed before dinner. We have a lot to catch up on, don't we?"

Part terrified and part hopeful, she longed to get the conversation over with. Not staying in touch with important people during her struggles made her feel ashamed.

"Where's Deandra?"

Mama Dee offered a reassuring smile, though it didn't quite reach her eyes. "Deandra won't be joining us, dear.

Something came up." The words hung in the air, and Harper felt the weight of disappointment pressing down on her chest.

As they moved further into the house, Harper couldn't stop thinking about the lingering concerns that weighed heavily on her mind: the social media posts implicating Judge Jackson in a possible PenCore kickback scheme, and her strained relationship with Deandra. For now, she pushed those thoughts aside, focusing on the present moment.

Mama Dee led Harper to the dining room, where the table was full of mouthwatering dishes of Southern comfort food.

Harper's eyes widened in awe as she took in the feast before her. A smile spread across her face, and she exclaimed, "Mama Dee, you've outdone yourself! This is exactly what I needed."

As they were about to sit down, the entrance of Judge Isaac Jackson was felt more than seen. His aura of authority was substantial, but the warmth in his eyes when he looked at Harper belied his stern demeanor.

"Counselor," he began, making Harper instinctively straighten. "A word?" He gestured toward his study, and she followed, footsteps echoing in the grand hall.

Inside, he waited for her to sit before fixing her with a gaze that had reduced many a defendant to stammers. Harper felt that familiar tug of unease, reminiscent of her rebellious school days.

"Harper," he started, his voice a deep timbre that had swayed countless juries. "This suspension is a matter of concern." He spoke of their sacred duty to the law, to the trust placed in them by clients and society. Each word weighed on Harper's heart.

She fidgeted, internally battling the urge to justify her actions against the wisdom he imparted. She knew he was right, yet years of suppressed resentment simmered beneath her surface.

Concluding their talk, he said, "Harper, you need to tread the path of integrity."

Acknowledging him with a solemn nod, Harper's features eventually softened into a reluctant smile.

"Dinner awaits, child." His tone was now infused with an affection that broke the tension.

As they stood up to leave the study, he leaned in and pressed a gentle kiss to her forehead and added, "That Turner is a piece of work. Shh."

Back at the table, Harper felt the weight lift off her shoulders, immersing herself in the warmth of the Jackson household. Their tactful avoidance of her recent past, clear-cut in their lively conversation, made her more appreciative of their unspoken understanding.

Before saying her goodbyes, Harper helped Mama Dee clean up in the kitchen.

"Harper, dear, are you lost in thought again?" Mama Dee's gentle voice interrupted her reverie. She stood in the doorway, her warm smile spreading across her face.

Harper let out a heavy sigh. "Ah, yes. Remembering all the of times the judge supported me." Her gaze drifted away for a moment as memories flooded in.

Mama Dee nodded knowingly. "He's always believed in

you. You're like a second daughter. His retirement..." She paused, her gaze drifting towards the study. "Well, it's been an adjustment for these past eighteen months. But I'm happy to have him home all to myself."

Harper's heart swelled with warmth as Mama Dee's lighthearted voice filled the room. She couldn't resist smiling, watching a grin spread across her face too.

"Though I'll admit," she let out a soft giggle and shook her head, "he's not very handy around the house."

"Really?" Harper raised an eyebrow, amusement flickering in her eyes.

"Absolutely," Mama Dee confirmed. "He tried to fix a leaky faucet last week and ended up flooding the bathroom instead."

Harper let out a guffaw as her mind's eye pictured Judge Jackson, usually so dignified and imposing, with his eyebrows furrowed in concentration as he attempted to fix the plumbing with his toolbox of wrenches and spanners. It reminded her that even great people had flaws, making the man she admired more human.

Sharing this moment with Mama Dee, Harper was flooded with gratitude for the Jackson family's steadfast support. They had witnessed both her highs and lows, yet their belief in her never wavered—despite her recent lapses in communication.

With the sun casting a gentle glow on the porch, Harper resolved to honor their faith in her by making each day count. However, the online allegations about the judge continued to cast a shadow over her thoughts.

Harper met Adam at Brother Juniper's the next day. The aroma of freshly brewed coffee wafted through the air, mingling with the scent of buttery pastries and crisp morning air.

Adam's mouth tightened into a firm line as his fingers fumbled with his glasses. "I can't help you," he said, his voice low and resolute. He looked around the café before continuing. "I'm too busy to be a part of whatever this is. I know we both want justice, but I've got another investigation that needs my attention."

His sudden dismissal surprised Harper. "Adam, people are being mistreated every day, and someone needs to do something about it. Don't tell me you're afraid of repercussions; I thought you were fearless! Talk to me."

After a long pause, Adam rose from his seat. "I have to go now, Harper. I wish you the best in your mission. Really, I do. Though mine is much bigger than this one." She noticed a folder sticking out of his bag with PenCore written on it and lunged for it.

Startled, Adam called out, "Hey! What are you doing?" But he did not stop her from taking the folder. He finally sat back down with a sigh.

Harper leaned forward, her heart racing in anticipation. "What did you discover?"

Adam's shoulders slouched, and he shook his head as he sat back down. "No, Harper! You can't take stuff out of people's bags." His voice carried a controlled urgency.

She slid the folder towards him. "I know. I'm sorry. The

PenCore story has been getting to me. Please, don't leave yet. You brought that folder because you weren't sure what would happen when you came here today, right?"

Adam's grip on his coffee cup tightened, his knuckles whitening. "Remember my exposé? I've dug deeper since then. But I'm wary of making accusations. The article got shelved, and now I think I might have stumbled onto something perilous. Maybe its cancellation was a blessing."

Harper bore her eyes into him. "Get to the point, Adam."

Taking a deep breath, he said, "I've compiled names of city officials who may be entangled with PenCore. It's an intricate network—politicians, police, council members, court officials, even judges."

Adam's voice dropped, almost drowned by the ambient noise of the café. "I've unearthed evidence of monetary exchanges—bribes meant to ensure a steady flow of inmates into PenCore's profit-driven facilities. But my evidence is from unverified, anonymous tips. It wouldn't stand a chance in court. Before I could bring anything to light, they silenced me."

Harper paled, absorbing the gravity of Adam's words. "This is... chilling."

Adam's lips pursed, and his brow furrowed. He leaned forward, arms crossed over the table as he explained in a low voice, "This is how these for-profit prisons work... they can charge the government whatever they want, as long as it's less than what it would cost the government to run the operation themselves. It's nebulous, and it allows them to prioritize profit over the well-being of their inmates."

Harper's mind raced through the implications as she muttered grimly, "More prisoners, more facilities."

"Exactly," confirmed Adam. "It's a vicious cycle, driven by greed."

As Adam spoke, Harper felt a surge of fury and revulsion. The notion of innocent lives ensnared in such a cold-blooded conspiracy was deeply unsettling. She knew she had to intervene, but the path forward was murky. A pressing doubt clouded her thoughts: in this twisted game, whom could she rely on? Her boss, Sam? He'd likely be irate, insisting she keep her attention undivided on Darrius.

"Let me see that list."

Adam paused momentarily before sliding the paper back to Harper. As her eyes darted over the names, her pulse quickened, her breathing grew shallow, and a knot tightened in her stomach. Her gaze froze on one name, making her surroundings feel as if they were spinning off-kilter.

"Judge Isaac Jackson," she declared, the name sounding like a personal affront.

Adam furrowed his brows in worry. "Something wrong?"

"Nothing," Harper lied, hastily folding the paper and shoving it into her bag. "This whole thing just really disgusts me. If what you found is true, there's an enormous problem."

"Agreed," Adam nodded solemnly. "There's still so much we don't know, though. You'll have to tread carefully, Brass."

Harper nodded and leapt up. "I need some air."

"Hey, wait—" Adam called after her, but Harper was already out the door, her mind reeling with the implications of Judge Jackson's involvement in the PenCore scheme. She needed answers, and she needed them now. No matter the cost.

As she walked down the sidewalk, her heels clicking against the pavement, she knew just who to call.

"Ethan, I need your help with something."

Harper continued, "I need you to look into the history of some convictions—specifically, the defendants, the judges who sentenced them, and which facility or prison they went to." She carefully avoided any mention of Judge Jackson.

"Interesting," Ethan mused. "Any particular reason?"

She bit her lip, glancing around to ensure no one was eavesdropping. "Met with Adam Burke today. He shared some troubling evidence of a kickback scheme involving city officials and PenCore. I can give you more detail in person."

Ethan's tone shifted to one of concern. "Wow, that sounds serious." He paused. "I'll get right on it, Brass. Anything else you need?"

Harper's heart pounded as she ended the call. "No, that's enough for now." As she stood on the sidewalk, the weight of the information heavy on her shoulders, she wondered what she would find—and if her trust in Judge Jackson had been misplaced.

The morning sun painted elongated shadows over Harper's office floor as she strode back and forth, lost in the maze of Adam's revelations. A soft rap on the door broke her concentration.

Ethan peeked in. "Morning, Brass." His composed demeanor provided a stark contrast to her internal storm.

"You have a file for me?"

"In my hand." Harper produced the paper Adam gave her, thankful for Ethan's unwavering support.

"I'll dig into this," he promised, sliding the document into his briefcase. "We'll get to the bottom of it."

She nodded, her voice shaded with concern. "Just watch your back, alright? This feels like we're diving into deeper waters than we're used to."

Ethan gave her a reassuring grin before turning serious. "What about Darrius Robinson? I know you're focused on PenCore, but…"

Harper felt a flicker of irritation. It was easy to get absorbed in the corruption scandal, overshadowing their cases. "He's still a priority," she replied shortly.

Ethan's voice softened. "Just making sure. We're a team, right?"

"Always," she said with a slight smile, watching him leave. Alone again, Harper leaned back in her chair, her thoughts heavy. Guilt over neglecting her personal life nagged at her, but she pushed it aside, focusing on the task at hand. The implications of PenCore's corruption and its ties to city officials loomed large in her mind.

Later, Ethan's message flashed on her phone. "*Progress made. Stay tuned.*"

As dusk turned to night, Harper worked tirelessly, her focus alternating between her computer and her notes. She was determined to avert a bleak outcome for Darrius, despite the daunting challenge ahead. Near midnight, Harper paused, her fingers weary from typing. She gazed out at the night sky, a mix of anxiety and determination stirring within her.

61

SEVEN

Ethan Cook's fingers raced across the keyboard, his gaze fixed intently on the screen as he navigated PenCore's digital labyrinth. In the stuffy room, he was in his element, uncovering layers of deceit to find the truth. He paused, stroking his stubbled chin, contemplating the enormity of his task.

Ethan, originally from Nesbit, Mississippi, had witnessed his small town evolve into a busy suburb for Memphis commuters, often humorously calling it "Tennissippi." His path to law started with the Shelby County Sheriff's Department and veered into the military, where he sought direction.

Returning from service, Ethan balanced law studies with investigative work at Sam Chapman's firm. He had grown to respect Harper's direct approach, their rapport marked by lighthearted banter. He nicknamed her "Tacks" much to her mock annoyance but secret amusement.

Known for his meticulousness and ability to unearth obscure details, Ethan became a key asset to the firm. Now, delving into PenCore, he faced a formidable challenge.

As he meticulously analyzed the data-laden spreadsheet, a sudden insight about PenCore's ownership struck him. With a mix of discipline and urgency in his voice, he called Harper. "Tacks, I've made a breakthrough."

She responded, "What've you got?"

"They've left some breadcrumbs. I've managed to trace the first few shell companies connected to PenCore. We're onto something, but I need more time to piece it all together.

"I've also gathered a list of defendants and their sentences through some well-placed favors and low-key inquiries within the courts. Rest assured, I've sanitized the list to ensure our objectives aren't obvious. We'll have a clearer understanding soon."

"Keep at it, Ethan. We need to uncover whatever they're concealing. While Darrius's case is crucial, there's a deeper issue with PenCore. A profit-driven company overseeing prisons and potentially bribing officials? It's too significant to overlook."

"Understood. I won't let you down, Harper."

Ethan's resolve deepened as he navigated the complex web of shell companies. His fingers moved swiftly over the keyboard, each keystroke a step closer to unveiling the truth hidden beneath layers of secrecy.

The task was daunting, with hours spent dissecting intricate financial records. Rubbing his temples, he felt the strain of the work. The deeper he looked into PenCore's network, the more complex the puzzle became, resembling the challenge of unraveling a Gordian knot. Yet Ethan was determined to find the key to unravel it.

In a moment of reflection, he tapped his pen rhythmically, breaking the room's quiet. "Meridian Holdings," he pronounced, noting it down. This entity was a new lead, but its significance was still enigmatic. With a determined grin, Ethan delved back into his research.

Standing on the train platform in downtown Memphis, Lucas Fairbanks's eyes widened as he stared at the sleek high-speed train before him. The impressive amenities offered by CytoLife Dynamics for his journey to Washington, DC were enough to make anyone feel a sense of awe. He paused for a moment to calm his nerves, reminding himself he was more than qualified.

A newly established rail service now dramatically shortened the journey from Memphis to Washington, DC with speeds exceeding 220 MPH. The previously daunting 12-hour trip was reduced to less than four hours, thanks to direct, nonstop service. Lucas, who had once been captivated by this swift gateway to the nation's capital, found his thoughts preoccupied elsewhere today.

"First-class cabin, huh? They really want you to feel special," a fellow passenger remarked, eyeing Lucas's ticket.

Lucas gave a tight smile. "Seems that way," he said, his

words not quite masking his anxiety.

As the train picked up speed, Lucas sank into the plush leather seat, his gaze fixed on the swiftly passing scenery. Thoughts of his mother, Harper, crept into his mind, stirring feelings of tension and unease about their strained relationship. The prospect of seeing her again left a bitter taste in his mouth.

Memories of his parents' divorce replayed in his thoughts. His father, Rob, was kind and gentle, yet often overshadowed by Harper's formidable will and ambition. Lucas felt a deep sense of abandonment, believing Harper had prioritized her career over her family. He also feared that Charlotte, his younger sister, was falling victim to the same emotional neglect he had experienced.

An attendant interrupted his trance, asking, "Can I get you anything to drink, Mr. Fairbanks?"

"Uh, just some water, please," he said, shifting his gaze away from the window.

While sipping his water, Lucas's mind drifted to the upcoming interview. While he hoped his military background would be attractive to CytoLife Dynamics, their sudden interest in him stirred a sense of unease. Excited yet puzzled, he pondered why they had specifically chosen him, particularly since he hadn't directly applied and knew there were numerous other qualified candidates.

Lucas was astounded by CytoLife's philanthropic reach as he scrolled through their website. Their extensive support of medical care in isolated areas, alongside scholarships and grants for the underprivileged, filled the screen. Equally notable were their global sustainability programs, fostered through governmental and academic alliances. With a deep exhale, he shut his laptop, sinking into the plush embrace of the high-speed train's seating.

"Your stop is approaching soon, sir." The attendant's voice cut through his thoughts once again.

Lucas murmured his thanks, gathering his belongings and heading towards the exit. His heart raced faster now, a mixture of anticipation and nerves coursing through him.

As the train pulled into the station and Lucas stepped onto the platform, he paused for a moment to gather his thoughts. He couldn't change the past or mend his relationship with Harper in an instant, but he could control his own future.

He muttered under his breath, "Here goes nothing," and strode forward with determination etched on his face.

The sleek, black sedan awaited Lucas as he exited the station, a tall, well-dressed driver holding open the door with a respectful nod. The bright sun glinted off the car's polished surface as Lucas approached, his heart pounding in his chest.

"Mr. Fairbanks," the driver said, extending his hand to help Lucas into the vehicle. "Welcome to Washington, DC."

Lucas thanked him, noting the man's professional demeanor and the subtle bulge beneath his jacket—a telltale sign of a concealed weapon. This was no ordinary chauffeur, and it only added to the intrigue surrounding CytoLife Dynamics.

As the car accelerated onto the highway, Lucas's mind wandered back to his time in special ops. His skills were honed to a razor's edge, shaped by experiences far beyond the ordinary. The prospect of a civilian job that could utilize his unique abilities intrigued him, despite his lingering doubts about why they had reached out to him.

Lucas's gaze returned to his watch, marking time impatiently as the car meandered down the serpentine road hemmed in by the lofty evergreens. Their shadows played across the tarmac, stretching and retreating like silent specters. Lucas estimated they must be somewhere deep in rural Virginia, at least eighty miles from the pulse of DC life.

The resort, aptly christened *the Evergreen*, sat secluded amidst lush foliage, its beauty both striking and tranquil.

As they neared the entrance, Lucas was captivated by the grandiosity of the atrium lobby, a three-story spectacle of glass that soared heavenward, mirroring the untainted wilderness. The opulence of the place provided a momentary distraction from his anxiety about the enigmatic job interview that awaited him.

"Quite something, isn't it?" the driver remarked, clearly noting Lucas's awe. "I've been driving guests here for years, and it never gets old."

"Definitely not what I was expecting," Lucas admitted, feeling a bit out of his element as they pulled up to the main entrance.

Once inside, he was greeted by a smiling concierge, who handed him a key card and offered directions to his suite. The interior of the resort was as lavish as its exterior, with polished marble floors, ornate chandeliers, and a grand staircase that seemed to float upwards, inviting guests to explore the opulence above.

Inside his luxurious suite, Lucas opened the balcony door and stepped outside, letting the crisp air wash over him. He leaned against the railing, eyes scanning the horizon for any sign of movement or impending change. He knew that waiting was a part of any operation, but this felt different—like the calm before an incoming storm.

"Mr. Fairbanks?" Hours passed, and then a soft knock on the door interrupted his thoughts, and Lucas turned to see a young woman dressed in a sleek black uniform standing in the doorway. "My apologies for the delay. Mr. Ross is ready for you now."

Relief swept through Lucas as he trailed behind the woman, exiting the suite. Despite the encroaching night, the resort's opulence remained undiminished. The luxurious furnishings, exquisite art, and elegantly attired guests all hinted at immense wealth and influence—attributes CytoLife Dynamics clearly had in abundance.

The choice of such a lavish, secluded resort for their headquarters was intriguing; Lucas surmised it provided them with much-needed privacy and an ideal setting to entertain affluent benefactors.

Pausing at a plain door, the woman announced, "Here we are." With a nod, she gestured for Lucas to enter.

The office was nothing like the rest of the resort. While still undeniably luxurious, it carried an air of cold efficiency. Dark wood furniture dominated the space, and a floor-to-ceiling window offered a breathtaking view of the moonlit forest beyond.

"Mr. Fairbanks, I presume?" A man in his early forties

stood near the window, his voice deep and commanding, capturing Lucas's immediate attention. His hair was cut short in a style that suggested order and precision, while his muscular build hinted at a history of physical discipline, likely military. Yet, it was the sharp, assessing look in his eyes—a gaze that seemed to weigh and measure with a single glance—that sent an involuntary tremor through Lucas. The air around the man crackled with an unspoken history, his entire demeanor echoing a past steeped in strategy and survival.

"Lucas Fairbanks," he confirmed, extending his hand for a firm handshake.

Felix Ross introduced himself, with an intimidating grip on Lucas's hand. Lucas held steady, returning the pressure without flinching.

"Have a seat."

Lucas paused, instinctively shifting into a firmer stance, but Felix's assertive attempt at intimidation subtly threw him off balance.

Tension filled the room as Felix stared at Lucas, trying to uncover his thoughts and secrets. Although surprised by the sudden intensity, Lucas quickly regained his composure, drawing on his training and the steeliness he'd inherited from his mother.

"Mr. Ross," Lucas began, his voice steady and strong. "I understand you need someone with my particular skill set for this job. However, I'd appreciate some transparency about what it is I'm signing up for." He leaned forward slightly, matching the intimidating posture of Felix.

Felix's lips curved into a sly grin. "Is that so?" He studied Lucas for a moment before continuing. "Very well, Mr. Fairbanks. We require someone capable of providing personal protection for key individuals within our organization. Your background and expertise make you an ideal candidate."

Felix was withholding information, and Lucas sensed it. He had many questions, but didn't want to appear vulnerable. Instead, he focused on maintaining control of the conversation. "Who exactly would I be protecting, Mr. Ross?"

Felix's smirk grew as he leaned forward, mirroring Lucas's position. "That information will be disclosed on a need-to-know basis, Mr. Fairbanks. Rest assured, you will be well-compensated for your discretion and loyalty."

Lucas could feel the challenge radiating from Felix, a test of his mettle and resolve. He refused to back down, his eyes never leaving Felix's probing gaze. Inwardly, he acknowledged his mother's influence, her relentlessness in the face of adversity serving him well in this moment.

"Alright," Lucas conceded. "But I expect full disclosure if I take this job. No more secrets or surprises."

A flicker of amazement flashed across Felix's face before he quickly masked it with a nod. "Agreed, Mr. Fairbanks. You'll find that we value loyalty and transparency, as long as it flows both ways."

Lucas locked onto the other man's piercing eyes and stood tall, refusing to bow before such a formidable presence. As he confirmed he understood, Lucas felt a surge of adrenaline course through his veins, electrifying every inch of his body in a wave of exhilaration.

Felix's expression was unreadable but showed begrudging respect for Lucas.

"Mr. Ross," Lucas began mindfully. "You haven't really asked me about my qualifications or experience."

Felix arched an eyebrow, his eyes never leaving Lucas's face. "We've done our research, Mr. Fairbanks. We know everything about you." He leaned back, fingers steepled together. "Besides, we've been watching you since you boarded the high-speed rail."

Lucas blinked, taken aback. He replayed his journey in his mind, searching for any missteps. He had been on his best behavior during the trip—staying alert, observing his surroundings, and maintaining a professional demeanor throughout.

Standing, Felix clasped his hands behind his back. His eyes, previously sharp, were now flat and emotionless. "Your conduct and awareness have been exemplary, Mr. Fairbanks," he said. "You passed our test."

Lucas's chest tightened as he processed this revelation. They had been evaluating him, monitoring his every move, even before the interview had begun. It was unnerving, but he couldn't deny the thrill it sent coursing through him. This job clearly demanded more than what met the eye.

"Alright," Lucas said, forcing his voice to stay even. "You've been watching me, and I've passed your test somehow. What details can you give me about this job?"

Felix allowed a small smile to cross his lips. "As I mentioned before, you'll be providing personal protection.

Your expertise in special ops will be invaluable to us."

"Who am I protecting?" Lucas pressed, uncomfortable with the vague answers.

Felix's smile slowly dropped from his face. "Need-to-know basis, as I said earlier," he stated tightly. "But I can assure you, the work will be challenging and rewarding."

Lucas considered the limited information he had about the opportunity. The chance to use his training and the pay made it seem too good to be true. Despite everything, Felix's evasiveness still bothered him.

Lucas, shoulders squared and posture rigid from his disciplined background, locked eyes with Felix. "Is there a reason for all this secrecy?"

Felix leaned in, his voice dripping with calculated charm yet underscored by a cold undertone. "Mr. Fairbanks, CytoLife Dynamics is at the forefront of biotech innovation. The nature of our work, and the potential it holds, makes what we do highly sought after—and not always by those with the best intentions. If you're to join our ranks, especially in a protective capacity, you'll need to understand and respect the confidentiality that comes with it."

Lucas's eyes darted for a moment, reflecting his internal struggle. He was eager, perhaps too eager, to prove himself beyond his service in the armed forces. Taking a deep breath, he extended his hand, making his decision.

"Alright, Mr. Ross. You've got yourself a deal."

Harper sat in the Vice & Virtue Coffee Shop, nerves on edge as she awaited Lucas. She folded the napkin in her lap, trying to still her trembling hands and project calm. Her eyes flicked to the window, observing the pedestrians outside as a distraction from her anxiety. This meeting was more than a casual coffee catch-up; it was a chance to mend her relationship with her son and begin anew.

"Mom?" Lucas's voice jolted her, and she saw him at the entrance. His tall figure and dark hair were unmistakable, a reminder of the bond they once shared.

Harper leapt to her feet, her face alight with joy as she ran towards Lucas. She flung her arms tightly around him and he returned the embrace before reluctantly stepping back. Her voice caught in her throat as she said, "Thank you for meeting me."

After they took their seats, she forced herself to maintain eye contact with her son, despite the discomfort it caused her. "So, how did your trip to DC go? How was the job interview?"

Lucas shifted in his seat, suddenly guarded. "It went fine, I guess. They offered me the job, and I signed an NDA, so I can't really talk about it." He looked away, avoiding his mother's gaze.

Harper's brow furrowed as she reached out and placed her hand on Lucas's arm. He pulled away.

Her voice was gentle, almost a whisper, filled with fear and worry. "Lucas, I just want to know you're okay," she said. "I know you're a grown man, and I don't want to interfere in your life, but I'm still your mother. I can't help but worry."

Lucas played with his ear, a visible sign of his growing frustration. Exhaling a heavy sigh, he locked eyes with Harper, his expression hardening. "Mom, I get it, and I'm grateful, but I need some room to breathe. Transitioning to civilian life isn't easy, and I have to figure it out on my own." His words were firm, yet his voice carried an undercurrent of regret.

Harper's response was no more than a whisper. "Does this mean we can't even see each other?" The mere thought of a complete disconnection from her son was unbearable.

A shadow of discomfort crossed Lucas's features. "Just for a little while," he conceded.

The words ripped through her heart like a jagged blade.

Her voice quivered as she asked, "You can't even tell me who you're working for?"

"Mom, you're an attorney. You know about NDAs."

In the seclusion of the coffee shop, Harper was keenly aware of the distance between herself and Lucas. Harper's heart ached for a way to close the gap, to heal the rift between them.

Memories flooded back of the day Lucas announced he'd enlisted in the Army instead of applying to colleges. Rob's face had fallen, but he'd embraced Lucas, giving him a reassuring pat. Harper, on the other hand, had been furious. She couldn't fathom his choice and believed it was a rebellious act against her. Despite Lucas's achievements in the military, she never fully accepted his decision. And now, once again, he was withholding details about another significant move in his life.

Harper looked expectantly at Lucas. "Will you move soon? What's the plan?"

Lucas shifted his weight and nodded. "Yeah, I'm getting on the train tonight. You know me. I travel light." He offered an assuring smile. "I'll contact you as soon as I can."

Harper gave a slow nod, feeling the lump in her throat. She realized Lucas had to make his own choices, and with a heavy heart, she let him leave. She watched him disappear down South Main Street, her heart aching with a bittersweet mix of hope and sorrow. In her own way, she knew she had to support him, even if it meant from afar.

"It's like trying to peel an onion, isn't it? All these layers of shell companies behind PenCore," Harper said to Ethan, her gaze focused on the computer screen in her office.

Ethan paused, a look of frustration crossing his face. "I've been chasing down leads, and it's a labyrinth. One name that keeps surfacing is Meridian Holdings. What it means is still unclear. But I've got someone, a secret source, who owes me. It's not something I like to cash in on, but it might be time. I'll reach out and see if they can provide some clarity on this."

Harper's expression was a mix of gratitude and concern. "Ethan, I appreciate your efforts immensely. The Darrius Robinson case is critical, but we can't overlook the potential of a bigger plot with PenCore, especially with possible kickbacks. We need to pursue every lead that might help Darrius."

Ethan met Harper's gaze, his expression resolute. "I'm in.

Adam Burke's info is just the tip of the iceberg. We need to dive deep and uncover the whole story."

Harper leaned in, her chest tight with worry. "What have you found so far?"

"Shelby County's courts have had their share of progress and abuses of power." He paused, then added, "Persistent racial injustices are still causing deep divisions, making it hard for the community to truly move forward."

Harper's eyes reflected her deep familiarity with the issues Ethan described. She let him unfold his findings, both out of respect for his work and to ensure their strategies aligned. "In light of all this, what do you suggest we do next?"

Ethan leaned back. "I'll reach out to my contact, try to shed light on these shell companies and their ties to PenCore. It's a complex maze, and we'll need all the help we can get."

Harper's tone sharpened, reflecting her urgency. "Ethan, don't hold anything back. I need the full story."

Ethan massaged his temples as if to ease an impending headache. "Alright, Harper. From what I've managed to piece together, both through official channels and... let's say, less conventional ones, it's clear that there were pay-offs and kickbacks."

Harper's stomach churned, her pulse quickening. "What about Judge Jackson?" she pressed.

Ethan hesitated; his voice colored with sorrow. "The records suggest he took kickbacks. He wasn't the most egregious, and it seems he stopped prior to his retirement."

He met her gaze. "Knowing your history with him, Harper... I'm sorry."

The weight of her mentor's apparent betrayal pressed down on Harper. The inevitable confrontation with Judge Jackson loomed large, filling her with dread.

She straightened, steeling herself. "Our priority is Darrius," she interjected, trying to channel her emotions into their immediate mission. "Tell me about his situation."

Ethan shook his head. "Honestly, it might be a lost cause. Darrius is in a tight spot, according to my sources, unless the police screwed up procedurally." He leaned in closer, his voice dropping to a whisper. "I also heard that his gang might actually want him to go to prison. Gangs are prolific inside, and he could be more useful to them behind bars."

Harper's heart ached for Darrius, but she felt helpless. Desperate for a change of subject, she hesitantly asked Ethan for advice about Lucas, mentioning their shared backgrounds.

"Rob is zero help, and we aren't really talking right now," she admitted. "You took a similar path in special ops. Should I be concerned about the NDA and mysterious job? He can't even tell me the name of the company."

Ethan considered her question for a moment, his gaze thoughtful. "The military can be a tight-knit community, and it's not unusual for former service members to transition into high-security civilian jobs that require NDAs. It could be something completely legitimate, Harper."

He added a note of caution, his voice growing more serious. "Still, keep an eye on any changes in his behavior or communication. Trust your instincts as a mother."

Harper nodded, feeling a mix of relief and lingering worry. However, she knew she had more pressing matters to address—like confronting Judge Jackson and fighting for Darrius's future. She prioritized focusing on what she could control, taking it one step at a time.

The sun had sunk low in the sky, casting long shadows as Harper approached the judge's house in Midtown. The elegant home seemed to mock her with the promise of a simpler time. She hesitated at the doorstep, her heart heavy with the knowledge of his involvement in the kickback scheme.

Gathering her composure, she knocked on the door. Mama Dee greeted her adoringly, enveloping her in a hug before ushering her inside. As they walked through the familiar halls, Harper couldn't help but feel like an intruder— the weight of her mentor's betrayal making it difficult to breathe.

Mama Dee guided Harper toward the room filled with leather-bound books and the faint scent of pipe tobacco. "Isaac's in his study."

Harper stepped into the study, bracing herself for the conversation with Isaac. He looked up from his desk, his expression weary but gentle, and stood to greet her.

"Judge Jackson," Harper began, maintaining a formal tone to mask her inner turmoil. "Thank you for agreeing to meet. I really appreciate you taking the time to... to let me pick your brain a bit."

Isaac studied her, a brief hint of relief passing over his features. He motioned for her to take a seat. "Of course,

Harper. Please, tell me everything you can."

She settled into the chair, her mind racing with thoughts she couldn't yet voice. Instead, she focused on framing her questions, carefully avoiding the heart of her suspicions for the moment.

She vaguely shared the details of her case, purposely avoiding what she knew about his involvement in the conspiracy surrounding PenCore. "Um, well, it's about a young man facing serious charges. There are potential irregularities in the case. How would you handle that?" She fiddled with the hem of her sleeve, shifting nervously in the chair.

Isaac paused, his eyes searching hers as if trying to decipher her intentions. "I'd say first and foremost, gather all the facts. Don't jump to conclusions. If there are any procedural errors or additional evidence, pursue them diligently."

As they talked, Harper found herself increasingly torn. She considered confronting him about the kickbacks and demanding an explanation. She also desired his guidance and wisdom, which had once been a source of strength and inspiration to her.

"You're quite the crusader, Harper," Isaac remarked with a half-smile. "The world needs more people like you." His words were ambiguous, leaving her to wonder if he was truly proud of her or anxious she might discover his role in the scandal.

"Thank you, Judge," she managed, her voice tight with unspoken emotion. She steadied herself, feeling the gravity of her decision weighing on her. "I think I need to reach out to the DA about possibly reducing my client's charges."

Isaac nodded; his expression was somber. "Tough task, considering your history with the DA's office. However, it's important to keep those lines of communication open. Especially when you've made a mistake and need to make amends."

Harper acknowledged the truth in his words, despite her lingering doubts and fears. She was determined to ensure Darrius received every chance at justice, regardless of the daunting odds.

Isaac reminded Harper, "Sometimes, we need to accept that things don't always go our way. However, it's important to keep fighting for what's right."

Harper slowly rose. "Thank you, Judge."

Isaac's eyes were both warm and sorrowful as he spoke with the reassurance she so desperately needed. "Always here for you, Harper. "

She knew she was standing at a crossroads between loyalty and betrayal—and she wasn't sure which side would triumph in the end.

Settling at her desk, Harper opened Darrius's file. Her fingers lingered on the document edges as she pondered strategies to aid her client amidst the complexities of the kickback scheme.

Her hands shook slightly as she held the phone, her forehead glistening with sweat. Grasping the gravity of the situation, she paused to compose herself. Her finger hovered briefly over the keypad before she steeled herself and dialed, mentally preparing for the conversation that lay ahead.

"Shelby County District Attorney's office. How may I direct your call?"

"Hi, this is Harper Brasfield, legal counsel." Her voice was steady despite the turmoil within. "I need to speak with the ADA Wilson about a case."

"Please hold."

Harper's gaze swept across her office, drifting over the familiar stacks of files and legal tomes. A sense of unease prickled at her, the unsettling feeling of being watched creeping over her. Rising from her desk, she moved to the window and tentatively peered out.

Outside, the street appeared ordinary with passersby and cars lining the curb. Yet her instincts suggested otherwise. Her eyes methodically scanned the scene, eventually settling on a dark sedan parked across the street. Its tinted windows made it impossible to see inside, but Harper couldn't shake the feeling that someone was observing her from within.

"Ms. Brasfield?" The voice jolted her out of her thoughts, forcing her to refocus on the call.

The sedan's engine roared softly as it pulled away from the curb. Harper watched the car vanish into the distance, a sense of unease lingering. Its departure left her with a trail of unanswered questions.

EIGHT

Hunched over his laptop, Adam Burke sat in the dim light it cast, waiting. The digital clock on his screen showed 2:45 a.m. The room was silent except for the steady hum of the air conditioner and the occasional rustle of papers on his cluttered desk. His heart raced with anticipation; after weeks of cautious messaging through a secure app, his anonymous source was finally ready to speak.

The shrill ringtone cut through the silence. Adam took a deep breath to steady himself and answered the call with a soft, "Hello."

"Call me Cam." The voice on the other end trembled, fear noticeable even through the electronic distortion despite the secure Beacon app they were using. "I work for a biotech firm specializing in CRISPR technology. Don't ask me which one, or I'll hang up."

Adam's heart raced. A genetic engineering insider could

be the lead he was desperate for. "Okay, Cam." He tried to keep his own voice calm. "Tell me what you know."

Cam hesitated before speaking again. "You have to understand. I'm terrified of coming forward. The people I work for… they're powerful. Dangerous." He paused, trying to catch his breath. "But I can't stay silent any longer."

"Listen, Cam." Adam's journalistic instincts kicked in. "I know you're scared. Try to focus on explaining the basics to me, alright? Pretend I know nothing about CRISPR."

"Alright," Cam exhaled, a trace of relief in his voice. "Think of CRISPR as molecular scissors, tailor-made for snipping away at our genes. It operates on a scale so minuscule, it's entirely out of sight, tweaking life's fundamental code hidden inside every cell. Imagine being able to precisely trim away the bits of DNA that lead to disease and seamlessly patching them up with healthy code. That's the promise of CRISPR—astounding and yet it carries the weight of great responsibility, for in the wrong hands, such power could also lead to unforeseen consequences."

Cam's words echoed his fears. The clarity from an insider made Adam grip his phone tighter and shut his eyes in resignation.

"Now, let's use sickle cell disease as an example. People with this condition have a mutation that causes their red blood cells to become misshapen, which can lead to various health problems."

As Cam explained, Adam paced the room, the inky night casting shadows across his apartment, mirroring the complex puzzle he was trying to unravel.

"CRISPR can correct this mutation by cutting away the faulty part of the DNA and replacing it with the correct sequence," Cam continued. "It's like fixing a typo in a manuscript—you remove the incorrect letters and replace them with the right ones. In fact, there's already one patient with sickle cell disease who has had their DNA modified. They cured her."

Despite Cam's benign portrayal, Adam felt the hidden horrors pressing in, demanding immediate action.

"Genetic manipulation extends far beyond fixing defective genes," Cam began, his voice tightening with gravity. "Consider the possibility of crafting entirely new organisms or altering current ones in radical, unnatural ways. Picture a virus, tailored like a precision missile to seek out specific ethnicities, or insects weaponized to deliver lethal venom. The potential uses stretch as far as the mind can wander, tethered only by the thin thread of ethical boundaries."

Adam sensed a mix of passion and fear in Cam's voice as he spoke about science. Listening, a sense of dread built within him, yet he knew he had to keep his fears from spilling over to Cam.

"Thank you, Cam," Adam said softly when the explanation was finished. "Now, can you tell me more about your work and why you're afraid?"

Cam's voice quivered, hardly above a whisper. "I... I can't say too much. There are irregularities occurring in my lab. The implications are enormous, and we all know it. We're working around the clock, under intense security and secrecy. I haven't seen my family in months." He took a shuddering breath. "I don't know who else to turn to."

Adam's voice was soft and reassuring as he spoke. "Is that why you reached out to me?"

"Partly," Cam admitted, his voice faint. "I saw your piece online and… I don't know, something drew me to you. I'm not really sure why I contacted you."

"Cam, you did the right thing," Adam reassured him, his heart aching for this man who was risking everything to expose the truth. "I'm here for you. We'll figure this out together, one step at a time."

"Look, I'll try to stay in touch. But I can't promise anything."

The last syllables of his sentence were so faint that Adam wondered if he had imagined them.

"Understood. Your safety is important. Just do what you can."

"Before I go—" Cam hesitated, then rushed forward, as if afraid he would lose his nerve. "I overheard something about core samples. No…wait? Pencore? Yes, I think I heard pencore samples. That's all I know."

"Pencore?" Adam repeated, his interest piqued. Sensing Cam's growing unease, he quickly added, "Thank you for telling me. I can imagine how hard this was for you."

The call ended abruptly, leaving Adam feeling uneasy and with more questions than answers. He stared at the cell phone in his hand, a chill running up his spine, unsure of what Cam's words meant.

Harper Brasfield sank into her chair, massaging her temples in a quiet act of surrender. As she scrolled through the endless streams of social media on her phone, each flick of her thumb was a testament to her weariness. She was hunting for anything related to PenCore, but the digital noise was overwhelming. Hours had passed in a blur of forums and comment sections, her focus sharp on unraveling the company's secrets.

A single post caught her eye amid the chaos. A social media user mentioned a relative who received exceptional care at a PenCore-run prison—better than what was available to the public. Intrigued, Harper dug into the post's details, which described a prison medical center that was more akin to a high-tech hospital, boasting state-of-the-art imaging and robotic surgery.

Surprise flickered across Harper's face. Advanced healthcare in a prison was unheard of and raised a multitude of questions.

Then another piece of the puzzle clicked into place. In the comments, an alleged former PenCore worker confirmed the medical wing's sophistication.

With each new piece of information, Harper's pulse quickened. She saved screenshots of the key comments and their authors' profiles, though she was cautious about trusting anonymous online sources.

They were edging toward something big. She could feel it. With renewed determination, she mumbled, "Ethan, found something," and drafted an urgent message.

Harper lay in the bed she once shared with Rob, their past swirling in her mind. She reminisced about their early dating days, when Deandra, her lifelong friend, often inadvertently became a third wheel. Rob had tried to make Deandra feel included by introducing her to his friends. This memory brought a fleeting smile to Harper's face, but it was quickly tinged with melancholy, a poignant reminder that those days were gone forever.

As the first light of dawn broke the horizon, Harper readied herself for the day and made her way to the office.

Settled at her desk, she sipped her lukewarm coffee, leaning against the window. The soft hum of the air conditioning filled the still room. Her thoughts wandered, navigating the complexities of Darrius's case, the PenCore investigation, and her frayed relationships, stirring a whirlwind of emotions inside her.

Deandra's silhouette filled the doorway, her expression a cocktail of anger and sorrow. Harper's heart raced. She hadn't been prepared for this confrontation.

Gathering herself, Harper's voice wavered, her fingers absentmindedly tucking a strand of hair behind her ear. "Dee," she began hesitantly. "It's early. What's on your mind?"

Deandra hesitated, her gaze flitting to the floor. "I needed to talk. Are you free?"

Harper nodded, motioning to the chair across from her desk. "Please, sit."

As Deandra settled in, Harper couldn't help but notice the tired lines marking her friend's face, each one echoing countless restless nights. Harper tried to ease the tension with light conversation about her recent cases.

Deandra's voice broke through the veneer of casualness. "Harper, we can't dance around this. There's something I've held back."

Harper steeled herself, sensing the gravity of what was to come.

Deandra met Harper's eyes, her own filled with hurt. "I'm upset, Harper. You've built walls around you. When Rob left, I expected you to turn to me, but instead, you shut me out. It hurt."

Harper looked down, feeling a rush of guilt. Memories of solitary nights with alcohol and snapping at Deandra weighed on her. The pain in Deandra's words was justified.

With a trembling voice and eyes brimming with tears, Harper said softly, "Dee, I didn't know how much I hurt you. Is there a way for us to heal?"

Breaking the heavy silence, Harper's voice quivered with remorse. "I've apologized to everyone at the firm, but I missed you. I want to make things right, even if I don't deserve your forgiveness."

Deandra stayed quiet, her gaze somewhere far off. Seeking to change the subject, Harper brought up her concerns about Lucas. "He's in DC now, and I haven't heard from him. It's worrying me," she confided.

At the mention of Lucas, a softer expression crossed Deandra's face. They both had a connection to him that Harper longed to reclaim. With a hopeful gesture, Harper extended her hand. "Dee, can we find our way back to each other?"

Deandra paused, the weight of her decision clear as day. "Before we can rebuild, there's something you should know."

Anxiety gnawed at Harper. "Tell me."

"I've been offered a position at the DA's office," Deandra confessed.

The room seemed to contract, the weight of Deandra's words pressing down on Harper. The thought of losing her as a colleague felt like a cruel twist of fate.

"Harper." Deandra's voice carried a tremor of concern. "I've always valued the work we do together, yet I find myself questioning if the path of criminal law is still right for me. Beyond that, the conflict with ADA Turner—it's not just about a single disagreement. Your recent actions, the intensity you've brought into the office... it's reflecting on both of us. It's complicating things for me professionally, and it's hard to ignore."

Harper's chest tightened, realizing her impulsive actions had unintentionally impacted Deandra's career. Tears blurred her vision as she said softly, "Dee, I had no idea. I'm so, so sorry."

Deandra's eyes betrayed a hint of envy, a sheen of unspoken grievances. "You're always in the spotlight, Harper. Even in the eyes of my own family. Where does that leave me?"

The sting of Deandra's words was sharper than Harper expected. She stepped in, her tone gentle. "I never meant to cast a shadow over you, Deandra. Your family... they've been my anchor. I didn't see that I might be taking up too much space."

Deandra withdrew slightly. "This isn't just about being

overshadowed. It's about me recognizing my need to step into my own light. Our friendship means the world to me, but I can't let it eclipse my own needs."

Harper's voice was thick with emotion. "I've been lost, Dee. But losing you? That's a nightmare. Please, tell me we can fix this."

A tear slid down Deandra's face. "We'll find a way, but it'll take work."

Harper smiled weakly. "And if you want to join the DA's office, I've got your back. Always."

A shared smile passed between them, full of memories. "Rawls Hall girls forever," they murmured in unison.

After Deandra left, Harper stood still, feeling the silence. She wasn't sure how to fix things between them, but she was determined to try. Their friendship meant too much to give up without a fight, and she was ready to do whatever it took to get them back on good terms.

Exhaustion shadowed Harper's eyes after yet another restless night. Sitting in her home office, thoughts of Deandra's biting words, her children, and the judge swirled in her mind.

Opening an email from Ethan, she sifted through the attached PenCore documents, hunting for elusive connections. Her fingers skimmed over the keyboard, searching for patterns among company names and contracts.

"You're better than this, Brass."

Despite her expertise, the links remained hidden. Harper

dialed Ethan. He answered on the second ring, voice groggy.

"Hey, Harper. What's up?"

"Can you meet tomorrow?"

"Just text the details," Ethan replied, muffling a yawn.

"Will do." A flicker of hope ignited within her, and she allowed herself a small smile.

The next day, Harper and Ethan hunched over her laptop, scrutinizing the documents spread before them like a jigsaw puzzle.

Ethan recapped their findings. "We can trace a line through cutouts and shell companies which leads to PenCore; it looks like Meridian Holdings owns it. It's documented, but not obvious."

Harper nodded and clarified, "Shell companies are often created for legitimate reasons like confidentiality, asset protection, or intellectual property management. But they can also be misused for illegal activities such as tax evasion or to hide the real owners."

"You were working with a contact at a federal agency, right? Harper recalled. "Have you uncovered any illegal activities by Meridian Holdings?"

"No," Ethan replied with certainty. "My contact at the agency—yeah, the one with the alphabet soup name—confirmed the list is solid. It's got every subsidiary under Meridian Holdings, and there's nothing shady on record."

Harper's lips curled into a wry smile. "Always playing it close to the vest with your informants, huh?"

Ethan shifted uneasily, his eyes darting away for a moment. He gave Harper a guarded look, his protective instincts mixing with affection. "It's for the best. Keeps things neat—distance and plausible deniability, Tacks."

Harper glanced at the list of names, reciting them aloud. Most were for industrial businesses, but a few caught her eye: LifeCore, GenenLabs, and CytoLife Dynamics. Ethan went through his documents to search for details on those three companies.

"LifeCore operates in the renewable energy sector, and GenenLabs focuses on alternative energy research in wildlife ecosystems."

"What do we know about CytoLife Dynamics?"

"Not much. There's nothing else here except that it's a biomedical research firm."

Harper opened their website, a sleek page bearing the company logo and marked with the slogan "Pioneering Today for a Healthier Tomorrow." Their mission was "to use cellular research to eliminate debilitating diseases, enhance life quality, and maximize human potential."

Harper's recognition flickered as she scanned the online articles. "Ah, yes," she recalled. "This company has made quite a name for itself with grand public health campaigns— vaccinating populations globally—and they also provide genetic testing kits. They've cultivated an impressive reputation."

Ethan nodded eagerly while Harper delved deeper into the documents.

Then, with a sudden burst of realization, Ethan declared, "Harper, it's Thomas Baxter. He's the key player at Meridian

Holdings."

Shock etched Harper's features. Thomas Baxter, the celebrated pioneer of Baxter Global, was a household name for his groundbreaking work in renewable energy. His effortless charm had graced many a talk show, captivating audiences and even prompting hosts to playfully propose he mediate international conflicts. Beyond the cameras, he was a titan, tirelessly championing for a greener planet.

"The darling of the green revolution," Harper exclaimed incredulously.

Ethan's expression mirrored her shock. "But what's his angle with PenCore?"

Harper leaned back, thoughtful. "Men like him command sprawling empires, often blind to the minutiae. I'd wager he's oblivious to PenCore's machinations."

Ethan's gaze drifted, contemplative. "We might consider consulting Adam Burke. He could have pieces of this puzzle that we're missing."

Harper expressed her doubt. "Adam was uncooperative last time, like pulling teeth. But you're right. We're at a dead end." A faint, unsettling premonition stirred within her, a whisper of caution that sent a tingle through her veins.

Days later, Harper sat in a corner of a cozy diner in Hernando, MS, far from Memphis. She constantly scanned the room, her eyes flicking from one unfamiliar face to another, searching for signs of recognition or danger. Ethan sat across from her, his laptop open and displaying a myriad of documents and notes.

"Here he comes," Ethan said, nodding towards the entrance.

Adam Burke slid into the booth beside Harper, glancing around anxiously. "Thanks for meeting me here," he whispered. "I'm trying to keep my head down."

Harper cut straight to the chase. "We need to pool our information. We're digging into PenCore, trying to piece together the alleged kickback scheme you mentioned."

"I'm telling you, it's real! I just—"

Harper held up a hand. "We believe you." She glanced at Ethan, who gave a confirming nod. "Let's go over what we've uncovered."

Adam looked strained. "I've shared everything about the kickbacks. What else do you want?"

"It's not just the kickbacks," Harper said, her voice quivering with urgency. "There's a bigger picture here. We need to collaborate to uncover the full story."

"I've got my own work to tackle. I don't need this added stress."

Harper reached out, her grip firm on his arm. "Hear me out.

"We suspect there's a calculated move to transfer prisoners to PenCore, driven by profit and potentially darker intentions. Our evidence? PenCore's facilities are stocked with advanced medical equipment—odd, considering Tall Trees' reputation."

Harper meticulously detailed their findings, keeping a

close eye on Adam's reactions. When she mentioned CytoLife Dynamics, she saw him stiffen, fingers tapping rapidly against the table.

Harper's intensity peaked. "PenCore, a corporation driven by profit, controls prisons. They've embroiled politicians and bureaucrats in a corrupt kickback scheme, ensuring a constant influx of prisoners and, thereby, profit. Yet, astoundingly, these same prisons provide superior healthcare compared to what our taxpayers get. Don't you find that awfully suspicious, Adam?"

Adam removed his glasses, massaging the bridge of his nose. "There's something... something I've stumbled upon. It might be connected, but it's still hazy. I've been diving into a new investigative series and..."

Ethan leaned in, his voice firm. "Share it."

Adam seemed torn, finally confessing, "It's all speculative right now. However..."

"Go on," Harper urged, her eyes fixed on him. "Whatever you say stays between us."

Adam took a deep breath. "I interviewed someone anonymously. He said he's from a biolab, but wouldn't divulge its name. He was terrified. He did mention PenCore once, adding the term 'samples' after it."

"Samples?" Harper repeated, aghast. "What does that mean?"

Adam looked as shaken as she felt. "I don't know. He insinuated the ramifications were staggering."

Ethan's eyes met Harper's, both reflecting a mix of fear and bewilderment.

She clutched Adam's forearm, her voice quivering.

"Adam, we need more. Can you connect us to him? Allow Ethan to set up some recording gear. We need every detail."

Adam hesitated, then rose. "I can't promise anything. He might not even contact me again. And honestly, he might've just been some prankster trying to spook me."

"But you believed him, didn't you?" Harper's voice was thick with emotion. "Just... think about it. We need to be prepared when or if he reaches out."

Adam paused, a flicker of hesitation crossing his face. He nodded, giving in, yet there was a quick rush to his agreement, a hurry to end the conversation that hung heavily in the air.

As darkness blanketed the city, Harper felt a foreboding certainty that this was merely the tip of the iceberg.

NINE

Adam Burke sat hunched over his desk, his fingers paused on the keyboard as he worked on an article about CRISPR. He reached for his mug, the coffee inside long gone cold and bitter, yet he drank it to stay sharp. Shaking off the lingering irritation from Harper's probing questions, he refocused on the article, determined to get back to what truly mattered.

CRISPR, the cutting-edge gene-editing tool, promises to revolutionize medicine and has ignited intense debates across the scientific and legal realms. Adam typed, aiming to simplify the complex topic. *While its potential is vast, from curing diseases to enhancing lives, it also raises ethical questions about the boundaries of human intervention.*

He remembered spirited debates with scientists. Some hailed CRISPR's breakthroughs, while others cautioned against overstepping nature's bounds. Yet they universally recognized the tool's potential to alleviate human suffering.

The key to understanding CRISPR is the difference between editing somatic cells, like lung or blood cells, and germline cells, such as sperm or eggs. **Adam elaborated.** *While somatic edits affect only the individual, germline edits impact descendants too. A prime example was the 2018 claim by a Chinese scientist of editing twin girls' genes to make them HIV-resistant, triggering global controversy.*

He then touched on the US legal landscape. *While germline editing isn't outright illegal here, it's heavily regulated. Research involving human embryo manipulation doesn't receive federal funding. Plus, clinics need FDA approval before employing gene editing in procedures like in-vitro fertilization. Yet the line of legality remains somewhat ambiguous.*

Adam concluded, highlighting global perspectives. *Internationally, countries' stances on genetic editing vary widely.*

Adam Burke paused, his fingers hovering over the keyboard. The CRISPR draft before him hinted at something momentous lurking beneath the surface. His research, fueled by an anonymous tipster whose revelations were as thrilling as they were disquieting, seemed on the verge of a major breakthrough.

He rolled his shoulders back, readying himself, the

excitement of the chase sharpening his focus. Truth-finding was his marathon, and despite the nerves, Adam was steadfast, buoyed by the cryptic promise of his sources' leads and the steadfast rhythm of his journalistic pursuit.

Several weeks after meeting Adam, Harper and Ethan sat on a weathered bench beneath the shade of a towering oak tree in Court Square, downtown Memphis. The square was a sanctuary amid the bustling city, its lush greenery, and dappled sunlight providing a sense of seclusion.

Harper's brow knotted as she watched a squirrel sprint up a tree. "Adam's been avoiding us like the plague." She'd tried to reach him countless times, only to be met with non-answers or halfhearted excuses.

"Seems like he's worried about revealing too much." Ethan leaned back on the bench, watching people pass by. "Either that or he thinks he's already overstepped his boundaries."

"Maybe," Harper mused, staring at the leaves above them, gently swaying in the breeze. "Yet that doesn't explain why he's gone radio silent on us."

Ethan suggested, "Maybe he found something that spooked him, or he's just covering his backside."

Harper took in his words, understanding the implications. "We can't bank on him now."

"We have enough to deal with as it is," Ethan finished.

"You're right, Ethan. We need to focus on the leads we've

already uncovered. Let's push forward without waiting for Adam. If he decides to come back and offer more insights, great, we'll take them. But for now, we've got to rely on ourselves."

Harper watched as Ethan scanned the park for any signs of eavesdroppers. His past experience had honed his instincts for surveillance and countersurveillance, making him wary of potential threats.

Checking at her phone, Harper stared at Lucas's disconnected number. A knot tightened in her stomach, a blend of worry and guilt swirling within her.

She lifted her gaze to find Ethan's forehead creased as he watched her.

"Lucas," she muttered, her voice not quite audible. Ethan waited patiently for her to continue. "His number isn't working. I'm not sure what to do."

Ethan shifted in his seat and offered a gentle suggestion. "Have you tried contacting Rob?"

Harper's expression was one of apprehension; the tension between her and Rob was thick enough to cut with a knife.

Harper sighed, running a hand through her dark hair. "I might have to," she conceded, her voice steeped with resignation.

"If you need help, let me know." Ethan placed a supportive hand on her shoulder.

"Thanks," she said, managing a weak smile before refocusing on their investigation.

Harper's fingertips tapped rhythmically on the wooden surface of their table at Bluff City Coffee Shop, setting the tempo for their investigative symphony. The place was cozy, with the rich scent of brewing coffee providing a comforting backdrop to the tension of their task. Piles of crinkled documents were strewn about, each page a potential clue in their sprawling investigation.

She caught Ethan's eye, who appeared to be lost in a maze of thought, and began to piece together the puzzle aloud. "Okay, let's string this together. We've got PenCore, infamous for its cutthroat operations, yet oddly providing top-notch healthcare in select institutions. There are whispers of their hand greasing the palms of city bigwigs, and then there's Meridian Holdings sitting at the top of this questionable pyramid."

Ethan leaned over, his finger hovering over a highlighted segment of a report. "And the captain of this ship is none other than Thomas Baxter, the billionaire whose name is synonymous with global philanthropy and the push for renewable energy. The guy's a headline darling. It's hard to imagine him keeping tabs on a prison operation."

Harper flipped through her notes again. "Then there's the wildcard, CytoLife Dynamics. A biotech firm dabbling in health research with a tenuous thread linking it to PenCore, all under Meridian's expansive umbrella."

Ethan's frown deepened as he pieced together the disparate elements. "We're staring at a jigsaw where the pieces don't seem to fit. But there's a picture here we're not seeing. What's the missing link?"

Harper's voice was a hushed thread of concern. "Ethan, think back to our last chat with Adam—his whole demeanor was off. And the way he spoke about his whistleblower, how spooked they were about something and they heard the words 'pencore samples'... it's troubling. He's avoiding our calls now, and we're in the dark about his research. Could it all point to something he's too scared to reveal?"

The gravity of her suggestion lingered between them, a specter of possibility that was as unsettling as it was undeniable.

Harper strode into her office, adrenaline pulsing, ready to confront Sam about Darrius's case. Despite the odds, her fervor for justice burned fiercely. She entered Sam's tight office space, capturing his gaze filled with curiosity edged with suspicion.

"Sam, about Darrius's case," she started, her voice firm.

Sam motioned to the opposite chair. She sat, poised and waiting.

After a beat, he prompted, "Well?"

"The ADA won't budge. They want Darrius to turn on his gang."

Sam's voice dripped with condescension. "Tough negotiations, huh? You always get so invested."

"Why assign this to me? Is there something you're not

telling me?"

Raising an eyebrow, Sam responded, "You're one of the best, Harper. But you always look for a deeper plot."

She shot back, "It feels like you're testing me. Pushing me towards some hidden agenda."

He sighed, exasperated. "It's not always a conspiracy, Harper. Just do your job."

"I am. Every day. But with cases like Darrius's, it's hard to just go by the book."

Sam rubbed his forehead, the lines of fatigue pronounced as he weighed her words. "I hope you're not chasing ghosts with wild theories. Focus on what's solid in Darrius's case. And remember, mitigating circumstances in a three-strikes case is next to impossible to argue. Just make sure your other cases don't fall by the wayside. They all deserve your full attention."

As Harper left Sam's office, her stride was steady, but her aura spoke of a hidden storm that threatened to leave her adrift.

Adam sat in his Midtown apartment, a tumbler of whiskey in hand, his gaze fixed on the shifting shadows on the wall. A blend of fear and hesitation clouded his thoughts, hindering his focus on the investigation.

His mind raced back to the enigmatic call from the whistleblower, the words "pencore samples" echoing incessantly. The ambiguity of the message burdened him.

Was he on the right track, or was he gambling everything on a baseless hunch?

Taking another sip, the whiskey's warmth scarcely countered the chill of dread enveloping him. While he had attempted to distance himself from Harper and Ethan, he couldn't shake the feeling that he possessed crucial information.

Adam's contemplation of the amber liquid, with its hint of smoky oak, was interrupted by a buzz from his phone. An alert from the Beacon app flashed on the screen. Shifting his focus, he opened the message from Cam.

I'm ready to talk.

TEN

The downtown law firm buzzed with the celebration of Deandra's new position at the DA's office. Amidst the lively chatter and clinking glasses, Harper stood by the window, her gaze lost in the fading light.

A sense of both pride and sorrow enveloped her. Deandra's ascent was a poignant reminder of the growing distance in their once-close bond. Harper swirled her drink, its amber reflections mirroring her inner conflict, and took a slow sip, questioning the reality of their vow to reconnect.

"Harper, darling, you look in need of a hug," came a soft voice from behind. Mama Dee, ever graceful in her emerald dress and pearls, approached with open arms. Her warmth and charm were a beacon in the Memphis legal scene, drawing people to her naturally.

Mama Dee was more than just Deandra's mother and Judge Jackson's wife. Her legendary kindness had made her a beloved figure. As she hugged Harper, the tension in Harper's shoulders eased.

She leaned into Mama Dee's embrace, soaking in the much-needed warmth and affection. "I really needed that," Harper murmured.

Mama Dee held Harper at arm's length, looking into her eyes with a tender gaze. "Nothing's too good for my honorary daughter," she said, her voice filled with maternal affection. "Let's get you a fresh drink and then find Deandra. Tonight's about making happy memories."

Harper nodded, allowing Mama Dee to lead her back into the lively crowd, a small glimmer of hope flickering within her.

As the party wound down, Deandra approached Harper with a beaming smile. Her tone light and teasing, she mentioned getting the job at the prosecutor's office despite their friendship's complications.

Harper chuckled, feeling a spark of hope ignite within her. Her heart fluttered at her friend's success. "Well, I always knew you were destined for greatness."

Deandra tugged at her arm. "Come on," she said. "Let's take a break from the noise."

Together, they navigated the thinning crowd and slipped into Deandra's office, closing the door behind them. The silence was a pleasant relief from the party noise.

Deandra leaned against her desk, a mischievous glint in her eye. "Remember when we used to sneak away to my dad's study to steal sips of his whiskey?"

Harper burst into laughter. "Lord, yes! And how we'd

make those awful faces, pretending we actually enjoyed the taste."

She rolled her eyes before adding, "Speak for yourself, Brass. I developed quite a refined palate."

The two friends dissolved into laughter as memories of their younger selves flooded back. Deandra continued between fits of giggles. "Or that time we put shaving cream in poor Mr. Thompson's shoes? I thought he'd have a heart attack right there in front of the entire school!"

"God, we were such little hellions." Harper grinned. "How Mama Dee never caught on to our schemes is beyond me."

"Maybe she did," Deandra mused. "She's always been pretty perceptive, you know. I bet she just let us think we were getting away with it."

Harper laughed in agreement. "She's holding court out there like the queen she is."

Sitting in the calm, a hidden fear gripped Harper. Amidst the flood of shared memories, she saw the fragility of their bond. The unspoken worry that they might not reclaim the closeness of their once-unshakable friendship weighed heavily on her.

Deandra cupped Harper's arm with her hand and spoke in a gentle voice. "Hey, no matter what happens or where our careers take us, you're my sister. We'll always find our way back."

Harper stared into Deandra's sincere gaze. The sentiment was so powerful, words were unnecessary. She simply nodded and mouthed a silent, *I love you*, before embracing her best friend. Despite the looming changes casting shadows of doubt, their friendship stood resilient, a constant amidst life's upheavals.

The buzz of Harper's phone interrupted their moment of connection. Pulling back, she glanced at the screen—a message from Rob.

Still no news from Lucas. I'll send updates if I get any.

A frown crossed her face, mirroring her concern. While frustrated by the lack of news, she found a small solace in knowing Rob was also waiting for word.

Harper pocketed her phone and said to Deandra, "Thanks. I needed this." Their eyes met in mutual understanding. Together, they stepped back into the office, where the party's lively chatter welcomed them, a stark contrast to their solemn interlude.

"Hey, Brass."

Hearing Ethan's serious tone piqued Harper's curiosity. She excused herself from Deandra, telling her she'd be right back, and huddled into an alcove with Ethan.

"What's going on?" Her eyes darted to the tablet he was holding with a look of anticipation.

Ethan sighed. His eyes lowered to the floor as he told Harper he had contacted a profile on the internet that had commented on PenCore. His voice was almost inaudible. "Knew it was a long shot. I still made sure no one could trace me."

Harper stared at Ethan, her mouth agape. She swayed slightly, revealing she had too many drinks. "You astound me," she said in awe, admiration flashing across her face. She shook her head to clear it, then gave him an ironic smile. "I thought I was the one always taking risks."

"Look at this," Ethan said, showing her the screen. It displayed his chat with diver09437, reportedly a former PenCore employee in Tennessee. The messages were succinct, confirming their suspicions and revealing the transfer of certain inmates to a specialized, out-of-state medical center.

Harper's lips formed a tight line as she considered the possibilities. "Do we have any additional details on this person?"

Ethan tapped the screen, highlighting the message where the stranger mentioned tracking down old coworkers.

Harper grew serious, her mind spinning with implications of this connection. "Keep pushing for more info. We need to learn everything."

Meanwhile, across town, Adam Burke's fingers trembled as he opened his phone to a secure message from Cam through the Beacon app.

Adam, I can't sleep at night, Cam's message began, a note of unease threaded through his words. *At work, we have stringent protocols.* He listed the rigorous security measures in place—keycard entries, video monitoring, comprehensive background checks. *But despite all these precautions, something feels off.*

Adam's heart raced as he typed the urgent reply. *Go on.*

I've seen reports on a colleague's workstation. It doesn't look like anything I'm familiar with. Something isn't right.

A chill ran down Adam's spine as he processed Cam's words. The lead was too crucial to ignore, despite the need for caution. *Tell me more.* His fingers trembled as he typed.

Can't say much more. But I'm willing to help. We need to do something.

Agreed, Adam responded, already planning in his mind. He sensed the hesitation in Cam's replies, as if he were weighing the risks of revealing more. He knew he had to tread carefully, but this information could be vital.

Look, Cam, I understand you're putting yourself on the line here, but if there's something untoward happening at that lab, we need to expose it. I promise not to publish anything until we have the full story. And I'll protect your identity. But I need your help. I need documented evidence.

Cam's response took longer than usual, and Adam couldn't resist feeling a knot of anxiety tightening in his stomach. Finally, a message appeared.

Alright. I can't just send you the documents outright. It's too risky.

Adam typed. *Take photos. Send them through Beacon. It's secure. Feel free to redact any identifying info. I need to examine these reports on my own.*

The silence stretched on for several agonizing minutes before Cam's reply arrived.

Okay. This stays between us. I can't bear the thought of someone finding out.

Trust me, **Adam assured him.** *Your secret is safe with me. We'll put a stop to this, whatever it is.*

Cam's reluctance was obvious, even behind the digital screen, but after another pause, he agreed. *Give me some time. I'll get you what you need.*

As Adam waited, his unease grew. What secrets would those documents reveal? What had Cam stumbled upon that was so dangerous and disturbing?

He paced back and forth in his small apartment, his mind racing with possibilities. The weight of responsibility settled heavily on his shoulders—both for uncovering the truth and for protecting Cam.

Days later, when the images finally arrived via Beacon, Adam felt a mixture of dread and relief wash over him. He was one step closer to unveiling the darkness lurking beneath the surface of gene editing.

Thanks, Cam. **A newfound determination took hold.** *I appreciate the risk you're taking. You're doing the right thing.*

Adam's heart raced as he opened the files Cam had sent him. The documents were a blur of scientific jargon and figures, but one page caught his eye—unredacted and filled with information that made his pulse quicken. There, in black and white, were the words "PenCore" and "CytoLife" alongside an extensive list of random numbers.

A vivid memory surged—Harper and Ethan debating CytoLife in a charged meeting weeks earlier. Adam remembered Harper's intensity as she said the name, her eyes wide.

Adam dropped his head in frustration, wishing he could make sense of the data. Despite the jumble of data, PenCore and CytoLife's inextricable link was painfully clear to him. And Cam seemed to be in the middle of the sordid mess.

Adam's eyes darted across the files, deciphering the terminology and charts. He noticed a recurring reference to "genomic sequences" and "gene editing" alongside mentions of PenCore samples. It was apparent to him, even with his limited understanding, that these were related to DNA experiments.

A knot formed in Adam's stomach as he stared at the screen, grappling with the magnitude of his discovery. A mix of fear, astonishment, and disbelief churned within him. While his journalistic instincts demanded clarity, another part of him yearned to escape this intricate maze of secrets.

He navigated to the CytoLife website, seeking some solace. Certain phrases stood out. *CytoLife's Genome Project focuses on mapping genetic diseases for early detection. Our over-the-counter kits empower individuals to explore their genetic health.* Their DNA research was indisputable, but its link to Cam's unsettling revelations remained elusive.

Then it dawned on him. CytoLife must be using PenCore inmates' samples for clandestine DNA experiments.

He had to focus. Harper needed to know. He braced for her anger, blame, and skepticism, but knew that together, they might unravel the ominous connection between PenCore and CytoLife.

Adam's hand trembled as he held the phone, his eyes fixed on the complex documents in front of him. The pages were dense with scientific jargon and intricate data he only partially understood. Before rushing to Harper with potentially misinterpreted facts, he needed Cam's insights.

He willed himself to stay focused and dialed Cam through Beacon.

"Cam," he began, trying to keep his voice steady despite the rising fear. "We need to discuss the files you sent over. It seems you overlooked some redactions. They indicate DNA experiments using samples from PenCore."

A tense silence stretched between them until Cam's voice, quivering with anxiety, broke through. "I... I have no idea what you're referring to." Adam could feel the genuine dread in Cam's response.

Adam's tone grew gentler, sensing the gravity of the situation for both of them. "Listen, Cam, I know this is frightening, but we have to understand the full scope of this. We stand a better chance if we're united. Can you help clarify these documents regarding the experiments?"

Cam hesitated, his voice shaking. "Adam, I've risked a lot getting you this far. I can't go on. It's too dangerous. I'm ending our communication."

"Cam, please—" Adam began, desperation plain, but the call had already ended, leaving him with a sense of rising urgency and frustration.

Adam knew he had to involve Harper, despite risking her anger. He hesitated, staring at the phone for a moment to gather his thoughts, then finally initiated the call. His heart thumped with anxious anticipation, each ring amplifying the tension as he awaited her answer.

"Brass." Harper's voice was sharp and unyielding.

"Harper, it's Adam. We need to talk. As soon as possible."

"Really?" Harper's response dripped with sarcasm, but Adam could hear a hint of concern underneath the scorn. "You've been ducking my calls for weeks, and now you suddenly want to talk?"

Adam's voice edged on desperation as he pleaded, "Harper, I know you're angry. But please, just listen to me. I have new information, and it's big. Bigger than anything you've come across. I think I know what's happening. We need to figure this out together."

Adam feared she would hang up on him during a long pause. Then he heard her exhale a heavy sigh, and he knew she was listening.

"Alright, Burke. Let's hear it."

Lucas Fairbanks, coffee cup in hand, stood on his cottage's veranda, mesmerized by the expansive beauty of the Evergreen. The resort, sprawling over 11,000 acres, was a secluded haven of luxury, a favorite among the world's most influential figures.

His cottage, tucked away on the property, offered more space than any place he had previously lived. Lucas stepped onto the verdant lawn, embracing the solitude. With eyes closed and arms outstretched, a brief grin crossed his face, quickly replaced by the sobering realization of the significant changes in his life.

The position at CytoLife had offered benefits beyond his wildest expectations: a handsome salary, a fortified company-issued Range Rover, and a generous allowance at a renowned clothing boutique.

Lucas had made his weapon choices swiftly: a Walther PDP secured at his hip and a trusty Smith & Wesson .357 snub nose as backup on his ankle. On the recommendation of his superior, Felix, he also included a Benelli shotgun in the SUV's armory. Although he felt a brief twinge of discomfort about the potential dangers ahead, Lucas's training and Felix's endorsement of his armament choice bolstered his confidence, reinforcing his readiness for whatever lay ahead.

Lucas surveyed the immaculate grounds of the resort, his eyes sweeping over the manicured lawns and the majestic glass exterior of the main building. The luxury he had grown accustomed to in his life seemed modest compared to this opulence.

The resort appeared almost surreal in its grandeur, boasting premier restaurants, a variety of outdoor activities, and an enticing casino. It had served as an exclusive playground for the affluent for over a century.

It wasn't all leisure and luxury for Lucas. He worked long hours under the watchful eye of his boss, Felix Ross—a man as calculating as he was ruthless. He filled Lucas's days with mundane, and at times degrading, tasks. But Lucas viewed each one as a challenge and accepted it willingly.

Felix had laid out strict instructions: Lucas was not to mingle with the guests or engage too closely with his fellow employees. He could enjoy the facilities, but only when they weren't busy and without revealing his occupation.

Lucas stood on the veranda, contemplating whether to enjoy the resort's offerings. Despite his fear, he couldn't resist his curiosity.

He took a step onto the soft grass, and with a breath of anticipation, he made his way towards the main structure. Passing by the Executive Medical Clinic, he made a mental note to confirm his physical—a perk Felix insisted he partake of sooner rather than later.

As Lucas strolled through the resort's lush grounds, a pang of guilt surfaced. He was here, immersed in luxury, while his mother, Harper, was probably embroiled in another dangerous situation. In military terms, she seemed to be a magnet for trouble. He attempted to push these thoughts aside, reminding himself that he couldn't control her decisions.

"Focus, Fairbanks," he whispered to himself, entering the grandeur of the lobby.

Lucas stood outside Felix's office, the formidable oak door exuding authority. Taking a deep breath, he braced himself, anticipating another evaluation.

"Enter," Felix's gruff voice commanded. Lucas pushed the door open to see Felix engrossed on his computer.

"Ah, Fairbanks," Felix said, gesturing towards a woman by the window without looking away from his screen. "I'd like you to meet someone." The woman, her blonde hair cascading down her back, stood gazing out over the resort.

"Dr. Rebecca Kent," Felix introduced. "She's vital to CytoLife, and you'll be her personal security."

Rebecca turned, her piercing blue eyes meeting Lucas's. She exuded confidence, her subtle smile hinting at amusement. "Mr. Fairbanks," she said in a smooth, slightly accented voice. "Pleasure to meet you."

Lucas stumbled verbally, his voice wavering. "Uh, likewise, you can call me Lucas."

She stepped closer, her presence overpowering. "Lucas," she said, a sultry smile playing on her lips. He struggled to maintain composure, feeling a rush of adrenaline.

"Very well, Lucas," she continued, her gaze intense. "I hope we'll work well together."

He nodded, barely managing a hoarse reply. Felix's voice cut through the tension. "Fairbanks, remember your role. Don't mess this up."

"Understood," Lucas replied, a thread of apprehension weaving through him. The faint pull towards Rebecca suggested they were on the cusp of navigating risky waters.

Exiting Felix's office, Rebecca tugged at his sleeve, her

gaze unwavering. "Let's take a walk. I want to know more about you, Lucas Fairbanks."

As they walked through the gardens, Lucas was torn between exhilaration and concern. He had navigated Felix's trials, but this new challenge—balancing his duty and developing attraction to Rebecca—seemed daunting.

Rebecca's voice, deep and captivating, broke the silence. "What do you truly want?"

Lucas hesitated, caught in her mesmerizing gaze, torn between candor and caution. The mutual attraction was unmistakable, adding another layer of complexity to his mission.

In the night's stillness, Harper, Ethan, and Adam met in a deserted corner of a lot that used to house the Mall of Memphis. Bathed in moonlight, their long shadows sprawled across the cracked pavement. Harper sensed the impending moments held the power to change their lives forever, their significance almost tangible in the silence.

Harper's eyes narrowed as she regarded Adam. "Nice of you to join us."

Adam rubbed the back of his neck anxiously. "Look, I'm sorry, Harper. I've got something you need to hear."

Harper uncrossed her arms and leaned forward in anticipation. "Alright, spill it."

"How familiar are you with CRISPR or gene editing?" Adam asked.

Ethan slowly blinked a few times. "Um… didn't you write an article?"

Harper stepped in calmly, softening her gaze on Adam. "Why don't you give us a quick explanation?" she asked. Her green eyes held a blend of curiosity and concern, intently fixed on him, seeking clarity.

"CRISPR allows scientists to edit living things' instruction manual, like editing a book's sentence with microscopic scissors. It edits the genes, which are the instruction manual for growth and function of living things."

Harper cut in suddenly, her curiosity piqued. "So the hope is that it can cure certain genetic diseases?"

Adam's face was etched with concentration as he nodded. He spoke of dual possibilities—the potential to alleviate widespread suffering, but also the risk of darker outcomes like bioweapons, super-soldiers, and human enhancements. His voice softened, his expression more inquisitive than conclusive.

Harper reached out, her touch light on his arm, urging him to continue. He hesitated, gathering his thoughts, before resuming his explanation.

"I've been in touch with someone called Cam. He's part of a CRISPR research team at a biolab. He seems troubled, like he's trying to ease his conscience. He's been leaking bits of information to me. Anyway, recently, he accidentally sent documents with incomplete redactions." Adam's voice shook with unease.

"These papers link him to CytoLife, a major player in DNA editing. And they mention PenCore samples, which connects back to something Cam mentioned in passing earlier."

Adam's voice was heavy with a grave certainty. "I'm certain of it now—they're conducting experiments on DNA samples from PenCore inmates." His words echoed with a chilling sense of impending doom.

Harper's face paled as she locked eyes with Ethan, both sharing a look of sheer astonishment. A storm of emotions—outrage, disbelief, and a dawning realization—raged within her. Their relentless chase for leads was finally yielding results. The puzzle pieces were coming together at last.

"Adam, do you realize the implications?" Harper's voice trembled, her words filled with both shock and a surge of adrenaline. "Our paths have converged. We can't turn back now."

Adam looked up, a reluctant resolve in his eyes. "I never meant to get this deep, but I can't ignore what's right in front of me. I'm in over my head now, whether I like it or not."

Ethan's expression hardened. "We're stronger together. We're facing a common enemy. It's time we combine our efforts."

Harper surveyed them both. "We have to act. Whatever is happening at PenCore and CytoLife needs to be brought to light."

Though her words were firm, her eyes betrayed the gravity of their task. The prospect of taking on a giant like CytoLife, especially if the rumors of inmate experiments were true, loomed large—a daunting yet necessary confrontation.

ELEVEN

In his office, suffused with the scent of leather and old wood, Felix Ross stood by the window, his silhouette stark against the setting sun. As a former Special Forces operative turned mercenary, his journey had led him to the secretive world of CytoLife, a shift prompted by a trusted associate's recommendation.

Now in his mid-forties, Felix was a synthesis of strategic acumen and mercenary ruthlessness. His tenure in special ops had refined his physical and mental prowess, earning him a revered position at CytoLife. Although often outwardly composed, he was a maelstrom of strategy and occasional warmth beneath his cool exterior.

During their initial meeting, the man behind CytoLife had seen something valuable in Felix—a shared penchant for cold calculation and ambition. It was a perfect alignment for his vision.

On the phone, Felix's words were laced with obligatory politeness. "We're making significant progress at the lab," he assured the caller, his back straight, voice respectful, but laced with hidden hostility. "Rest assured, secrecy is paramount. There's no suspicion."

He ended the call with a headache, resentful of being treated as a subordinate despite his vital role in the lab's success. The man on the other line wielded power and influence, but relied on Felix to actualize his vision. Navigating the man's interference was taxing, but Felix knew greater tasks demanded his focus.

Felix left his office, striding down the corridor towards the bunker's concealed entrance. His mind churned with thoughts, each echoing his frustration. Only upon reaching the "High Voltage" sign did he compose himself, reflecting on the bunker's history as a Cold War relic.

The Evergreen Resort, now the face of CytoLife, held an air of vintage opulence. Beneath its lavish veneer, however, lay the hidden bunker. Initially designed as a nuclear fallout shelter for government officials, it now served as the bedrock for CytoLife's covert operations. The bunker, spanning the size of two football fields, was a marvel of engineering, boasting an auditorium, living spaces, a prison, medical facilities, and a cafeteria, all designed to withstand a nuclear blast.

Though the Evergreen Resort boasted being the headquarters for CytoLife Dynamics, beneath its grandeur lay the company's surreptitious endeavors, known to only a select few, including Felix. He marveled at the foresight of the visionary who had secured this sprawling underground facility, providing a well-equipped base for their illicit work.

Descending into the bunker, Felix inhaled the cool, damp air, allowing the solitude to soothe his frayed nerves. "Out of sight, out of mind," he mused, appreciating the bunker's obscurity and the ingenuity of its Cold War origins.

Reemerging, Felix's demeanor was calm, his internal storm quelled. As he stepped back into the resort's corridor, he nearly collided with Lucas and Rebecca, who rounded the corner unexpectedly.

"Where the hell did you come from?" Felix barked at Lucas, his eyes narrowing with suspicion. A sheen of sweat glistened on his forehead, betraying his earlier frustrations.

"Uh, I was just—" Lucas stuttered, taken aback by Felix's sudden appearance and gruff demeanor.

"Never mind," Felix cut him off, his jaw tense. "What are you doing here? Is there nothing more useful for you to do?"

"We were just—" Rebecca began, but Felix shot her a pointed look that silenced her mid-sentence.

"Listen, Fairbanks," he said, addressing Lucas directly. "I don't have time for your little games. Stick to your job and keep your nose out of things that don't concern you. Understood?"

"Understood," Lucas mumbled, confusion clear in his furrowed brow.

With a final glare, Felix stormed off down the hallway, leaving Lucas and Rebecca in his wake. The tension in the air dissipated as they exchanged puzzled glances.

"What was that?" Lucas asked as Felix disappeared.

"Nothing to worry about," Rebecca replied, trying to sound nonchalant. "Just another door to the lab. You're aware of how secretive things are here."

"Right," Lucas agreed, though doubt lingered in his voice. "Felix seems... unreadable most of the time. Not exactly friendly, either."

"Best not to take it personally," Rebecca advised, offering him a reassuring smile. "Let's get going. There's work to be done."

As they walked away, Lucas glanced back at the strange door from which Felix had emerged. He had a nagging intuition that there was more to it. He felt like he was missing something, but he focused on the task and the woman next to him, dropping the matter for now.

Seated at his desk in *The Bluff City Standard's* newsroom, Adam Burke was deep into an article about CRISPR and genetic editing. A recent piece in *The Guardian*, highlighting ethical concerns around designer babies and eugenics, caught his attention.

"Ben," he called out to his editor, buried in paperwork. "Did you catch this piece in The Guardian? It's raising some serious points about CRISPR's misuse."

Ben looked up, adjusting his glasses. "Oh? Sounds like you might be onto something concrete this time, not just shadow-chasing."

Adam flashed a wry smile, keeping his investigation with

Harper into CytoLife's questionable activities to himself. "Here, have a look," he said, turning his laptop towards Ben. "It outlines the dangers of genetic manipulation and potential catastrophic outcomes."

Ben peered at the screen, his interest piqued. "Interesting angle," he mused. "But we need more than opinions, Adam. Bring me hard evidence."

"Understood," Adam responded, his mind on Harper and their joint endeavor. "I'll dig deeper."

"Keep me posted," Ben said before returning to his documents.

Adam took a thoughtful sip of his coffee, the weight of his findings, and thoughts of their informant, Cam, heavy on his mind. "We can't let this slip away," he muttered. He recalled his near miss with the PenCore story, thwarted before it could gain traction. This time, he was resolved to see it through.

His focus returned to his research, the hum of the newsroom fading into the background. Suddenly, his phone buzzed—an urgent message from Harper. "Adam, we're running out of time. We need to know what's going on at CytoLife."

Adam's response was swift and resolute: "I'm on it." He was committed to uncovering the truth, mindful of maintaining discretion in their investigation. Leaks could jeopardize everything.

The silence from Cam, their crucial informant, added to the tension. Despite repeated attempts to reach out, all they were met with was an unsettling quiet.

As time went on, Lucas and Rebecca increasingly found themselves in each other's company, a byproduct of his role as her personal security. His training was transparent in everything he did, from his deliberate actions to his unwavering focus. Daily, he rigorously checked their vehicle and surroundings, adopting various security tactics to evade surveillance, his meticulousness unwavering. The bulletproof Range Rover he used underscored his dedication to her safety, hinting at the underlying risks in their work with CytoLife, though Rebecca seldom shared specific details.

Lucas often contemplated asking why a scientist like Rebecca needed such extensive security. But whenever he was about to voice the question, he held back, considering it outside his professional boundaries. His main focus was to maintain a secure environment for their operations. However, as weeks passed, the distinction between the professional and personal softened. Rebecca's laughter started to brighten the normally subdued halls, and her smile was more frequently cast in his direction. Lucas couldn't help but feel a growing tension, fully aware of the complexities such emotions entailed.

"Lucas," Rebecca said one day as they walked down a pristine hallway toward the lab. "You're always so serious. Has anyone ever told you that?"

"Ma'am, it's my job to be serious," he replied, trying to suppress a smile. But her laughter was contagious, and soon both of them were chuckling.

"Please, just call me Rebecca," she insisted, her smile softening the formal air between them.

"Alright... Rebecca."

In moments when their guard slipped, their connection seemed real, not just a byproduct of their constant proximity. Rebecca's enigmatic nature, coupled with the allure of something unspoken lingering beneath her exterior, drew Lucas in. His fascination with her grew, fueling a deeper desire to unravel the mysteries she held. Their interactions, laced with a subtle flirtation, walked a fine line between professional responsibility and personal attraction, fueling an undercurrent of unspoken tension.

When Rebecca was performing her work duties, Lucas would stay at his post in the security surveillance station within CytoLife, monitoring her from a distance. The sealed doors that led to the private laboratory fascinated him.

"Rebecca, why can't I come in with you?" he asked one day, his curiosity getting the better of him.

"Lucas," she replied with a laugh, "you're too valuable out here making sure everything stays secure. Besides, it's just boring science stuff in there."

Despite understanding her reasoning, Lucas couldn't shake a sense of disappointment as the lab's secrets loomed in his thoughts. Meanwhile, his duty to ensure Rebecca's safety persisted, mingled with unresolved questions.

Lucas sat in the dimly lit security monitoring station, his eyes scanning the various monitors before him. As the constant hum of electronics filled the air, Rebecca dominated his thoughts. She intrigued him, and he wanted to know more about who she was beyond her professional exterior.

He discreetly opened a private browser on his phone, scanning for information on Dr. Rebecca Kent. He soon found her CV, showcasing her stellar background in molecular biology and biomedical research. Her prestigious academic journey, including a PhD from Oxford and tenure at Cambridge, was striking.

Impressed, Lucas murmured, "What a résumé."

Her digital presence was minimal, with only a few interview images available. Clearly, discretion was paramount—likely due to proprietary research and patents.

Lucas then found interviews where Rebecca discussed CRISPR's potential. Her fervor was clear, her expertise undeniable. Yet the passionate scientist in the videos seemed worlds apart from the enigmatic woman he guarded.

"CRISPR has the potential to revolutionize medicine as we know it," Rebecca explained, enthusiasm lighting up her eyes during the interview. "Imagine a world where we could eradicate genetic disorders, eliminate debilitating diseases, and even enhance our own capabilities. The possibilities are limitless."

The interviewer skeptically asked about the ethical implications of the technology.

"Of course," Rebecca replied without missing a beat. "But we must not let fear hinder progress. As long as we continue to research responsibly, the benefits of CRISPR far outweigh the risks."

"Who are you, really?" Lucas wondered, trying to reconcile the enigmatic woman he worked so closely with and the enthusiastic scientist in these videos.

Despite his growing admiration, Lucas still found himself puzzled by Rebecca's true nature. He desired to understand her more, but he had to be cautious.

The mysteries behind those closed doors sparked his anticipation, but he knew the dangers of prying. "Focus on the job," Lucas muttered, closing the browser and shifting his gaze back to the security monitors.

Lucas leaned against the sleek black Range Rover, waiting for Rebecca. Despite the beauty of his surroundings, he felt a nagging sense of unease. Thoughts of Felix emerging from that strange door weeks ago still haunted him. He shook his head, trying to dismiss the thought.

"Good morning, Lucas," Rebecca greeted as she emerged from her luxurious home within the private estates of the Evergreen, dressed impeccably in an elegant pantsuit. Her long blonde hair, pulled back into a neat ponytail, accentuated her delicate features.

"Morning, Rebecca," he replied, opening the car door and holding it out for her. As she slid into the passenger seat, he caught a faint whiff of her perfume, a subtle scent that stirred something deep within him. He shut the door and slid behind the wheel, chastising himself silently for being so affected by her presence.

"Thank you," she said softly, shooting him a warm smile that made his heart race. He had to remind himself to keep his attraction hidden, especially from Felix, who would have no patience for distractions.

"Anytime," he replied, forcing a casual tone as he started the engine and drove them towards CytoLife.

"Lucas," Rebecca began, her voice taking on a more serious tone. "I've been thinking about our last conversation on CRISPR, and I wanted to discuss it further with you."

"Sure thing," Lucas said, focusing intently on the road ahead. He relished these cerebral exchanges—they weren't just enlightening about her work; they also peeled back layers of her poised professional exterior, revealing the person underneath.

"Many people fear the unknown, and it's natural to be cautious," she explained, her words measured. "Like I said before, we mustn't let fear stand in the way of progress. CRISPR could bring significant benefits to humanity."

Lucas nodded, stealing a glance at her as they discussed the possibilities and ethical implications of gene editing. As they delved deeper into the subject, he found himself captivated by her passion and intellect, making it difficult to keep his emotions in check.

"Rebecca," he ventured hesitantly, "I understand the benefits, but have you ever considered the potential dangers of this technology?"

"Every brilliant invention comes with risks," she replied,

not shying away from his question. "But if we proceed responsibly, the rewards far outweigh the dangers."

He respected her candor, but it did little to quell his growing concerns. Their conversation continued until they reached CytoLife, where Lucas dutifully escorted her inside.

"Thank you for the ride," Rebecca said as they parted ways, her eyes lingering on him for a moment longer than usual.

"My pleasure," Lucas replied, watching her walk away before turning to assume his post at the security monitoring station.

In the tranquility of his cottage, Lucas immersed himself in CRISPR research. Conversations with Rebecca had ignited his interest, along with his suspicions about CytoLife's hidden activities. He was particularly drawn to critiques of gene editing.

Terms like "unintended consequences" and "irreversible alterations" resonated as he read about the potential perils of tampering with DNA. While the technology heralded incredible potential, the looming threats of misuse, harmful mutations, and unforeseen repercussions weighed heavily on him. The implications for CytoLife's undertakings sent a shiver down his spine.

When Lucas saw Rebecca again, he took the chance to express his concerns. In her inviting living room, wine glasses in hand, Lucas warily brought up the issue by saying with care, "I've been checking out some pieces on the risks of CRISPR. There's worry out there about unexpected problems."

Rebecca raised an eyebrow, but didn't appear surprised. "There are always naysayers, Lucas. People who fear progress and change." She took a sip of her wine and continued, her voice firm. "But I truly believe that the advancements we make will benefit humanity far more than any potential pitfalls."

Rebecca set her glass down, her gaze inquisitive. "Lucas, do you feel you grasp the full mechanics of CRISPR, or is your understanding based on what's available online?"

Lucas, with a humble smile, replied, "Honestly, I've only scratched the surface with online resources. The intricate details elude me."

Rebecca's eyes softened as she acknowledged Lucas's honesty. "CRISPR works on a scale that's invisible to the naked eye," she explained, her voice suffused with excitement. "It's like precise molecular scissors, paired with a GPS that hunts down a specific DNA sequence. To get inside the human body, vectors like viruses are often used—they can deliver the CRISPR system to the targeted cells. Once inside, it can cut, add, or edit pieces of the genetic code, like tweaking the most fundamental script of life itself.

"In layman's terms," Rebecca added, her smile making the complex science more approachable, "think of CRISPR as a highly advanced editing tool. It's like having a tiny surgeon who can find and fix specific errors in our DNA. And the virus part? It's like a special delivery service that safely brings this tiny surgeon directly to where it's needed in our body."

"Even if there are unintended consequences?" Lucas pressed, feeling a strange mix of admiration and unease at her unwavering conviction.

"Every new technology has its risks," she replied, rolling her eyes. "Do you remember the case of the Chinese scientist who went to jail for creating CRISPR embryos? It was absurd to punish him for pushing the boundaries of science. We've made significant progress since then." She gestured around the room, as if the opulence surrounding them was proof enough of their noble pursuit.

Rebecca's voice carried a faint trace of condescension. "People were once afraid of electricity and telephones. But now, can you even imagine our lives without them?"

Lucas nodded slowly, finding her words both comforting and unsettling. As he listened to Rebecca extol the virtues of CRISPR, he couldn't help but wonder if they were venturing down a perilous path, reminiscent of the eugenics debates of the past.

Rebecca leaned back, a sly smile playing on her lips. "The truth is, Lucas, the legislation governing CRISPR is lagging behind the science. And I'm rather glad about that." She studied his face, gauging his reaction.

Lucas's brows furrowed. "But doesn't that leave room for the technology's misuse? Your intentions might be noble, but what about those with less honorable agendas?"

She conceded with a nod, her eyes narrowing thoughtfully. "True, the potential for misuse exists. But think of the benefits: eradicating diseases, eliminating birth defects, even enhancing human capabilities. The upsides are immense. And let's not confuse this with eugenics. That was about limiting life. We're about enhancing it."

Her conviction was notable, yet Lucas remained unsure. He hesitated, his analytical mind urging caution, reminding him of history's lessons about the fine line between scientific advancement and ethical boundaries. "I understand your perspective, Rebecca. And I truly hope you're right."

Rebecca's eyes sparkled with the fervor of someone who truly believed in the path they were on. She held Lucas's hands, infusing her grip with earnest passion. "Believe in me, Lucas," she urged, her voice imbued with the certainty of the devoted. "We're on the verge of something that transcends mere scientific progress. It's a transformation at the very core of existence. Our work is about to turn the tide on how we understand genetic destiny."

Her fingers tightened around his with intention, her touch conveying excitement and camaraderie. "It means the world to me that you're here, that our paths have aligned at this pivotal moment. Your presence, it's... it's serendipitous," she said, leaving the depth of her statement hanging between them, an invitation to the unknown.

Lucas paused, searching her eyes for answers. "Rebecca, I have to wonder... why the need for dedicated security?"

A shadow passed over Rebecca's face, hinting at concealed truths. "In our world," she murmured, her tone laden with caution, "every leap forward carries risks. Not all will champion our cause. Some might even perceive it as a menace."

Lucas leaned in, his instincts on high alert. "This isn't just about business rivalry, is it?"

Her stare intensified, a silent prelude to her words. "In our realm, allegiances are fluid. What I need from you is unwavering protection and trust. And I hope you can place the same trust in me."

TWELVE

As the sun dipped low at Leesburg Executive Airport near Washington DC, elongating the shadows, a sleek Gulfstream G650 touched down gracefully. Inside the luxurious cabin, the man by the window let out a deep sigh, his thoughts a complex tapestry of reflective memories and contemplations about the future. In his heart, sadness, and hope were intermingled, capturing the essence of his losses and the potential of what was yet to come.

"Welcome back, sir," said one of his assistants, a young woman with a warm smile. "How was everything?"

"Excellent as always, thank you," he replied, his posh English accent smooth and refined. He stood up, straightening his tailored suit, and made his way to the exit. The cabin crew and assistants, ever attentive, hurried to gather his belongings and see to his needs.

The lead assistant announced they were ready to transfer

to the helicopter and would arrive at CytoLife by two o'clock.

"Understood," the man replied.

As the man stepped onto the tarmac, a gentle breeze tousled his silver hair. He took a deep breath, and a wave of nostalgia hit him. Carried back to days past, visions of the expansive green fields of the English countryside from his youth filled his mind, along with the scent of fresh-cut grass from his family's ancestral estate.

His mother, Francesca, had spent hours with him relaxing in the gardens. She had listened to his stories, offered whatever wisdom she could muster, and held him close, as if trying to imprint the feel of his small body against hers as a memory she could carry with her into the darkness.

"Remember, my dearest," she would tell him, her breaths coming in shallow gasps. "I will always be with you, even when you can't see me. You are my heart, and nothing can ever change that."

By the time Francesca succumbed to her illness, the estate had already been fading into gloom for weeks. The once-vibrant halls had fallen silent, and the rooms grew cold and uninviting. The man and his father were left to face the gaping chasm left by Francesca's absence, their grief an unwelcome companion that refused to leave.

As the years had passed, the boy grew into a young man, bearing the burden of his sorrow and isolation with each stride. He had watched as his father gradually decayed under the strain of his grief.

Several years later, when the young man was twenty-two, his father succumbed to his broken heart, leaving his son to inherit the vast estate and family fortune.

Determined to honor both his parents' memory, the young man threw himself into modernizing the estate and safeguarding their fortune. He had sought the most innovative technologies and investment strategies, transforming their family legacy into a thriving empire that spanned across continents.

The man's chest tightened as he felt the familiar ache of a distant memory. He closed his eyes as he tried to push away the pain so he could focus on the present. When he opened them again, his mouth had curved into a faint smile, and his gaze shifted back to the activity in front of him on the tarmac.

He looked over to see his head of security approaching, a tall man with an air of authority. "Ah, good to see you again, James," he greeted kindly, shaking the man's hand.

"Likewise, sir," James said, returning the firm handshake. "Your helicopter is ready whenever you are."

"Thank you," the man replied, nodding towards the EC155 helicopter waiting nearby. As they walked, he made a point of engaging with those around him, asking after their families and making them feel valued. He genuinely enjoyed connecting with people, holding court with grace and charm.

He surveyed the scene before him, taking in the army of security personnel and staff that surrounded him. This was his world—a life of luxury and power, built on the foundation of his family's vast fortune and influence.

"Let's not waste any more time," he said decisively, climbing into the helicopter. Once aboard, he settled into the plush leather seat and donned his headset. His assistants, ever diligent, joined him with their tablets and briefcases in hand.

As the helicopter lifted off, the man turned his attention to the various ongoing projects under his control. His assistants provided updates on business matters, investments, and philanthropic endeavors. His staff cherished and admired him, and were eager to serve his needs. They all appreciated the opportunities he gave them.

"Thank you for your hard work," he told them sincerely, as the helicopter hummed through the air. "I couldn't do any of this without you."

"Of course, sir," one assistant replied, her eyes shining with admiration. "It's an honor to work for you."

With each mile that passed beneath the helicopter, he felt himself drawing closer to the world he had created and the legacy he intended to leave behind. He knew whatever challenges lay ahead, he would face them head-on, guided by the lessons of his past and the hope for a better future.

The EC155 helicopter descended smoothly onto the helipad, surrounded by immaculately landscaped gardens. Even from a distance, the grandiosity of the surroundings was undeniable. As the rotor blades slowed to a stop, the man—exuding authority and wealth—stepped out onto the lush grass.

A team of impeccably dressed staff members approached, smiles on their faces and hands extended in welcome. The man greeted them graciously, remembering not just their names, but personal details about each of them as well.

"Charles, how's your daughter's ballet lessons coming

along?" he asked one gentleman.

The man beamed with pride. "Very well, sir. They just promoted her to the next level. Thank you for asking."

"Ah, wonderful news! And Emma," he turned to a young woman, "how did your gardening project turn out?"

"Fantastic, sir. Your advice about the roses really made all the difference."

As they continued toward the impressive building, the man couldn't help but take in the beauty of his surroundings—a testament to his success and the life he had built for himself.

Upon entering the building, Felix Ross waited in the grand foyer. He bowed respectfully and led the man into a lavishly furnished sitting room next to his own office. Plush armchairs and gleaming dark wood furnishings created an atmosphere of elegance.

"Welcome back, sir," Felix said deferentially. "I trust your journey was comfortable?"

"Indeed, it was." The man settled into an armchair, looking expectantly at Felix. "Now, what updates do you have for me regarding the lab here at CytoLife?"

"Everything is progressing as planned," Felix replied, maintaining an attentive posture. "Our latest experiments show great promise, and the team works tirelessly to achieve our goals."

"Excellent." The man leaned back in satisfaction. "You know, the potential of science to change the world has always fascinated me."

He dove into a montage of stories detailing his brush

with the global elite, including extravagant parties, geniuses, and future breakthroughs. As he reveled in the past, the man remained oblivious to Felix's glances drifting away, assuming his perfunctory nods meant genuine interest.

Inwardly, the man felt a swell of pride and nostalgia as he recounted these experiences. He had come so far from the grief-stricken boy of his youth. And while sadness still lingered in the corners of his heart, the promise of scientific advancement offered hope for a brighter future.

"Truly, our work here has the potential to revolutionize not just our own lives, but the lives of countless others," he mused, a determined glint in his eyes. "I look forward to seeing what we can achieve together."

"Indeed, sir," Felix replied, his voice steady. "We are all committed to bringing your vision to fruition."

"Good," the man said, pleased. "Now, let us continue this discussion over dinner. I have a feeling tonight will be one to remember."

"Shall we proceed to the labs, Felix?" the man asked with enthusiasm. Felix agreed and led the way out of his office.

As they traversed the sleek, modern corridors of CytoLife, the man's excitement grew. He felt a renewed vigor coursing through him, expecting to witness innovative scientific advancements firsthand. He glanced at Felix, hoping to see a shared enthusiasm. However, his expression remained unreadable, and the man assumed it was just his professional demeanor.

Breaking the silence, Felix spoke up, his tone casual yet probing. "How have you been managing the inquiries about

CytoLife's work? There must be a lot of curiosity about our mission."

The man chuckled, the sound echoing off the pristine walls. "Oh, Felix, dealing with curiosity comes with the territory. You know, the usual spiel about pioneering today for a healthier tomorrow. I assure you, I've been handling the press and any... shall we say, overly inquisitive minds with the usual finesse."

He paused, a hint of amusement in his eyes. "Of course, they ask about our grand health campaigns and genetic testing kits. I just reiterate our mission: eliminating diseases and enhancing life quality. It's all about maximizing human potential, after all."

Felix nodded, his expression still controlled. "And no one has questioned the deeper implications of our work? No whispers of... eugenics, perhaps?"

The man's smile didn't waver as he replied, "I make it clear that we're worlds apart from such outdated concepts. Like Dr. Kent, I emphasize enhancement over limitation. It's all about perspective, Felix. We're shaping a brighter future, not delving into the dark past."

His words were smooth, practiced—a reflection of his confidence in controlling the narrative, and he felt assured in his ability to guide the direction of any conversation about CytoLife's work.

Finally, they arrived at the entrance to the lab. Just as they were about to enter, a tall figure with dark hair and sharp features appeared in the hallway, seemingly out of nowhere. The man became intrigued by his powerful presence as soon as he saw him.

"Ah, you must be Lucas," the man said amiably, extending his hand. "I've heard much about you."

"Thank you, sir," Lucas replied with graciousness. The man could tell he had an impeccable upbringing because he seemed desperate to make a good impression.

Felix cleared his throat, drawing Lucas's attention back to him. "Lucas, allow me to introduce Mr. Thomas Baxter."

Lucas reacted with sudden realization and awe at his identity, causing the man to silently brim with satisfaction. After a moment of reverence, Lucas extended his hand for a greeting once more, this time displaying an even greater level of respect than before.

"Mr. Baxter," he finally said in admiration. "It's an honor to meet you, sir."

"Likewise, Lucas," Baxter replied, clasping Lucas's hand intensely. His blue eyes sparkled with genuine interest as he continued. "I've heard remarkable things about your work here. Your background, combined with your dedication to our cause, is truly commendable."

A proud smile spread across Lucas's face. "Much appreciated, Mr. Baxter."

"Keep up the excellent work, Lucas," Baxter encouraged him. "I have high hopes for your contributions to our mission here at CytoLife."

"Very well, we must be on our way," Baxter said, giving Lucas a friendly pat on the shoulder. "Take care, and until we meet again."

"Goodbye, sir." Lucas nodded politely and watched as Baxter and Felix disappeared into the lab.

Inside the lab, Baxter marveled at the sleek, advanced equipment and futuristic surroundings. He turned to Felix, eyes alight with enthusiasm. "Felix, you've truly outdone yourself in assembling this team and creating this space. It's clear that my money has been well spent."

"Thank you, Mr. Baxter," Felix replied. "We've gathered the best minds in DNA editing, all thanks to your support."

Baxter walked over to a row of monitors displaying real-time data from ongoing experiments. Tapping his fingers against the pristine countertops, he said, "I believe we stand on the precipice of greatness, Felix. The work being done here could redefine the very essence of human existence. I know that my investment will yield monumental results."

"Indeed, sir," Felix agreed. "Your vision drives us all."

Baxter continued deeper into the lab, his eyes taking in every detail with an almost childlike wonder. Felix followed closely behind. They stopped outside a glass-walled office with the name *Dr. Rebecca Kent* etched on the door.

"Ah, Rebecca," Baxter said, his face lighting up as he spotted the young scientist inside. "Let's see how our brilliant lead scientist is faring."

As they entered, Rebecca looked up from her work, her blonde hair catching the light and framing her kind face. A warm smile bloomed across her lips as she rose to greet Baxter. "It's wonderful to see you again."

"Likewise," Baxter replied, embracing her briefly before stepping back to observe her more closely. "How goes the research?"

"Very promising," Rebecca assured him, her voice laced with excitement. "We've made significant strides with CRISPR technology and gene editing."

"Tell me more," Baxter urged, locking his eyes onto hers.

"Of course, please." Rebecca gestured to a nearby whiteboard filled with diagrams and notes. "We're focusing on using CRISPR to manipulate stem cells, essentially resetting their age clock. For example, we can take a fifty-year-old cell and revert it to the state of a one-year-old cell."

"Remarkable," Baxter said, studying the whiteboard. "So, how does this relate to mitochondrial aging, epigenetics, and DNA repair?"

Rebecca leaned in, ready to explain. "Think of mitochondria as tiny power plants within our cells. As we age, they start to wear out, affecting our energy and overall health. But what if we could rejuvenate them?"

Baxter nodded, trying to follow. "And epigenetics?"

"Imagine our DNA as a vast library," Rebecca continued. "Epigenetics is like using bookmarks. It tells our body which parts of the DNA to read and which to skip. These bookmarks can be influenced by our lifestyle, surroundings, and even by events in our ancestors' lives. Our goal is to learn how to place these bookmarks more strategically."

"And DNA repair?" Baxter asked.

"It's about mending our body's instruction manual," Rebecca replied. "We have proteins that act as repairmen, fixing damaged parts. By enhancing this natural process, we can help cells recover faster from damage."

Clearly impressed, Baxter said to Rebecca, "You have a gift for making complex topics understandable. Outstanding explanation, Rebecca."

"Thank you, sir," she said, blushing slightly under the praise.

Baxter looked intently at her. "Given all this, how close are we to unlocking the ultimate therapy?"

Rebecca's enthusiasm was undeniable. "We're almost there. Our team is perfecting a method that might not only slow down aging considerably but also tackle some major diseases. Imagine a world where we have more control over our health's destiny. That's what our team, and others worldwide, are striving for every day."

"Remarkable," Baxter murmured, his gaze never leaving her face. "Your brilliance truly knows no bounds, my dear. It's been such a pleasure listening to you explain these complex matters in such an elegant and comprehensible manner."

"Thank you," Rebecca replied, a warm smile gracing her lips. "I've always believed that it's important to make knowledge accessible. And what better way to do so than by breaking down complicated concepts into simpler terms?"

"Truly fascinating," Baxter mused, his fingers tapping thoughtfully on the table as he considered her words. "The potential of your work is staggering, and I'm confident that our investment in this project will have far-reaching implications for the betterment of humanity."

A warm blush spread across Rebecca's cheeks as she took in Baxter's compliment. Her eyes sparkled with pride, appreciation, and determination, reflecting her unwavering dedication to their shared vision.

"Thank you, I truly mean it," Rebecca replied. "Your support means the world to me, and I promise our efforts will not be in vain."

Baxter could see, now more than ever, that their partnership was destined for greatness, and he couldn't have been prouder to play a part in it.

"Rebecca," he said, his voice warm with fondness, "the pleasure has been all mine. Now, I must be off. We'll continue this discussion soon, yes?"

"Of course." She stood with graceful ease, smoothing her lab coat as she walked towards him with measured and confident steps.

As they met, Baxter leaned in and pressed a tender kiss to each of her cheeks.

"Would you care to join me for dinner tomorrow night?" he inquired, his eyes searching hers for an answer.

"Yes, Papa," Rebecca responded without hesitation, her smile warm and genuine.

"Excellent," Baxter said, pleased with her response. He clasped her hand briefly, giving it a reassuring squeeze before releasing it. "I look forward to our time together. Goodbye for now, my dear."

Each time Baxter gazed at Rebecca, he was swept back in memories of her mother, Constance. Rebecca's long, blonde hair and intense gaze were striking echoes of Constance. She had been his haven, a reprieve from life's burdens, and her sudden departure had plunged him into profound grief.

In Rebecca, he found both a poignant reminder of his

loss and a connection to the present. Her spirited resilience reflected Constance's own, yet Baxter could sometimes discern a subtle fragility in his daughter. This combination brought him comfort and concern in equal measure.

Rebecca's dedication to their shared vision at CytoLife was unwavering. However, Baxter occasionally noticed flickers of doubt in her eyes, hinting at unspoken struggles. He was conflicted, torn between his desire to protect her and involving her in a quest that could unearth disconcerting realities.

Navigating the ethical intricacies of their pioneering research, Rebecca represented both a link to his cherished memories of Constance and a guiding light towards a future brimming with possibilities and challenges.

Thomas Baxter's life had been profoundly enriched by his union with Constance Kent, a woman whose outer beauty was a mere reflection of her inner warmth.

"You've brought such joy to my life," he'd once whispered to Constance during a dance under the stars, with a sleeping infant Rebecca nearby.

"You've done the same for me," she had responded, her eyes moist with emotion.

Their days had been filled with happiness and the joys of parenthood. But fate had been cruel, and Constance's sudden passing because of a car crash left Baxter to care for their daughter on his own.

"Promise me," Constance had declared in her last moments. "Promise me you'll take care of our little girl."

"I swear it," he choked out through his tears, clutching

her hand tightly. "I will do everything in my power to give her the life she deserves."

With newfound resolve, Baxter immersed himself in fatherhood, enveloping Rebecca in love and care. Determined to shield her from the isolation he had known as a child, he committed to giving her the best life possible.

"Goodnight, my dear," he'd murmur to Rebecca every evening, embracing her as tenderly as he had Constance. "Always know that my love for you is boundless."

As time passed, Baxter drew comfort from his growing bond with Rebecca, viewing their moments together as a living tribute to his love with Constance. While the pain of Constance's absence lingered, he found solace in the realization that their love lived on through their daughter.

One tranquil evening, as the horizon blazed with hues of a setting sun, he murmured, "Constance, I hope you see us and know how our love has endured."

In the triumphs of CytoLife, Baxter glimpsed the potential for a life liberated from the shackles of mortality. Armed with CRISPR technology, he envisioned a future free from human frailties, where he could extend life well beyond its natural limits.

His hands tightened as visions of a future free from death's grip, a future where his legacy could thrive indefinitely without the looming specter of mortality, overtook him.

He imagined a world reshaped by his aspirations, with humanity thriving under his wise guidance. In this envisioned utopia, he saw himself as immortal, not just through his accomplishments, but in actuality. Dodging the finality of death, protecting Rebecca from the sorrow of loss, and eternally shepherding the idyllic existence he planned to forge fueled Baxter's unwavering resolve. His image in the mirror bore an air of calm determination, a silent vow for a future unmarred by human fragility.

And as Baxter exited the lab, he whispered a muted plea, seeking a reprieve from his sorrows.

"Goodbye, Papa," Rebecca uttered, watching him leave her office with his characteristic authoritative presence. Amidst the intricacies of their mission, she felt a surge of pride for the deep bond they had cultivated over the years.

Memories of her childhood often resurfaced during their time together, highlighting the strong connection they had always shared. He had spared no expense in her upbringing, providing the best education and surrounding her with mentors who nurtured her intellect and diverse interests. Their relationship had grown stronger over time, forming a steadfast link of trust and affection.

Many evenings were spent in their study, engaged in lively discussions on everything from literature to the mysteries of the universe. His eager mentorship had always matched Rebecca's relentless thirst for knowledge.

In the tranquility of her well-appointed office, she felt the lingering presence of her father, a comforting yet somewhat overwhelming embrace. She stood at the crossroads of deep love for him and their shared ambitious vision for CytoLife.

Her eyes moved over the neat files and advanced equipment that filled the room, each one fueling her fervent belief. Their every advancement brought them closer to their bold goal, a task she embraced with unyielding dedication and resolve.

In these moments of solitude, Rebecca indulged in a brief daydream: a future where their dreams for humanity were realized, and where her father, her ever-present guide, looked upon their transformed world with satisfaction. Her commitment was unwavering, often bolstered by Baxter's rare but treasured signs of approval. The ethical complexities and potential consequences of their work were momentarily eclipsed by her strong conviction and deep bond with her father.

However, beneath her resolute exterior, occasional doubts stirred, waiting in the shadows of her mind. For now, Rebecca chose to focus on their achievements and the precious time spent with her father, her ally in this bold journey to reshape the future.

At Harper's law firm in Memphis, she observed Ethan Cook's gaze fixed on his computer, the screen's glow casting faint shadows on his face. Rapidly, his fingers skimmed the keyboard, uncovering the links between CytoLife and PenCore. The quiet space was filled only with his steady typing and the occasional hum of an air conditioner.

"It's not adding up," he remarked, his eyes darting over

the digital data. His days-long dive into the companies had revealed more mysteries than clarity. A deliberate obscurity seemed to cloud the facts.

"Harper," he called without looking up. Her footsteps approached, and he briefly turned to her, pointing at the monitor. "I think Baxter's just the face of this. The real movers? These mid-level execs in the shadows."

"Using inmate DNA in tests?" Harper's voice held a note of disbelief.

"Seems so." Ethan nodded, weary eyes never leaving the screen. "They're hiding something big."

"We'll uncover it," Harper assured, touching his shoulder briefly before resuming her work.

As Ethan resumed his investigation, Harper's phone buzzed, drawing her attention away from her documents. She glanced at the caller ID before answering, her expression turning serious. "Yes?"

"Ms. Brasfield," the voice on the other end said, his tone grave and measured. "I have some troubling news to share with you."

"Go on," Harper replied, her grip tightening around the phone as a chill ran down her spine.

"Darrius Robinson has died in custody."

The words struck like a lightning bolt, leaving Harper momentarily breathless. Her mind raced, processing the devastating news, but all she could manage was a strangled whisper, "What happened?"

"Details are still coming in," the caller said. "But it appears there was an altercation with another inmate. I'm afraid Darrius didn't survive."

"Thank you for letting me know," Harper said, her voice inaudible. As she hung up, she stood in stunned silence, the weight of the revelation bearing down on her like a crushing tide.

"Harper?" Ethan called out, sensing the shift in energy. "What's wrong?"

"Darrius..." she choked out, tears welling in her eyes. "He's... he's dead."

Ethan stared at her, his own shock mirroring hers, as the reality of the situation settled upon them both. In that moment, their investigation took on a new urgency, fueled by the haunting specter of the young man whose life someone tragically cut short.

As they grieved the loss of their client, a burning determination set in. They would unravel the truth, no matter the cost.

THIRTEEN

Harper sat in her living room's silence, the flicker of a candle casting shadows as she mulled over Darrius's fate. Cradling a wine glass, she pondered his life sentence, a victim of the unforgiving three-strikes law. Her calls for a plea bargain were rebuffed by the unyielding Assistant District Attorney. Even a glimmer of hope for leniency, hinging on Darrius's cooperation against his gang, vanished quickly. Now, he was dead.

The shrill ring of the phone jolted her from her thoughts. She set down her wine and answered hesitantly. "Hello?"

"Harper? It's Irene, Darrius's mama," said the voice, strained with a mix of grief and resolve. "Before everything fell apart, Darrius gave me your number." Irene's voice cracked. "He said you were different, that you actually cared. It's taken me this long to find the courage to call."

"Irene, my heart goes out to you," Harper responded,

bracing herself for what came next.

Bitterness colored Irene's words. "They think it was gang violence. My boy... he was lost to me long before this, ever since he got caught up in that life."

Harper's grip tightened on the phone, the weight of Irene's sorrow indisputable. "Ms. Robinson, your loss is unimaginable. Darrius should have had a different path."

"Harper, did they really give him no chance? No plea deal without betraying his gang?"

Harper paused, hesitant to divulge the bitter truth. "Yes, that was the case. But I'm not sure it would've changed the outcome. He was trapped, Irene."

"Perhaps," Irene sighed, resignation in her tone. "But a chance is a chance, no matter how small. You tried for him, didn't you?"

"I did, Irene. And it haunts me that it wasn't enough," Harper admitted, her voice thick with regret.

"Thank you for that, Harper. In this broken system, trying means something. It's a cold comfort, but it's all I have now."

After hanging up with Irene, Harper found herself gasping for air. The room's oppressive silence enveloped her, punctuated only by the subtle tremble of her hand as she placed the phone aside.

"Why didn't I do more for Darrius?" she uttered to the empty room, a pang of guilt eating at her for having been so consumed by the PenCore conspiracy.

Drawn to the liquor cabinet, her unsteady hand poured bourbon into a glass. Its golden hue glinted in the dim light.

Though she recognized it wasn't a solution, the fiery warmth offered a fleeting escape from her internal tempest.

"What a disaster," she murmured, tears brimming. The bourbon's burn provided a brief relief, but couldn't quell the rising tide of despair.

"Perhaps it's time for a new chapter," she wept. "Maybe this isn't my fight anymore."

Overwhelmed, Harper crumpled to the floor, the glass tumbling and shattering beside her. Amidst the shards, she pondered if she'd ever mend the broken pieces of her existence.

The unexpected sound of the doorbell roused Harper. Brushing away her tears, she shakily got to her feet, bracing herself for the visitor. With a steadying breath, she swung the door open.

"Dee," Harper cried, as a wash of relief flooded her at seeing her long-time friend. Deandra's worried expression and tense body language made it clear to Harper that she had received news about Darrius.

"I got here as soon as I found out about Darrius," Deandra said, stepping in without waiting. "I'm so, so sorry."

"Thank you," Harper replied softly as the two moved into the living room. The weight of Deandra's concern was undeniable.

"Do you recall that case from a few years ago?" Deandra gestured for Harper to sit beside her. "You exposed the tampered security footage? Harper, your defense was masterful. That man owes his life to you. I want you to remember that you're still the formidable 'Brass' everyone admires."

Harper settled next to Deandra, warmth flooding her as she remembered that triumph. The appreciation for her friend's timely reminder was immense. But internally, Harper grappled with a sense of displacement.

"Dee, our dynamic has shifted recently," Harper began, her voice streaked with emotion. "I want you to know I cherish our bond. I yearn for the days we once enjoyed."

Tears welled in Deandra's eyes as she squeezed Harper's hand. "I wish for that too. Always."

Harper's mind shifted to the looming confrontation with Judge Jackson, Deandra's father. The thought of its potential effect on Deandra weighed heavily on her, yet she understood its necessity. For now, she embraced this brief respite, a chance to heal the rifts carved by time and circumstance.

"Your presence means the world, Dee," Harper murmured, choked up. "I'd be lost without you."

"We've got this." Deandra's eyes shone with affection. "Rawls Hall girls… we always find a way."

As they drew comfort from each other, a glimmer of hope sparked in Harper. The road ahead was challenging, but with Deandra's support, she believed she could regain her fire and purpose as a lawyer.

Harper gazed as the daylight played upon the hardwood floors of her home office, where papers and legal documents lay strewn in chaos. Her eyes, distant and reflective, seemed to pierce through the window to something far beyond the visible.

A gentle knock on the front door broke her reverie, and she saw Ethan standing in the doorway, his face etched with concern. "Harper, I've got some news about what happened to Darrius."

She sighed heavily, bracing herself for what he was about to say. "Let me guess, another gang hit?"

"Unfortunately, yes," Ethan said as he stepped inside. "My sources confirmed it was a rival gang that took him out while he was in custody. The Tennessee Bureau of Investigation is officially involved now, since it happened under the County's watch."

"God, not again," Harper muttered, rubbing her temples. "When will this ever end, Ethan? The racial disparities, the disproportionate sentencing by the courts—these kids are born into a world where they have no chance! They're trapped in generational dysfunction, trauma, and poverty. Memphis has such a tragic history, and it just keeps repeating itself."

"There's more. The city is protesting over Darrius's death. People are angry, and rightfully so."

Harper slammed her fist onto her desk, making pens and paper clips jump. "Damn it!" She took a deep, shuddering breath, fighting back tears. "These kids keep falling through the cracks, and we're failing them. I'm failing them."

"Harper, you can't blame yourself for all of this," Ethan said softly, placing a comforting hand on her shoulder. "You've done everything you can for your clients."

"Have I, though?" she pleaded. "I couldn't save Darrius."

Ethan sighed. "I know it's hard, and it might not seem like it now, but we need to keep moving. We're doing the best we can, Harper."

"Sometimes it just doesn't feel like enough." She looked at him, her eyes pleading for some kind of answer he couldn't provide.

"I know," he murmured. "But we can't give up. That's not who we are." He paused, glancing towards the door before turning back to her. "I should get going. Just wanted to let you know the latest."

"Thank you, Ethan." Harper offered him a weak smile as he left.

She felt an icy resolve taking root within her, a determination to fight against the injustice that plagued her city and the young lives caught in its grip.

After a fitful night, Harper mustered the strength to immerse herself in her routine, hoping to combat the engulfing sense of helplessness. Her absence from the office would raise eyebrows, and she couldn't afford that.

Her desk at the firm was a chaos of papers and folders, mirroring the recent upheaval. Harper's face showed sorrow lined with determination. She sat alone, yet the implied support from her colleagues was visible. They exchanged empathetic looks from their desks, respecting the space around her. Deep down, Harper yearned for the comfort of a hug, for any sign they understood her battle. But an unspoken rule of professional distance kept them at bay, honoring the tough exterior she presented.

A gentle tapping on her doorframe jolted her out of her reverie. "Come in," she said. Sam, her boss, was standing there with a worried expression on his face.

"Harper," he said cautiously, walking into her office.

"Sam." She offered a tired smile, guiding him toward a side chair. "What brings you here?"

"Your well-being, for starters," he replied, taking a seat. "You've been pushing yourself too hard lately. Maybe it's time to take a break."

"Maybe," she admitted, rubbing her temples. "But I can't help but feel like there's more I could have done for Darrius."

Harper caught the unease in Sam's voice as he exhaled a heavy sigh, his words laced with discomfort. "Harper," he began hesitantly. "You did everything in your power. Nobody could have predicted this outcome."

She sensed his struggle to offer comfort, the unspoken acknowledgment of their shared helplessness hanging in the air between them.

"Speaking of which," she said, her voice tense. "You never told me how we got Darrius's case."

Sam hesitated, his eyes flickering away from hers. "It came from JusticeGuard, a legal defense fund that promotes civil rights and equality. They work with people like Darrius."

"JusticeGuard?" Harper recognized the name, but her thoughts were too muddled to press Sam for details.

"Harper, I respect your brilliance, but you always seem to burn yourself out. That's not healthy."

He stood up, placing a hand on her shoulder. "Take some time off. You deserve it."

"Thank you, Sam. I'll consider it," she replied.

Sam nodded. "Please do."

Days later, Harper sat in Comeback Coffee, a downtown café, with Adam and Ethan. The tension in the air was apparent as they discussed CytoLife's interest in DNA samples from inmates.

"Based on the reports Cam sent me," Adam said while his eyes scanned the documents before him, "it appears they're looking for specific genetic markers. But I'm not sure why."

"Genetic markers?" Harper's stomach churned at the thought. "What could they possibly want with that information?"

Adam cleared his throat before beginning. "Think of genetic markers as unique signatures woven into our DNA. They tell us much about a person's characteristics, health, and behaviors. You've heard of those ancestry tests, right? They're based on these very markers. My investigative research has uncovered that scientists are exploring behavioral genetics, attempting to decode how specific genes may affect our choices, actions, and vulnerability to influences."

Harper's eyes widened in understanding, the implications sinking in. "So, they could be using these markers to, say, influence how people think or act?"

Adam nodded solemnly. "It's a disturbing possibility, but as far as I know, I haven't come across any concrete studies like that happening here. However, we can't rule out the global reach and the potential consequences of such research."

"I guess the advanced medical units inside the PenCore prison facilities make a little more sense now," Harper said.

"Whatever their intentions, it can't be good," Adam replied grimly. "I'll reach out to a source at the University of Tennessee to interpret these reports. Confirm this is what they're after."

"Good," she said, clenching her fists. "The more we know, the better equipped we are to stop them."

"Agreed," Ethan chimed in, his voice steady. "Let's keep digging. We need to sort this out."

Harper felt a chill at the thought of DNA experiments being conducted on inmates. A sense of dread filled her as she remembered the historical atrocities of medical experimentation, from the Tuskegee syphilis study to the appalling human trials of World War II.

The phrase "playing God" seemed too mild for what she envisioned. The notion of using inmates, a vulnerable group in society, for such research raised profound ethical questions. Were they informed? Did they truly have a choice in the matter?

Thomas Baxter often stood atop the Baxter Global tower, gazing over the city below—a testament to his mission to correct the world's ills. Each time, the view reignited his dedication to eliminating violence, corruption, and the inevitability of death.

His drive was born from personal loss: the early deaths of his parents and his wife's tragic accident. These sorrows transformed his fear of mortality into a relentless quest to save humanity from its own destructive tendencies.

Baxter, renowned in the alternative energy sector, aspired to achievements far beyond earthly recognition. His wealth and influence were merely instruments in his pursuit of societal betterment. He was part of a secret coalition, even more elusive than the famed Bilderberg meetings, united in their commitment to hope and progress.

This group laid the groundwork for Baxter's utopian vision, with CytoLife at the forefront of conquering human frailty. His daughter Rebecca, a brilliant geneticist, was the linchpin of his plan. Her groundbreaking work in genetics not only resonated with his aspirations but also accelerated them, hinting at a future where humanity transcended its inherent limitations.

Despite challenges, Baxter's conviction never wavered. He envisioned a future where human shortcomings were overcome, and longevity was a gift for the chosen leaders. His most treasured moments were those spent with Rebecca, his intellectual equal and co-visionary.

In the seclusion of the Appalachian Mountains, the private estate at Evergreen offered Baxter a serene retreat. Here, in his opulent study surrounded by ancient tomes, he indulged in the rich scent of leather and old paper, each book a symbol of mankind's enduring pursuit of knowledge.

"Papa?" Rebecca's voice echoed softly, her silhouette

framed by the sun's golden embrace streaming through the door.

"Ah, my dear," Baxter greeted, his affable smile masking the relentless drive that fueled him. "Come, we must deliberate on the advancements in our DNA research."

Rebecca entered and gently closed the door, ensuring their confidentiality. "Absolutely. Our team has made significant headway in pinpointing genes linked to unfavorable behaviors. I believe we're on the brink of mitigating their influence."

"That's promising," Baxter acknowledged, pondering the ramifications.

Rebecca hesitated for a moment, her eyes searching her father's. "Papa, do you ever wonder if we're playing with forces we don't fully understand? What if there are unintended consequences?"

Baxter, ever the orator, placed a reassuring hand on her arm. "My child, every great leap in history has been accompanied by doubts. Our intentions are noble, and I heartily believe that the path we've chosen is for the greater good."

Rebecca nodded, though a shadow of uncertainty lingered. "I trust you, Papa. But the weight of what we're undertaking sometimes overwhelms me."

Understanding her concerns, Baxter continued, "Our endeavors are indeed monumental, but remember, we're doing this for a brighter tomorrow."

Their shared dream was visible in their discussions. Rebecca affirmed, "We're striving for the common good. The world requires guidance, and we're poised to provide it."

"How's Felix adjusting? Quite the fortuitous find, wasn't he?" Baxter mused.

Rebecca's laugh was laced with irony. "Felix? He's the epitome of an exemplary robot. His commitment to CytoLife is, shall we say, unwaveringly mechanical. He may not be bursting with personality, but his efficiency is unparalleled."

Baxter nodded, seemingly missing the sarcasm. "Together, we will redefine humanity's trajectory, promising a brighter era for all."

As they stood side by side, Baxter's conviction was indisputable. Yet, as he gazed at Rebecca, he felt no apprehension, no inkling of the potential repercussions of their vision. He genuinely believed their mission was just and that they held the blueprint for humanity's salvation.

The revelations about CytoLife's questionable intentions with prisoner DNA samples troubled Harper. She pondered the obscured ambitions behind them, and how they intertwined with her personal relationships. The burn of her drink offered a momentary escape from the storm within.

"Damn it all," she muttered, sinking into a slump, her hand cradling her forehead in a moment of frustration.

As twilight settled, Harper felt an urgency to act. She dialed a long-known number. After three rings, a recognizable voice responded.

"Isaac? It's Harper. We need to discuss something."

Judge Isaac Jackson sounded both surprised and somewhat relieved. "What's troubling you?"

"It's significant, Isaac. Potentially with vast implications. I believe you can help me navigate this." Harper's voice quivered, revealing her hesitation.

After a contemplative silence, Isaac responded, "Come by tomorrow evening. We'll discuss it then."

Harper thanked him and hung up, feeling her pulse race. She didn't know how Isaac would react to her revelations, but confronting the truth was vital.

Harper took a final sip of whiskey, allowing the warmth of the liquor to settle her nerves for the evening. She spent a restless night, thoughts swirling, before the dawn broke.

The following day, her drive to the Jackson residence felt almost trance-like, the familiar cityscape a silent witness in the distance. As she arrived and parked her car, Harper noticed her hands trembling slightly, a physical manifestation of her internal turmoil.

Taking a moment, she fortified herself, remembering the grit that earned her the moniker "Brass." She rang the doorbell, her courage momentarily faltering.

The door revealed Judge Jackson, his visage reflecting fatigue and seriousness. But seeing him fortified Harper's resolve. They had to confront the truth, regardless of the aftermath.

"Evenin', Harper," he said, stepping aside to let her in. "Come on in. Let's talk."

FOURTEEN

As she entered the judge's home, Harper's mind drifted back to a time when she was on the brink of flunking out of college, her life veering off course as parental neglect and bitterness fueled her rebellion. She could still hear Judge Jackson's words echoing in her memory, his stern expression softened by the warmth in his eyes.

In his deep voice, he'd said, "Harper, I know you're going through a tough time, but you can't let it consume your life like this."

Tears had welled up in Harper's eyes, her shoulders slumping under the weight of his words. The judge had never given up on her, even when she did everything in her power to push him away.

"Brass, listen to me," he continued, using the nickname Rob had given her. "You've got so much potential, and I won't stand by and watch you waste it. You owe it to yourself to succeed."

Jolted back to the present moment, Harper stood in Judge Jackson's foyer. He wordlessly guided her to his study, where they both sat down on the worn leather sofa, its cushions molded from years of late-night conversations and heart-to-hearts.

"Judge," Harper began, her voice cracking with the effort to maintain her composure. "I don't know what to say or how to begin."

"Take your time, Harper," he said, his voice low and steady. "We're here to talk, and I'm here to listen."

Judge Jackson patted Harper's leg gently, a simple gesture that spoke volumes. A heavy silence hung between them, the air thick with unspoken tension and emotions running high.

Her breath hitched in her chest, and she struggled to find the words to express the pain that threatened to consume her. "Judge... it's just... Darrius. He was killed while in jail, and I couldn't do anything to save him."

The judge's eyes widened in shock, his own heart obviously aching at the news. He might have never met Darrius, but she knew he understood it was yet another life that was entangled in a cycle of violence.

"Harper, listen to me," the judge said softly, his voice firm despite the sorrow filling his words. "I spent my entire professional life trying to help young men like Darrius. I became a lawyer, then a judge, so I could make a difference. But we can't save everyone."

He paused, taking a deep breath before continuing. "I remember this one young man, not much older than Darrius, who found himself in a similar situation. He'd gotten caught up in a gang, facing years behind bars. But I saw something in him, a spark that told me he could change if given the chance."

Harper's sobs gradually subsided as she listened to the judge recount the story of the young man he had saved from the clutches of the broken system. Touched by his words, she wiped the tears from her cheeks and gazed into his eyes, finding solace in their warmth.

With a slight smile, Judge Jackson shifted gears, deciding to lighten the mood. "You know, Harper, if it wasn't for Mama Dee's strength and encouragement, I might have thrown in the towel a long time ago."

Harper managed a small smile, her tear-streaked face reflecting the deep appreciation she had for the woman who had acted as a mother figure to her.

"Ah, that woman," he continued, chuckling softly. "Mama Dee never let me give up, no matter how many times I was beaten down. I remember once when I was at a legal conference, and someone made a crude joke about me being the token black man in attendance. It hurt, but Mama Dee reminded me that my presence there challenged their ignorant beliefs, and that I was making a difference."

"Where is Mama Dee now?" Harper asked, wiping away lingering tears.

"Out for the evening with her church group," he replied. "She'll be back later tonight."

As the conversation wound down, Harper's thoughts retreated inward, bracing herself for the inevitable confrontation ahead. Her heart pounded with apprehension, tempting her to back down to preserve their relationship. Yet the weight of truth, amplified by recent events, left her no choice but to face what lay ahead.

"Judge..." she began hesitantly, her voice shaking slightly. "There's something I need to talk to you about. Something important... and difficult."

His brow furrowed with concern, and he leaned forward, giving her his full attention. "Of course, Harper. You can tell me anything."

Judge Jackson stood up and walked over to a small bar cart by the window. "Would you like something to drink?" he asked, reaching for a bottle of bourbon.

"Nothing for me, thanks," Harper replied, her voice firm. "I need to keep a clear head."

The judge hesitated, catching the seriousness in her tone. He set the bottle back down and returned to the leather sofa, his eyes searching hers. "What's going on, Harper?" he asked softly. "Is this about your divorce from Robert? Or are you still worried about your kids?"

Harper shook her head, feeling a knot tighten in her stomach. "It's not just that, Judge," she admitted, her hands twisting in her lap. "I'm struggling with everything. The divorce, my drinking, the fact that my kids won't talk to me... I don't even know if my reputation at the law firm will ever recover."

"Listen, Harper," the judge said, his voice soothing and paternal. "These things take time. Your children are hurting too, but they'll come around, eventually. You're their mother, and they love you."

"There's more," she continued, her voice trembling

slightly. "I've been trying to repair other relationships too, including with Deandra. We used to be so close…"

"Deandra loves you like a sister," Judge Jackson reassured her. "You two have been through so much together. It's only natural that there'd be some bumps along the way." He paused, then said with a hint of amusement in his voice, "Speaking of Deandra, do you remember that time when you two got into a huge argument over some silly teenage drama? You both refused to speak to each other for days."

Harper's eyes widened as the memory came flooding back. "Oh, my goodness, I had forgotten about that!"

The judge chuckled. "Mama Dee sure had her hands full with you two. She finally had enough and locked you both in the pantry until you sorted things out."

Harper laughed at the recollection. "I remember that! We were so stubborn, but after sitting on bags of flour and canned vegetables for hours, we couldn't help but start talking again."

"Mama Dee always knew how to handle situations like that," the judge said fondly. "She's wise beyond her years and strong as an ox."

"Absolutely," Harper agreed, her laughter fading as she grew serious once more. She took a deep breath and looked at the man who had provided the support and guidance of a father. "Judge… Isaac, I just want to say thank you for everything you and Mama Dee have done for me over the years. I feel guilty for taking both of you for granted."

The judge looked surprised by her sudden shift in tone. "Harper—"

"Please, let me finish," she interrupted, her voice

wavering. "You two have been there through it all: college, marriage, watching me start a family, helping me get a job. I can't express how grateful I am for your constant love and support."

Judge Jackson looked at her, his eyes misty but sincere. "Harper, there's no need to feel guilty. We love you like a daughter, and we've always been proud of the person you've become." He reached over and squeezed her hand, offering comfort and understanding.

"Thank you," she muttered, feeling the weight of what was still left unsaid bearing down on her shoulders. In that moment, she realized just how much love and support she had in her life—and how much she would risk protecting it.

"Harper," he said gently, his deep, gravelly voice carrying the weight of years of wisdom and experience. "I know you need support, and I'm here for you. Always have been, always will be." He paused, searching her eyes for clues. "But there's something else going on, isn't there? Something you're not telling me."

"Isaac," she replied, her voice quivering. "There's something I've discovered, something I need to share with you. And I'm not sure how to say it."

"Whatever it is, Harper, you can tell me," he said gently, concern etched into his features. "I promise, no matter what it is, I'm here to help."

"Alright, Isaac," she said, her voice wavering but determined. "I need to tell you what I've learned since taking on Darrius's case."

She reached into her bag and pulled out a stack of

carefully organized documents, her hands trembling as she laid them out methodically on the coffee table before them. Each sheet felt like a brick, building a wall between her and the man who had always been her rock.

Judge Jackson's eyes flicked over the papers, his expression guarded but attentive. "Harper, you can talk to me about anything, you know that. Just say what's on your mind."

"Isaac," she began, her voice tight with emotion. "These papers are from my investigation into Darrius's case. They reveal a connection between the private prison company PenCore and a horrifying conspiracy involving medical experimentation on inmates. And Isaac... you're involved."

"Go on," Judge Jackson replied, his voice weak, his eyes locked on hers.

"When he was a teen, they sent Darrius to Tall Trees, a juvenile facility owned by PenCore." Harper continued, her voice gaining strength as she delved into the facts. "It's a place where young men like him are beaten and mistreated, all while PenCore profits from their suffering." Whispering softly, her voice cracked with emotion. "I don't want to believe it, but the evidence is here. You... you took money from them, didn't you?"

"Harper..." he finally choked out, his voice fracturing, his eyes clouded with pain and regret. "I... I never meant for any of this..."

Harper leaned forward, her voice steady and strong as she continued to outline the case against PenCore. "Isaac, the government has allowed private corporations like PenCore to take over the operation of prisons and correctional institutions. It's a way for them to wash their hands of any responsibility and just pay someone else to handle it."

"Because of this," she went on, "PenCore has operated with little oversight, turning these facilities into profit machines at the expense of the people they're supposed to be helping."

Judge Jackson seemed to shrink before her eyes, his face a mask of pain and shock that Harper struggled not to respond to. She forced herself to stay focused, knowing that what she had to say next would cut even deeper.

"Isaac," she said, her voice catching slightly despite her best efforts. "PenCore is using the inmates in their facilities for medical experimentation."

Harper's eyes blazed with a fierceness that belied the tremor in her voice as she continued. "Experimenting on people without their full knowledge or consent is not just unethical, Isaac. It's illegal. It's monstrous. We're talking about taking away human rights, treating them like lab rats!" She slammed her fist down onto the table, causing the papers to scatter.

Judge Jackson's face crumpled, tears welling up in his eyes as he fought to hold back an anguished sob. "I swear, Harper," he choked out, "I swear to you, I was unaware. There's so much beneath the surface, complexities you couldn't possibly understand. How could I have known? How could anyone?"

"Please, Isaac," Harper said gingerly, her anger softening ever so slightly as she saw the devastation etched into every line of his face. "Just tell me what happened. How did you get involved with these people?"

The judge swallowed hard, his chest heaving as he struggled to pull himself together. "I can't... I can't explain it all right now," he managed, looking at her with pleading eyes. "But please, Harper... please believe me when I say I didn't know about any experiments! I would never knowingly be a part of something so vile!

"Harper, please," he begged, his face a mixture of anguish and desperation as she began to pack up her things to leave. "Let me try to explain. Just give me a chance to make this right."

"Make it right?" she spat, shaking her head in disbelief. "How can you possibly make this right? Lives have been ruined, destroyed! And for what? Money?"

Harper's chest heaved with a mix of anger and exhaustion as she stood in the doorway, her hands shaking. "I can't... I can't do this right now, Isaac," she exclaimed hoarsely, unable to look him in the eye. "I need some time."

"Harper, please," Judge Jackson pleaded, his voice breaking. "Let me explain. Don't leave like this."

"Isaac, I can't..." Harper choked out, her voice trembling with emotion. "I'm upset, tired... I need some rest." She turned away, avoiding his pleading eyes.

"Harper, hold on," Judge Jackson said, his voice strained. "Let me explain. Don't just walk out."

The mix of anger, betrayal, and sadness was too much to handle right then. She shot a final, disappointed look at the man who had been her mentor for years, and quickly left the house, leaving a distraught Judge Jackson behind.

A few days later, Harper sat at her kitchen table, sunlight casting shadows on the polished wood. Her hands trembled as she unfolded a letter from Judge Jackson.

Dear Harper,

I can't express my sorrow for the revelations about PenCore and the medical experiments. I swear, I never knew. Young men like Darrius being subjected to such horrors breaks my heart. Knowing I played a part in their suffering is a weight I can't shake off. I've always aimed to uphold justice, but my ties to PenCore have darkened my legacy. I hope you can believe that I truly didn't know.

Tears welled in Harper's eyes as she absorbed his words. The weight of her anger wavered, replaced by a sliver of sympathy. But Harper grappled with reconciling her image of the judge with this newfound reality.

Being one of the few black judges, I felt a vast responsibility. I believed that by joining this scheme, I could make a difference. They presented Tall Trees as a beacon of rehabilitation. Despite my reservations, the vision of helping these young men blinded me to the moral dilemma.

Anguish welled up in Harper. The judge's intentions, albeit misguided, stemmed from a desire to help. But the magnitude of the betrayal stung. She continued reading.

Over time, I heard rumors about the facilities being nothing like what I had been promised. It bothered me, especially when my colleagues bragged about taking the bribes. They seemed not to care about the people they were sending to PenCore facilities.

I cared, Harper. I did. I tried to expose the corruption by feeding information to an investigative journalist, aiming to shine a light on the darkness, even if my motives weren't entirely pure.

Harper, I know my actions are inexcusable, and I cannot begin to express how much I regret them. These choices have tainted a lifetime of trying to do good, but please believe me when I say that I never knew the true extent of PenCore's depravity. If I had known, I would have fought against them with everything I had.

Please know that I'll do everything in my power to make amends for my actions. I pray that the truth will come to light, and that those who've suffered at the hands of PenCore will find some measure of justice.

Harper's emotions churned. The judge's admission was a double-edged sword, revealing his flaws but also his humanity. Tears streamed down her face. "Isaac," she declared, "how could everything be so complicated?"

After finishing the judge's letter, Harper sat in silence, the gravity of his confession weighing heavily on her. Torn between confronting the situation or retreating into solitude, she felt overwhelmed.

As the days passed, the allure of solitude in her dimly lit home and the temporary comfort of a whiskey glass grew stronger, rendering Harper increasingly immobilized. Yet, despite her desire to withdraw, the urgent need to address and dismantle PenCore's complex network of influence persisted in her mind, compelling her to act.

The emotionless beep of the voicemail contrasted sharply with the contents of Dee's message, sending a shiver down Harper's spine. Dee's voice, laden with sorrow, made Harper's heart sink.

"Harp, it's Dee. Call me back now." Dee's voice cracked, a mix of urgency and partially contained anger coloring her words. "Daddy's gone. He died in his sleep. Please, come as soon as you can!"

Harper replayed the message, each time hoping for a different outcome. But the truth was unchangeable. Learning of Judge Isaac Jackson's sudden passing through Dee's tearful, strained words struck her with an overwhelming sense of shock.

Numbly, she found herself at the Jacksons' front door, disheveled and reeking faintly of alcohol, yet those details seemed insignificant compared to the magnitude of their loss.

Before she could knock, Deandra opened the door, her hands trembling. "They're saying he went peacefully," Deandra murmured.

Without a word, Harper stepped in, and they clung to each other, collapsing to the floor in a shared grief. Their silent embrace spoke volumes, their tears intermingling.

"This can't be happening," Harper exclaimed into the void of their sorrow.

Over forty years had passed since Harper first gestured to Deandra to join her for lunch, a simple act that had spawned a lifetime of friendship. Fleeting images flickered through Harper's mind—giggling fits at high school proms, boundary-testing escapades in college, and the eventual steadying into adulthood.

Isaac and Mama Dee had always embraced Harper with the same warmth they showed their own family, making Deandra more than just a friend—she was the sister Harper never had. However, Harper had recently retreated, erecting barriers to shield herself from vulnerability. The revelations about Isaac had shaken her, a discordant note in her already unstable perspective, and his death left a void too vast to comprehend.

This wasn't a time for self-blame; it was a time to grieve alongside those who were family in all but blood. "Where's Mama Dee?" Harper asked softly. Dee took her hand, leading her to the study, a wordless reminder that in their shared sorrow, they remained united.

They found Mama Dee sitting in Isaac's chair, her eyes red-rimmed but dry. She looked up as they entered, her gaze flicking between the two women.

"Y'all come on in and sit down," she said, her voice steady despite the grief that weighed heavily on her shoulders.

"Isaac would've wanted us to be together," Mama Dee replied, her voice quavering ever so slightly. "Now, we got some plans to make. We need to pick out a suit for my Isaac."

Harper nodded, blinking back fresh tears. Despite the turmoil she felt inside, she knew she had a responsibility to honor the man who had played such an important role in her life—even if his actions had left her reeling.

"Alright, Mama Dee," Harper said, steeling herself. "We'll do whatever we need to do. We'll get through this together."

Harper, Deandra, and Mama Dee sat together in solemn silence. The air was heavy with grief, but also filled with an unspoken tension that seemed to cling to every surface. Harper stared down at her hands, processing the whirlwind of emotions that threatened to overwhelm her.

"Y'all," Mama Dee said finally, breaking the silence that had settled over them like a thick fog. "There's something I need to discuss with you both, something important." She took a deep breath, steeling herself for what was to come.

"Girls," Mama Dee began, her eyes fixed on some distant point beyond the room. "I know things have been... difficult lately, to say the least. We've all lost so much, and we're still trying to make sense of it all. But I want you to know—" She paused, swallowing hard. "I want you to know that no matter what happens, we're going to stand together, like we always have."

Deandra reached over to grip Harper's hand, her eyes glistening with unshed tears. "We're family, Mama Dee," she mumbled. "We'll get through this—together."

"Thank you, baby girl." Mama Dee smiled sadly, but there was a fierce determination in her eyes. "Now, there's something I need to share with you. It ain't gonna be easy to hear, but I believe it's important for us all to face the truth— even when it hurts."

Harper felt her heart tighten in her chest, anxiety rippling through her like waves on a storm-tossed sea. She braced herself, knowing that whatever Mama Dee had to say, it would surely test the bonds that held them together.

"Alright, Mama Dee," she whispered. "We're listening."

FIFTEEN

Adam Burke stood on the steps of the University of Tennessee's Biochemistry & Cellular and Molecular Biology building in Knoxville, reflecting on how much had changed since he was a student here. The crisp fall breeze brushed against his face as he took in the familiar sights of the campus, feeling both nostalgic and apprehensive.

"Adam? Adam Burke?" Meera Kapur called out, her voice warm and inviting. She appeared from around a corner, her dark hair pulled back into a neat bun, and her lab coat fluttering in the wind.

"Meera! I can't believe it's been so long," Adam greeted her, extending his hand for a friendly shake. "How have you been?"

"Busy, but that's the life of an assistant professor," she replied with a laugh. "I heard you've been making quite a name for yourself as an investigative journalist."

"Trying my best," Adam said modestly. "Do you remember that old coffee shop we used to frequent near the library? I still miss their pumpkin spice lattes this time of year."

"Ah, yes, Java Junction!" Meera exclaimed. "I still go there during my breaks. They've expanded now, and added some great outdoor seating."

"Sounds like it's worth a visit while I'm here," Adam mused. "But let me get to the reason I reached out to you." He hesitated for a moment before continuing, "I've come across some confidential reports involving CRISPR-cas9 technology, and I could use your expertise in understanding them."

Meera's eyes lit up with enthusiasm. "Of course, I'd be happy to help. Let's head to my office, where we can discuss it further."

As they walked down the hallway, Meera began explaining the basics of DNA editing.

"Sounds incredible," Adam remarked, careful not to let on how much he already knew. He felt it would be simpler to tell Meera as little as possible.

"It is," Meera agreed, her voice full of passion. "Imagine a world where we could eradicate cancer or prevent Alzheimer's. The possibilities are endless, and that's what drives me to study this field."

"Still," Adam interjected, "such power also brings the potential for misuse, doesn't it?"

"True," Meera admitted as they entered her office. "But most scientists in this field are committed to using CRISPR ethically and responsibly."

"Let's hope so," Adam murmured, his thoughts turning to the DNA reports he had yet to reveal to her. "Here," Adam offered, pulling out the reports from his bag. "These are the ones I was talking about." He handed them to Meera discreetly, careful to hide the fact that he had duplicated them and removed any identifying information. "It looks like they're researching specific genetic markers. I was hoping you might recognize them or their purpose."

As Meera examined the documents, Adam observed her closely. Her eyes moved expertly over the pages, and for a moment, her brow creased—a subtle indicator of either concern or recognition. Then, regaining her composure, she looked up at Adam with a mix of professional curiosity.

"I've noticed an unusual marker here, one that's new to me," she began, her tone reflecting her scientific expertise. "I've heard discussions in the academic community about teams globally trying to identify genes related to behavior. This could be related to those initiatives. Can you share more about the origin of these documents?"

"Let's just say it's background for something I'm working on."

"Fair enough. Let me explain what genetic markers are, in case you're not familiar with them," Meera offered.

Adam nodded, his expression a mix of apprehension and necessity. "Go ahead," he said. Deep down, he knew the basics of genetic markers, but needed Meera's expertise to confirm his suspicions.

"In simple terms, genetic markers are DNA sequences with known locations on chromosomes. They can identify variations, track inheritance patterns, and diversity." She paused, making sure Adam was following along.

"Okay. So why are they important to study?" Adam asked.

"Genetic markers are like signposts within our DNA," Meera elaborated. "They can tell us much about who we are and where we come from. For instance, they offer insights into genetic diversity and our evolutionary past. This knowledge is crucial in understanding how different populations have evolved over time."

Adam consciously eased his posture, listening intently as Meera detailed the scientific applications of CRISPR technology. He aimed to fully understand, despite his prior research and the insights Cam had shared.

"In the medical field, these markers are invaluable. They can predict how a person might react to certain medications, allowing for tailored treatment plans. This aspect of personalized medicine is revolutionizing healthcare, making treatments more effective and reducing the risk of adverse reactions."

Despite its compactness, Meera's meticulously arranged office reflected her approach to teaching: descriptive yet precise. Adam was impressed by her skill in breaking down complex subjects into understandable pieces.

"Beyond medicine, genetic markers play a significant role in genealogy, helping individuals trace their ancestry and familial connections. They are also pivotal in forensic science. By analyzing genetic markers at a crime scene, investigators can identify suspects or victims, making it a powerful tool in solving crimes.

"Each of these applications underscores the importance of studying genetic markers. They're not just codes in our DNA; they're keys to unlocking a wealth of information about our health, history, and identity."

Meera leaned back and steepled her fingers, her smile radiating a clear passion for the subject at hand.

Adam nodded, taking in the information. He felt uneasy considering the implications of such knowledge in the wrong hands. However, he pushed these thoughts aside for now, focusing on Meera's explanation.

"By analyzing genetic markers, we can gain valuable insights into our own biology and the world," Meera continued, her enthusiasm for the subject shining through. "But, like all scientific advancements, there is the potential for misuse."

"Right," Adam murmured, wondering just how far some might go in their pursuit of power and control.

"Of course, most researchers in this field are committed to using their knowledge ethically and responsibly," Meera assured him, sensing his apprehension. "The information we gather from studying genetic markers can be used for a greater good."

Adam's mind churned with the implications of Meera's explanations, enthusiasm warring with unease. He could see how this kind of research could revolutionize medicine and change the world for the better. Yet, lurking in the recesses of his thoughts, was the potential for a more sinister application—eugenics.

"Your passion for this field is truly inspiring," Adam said, forcing a smile as he tried to shake off his darker musings. "It's incredible what science can uncover."

"Thank you," Meera replied, beaming. "There's always something new to learn, and that's what makes it so exciting." Then her brow furrowed with concern, and she asked, "Are you okay? You look a little spooked."

"Ah, it's nothing," Adam replied, attempting to dismiss his unease with a weak laugh. "I think my blood sugar's low. You know how it is when you're running on coffee and not much else."

"Of course," Meera said sympathetically. "Here, I have some snacks in my desk if you'd like something to munch on." She pulled open a drawer, revealing an assortment of granola bars and trail mix.

"Thanks," Adam said gratefully, accepting a granola bar and taking a bite. He hoped the snack would help settle his nerves and allow him to focus on the task at hand.

"See, your body tells you what it needs," Meera joked, gesturing at the granola bar. "Maybe we should study your DNA to find out why you're prone to low blood sugar."

They both chuckled at her lighthearted jab, and Adam felt some of the tension in his chest ease. He knew he needed to stay focused on uncovering the truth behind the DNA reports and not let his imagination run wild with frightening possibilities.

"Thanks again for your help," he said, finishing the granola bar and wiping the crumbs from his hands. "Your insight has been invaluable."

"Anytime, Adam," Meera replied politely, her eyes

hinting at a subtle concern. "I'm always here if you have more questions or think of anything else."

Adam paused before refocusing on Meera. "There's something else on my mind," he said, his voice betraying a hint of tension as he deliberated over his next words.

With a tilt of her head, Meera signaled him to proceed.

He hesitated, then ventured, "Is it conceivable to use genetic marker knowledge for... well, for manipulating genetic outcomes on a large scale? For choosing traits or controlling groups?" The word he avoided hung unspoken between them.

"Are you hinting at something akin to eugenics?" Meera interjected, her tone serious, eyes sharp with intellect.

Adam nodded grimly, relieved she understood. "Yes, could these markers be exploited to, say, enhance conformity, or to make a population more susceptible to certain conditions?"

Meera's expression turned contemplative as she pondered Adam's inquiry. "In theory, advanced gene-editing techniques have the potential to modify DNA traits," she began with caution. "This could involve altering characteristics for compliance or targeting specific groups with diseases. It's a complex and morally ambiguous area. But it's crucial to note that these are not the objectives of ethical practitioners in my field."

A look of concern etched onto Adam's face. "But in your field," he ventured carefully, "is it possible that some might overstep ethical lines in pursuit of progress?"

Meera leaned back in her chair, her gaze introspective. "There are whispers," she admitted in a measured tone.

"Stories circulate about research conducted in less-regulated areas, where ethical guidelines are more... relaxed. However, these are just stories, often lacking concrete evidence. Our community tends to be highly skeptical of such rumors." Meera shifted in her seat, her hands absently brushing away nonexistent crumbs from her lap.

Adam felt a chill of apprehension as he absorbed her words. While Meera's assurance that her colleagues upheld strict ethical standards was somewhat comforting, it didn't completely alleviate his concerns. The possibilities that such technology could be misused by less ethical hands lingered ominously in his mind, especially considering what Cam had uncovered at CytoLife.

"Thank you, Meera," he said, forcing a smile to hide his unease. "I appreciate your candor and expertise. You've given me a lot to think about."

Meera returned his smile, though her eyes held a hint of confusion. "You're welcome, Adam. I hope I've been able to ease some of your concerns. Just remember that science can be both fascinating and terrifying, depending on how it's used. It's up to us to ensure that it's used responsibly."

"Of course," he agreed, extending his hand for a farewell handshake. "Thank you again for your time. I'll keep in touch if I have any more questions."

"Take care of yourself, okay?" Meera insisted, her handshake firm. He felt the weight of her concern as he walked away, sensing the warmth of enduring friendship in her look.

Adam paused outside Meera's office, his mind a

whirlwind of apprehension. The immense potential of genetic manipulation weighed heavily on him, a potent tool that could either heal or devastate. The gnawing suspicion that CytoLife's intentions were far from benign refused to leave his thoughts. Steeling himself, he took a deep breath and sent a quick message to Cam through Beacon: "We need to talk ASAP."

Knowing that Cam had gone silent, likely driven by fear, Adam hoped for a response this time. He needed to make sense of the staggering insights he'd just gained. As he slipped his phone back into his pocket and walked away from the campus, his thoughts raced, consumed by the vast and complex consequences of gene-editing technology.

Baxter surveyed the opulent suite inside the Evergreen Resort, a sense of satisfaction in his posture. The room buzzed with laughter and the gentle clink of crystal glasses. Influential figures, impeccably dressed, mingled amongst each other, their conversation filled with the energy of ambition.

"Thomas, this gathering is a testament to your vision," a man remarked, raising his glass. "We are shaping the future."

"Indeed," Baxter replied, his voice rich with confidence. "Faced with overpopulation, climate change, and resource scarcity, it falls to us to take decisive action."

The room hummed with agreement, each person there convinced of their role as saviors of humanity.

"But," Baxter interjected, his eyes narrowing thoughtfully, "not everyone may embrace our solutions."

A bald-headed man in designer glasses took a sip of his whiskey. "Progress often requires sacrifice, doesn't it?"

Baxter offered a knowing nod. "Yes, and it's our duty to make these tough decisions. Humanity teeters on a precipice, and we are the only ones who can guide it safely."

He paused, letting his gaze drift across the room. "However, let me be clear. We're not dabbling in the shadows of a dark past. This isn't about limiting or removing—it's about enhancing and advancing humanity."

His eyes locked onto those of his guests, a practiced charisma in his stance. "We're not echoing eugenics; we're forging a path to a brighter, more robust future. We're adding to humanity's potential, not subtracting. Our work is the next step in human evolution, a leap forward, not a step back."

The guests nodded, any earlier hesitations melting away beneath Baxter's persuasive eloquence. With a smug satisfaction, he recognized their eagerness, merely restrained by fear, and how skillfully he nudged them toward the destinies they desired yet dared not pursue alone. His visionary leadership was not just necessary; it was inevitable. Preempting objections with ease and painting a compelling picture of progress, Baxter stood unrivaled. In that room, he was the undisputed maestro, orchestrating a symphony of ambition and influence, guiding each note with the precision of a seasoned conductor.

Baxter's announcement had captivated the room, and he seized this moment to further enthrall his audience. "I have yet another significant revelation," he declared, his voice resonating with a mix of gravity and pride. "Dr. Rebecca Kent of CytoLife is at the helm of a groundbreaking venture in DNA editing through CRISPR technology."

The room stilled, anticipation hanging in the air.

Baxter continued, his words painting a picture of a transformative future. "Imagine the power to reshape the very essence of life. We stand on the threshold of solving overpopulation, addressing resource scarcity, and eliminating diseases with unmatched genetic precision."

A collective murmur, a blend of awe and uncertainty, swept through the attendees.

Baxter, sensing their hesitancy, leaned in, his expression earnest. "These are not just lofty ideals; they are concrete results born from our collective endeavors, discussed and refined right here." His sweeping hand gesture included everyone present, his penetrating gaze seeking to dispel any lingering doubts. "Together, we possess the capability to enhance humanity, to refine our species by augmenting our strengths and mitigating our weaknesses."

His next words were decisive. "Our immediate task is to cultivate a society ready to embrace this new era. Dr. Rebecca Kent is uniquely qualified to lead us on this mission. Her unwavering commitment and resolute focus are unparalleled."

Intrigue sparked in the eyes of a distinguished attendee. "Dr. Kent sounds like an exceptional scientist."

Baxter nodded. "Her work is indeed extraordinary. I propose a comprehensive presentation to showcase how her research aligns with our collective objectives. Would that be of interest?"

The response was instantaneous and emphatic. A chorus of "Absolutely" resonated around the room, signifying their eagerness to witness the fruits of their ambitious collaboration.

"Excellent," Baxter said, his eyes drifting over to Felix, who had been silently observing the proceedings from a shadowy corner of the room. "Felix, would you be so kind as to coordinate with Dr. Kent and set up a meeting? I'm sure she'd love to share her findings with our esteemed colleagues."

"Of course, Mr. Baxter," Felix replied, voice smooth and controlled as he stepped forward into the light. "I'll make the arrangements right away."

"Thank you, Felix," Baxter acknowledged, then turned to address the assembly at the table. "Ladies and gentlemen, we stand at the threshold of a groundbreaking era. Together, we will sculpt a new world—one where disorder yields to a structured harmony, and humanity flourishes under our stewardship."

With Felix discreetly exiting to execute his orders, the group raised their glasses again. Their faces glowed with the exhilarating sense of control and ambition. Amidst this atmosphere of charged anticipation, Thomas Baxter basked in the realization of his dominance. He was acutely aware that the fate of the world was now intricately linked to his vision and actions.

In Judge Jackson's study, Harper and Deandra waited, their curiosity piqued by Mama Dee's insistence on meeting before the judge's funeral.

"Alright, now," Mama Dee began, her voice a mix of steadiness and emotion. "I know it's hard, especially now, but there's something you both need to hear."

Harper and Deandra shared a glance, their anticipation crystal clear. Mama Dee paused, gathering her thoughts before excavating the past.

"Back when Isaac and I were newlyweds, just starting out, we had big dreams. He was studying law, on his way to becoming the respected judge he was. And I was there, every step of the way," she reminisced, her eyes reflecting years of shared life and love.

As she continued, the room seemed to echo with visions of their past. They could almost see a younger Isaac, driven and ambitious, and Mama Dee, his steadfast pillar of support.

"Isaac was brilliant, but he needed grounding, and that was my role. I was the anchor in his life." Her voice carried a blend of pride and nostalgia, her eyes moist with memories of their journey together.

Harper listened intently, her heart swelling with gratitude for the woman who had been like a second mother to her. She knew how much Mama Dee had sacrificed for her family, and she couldn't help but be in awe of her strength.

"Isaac was a good man, but he wasn't perfect," Mama Dee continued, her tone shifting to one of solemnity. "He made mistakes, like we all do. And I'm about to share with you one of those mistakes—one that has haunted him, and me, for years."

Deandra's expression turned thoughtful, struggling to fathom what urgency could overshadow their current sorrow. Beside her, Harper felt a tightness in her stomach, a blend of uneasy anticipation and apprehension. They both waited, silent and tense, for Mama Dee to unveil a long-concealed truth.

Mama Dee drew a deep breath, her eyes warm as they rested on Deandra. "When you came into this world, Deandra, it was a joy unlike any other. You've always been our light." She reached out, affectionately squeezing Deandra's hand.

"We hoped for more children, but it wasn't meant to be," Mama Dee said with a soft voice shaded with a hint of melancholy. "Then Harper entered our lives, bringing another kind of joy."

Harper's lips curved in a fond smile at the memory. From the day she and Deandra had become friends, she had felt an immediate kinship. She had often found comfort and acceptance in the Jackson household, a stark contrast to her own family dynamics.

"Deandra brought you home, and you just fit right in," Mama Dee recalled, her tone filled with warmth. "To Isaac and me, you were like a second daughter. We felt blessed that Deandra had someone like you in her life."

Harper's eyes welled up, remembering the countless times the Jacksons' home had been her refuge, a place of unconditional love and understanding.

"Y'all were inseparable," Mama Dee said, chuckling softly. "All those sleepovers, the secret clubs you made up, the adventures you went on—you two were thick as thieves."

Deandra laughed through her tears, nodding in agreement. "We were pretty wild, weren't we?"

"Wild? More like unstoppable!" Mama Dee exclaimed,

her laughter joined by Harper's. "I remember one summer, y'all built a treehouse in the backyard. Isaac thought it was the craziest idea, but he couldn't say no to his girls. So, there we were, all four of us, hammering away at that old oak tree."

"Didn't it end up being more like a glorified platform than an actual treehouse?" Harper asked, her laughter causing the tears to roll down her cheeks.

"Sure did," Mama Dee confirmed, wiping away her own tears. "But that didn't stop you two from spending hours up there, whispering secrets and planning your futures.

"Isaac loved you both so much," Mama Dee said softly, her voice thick with emotion. "And I know he's watching over us now, proud of the strong, beautiful women you've become."

Harper reached for Deandra's hand, squeezing it tightly as they shared a silent understanding. They had gone through so much together, and now, faced with this unthinkable loss, they discovered comfort in the unbreakable bond they had formed all those years ago on a playground in Memphis.

Mama Dee paused, her breath hitching as tears glistened in her eyes. She looked at Harper and Deandra, both tensely perched on the edge of their seats, bracing themselves.

Gathering herself, Mama Dee said, "I need to tell you something important. Isaac was coerced into accepting bribes from PenCore, pressured to send people to their facilities."

Deandra gasped, shock and confusion etching her face. Harper, her expression clouded with sorrow, recalled her intense confrontation with the judge and his subsequent letter of confession and apology.

"Harper," Mama Dee's voice wavered, "the night you and Isaac argued, he was distraught. He told me about the argument, how you uncovered his involvement in the scheme."

Deandra, her emotions spilling over, turned to Harper. "You knew and didn't tell me?"

Mama Dee intervened. "Deandra, let me finish. It's not that simple."

As Deandra sat back, trembling, Mama Dee continued. "Isaac was tormented by guilt. He absolutely regretted his actions, especially how it could affect both of you."

In a softer, sadder tone, she added, "I believe his heart was broken by the revelation and the pain it caused, particularly to you, Harper."

Harper bowed her head, grappling with a mix of guilt and grief. She hadn't fully realized the impact of her confrontation on Isaac.

Mama Dee shared more with a heavy voice. "Years ago, Isaac confessed to me about the bribes. He felt trapped, convinced it was a 'necessary evil.' But it weighed on him, terribly."

Mama Dee couldn't help but let out a small chuckle, lightening the somber mood for a moment. "I remember finding extra money and jumping to the conclusion that Isaac was dabbling in some risky business or secret investments," she recounted, a hint of amusement in her voice despite the gravity of the situation. "I stormed into his office, ready for a confrontation, only to find him there, looking so overwhelmed, like he was carrying the weight of the world."

Harper smiled along with Deandra, who brightened at the memory of her father. Mama Dee's storytelling, despite unveiling past hurts, vividly brought their shared humanity to life.

"Anyway," Mama Dee continued, "once he realized I wasn't about to let him off easy, he broke down and confessed everything. Told me why he felt compelled to take them bribes and how it was eating him up inside." She paused, wiping away a tear that had escaped her eye. "I could see the pain in his heart, and I knew we had to make things right."

Harper and Deandra clasped hands. Judge Isaac Jackson was a decent man who had been led down a difficult path, and now it was clear just how much he and Mama Dee had tried to atone for those choices.

"Your father," Mama Dee said, her voice filled with love and pride, "struggled every day with the guilt of what he'd done. But together, we fought to make amends—even if it meant keeping secrets from those we loved most."

Her voice, now fainter, wavered and then faded. "With my Isaac gone, there's no telling whether the bribery scheme will come to light. I wanted you girls to hear it from me first..." Mama Dee inhaled sharply, her eyes alight with a resolute spark. "Listen closely now because there's more," she said with a firm tone, leaning forward. "I've always had a knack for finances. When Isaac and I married, managing our money was my domain.

"Years back, after Isaac's confession about the bribes," Mama Dee went on, "I made a choice. I couldn't undo his actions, but I could make a difference. So, I diverted the bribe money into something worthwhile."

Harper and Deandra exchanged intrigued glances as Mama Dee's face lit up with a mischievous smile. "That money became the seed for JusticeGuard, a fund to help young people who can't afford proper legal defense. I've been the silent benefactor, ensuring they receive the advocacy they need."

Deandra gasped softly, while Harper's eyes shone with new understanding.

"Isaac never knew JusticeGuard's true origin," Mama Dee added, her voice a blend of firmness and compassion. "He might not have agreed, so I kept it secret. It was my way of tipping the scales back towards justice."

She reached out, her hands enveloping Harper's and Deandra's. "When Darrius's case came up, I saw an opportunity. I nudged Isaac to recommend it to Sam for you, Harper. He thought he was just helping you. He never knew about my deeper involvement."

Harper was awestruck, realizing the extent of Mama Dee's secret fight for justice. "Thank you," she managed to say, her voice laden with gratitude.

Mama Dee squeezed their hands tenderly. "You're welcome, my dear. We're in this together—for Isaac and for those wronged by the system."

A heavy silence filled the room, the clock's ticking the only sound. Deandra broke the stillness, her voice soft but earnest. "Mama, why did you do all this?"

"Because it was right," Mama Dee replied, her voice

unwavering. "Isaac believed in justice, despite his flaws. And so do I. Sometimes I wonder about the effectiveness of our efforts in such a flawed system," she mused, her gaze reflective. "But in my heart, I always knew it was the right thing to do. It was my way of trying to set things right in whatever way I could."

Harper studied her friend's face, noting the mixture of confusion and admiration that flickered across her features. Deandra's heart was always in the right place, but this was a lot for anyone to take in. She could almost see the cogs turning in Deandra's head, each piece of information slotting into place slowly, deliberately.

"Did Sam ever suspect anything?" Harper asked, curiosity getting the better of her. "Did he ever question why Isaac wanted him to assign Darrius's case to me?"

Mama Dee shook her head. "As far as I know, Sam thought he was doing an old friend a favor. He never questioned Isaac's motives or my involvement. Sam probably just thought JusticeGuard was paying the legal bills."

"Wow," Deandra murmured, leaning back in her chair. "This is... a lot to process." She glanced at Harper, her brow furrowed. "And you had no idea, either?"

"None," Harper admitted, feeling a pang of regret. "If only I'd known, maybe I could've done more to help. But what matters now is how we move forward and continue fighting for justice."

"Absolutely," Mama Dee agreed, her gaze steady. "We can't change the past, but we can still make a difference in the future."

After a moment that stretched out between them, Deandra's voice, soft and laden with the gravity of their conversation, broke the silence. "I have so many questions," she murmured.

"Me too," Harper admitted, her gaze steady on Mama Dee. "But there's something else I need to know first." Her chest rose slightly, a silent battle to keep her emotions in check. "Mama Dee, did Isaac tell you everything about the argument we had?"

Mama Dee furrowed her brow, confusion clouding her face. "He told me you found out about his involvement with PenCore and confronted him about it. But he didn't go into details."

Harper nodded, her heart heavy with the weight of what she still needed to reveal. "There's more to it than that, but... before we get into all of that, did Isaac ever mention writing a letter to me that night?"

"Ah, yes," Mama Dee recalled, her expression softening. "He was adamant about writing you a letter, though he wouldn't let me read it. I thought it might be his way of apologizing for his actions."

"Did you ever see the letter after he wrote it?" Deandra asked, curiosity piqued.

"No, child," Mama Dee replied, shaking her head. "He must've hidden it somewhere before... before he passed."

Harper's eyes drifted around Isaac's study, pausing on his meticulously arranged law books and the photographs filled with smiles. The weight of her discovery about PenCore and the DNA evidence loomed over her. With Mama Dee and

Deandra already grappling with Isaac's complex legacy, she dreaded adding to their grief.

"Harper, you seem troubled," Deandra noted, her expression marked by concern. "Is there something else?"

Harper paused; the words caught in her throat. "Yes," she finally murmured, reluctance clear in her voice. "But maybe we should wait until after Isaac's funeral."

Deandra reached out, her grasp reassuring. "We can handle it, Harper. No secrets between us anymore."

Mama Dee's voice, steady and strong, resonated in the room. "Harper, you're family. We need to face this together, whatever it is."

Nodding in understanding, Harper replied, "I will tell you, just not yet." She looked at Mama Dee, her eyes seeking solace. "First, we should honor Isaac."

Mama Dee gave Harper a knowing look, then agreed with a gentle nod. "He deserves a fitting farewell. Let's get his favorite gray pinstripe suit ready. And then, child, you can unburden your heart."

"His favorite," Deandra echoed softly, a bittersweet smile touching her lips as they left the study.

As Harper followed, her mind was a whirlpool of unspoken truths. The gravity of PenCore's sinister activities weighed on her, but she knew the time for revelation would come. Now, they needed to focus on honoring Isaac and preparing themselves for the challenges that lay ahead.

SIXTEEN

Harper awoke with a start, the remnants of her hangover pressing down like a heavy blanket. She groaned, her hands instinctively moving to her aching head as she struggled to sit up. The room spun, a cruel reminder of last night's overindulgence in bourbon.

"Damn it," she muttered, squinting against the harsh morning light.

The day of Judge Isaac Jackson's funeral hung over her, adding to the gloom of the morning. But it wasn't just the sorrow of saying goodbye to her mentor that troubled Harper. Her life seemed filled with regrets: a failed marriage, a widening gap with her children, and the daunting truths about PenCore and Isaac's involvement.

"Get it together, Harper," she uttered to herself, fighting to clear the mental fog. "One step at a time."

Summoning her willpower, Harper rose from the

bed, leaning on the dresser for support. She headed to the bathroom, splashing cold water on her face, bracing herself for the difficult conversations with Mama Dee and Deandra that would have to wait. Today was about honoring Isaac.

At Elmwood Cemetery, mourners filled the space, their dark clothes matching the cloudy sky. The elaborate funeral reflected Isaac's status as a respected African American judge. White chairs surrounded the polished mahogany casket, adorned with a majestic floral arrangement.

Harper found her place among the mourners, her heart constricting as she watched Mama Dee and Deandra approach the casket. Mama Dee's usual radiance was absent, replaced by a stony, unfamiliar calm. Deandra, eyes brimming with tears, gently touched the casket, her fingers quivering.

"Isaac." Mama Dee's voice trembled, laden with sorrow.

Throughout the funeral service, Harper attempted to immerse herself in the heartfelt eulogies for Judge Jackson. Speakers reminisced about his dedication to civil rights, his passion for public education, and his influential leadership in Memphis.

The somber melody of "Amazing Grace" filled the air, its notes weaving through the mourners' subdued whispers and soft cries. Seated behind Mama Dee and Deandra, Harper felt the comforting touch of her boss, Sam Chapman, his hand gently resting on her knee, a gesture she acknowledged with a silent, appreciative squeeze.

Harper had invited her ex-husband, Rob, and their daughter, Charlotte, to attend. Casting a discreet glance towards the back, she noticed them, seemingly oblivious to her gaze. Their isolated presence in the crowd underscored her sense of detachment.

Thoughts of Lucas intruded, sharpening her sense of loss. His absence left a void in the tribute to the man who had been a father figure to them. Harper's heart ached for the unity her family once had.

"The judge was a steadfast advocate for civil rights and public education," a speaker's voice echoed, filled with respect. The crowd nodded in agreement, many visibly moved by the tribute.

As the ceremony concluded, mourners queued to offer condolences. Harper watched from a distance, observing the genuine grief etched on their faces. They shared anecdotes of Isaac's generosity, his integrity, and his indelible impact. Yet, for Harper, these accolades were weighted with the knowledge of his hidden misdeeds, creating an unsettling contrast that gnawed at her conscience.

"Harper," Sam murmured, leaning in with concern. "You holding up?"

Harper managed a weary smile, her voice melancholy. "I'll manage, Sam. There was so much left unsaid with Isaac."

Sam gave her a knowing look, his eyes filled with empathy as he comprehended the inner turmoil behind her words. "Take your time to process, Harper. Remember, you're not alone in this."

Harper nodded, her eyes briefly meeting Sam's. She glanced away, allowing herself a moment of intimate reflection before leaving the cemetery.

The Jackson home buzzed with muted conversations

as a select group of mourners congregated for a private commemoration following the burial. The grandeur of the old Midtown residence now echoed bittersweet memories. Its usual vibrancy dimmed by the shroud of loss.

Mama Dee moved among her guests, her eyes red and her once-lively demeanor subdued by the day's sorrow. Deandra, normally the life of any gathering, remained downcast, her thoughts seemingly far away.

As Harper looked around, she felt a deep sympathy for Mama Dee and Deandra, who had become like family to her. Doubts and questions about Isaac's death lingered in her mind, casting shadows over her grief. "Could there be more to it?" she pondered silently, trying to dismiss the thought as mere conjecture.

The home's rich wood paneling and the scent of polished antiques and fresh flowers created a comforting, albeit somber, ambiance. Guests wandered in and out of the study, admiring the memorabilia that chronicled Isaac's distinguished life.

One mourner approached Harper, breaking her reverie. "Isaac had a way of filling a room, didn't he?" they said softly, offering a comforting touch.

Harper nodded, a small smile breaking through her solemnity. "He certainly did. His presence was larger than life."

"Harper, we're all here for you too, you know," another mourner offered. "Isaac was like a father to you. And Deandra... well, you two are practically sisters."

"Thank you," she mouthed, her throat tight with emotion.

One by one, friends and colleagues rose to pay tribute to Isaac, their voices filled with emotion and gratitude. A former law clerk spoke of his dedication to public service, while a fellow attorney praised his unwavering commitment to civil rights and social justice.

"Isaac was a force to be reckoned with in the courtroom," one speaker declared, "but he was also a loyal friend and mentor to so many of us."

Throughout the speeches, Mama Dee sat in her favorite armchair, her eyes glistening with pride and sadness. Though she looked weary and frail, there was a strength about her that seemed to hold the room together.

When a lull fell over the gathering, Harper felt a sudden surge of resolve. She couldn't let this moment pass without expressing her own admiration and love for the man who had played such a pivotal role in her life.

"Isaac was like a father to me," she began, her voice quavering slightly as she fought back tears. "He believed in me when no one else did, and he taught me everything I know about the law—and about life.

"His wisdom, integrity, and compassion made him not only a successful judge but a truly exceptional human being." As she spoke those words, a pang of guilt twisted inside her, a reminder of the secrets she still harbored. But now was not the time to expose them. Now was the time to honor Isaac's memory and celebrate the good he had done. "Memphis has lost a shining light, but I know that Isaac's legacy will live on through all of us who were touched by his kindness and wisdom."

As she finished speaking, Harper looked toward Mama Dee, who met her gaze with a tearful smile. The older woman rose slowly from her chair and addressed the room.

"Thank you all for your kind words about my dear Isaac," she said, her voice thick with emotion. "He would be so proud to know how much he meant to each of you. I am grateful beyond measure for the love and support that has been shown to our family during this difficult time.

"Isaac was a wonderful man—a loving husband, a devoted father, and a loyal friend. We will miss him dearly, but we will carry on, honoring his memory by continuing his work and striving to make our community a better place for all."

As Mama Dee finished speaking, the room erupted in muted applause, and Harper felt a swell of admiration for the woman who had lost so much yet remained so strong. She couldn't help but think how wisely Isaac had chosen in marrying her, a testament to the depth of their bond.

As the evening wore on, the mourners drifted away, leaving behind a bittersweet emptiness. Mama Dee, exhausted, but still unwilling to let go of the night, lingered in the parlor, savoring the last vestiges of warmth and camaraderie before facing the cold reality of life without Isaac.

"Tonight, we honored him well," she murmured, her eyes distant and full of grief. "But tomorrow is another day. And there is still so much work left to do."

As the last of the mourners left, Harper, Deandra, and Mama Dee gathered in the now-still parlor. The air was heavy with the lingering echoes of laughter and tears.

"Daddy would've loved tonight," Deandra said softly, her eyes glistening with unshed tears. "He always enjoyed a good gathering."

"Remember that time he organized the neighborhood block party?" Harper added, a wistful smile playing on her lips. "He insisted on grilling for everyone, even though he'd never touched a barbecue before in his life."

Mama Dee chuckled, the sound warm and bittersweet. "Oh, I remember. The burgers were charred black on the outside and raw in the middle. But no one had the heart to tell him. We just ate them with lots of ketchup and pretended they were delicious."

The three women shared a moment of laughter, finding solace in the memories of the man they all loved so dearly.

Without warning, the front door opened, and Lucas stepped into the house, a somber expression on his face. Shock rippled through the room, and Harper felt as if she'd been punched in the gut; his sudden appearance left her reeling.

"Lucas?" she breathed, her voice faintly audible.

"Hi, Mom," he replied quietly, meeting her eyes for a brief second before glancing away.

Without thinking, Harper crossed the room and pulled Lucas into a tight embrace. He hesitated for a moment, then hugged her back, the warmth of his body a stark contrast to the cold void that had settled in her heart since their estrangement.

"Lucas, my boy," Mama Dee exclaimed, her voice thick with emotion. "We've missed you."

"Good to see you, Lucas," Deandra added, giving him a teary-eyed smile.

"Sorry I didn't call," he said, his voice low and shaded with regret. "I saw the notice online and... I just had to come."

"Your presence means more than any phone call ever could," Mama Dee assured him, embracing him in her motherly arms. "Isaac loved you like a grandson, and he would be so glad to know you're here."

Lucas nodded, his eyes welling up as he looked around at the three women who'd been such an important part of his life. For a moment, their shared grief bound them together, eclipsing the distance that had grown between them.

"Come," Mama Dee said gently, guiding Lucas towards the sitting area. "Let's eat and share some stories about Isaac. We've got plenty to tell, and I'm sure you have a few of your own."

As they sat together, sharing stories of Isaac, Lucas's stoic demeanor slowly softened. Tears softly streaming down his cheek, he listened to Deandra recount a fond memory of the judge teaching her to play chess. Harper watched him closely, her heart aching at the sight of her son so raw and vulnerable.

"Isaac taught me how to drive, you know," Lucas suddenly interjected, swallowing the lump in his throat. "Mom was working. And Dad... well, he gave up teaching me so I asked Isaac. He took me out in that old Chevy of his, insisting I learn on a stick shift."

Deandra laughed through her own tears. "I remember that! You stalled it about a dozen times before you got the hang of it."

Lucas cracked a smile, recalling the day. "He was so patient, even when I accidentally backed into that fire hydrant."

Harper listened, feeling a pang of guilt at having missed these moments in her son's life. She'd been so consumed with her career, so focused on righting wrongs in the courtroom, that she'd neglected her own family.

"Lucas," she began haltingly, trying not to sound accusatory. "We've all been worried about you. Why didn't you reach out? Just...to let us know you're alright?"

He shifted uncomfortably under her gaze, clearly struggling to find the right words. "I've been... busy, with work. It's complicated, Mom. I can't really talk about it."

"Complicated?" Harper echoed, her voice tight with frustration. She wanted desperately to reconnect with her son, but the wall of secrecy between them felt insurmountable. "What kind of job is so secretive that you can't even tell your own mother what you're doing? I understand the NDA, but—"

"Harper, now's not the time," Mama Dee gently chided, placing a calming hand on her arm.

"Right," Harper relented, forcing herself to let the matter rest. For now, at least. "I'm sorry, Lucas. I didn't mean to pry."

Lucas offered her a small smile, his eyes conveying an apology she knew he couldn't voice.

Mama Dee's warm eyes settled on Lucas as she gave him a tender squeeze on the shoulder. Her genuine concern and curiosity about his life were obvious. "We've missed you so much, Lucas," Mama Dee drawled. "Tell us what you've been doing lately."

"Thank you, Mama Dee," Lucas replied, managing a grateful smile. "I've found myself a great job—really fulfilling work. I'm loving it."

Harper studied her son's face, searching for any hint of the truth hidden behind his guarded expression. She could sense he was holding something back, but knew better than to push him further.

"That's wonderful to hear, dear." Mama Dee beamed, her eyes shining with pride. "You deserve all the happiness in the world."

As the gathering wound down, Harper couldn't help but feel a pang of loss at the thought of Lucas leaving again. The emotional distance between them weighed heavily on her heart, and she longed for the chance to bridge the gap.

"Lucas," Harper ventured hesitantly, "why don't you stay with me while you're in town? We have a lot of catching up to do."

He shook his head, his gaze apologetic. "I appreciate the offer, Mom, but I've already booked a room at the Peabody. And I won't be here for long." The words stung, but Harper masked her disappointment with a tight-lipped smile.

"Of course," she said, trying to keep her voice steady. "I understand. It's just... I miss you, Lucas."

"Me too, Mom," he sighed, his eyes softening. "Maybe we can grab coffee or something before I leave?"

"Great," Harper said with a smile, though she felt a pang of sadness at the realization that she didn't even have her son's new phone number. "Just call me when you're free, okay?"

"Of course," Lucas agreed before saying his last goodbyes and leaving the house.

Baxter stood by the windows of the Evergreen Resort's lavish conference room, his silhouette commanding against the backdrop. As Felix and Rebecca entered, their expressions reflected the seriousness of the upcoming presentation.

"Rebecca," Baxter began, his voice resonating with authority, "we are addressing a select circle of influential leaders. Their support is pivotal for our project at CytoLife. They expect nothing short of groundbreaking from us, and we must deliver."

Felix, eyes fixed on Baxter, acknowledged the importance of the meeting. "This assembly wields the power to advance our mission. Your presentation is crucial in securing their backing."

Determination shone in Rebecca's eyes, the scale of the opportunity energizing her. "I'm ready to unveil our latest breakthroughs. We've identified genetic markers influencing traits like assertiveness and aggression. Modifying these can reshape societal norms, fostering greater compliance and reducing violence."

A flicker of approval lit Baxter's face. "And our longevity research?"

"Progressing rapidly," Rebecca assured. "We're close to extending human life significantly, nearing what was once mere fantasy."

Baxter's excitement was unmistakable. He clapped his hands once, decisively. "Splendid! Let's make sure our guests grasp the magnitude of our achievements. Their endorsement is key."

As Baxter leaned closer, his gaze intense, pride swelled within him. Observing Rebecca articulate their advances, he reveled in her brilliance. Their familial connection remained hidden, yet this secret bond only heightened his satisfaction in their shared endeavor.

"Break it down for me, Rebecca," Baxter urged with a commanding tone, "as if you were explaining to someone completely unfamiliar with genetics."

Rebecca nodded, her demeanor calm. "We've identified genes that influence behavior, particularly those linked to aggression, defiance, and compliance. Our technique modifies these traits, subtly guiding individuals towards more conforming and passive behaviors."

"It's important to note," she continued, "that this doesn't strip away one's personality. Memories, passions, goals—they all remain intact. The modification simply reduces the intensity of their reactions, leading to a more harmonious society."

Baxter listened intently, his nod signaling satisfaction with her explanation. "That's the clarity we need for the presentation. It's crucial our audience understands and supports the scope of our work."

Rebecca's face reflected the gravity of their project. "I can handle this. We'll get our point across."

Felix, his stance relaxed yet attentive, chimed in. "That's

a comprehensive overview, Rebecca. It should resonate well with our audience."

Baxter noted Felix's consistently composed presence, a necessary trait considering his crucial role in their operation. "Thank you, Felix," Baxter acknowledged, appreciating his steady support.

Rebecca responded with a brief nod, acknowledging Felix's comment.

Baxter's footsteps echoed across the ornate room. The afternoon sun bathed the space in a warm, golden glow, yet his thoughts were shadowed by the gravity of the upcoming presentation. Rebecca's voice, infused with a blend of hesitance and hope, broke his reverie. "Papa, what if we show them the human trials? It could truly illustrate the extent of our achievements."

Baxter halted, turning to face her. His eyes, sharp and penetrating, tunneled into hers, weighing the implications of her suggestion. After a thoughtful pause, he spoke mindfully. "Our progress is indeed extraordinary, Rebecca. But revealing the human trials now? It's a bold step. Perhaps too bold."

Rebecca advanced, her conviction absolute. "We're on the brink of a new era. Shouldn't we let them witness the real-world impact of our work?"

Memories of a younger Rebecca, her laughter echoing as she rode on his shoulders, momentarily softened Baxter's gaze. The vows he had made to protect her future and their shared legacy bore down on him. As he straightened his shoulders, his eyes locked onto hers, filled with unwavering determination. "Our innovations are revolutionary, but we must be strategic. Presenting human trials could provoke doubts and fear."

Observing the fervor in Rebecca's eyes, Baxter recognized her deep commitment. "Understood, Papa," she conceded, nodding slowly. "We'll focus on the science for now. The world will grasp our vision eventually."

Baxter's smile was tender as he placed a comforting hand on her shoulder. "Patience, my dear. Our time will come. For now, let's proceed with caution and conviction."

Standing together, they faced the imminent challenge of revealing their groundbreaking work—a disclosure set to irrevocably alter human destiny.

As they resumed their preparation, Baxter sensed an undercurrent of apprehension in Rebecca. He understood the profound impact of their research, the ability to reshape society fundamentally. Yet he also recognized the enormity of their responsibility, the potential for their work to be misunderstood or misused. He wondered if these same thoughts weighed on Rebecca, silently shaping her dedication.

SEVENTEEN

Harper's home lay in disarray, mirroring her depression. As she entered the living room, the familiar creak of the floorboards under her feet felt reassuring.

Determined, she gathered the bottles, symbols of her recent anguish, and tossed them into the trash. Their clinks marked a turning point. "Enough," she said intently, sealing the bag.

As Harper cleaned, a sense of control over her reactions emerged. Resolved, she planned a dinner with Mama Dee and Deandra, facing the issues head-on. The room's return to tranquility signaled the start of her own journey toward resolution.

She dialed the Jacksons and invited them to dinner. It was time for honesty.

"Are you free for dinner at my place this Wednesday?" she asked, trying to keep her voice steady. "There's something I need to discuss with you and Deandra."

"Of course, darlin'," Mama Dee replied fondly.

Harper then called Deandra, who agreed with a hesitant, "Sure, Harper. I'll be there."

Satisfied but nervous, Harper hung up and began planning the meal in her head. She wanted something comforting and familiar that would ease them into the difficult conversation ahead.

Harper had just set her phone down when a knock at the door disrupted her thoughts. Opening it, she found Ethan, his expression etched with worry.

"Ethan, what's wrong?" Harper asked, noting his troubled look as she let him in.

"It's Adam. He sounded really on edge during our call. He's insisting on a meeting as soon as possible," Ethan reported, his voice uneasy.

Harper's pulse quickened. "Did he say why?"

"He mentioned something about new information from his contact on those DNA reports," Ethan replied, his worry visible. "He was vague, but whatever it is, it's got him rattled."

Concern crept into Harper's voice. "We need to meet with him then. Maybe it's a lead we can work with."

As they settled into her now-tidied living room, Harper's mind was abuzz with possibilities, each more unsettling than the last. What had Adam unearthed that had left him so shaken?

Harper leaned forward, determination in her eyes. "Ethan, where are we on breaking through CytoLife's corporate veil?"

Ethan, pacing restlessly, exhaled in frustration. "Harper, it's like hitting a wall. There's nothing concrete linking them to anything illicit." He paused, a mix of exhaustion and self-doubt in his voice. "I'm starting to question if I've lost my touch."

Harper, deep in thought, shook her head. "We can't let this slip away. This might be our only shot at unraveling the PenCore mess." A sudden idea sparked in her mind. "Wait, I think I know someone who might help."

"Who?" Ethan asked, hope flickering in his eyes.

"His name is Neon. He's a former client of mine," Harper explained. As she spoke, memories flooded back. Neon had been a hacker, one who'd infiltrated the systems of St. Jude and FedEx. Yet, instead of causing havoc, he'd simply informed them of their vulnerabilities, leading to an embarrassed silence and a quick, quiet deal. Harper had successfully defended him, securing time served and a slap on the wrist.

"Are you sure he'll help?" Ethan asked doubtfully. "I mean, if he only contacted those organizations to warn them—"

"Trust me," Harper interrupted, her voice firm. "Neon's got a good heart, and he owes me one. Besides, we're not asking him to do anything nefarious—just to help us find the truth."

A warm, familiar drawl greeted her as Neon answered the phone. "Well, if it isn't the esteemed Harper Brasfield. To what do I owe this unexpected pleasure?"

"Neon," she began, a slight smile creeping across her face. "I need your particular expertise."

"Ah, Miss Brasfield," he chuckled. "Are you tryin' to corrupt me once again? I thought we left my dark days behind."

"Consider it a favor for an old friend," she replied, her tone softening. Harper glanced over at Ethan before continuing. "We have a hypothetical situation we'd like your input on."

"Go on," Neon prompted, his curiosity piqued.

"Let's say there's a company, and it's proving difficult to find any information on their real operations, particularly their lab work. Hypothetically, of course. Would you be able to help?" Harper asked, tiptoeing around the details.

"Miss Brasfield, you know I can't resist a wonderful challenge," Neon said with a hint of amusement. "Put me on speakerphone, would ya? I'd like to meet your associate."

"Of course," Harper obliged, pressing the speaker button and setting her phone down on the table. "Neon, meet Ethan Cook. Ethan, this is Neon."

"Charmed, I'm sure," Neon said smoothly. "Now, about this hypothetical situation..."

Ethan jumped in, explaining their predicament, using jargon that went straight over Harper's head. She watched as the two men conversed in their own language, their words weaving together like an intricate dance.

"Alright, friends, let's get down to business. Ethan, you're the tech-savvy one, so I'll be speaking your language."

"Fire away," Ethan replied, leaning forward expectantly.

"Let's see if we can thread the digital needle," Neon suggested, his voice heavy with determination. "Ethan, hand me the access to their network topology."

"I'm on it," Ethan said eagerly, tapping away at the keyboard. "Check this out. I've mapped a transaction to BluePulse Technologies. Seems like they have some sort of agreement with CytoLife Dynamics."

"BluePulse could be key," Neon mused aloud as he worked through the data. The room was filled with the cacophony of Ethan's clacking keys and Neon's murmured instructions over speakerphone.

Suddenly, Neon hooted in triumph. "Got something! Looks like BluePulse provided some high-tech surveillance equipment for CytoLife. Does that help?"

"Absolutely," Harper agreed, her brain spinning rapidly with possibilities.

Ethan expressed his gratitude. "Thank you for your assistance, Neon. Should you come across any further information, please call me directly, alright?"

"Consider it done, Ethan," Neon said, his tone shifting back to its earlier warmth. "And, if you ever want to learn more about the art of hacking, just call me."

Ethan flushed, but managed a smile. "I'll keep that in mind."

"Take care, both of you. I'll be in touch soon," Neon said before hanging up.

As the connection severed, Harper and Ethan exchanged glances, the weight of their discovery settling in. They now had a tangible link, and it felt like the first step toward unraveling the conspiracy that had entangled them.

Later, Ethan's phone rang. The caller ID showed Neon's name, bringing a small smile to his face despite the tense situation.

"Hey there, handsome," Neon drawled flirtatiously. "I have some news for you about that little project we discussed."

"Go ahead, Neon," Ethan replied, trying to focus on the task at hand even as his cheeks flushed.

"We know BluePulse Technologies provided advanced surveillance equipment to CytoLife. I took a creative stroll through their digital archives and found correspondence between them and a man named Felix Ross. Turns out he's the contact at CytoLife."

"Interesting," Harper mused, listening in on speakerphone. "What else did you find?"

"Unfortunately, not much. Whoever this Felix guy is, he's brilliant and careful. But I'm sending everything I found to you via a secure file-sharing app."

"Thank you, Neon," Harper said sincerely. "We appreciate your help more than you know."

"Anytime, darlin'," Neon replied smoothly. "Just remember you're corrupting poor little ol' me."

"Of course," she chuckled. "Wouldn't want to forget that."

"Alright, I'll let you two get back to work. Stay safe out there," Neon said, his voice softening. "And Ethan? Don't be a stranger."

"Never, Neon," Ethan assured him, a small smile playing on his lips as he hung up the phone.

Harper's heart pounded as she tapped the screen, her anticipation clear. The secure app beeped, signaling the download of Neon's files. Ethan, seated beside her, leaned forward, equally focused.

"Let's see what we've uncovered," she said, opening the first file. Her expression turned into a frown as she reviewed the information on BluePulse Technologies' advanced surveillance equipment supplied to CytoLife. "This level of tech seems excessive," she commented, looking up at Ethan, who could only offer a noncommittal shrug.

"Maybe it's linked to their hidden experiments," Ethan suggested, his tone laced with concern.

"Possibly," Harper conceded, her gaze fixed on the screen as she sifted through the technical details. Something was amiss, but what exactly remained unclear.

The next file revealed details about Felix Ross. The images depicted a man with a commanding presence and a background hinting at military or mercenary work, now deeply involved with CytoLife, yet absent from public records.

"Check this out," Harper motioned to Ethan, pointing at the dossier. "Felix Ross. Our mysterious CytoLife connection has quite a past."

Ethan peered at the photos. "Intriguing," he murmured, tapping thoughtfully on the table. "What else have we got?"

"Let's see what's next," Harper suggested, flipping to the following photo. She gasped at the familiar backdrop: The Evergreen Resort, a luxurious sanctuary nestled in the hills outside DC. The photograph, taken at a charity ball years before, showcased Felix standing next to Thomas Baxter and a woman named Rebecca Kent. Thomas, his arm affectionately draped over Rebecca's shoulder, beamed proudly. Given Baxter's renown as a philanthropist and head of Meridian Holdings, his ties to CytoLife were not unexpected.

"Look at this," Harper declared, showing Ethan the

photo. "Thomas Baxter with Felix Ross and Dr. Rebecca Kent."

"Rebecca Kent?" Ethan echoed, his eyes narrowing. "She looks... familiar."

"Could be another lead," Harper mused, her mind racing as she tried to fit the pieces together. "We need to find out more about her and her connection to Baxter and Felix."

Ethan's fingers flew across the keyboard, searching for any information on Rebecca Kent. Within moments, he had found a series of videos from a few years ago where she was interviewed about CRISPR technology. He clicked on one, and Harper leaned in to watch.

"CRISPR has the potential to revolutionize medicine as we know it," Rebecca said confidently, her blonde hair falling in soft waves around her face. "By editing specific genes, we might eradicate genetic diseases, improve crop yields, and even reverse the effects of aging."

"Sounds too good to be true," Harper muttered, her eyes narrowing as she watched Rebecca extol the virtues of DNA editing.

"Of course, there are those who question the ethics of such research," the interviewer pressed, leaning forward in his chair. "Some even draw parallels to eugenics. How do you respond to such comparisons?"

Rebecca met the question with a calm, unwavering gaze. "It's a common misconception, but what we're doing is fundamentally different from eugenics. That was about limiting life, often based on prejudiced ideologies. Our work is about enhancing life, responsibly and ethically, for everyone. We're not trying to play God. We're simply using the tools that science has given us to fix what's broken and improve what can be enhanced. The goal is to alleviate suffering, not to judge or categorize humanity."

Her reply was measured, reflecting both her deep understanding of the subject and her practiced ability to navigate such sensitive accusations. She continued, "Like any groundbreaking science, CRISPR requires careful ethical consideration. But shying away from its potential because of unfounded fears would be a disservice to the countless lives we could improve or even save."

"Responsibility?" Harper scoffed, her heart pounding with anger. "Exploiting people for their twisted experiments is their idea of responsibility?"

"Harper, listen," Ethan said, pausing the video. "This is big. If Baxter knows Felix—who's running the lab—and this Rebecca is advocating for the very technology they're using... This could be the evidence we need."

Harper twiddled her fingers, attempting to calm her frantic thoughts. The gravity of their predicament pressed heavily upon her, a mix of frustration and fear eating away inside. She met Ethan's gaze and found her own turmoil reflected in his eyes.

"Everything's coming together," she said, her voice thick with emotion. "Baxter, Felix, Rebecca... We're getting closer to exposing CytoLife's real agenda and whatever the hell they're doing behind closed doors."

"Let's not get ahead of ourselves," Ethan cautioned, his voice wavering slightly. "We need to keep digging and follow every lead."

"You're right," Harper agreed, her expression hardening. "We have to be thorough, absolutely certain before we go public with this information. But goddamn it, Ethan, we're going to bring them down. We'll make sure they pay for what they've done."

"Damn straight," Ethan replied, a fire burning in his eyes.

Across town, the buzz of Adam Burke's phone cut through the silence of his cluttered office, pulling him from intense concentration. He glanced at the Beacon app with a frown, hoping to see Cam Roberts—the elusive whistleblower he'd been tracking for weeks. Adam braced himself as he picked up the call.

"Adam? It's Cam," he said hesitantly when the call connected. "I'm sorry I haven't been in touch. I'm just... scared."

"Cam, it's okay," Adam replied, his voice calm and reassuring. "I understand how dangerous this is for you. But we need to know what's really going on inside CytoLife. You're our only connection."

"Adam, I don't know if I can do this anymore. What if they find out I've been talking?"

"Listen, I've had someone confirm that the DNA reports you provided show that your lab is studying genetic markers," Adam said gently but decisively. "That's big news, Cam. But do you have any idea what they're doing with this information?"

Cam paused, seemingly measuring the danger of speaking further. Sensing Cam's reticence and the imminent threat of a click, Adam cut in swiftly. "Cam, I know you're scared, but we need your help. If something sinister is going on at CytoLife, we have to expose it."

"Okay," Cam murmured. "I'm not entirely sure of their ultimate goal with these genetic markers, but from what I've seen, I believe they're targeting ones associated with human behavior. The lab is a maze of secrets—overwhelming, complex—"

"Cam, I need you to tell me what you've seen," Adam urged gently. "You can trust me."

"Alright," Cam mumbled. "There's so much secrecy in the lab. It's like they don't want anyone to know what's really going on. Part of it is even underground, in a bunker. And Rebecca... the lead scientist, she has a personal bodyguard."

"Strange, but not unheard of. What else?" Adam asked, his curiosity piqued.

"Th-there's more," Cam continued, his voice trembling. "I... I've seen bodies being removed from the lab. They take them down into the industrial furnace."

"Wait, what? Bodies?" Adam's stomach churned, and he suddenly felt sick. "Repeat that, please."

"Y-yeah," Cam stammered. "Bodies. I don't know who they are or why, but I've seen it more than once."

"Cam, listen to me," Adam said resolutely, trying to keep his own panic at bay. "I promise I'll do everything I can to help you. But right now, we both need to stay calm."

"Okay. Okay, I'll try. Please, just... don't let anyone find out I'm talking to you."

"I won't," Adam reassured him. "Stay safe, and keep in touch."

"Thank you, Adam," Cam said, his gratitude obvious even through the phone.

As he hung up, Adam took a moment to process the horrifying information he'd just received. Bodies disappearing into an industrial furnace? What on earth was happening at CytoLife?

As the reality of what they were up against sank in, Adam felt a renewed sense of determination. He was tempted to just drive to Harper's, but called first.

"Harper, it's Adam," he said urgently when she picked up. We need to meet ASAP."

"Ethan told me you had more information on the DNA reports—"

"Yes, yes, but…I just talked to Cam. It's worse than we thought."

"Alright," Harper replied, her voice tight with concern. "Come to my place tomorrow. I'll make sure Ethan is here, too."

"Thanks, Harper. See you then."

As Adam lay in bed, the images kept playing through his mind. He saw terrible things—bodies being pushed into fires. No matter how much he tried to push his thoughts away, he was convinced something sinister was happening in Cam's laboratory—and they must be stopped. But how could he expose them without evidence?

EIGHTEEN

Lucas emerged from the grandeur of the Peabody Hotel into the crisp Memphis air. He paused briefly, his eyes tracing the brooding gray sky above, a stark contrast to the lavishness he had just left behind. Pausing to collect his thoughts, he settled into his rental car, his mind focused on the journey ahead.

Navigating through the vibrant streets of downtown Memphis, he felt the city's pulse envelop him. The drive towards Midtown brought a different kind of familiarity. As he approached the new house where his father and sister had recently relocated post-divorce, memories surfaced. The house, nestled in a serene, tree-lined street, stood proudly among its neighbors—echoes of old wealth and Southern charm.

Lucas pulled up to the brick home, its dignified presence a new backdrop to his family's latest chapter. A wave of nostalgia swept over him as he thought of his father and Charlotte, now his only allies in a family reshaped by recent events. Recollections of past moments with them, a blend of comfort and laughter, brought a gentle, reflective smile to his lips as he stepped out of the car, ready to reconnect.

He rapped gently on the door, and within seconds, it swung open to reveal his younger sister, Charlotte, her eyes lighting up at the sight of him. "Lucas!" she exclaimed, embracing him tightly. "I can't believe you're here!"

"Hey, Charlie," he replied affectionately, tousling her hair. "It's been too long."

"Too long?" she teased, playfully punching his shoulder. "You're the one who changed his phone number and went off the grid! I didn't even know if you were alive!"

"Sorry about that," Lucas said, a hint of guilt crossing his features. "Things have been... complicated."

Charlotte's demeanor shifted as she lowered her voice. "Harper's struggling, Lucas. She's more stressed than I've ever seen her. I've talked to her on the phone, and I've visited her place. It's a mess."

"Mom's always been on some crusade or another," Lucas replied skeptically. "What makes this any different?"

"Something's changed, Lucas. I think she's in over her head this time." Charlotte's eyes filled with concern as she looked up at him.

Lucas frowned, recalling the days when their mother's drinking had caused similar chaos in their lives. The memory of those dark times hung heavily in the air between them. "You think she's back to...?"

"I don't know," Charlotte said faintly, shaking her head. "But whatever it is, it's not good. I haven't seen her like this in years."

Looking at his sister's troubled face, Lucas felt a familiar protectiveness rise within him. He gave her shoulder a reassuring squeeze. "Hey, we'll figure it out, okay? We always do. In fact, I'm on my way to meet her for coffee."

"Thanks, Lucas," Charlotte said, her eyes shining with gratitude. "I just wish Dad was here to help. He had to go out of town for work."

"Did he say when he'd be back?" Lucas asked, concerned.

"Next week, I think. But you should definitely call him. He'd love to hear from you."

"Will do, Charlie," Lucas promised, feeling a twinge of guilt for being so absent from his family since taking the new job. He knew he needed to be more present—for Charlotte's sake and his own.

"Okay, Mr. Big City," Charlotte teased, poking him playfully in the ribs as they stood on the front porch of their father's home. "Don't forget us little people when you're off living your fancy life."

"Of course not, Charlie," Lucas chuckled, feigning indignation. "I wouldn't dream of it."

"Promise me you'll stay in touch this time," she demanded, trying to sound stern but unable to suppress a smile.

"Cross my heart," he vowed, drawing an imaginary X over his chest. He ruffled her hair again teasingly, and she swatted at his hand, laughing.

"Alright, get out of here before I get sentimental,"

Charlotte said, rolling her eyes and giving him a gentle shove toward his car. "You've got a mom to see."

"True," Lucas agreed, suddenly feeling the weight of the upcoming meeting with Harper. Before climbing into his car, he gave his sister a tight hug and whispered, "Take care of yourself, Charlie." As he pulled away from the curb, he glanced back to see her waving goodbye, a bittersweet smile on her face.

Lucas's journey to the Peabody Hotel was a short one, yet each moment stretched out as he mulled over the impending meeting with his mother. Arriving at the hotel, his steps quickened through the opulent lobby, driven by a mix of apprehension and urgency.

The aroma of fresh pastries and rich coffee from the in-house deli and bakery enveloped him as he entered, offering a brief respite from his racing thoughts. The soft melodies of a piano playing in the background added to the welcoming atmosphere.

Through the gentle hustle of the hotel's morning crowd, he spotted Harper. She sat alone by a window, her attention seemingly captivated by the rising steam from her cup. Her body language spoke volumes, betraying a tension that made him pause. For a moment, Lucas's heart softened, empathy replacing the trepidation he had felt.

Stoic and determined, he navigated through the tables towards her, preparing himself to bridge the distance that time and circumstance had placed between them.

"Mom," Lucas greeted with a hint of hesitation.

Harper's eyes softened as she looked up. "Lucas." Her

expression was a blend of surprise and a flicker of hope. "You came."

He nodded, taking the seat opposite her, the weight of unspoken words hanging between them. Lucas's fingers traced the rim of his coffee cup, betraying his inner turmoil as he grappled for the right words to bridge their strained relationship.

Harper glanced upwards momentarily, absorbing the grandeur of the ceiling before refocusing on her son. "This place, its pastries... always a treat," she said, her attempt at lightness barely masking the underlying tension.

Lucas recognized the deflection for what it was, mirroring his own reluctance. Taking a steadying breath, he decided to address the elephant in the room.

"Charlotte's worried about you," he ventured gently, his eyes studying her for any telltale signs of distress.

Harper's eyes lowered. "It's been challenging," she conceded, her voice a soft murmur. "But I'm coping."

Lucas's expression tightened with concern. "But are you? Really?" he pressed, unable to mask his worry. "Charlotte paints a different picture."

Harper's defense rose instinctively, streaked with a hint of vulnerability. "Life's never easy, Lucas. You know that."

"I want to understand, to help if I can," he said earnestly, his fists unconsciously clenching on the table. "I just don't want to be dragged into another one of your battles."

Harper reached across the table, her hand seeking his. "Lucas, please, just hear me out—"

"Mom, just one thing," he cut in, his gaze unwavering. "Is

this like before, or is it something else?"

Her response was a whisper, laden with emotion. "It's different this time, I promise."

Lucas paused, a war of emotions playing out in his heart. After a moment, he slowly grasped her hand. "Okay, let's talk," he agreed, taking a tentative step towards mending their fractured bond.

"Lucas, the case I'm working on, it's unlike anything I've encountered. It's... it's legitimately disturbing." Her words were laced with a tremor of fear. "Remember Darrius, the young man who died in jail? He was my client."

Lucas's nod was somber. "Yeah, I saw the news about it."

"The investigation into his case unearthed a corruption scheme, but that's just the surface," Harper continued, her voice fraught with tension. "There's more, something much darker. Rumors of nonconsensual medical experimentation. People being used as test subjects without their knowledge or consent."

A heavy silence fell. Lucas grappled with the enormity of what his mother was revealing, a far cry from her usual legal battles. The air between them felt charged with the gravity of her words.

"Mom, that's horrific," Lucas hissed, his voice strained with disbelief. "But why are you involving me in this?"

Harper's eyes pleaded with him for understanding. "I need you to see the seriousness of this, Lucas. This isn't just a legal fight; it's a battle to protect innocent lives. I don't want to pull you into my struggles, but you deserve to know the reality of what I'm facing."

Lucas processed her words, the sincerity in her voice resonating with him. This was more than a legal endeavor for Harper; it was a moral imperative, a fight against an injustice that threatened to consume her.

"Mom," Lucas began, his tone cautious yet supportive. "I can see this is eating at you. I appreciate your honesty. But I'm not sure how I fit into all this. You haven't given me much to work with."

He watched Harper closely, half-expecting her to show frustration at his hesitancy. Instead, he saw only a deep-seated worry, a mother grappling with how much to share with her son.

"Lucas, right now, I can't share everything," Harper admitted, her voice unsteady. "Just please, keep an open mind. When the time is right, you'll know everything."

Nodding, Lucas felt a twinge of concern. He was all too familiar with his mother's habit of diving headfirst into danger. This time, though, the gravity in her tone suggested a threat that was both real and imminent.

"Alright, Mom," he responded, gently squeezing her hand. "Just promise me you'll be careful."

Harper's eyes brimmed with gratitude as she faced Lucas. A faint smile flickered on her lips. "Thank you, Lucas. I promise to be careful."

Throughout their conversation, Lucas grappled with a lingering disquiet, sensing his mother was on a perilous trajectory, navigating murky waters with no clear way back. He mentally cataloged the scant details she divulged, vowing to stay vigilant against any signs of her situation spiraling out of control.

Harper's voice, breaking the muffled clatter of the café, drew Lucas's attention back. Her eyes briefly met his before darting away. "Lucas, there's something else I need to say..."

He felt a familiar knot in his stomach, recognizing the telltale guilt shadowing her expression. Steeling himself, he prepared for a conversation they had circled around many times before.

"Lucas, I'm sorry for how things were with you and Charlotte," Harper began, her voice thick with emotion. "I let my career overshadow my role as your mother. I wasn't there for you as I should have been."

Lucas felt an uncomfortable heat rise in his cheeks. They had trod this path before, but Harper's tone carried a newfound depth of regret.

"Mom, it's okay—" he tried to interject.

"No, Lucas, it's not," Harper cut him off, tears glimmering in her eyes. "And Charlotte... how is she? I miss her terribly."

Lucas paused, choosing his words with care. "I saw Charlie today, actually."

Surprise and a hint of longing flitted across Harper's face. "You did? How is she?"

"She's adjusting to the new situation," Lucas replied gently, recalling his sister's resilience. "She just needs time, Mom."

Harper nodded, her expression a mix of resignation and hope. "I hope she can someday understand why I made the choices I did."

"Give her time, Mom," Lucas said softly, his hand reaching out to cover hers. "She'll come around, eventually."

Lucas shifted in his seat, his smile a faint effort to ease

the somber mood. "I should get going," he said, glancing at his watch. "There's a lot on my plate right now."

Harper nodded, her expression riddled with sadness yet understanding. "Of course, Lucas. I'm just grateful we had this moment together."

"Me too," Lucas agreed, his voice warm with sincerity. He hesitated, then added, "Here's my new number. I know I've been hard to reach."

Surprise and gratitude danced in Harper's eyes as she accepted the piece of paper. "Thank you," she said softly, her hand trembling. "This means a lot to me."

Lucas stood. "Take care of yourself, okay?" he asked, his voice earnest.

"I promise," Harper said carefully, clutching the paper like a precious gift.

He leaned in for a brief hug, a gesture that bridged some of the distance between them. "I'll see you around, Mom."

"Goodbye, Lucas," Harper replied, her voice scarcely above a whisper.

Lucas stepped out into the bustling lobby, the weight of their conversation lingering. Yet, amidst the heaviness, a subtle current of optimism began to flow. Perhaps, in these small steps, they could slowly rebuild their strained relationship—one awkward meeting at a time.

NINETEEN

Harper and Ethan leaned over a coffee table strewn with a chaotic mix of documents and images. Exhaustion creased Harper's brow, the cumulative toll of Darrius's tragic end, Judge Jackson's heart-wrenching admission, and the latest disturbing findings weighing heavily on her.

Ethan's voice broke the silence, somber and reflective. "You remember this photo, right?" He pointed to an image of Baxter, Felix, and Rebecca, impeccably dressed at a high-profile charity event. "It doesn't prove anything concrete, but it certainly illustrates their connection."

Harper nodded, her eyes tracing the figures in the photo. "It's a start, but we need to proceed with caution. This photo alone isn't enough. We can't risk alerting them prematurely." A mix of determination and wariness echoed in her voice. "However unsettling, we must pursue this lead, wherever it takes us."

She glanced at the clock. "Adam should be arriving soon. He might have more for us."

As if on cue, the doorbell rang. Harper rose and opened the door to find Adam, his face etched with concern and weariness. He stepped inside, fidgeting just inside the entryway.

"Thanks for coming, Adam," Harper said as she shut the door. "We've got a lot to unravel here."

"I'm all too aware," Adam responded, his voice carrying the seeming weight of countless sleepless nights.

Ethan gestured towards the living room. "Let's sit down and sort through this together."

Adam paced Harper's living room like a caged animal, his eyes darting around the space as if searching for an escape. The dark circles under his bloodshot eyes spoke volumes of his mental state. He raked a hand through his disheveled hair, drawing in sharp, shallow breaths.

"Adam, take a seat," Harper said gently, her voice carrying the reassurance of a mother calming a child after a nightmare. "You're safe here."

He hesitated, but eventually sank into an armchair, his limbs trembling with residual adrenaline. Harper sat down opposite him, her gaze never leaving his face. She exuded a calm strength, and her steady presence seemed to ground him.

Adam shifted in his seat, gathering his thoughts. "I spoke to a molecular biologist from my college days at UT," he began, his voice steadier yet gripped with concern. "She's an expert in genetic research."

Harper's attention sharpened. "And what insights did she offer?"

Adam recounted Meera's explanation of DNA collection and genetic markers' role in research. "She acknowledged rumors of unethical practices but emphasized the scientific community's commitment to ethical standards," he explained. "But it's what she didn't say that worries me." Adam paused. "I suspect CytoLife might be covertly analyzing prisoner DNA to manipulate behavioral traits."

The weight of his revelation lingered heavily in the room. Harper observed the fatigue on Adam's face, recognizing the familiar signs of a relentless quest for truth.

"Adam," Harper said, her voice imbued with a mix of concern and assurance as she reached out to him. "Your dedication is appreciated, but remember, you're not in this alone. We stand together in this."

Adam's eyes met hers and then Ethan's, a flicker of relief softening his features. "Thanks," he said, his voice full of sincerity. "I'm grateful to have you both on my side."

"Alright," she began, folding her hands on her lap. "I know you're scared, but we need you to tell us everything you know. What did Cam tell you?"

Harper noticed Adam gulp, his throat working with nervous tension. He glanced between her and Ethan, a silent battle playing out behind his eyes.

"Adam," she began, "we can't protect ourselves or anyone else unless we have all the information."

Her words broke through his hesitation, and he nodded. With a deep, steadying breath, he recounted his conversation with Cam, his voice low and hushed, as if afraid of being overheard.

"Cam called me last night, almost in tears. He was terrified that someone from CytoLife would find out he's been talking to us. He sounded... desperate."

"Desperate enough to tell you more?" Ethan asked, leaning forward intently.

"Y-yeah," Adam's voice wavered, his distress clear. "Cam mentioned they were isolating behavioral genes. But what's worse," he paused, swallowing hard, "he saw something horrifying. Bodies being secretly moved to the lower levels of CytoLife."

"Bodies?" Harper's pulse quickened, her mind grappling with the dreadful implications. "Do we have any idea who they were, or why... why this was happening?"

"Cam couldn't pin down the details," Adam confessed, his hand instinctively massaging his temple. "He only caught a fleeting glimpse, but he was certain. They were human remains, and they were being taken to industrial furnaces."

"Industrial furnaces?" Ethan blanched at the thought. "That's their method of erasing evidence—burning it."

Harper felt a cold shiver run down her spine. "We need to uncover the identities of those victims, find out why they met such a horrific end. Nobody should be disposed of like that."

Harper clenched her fists as she forced herself to focus. The echoes of Cam's frightened words reverberated in her mind, and she knew they had to tread carefully. She glanced at Ethan and Adam, their faces etched with concern and determination.

"Alright," Harper said, "we've got to map out our plan. CytoLife's entanglement in this is deeper and more dangerous than we thought. It's imperative we put a stop to their actions."

Ethan nodded, his expression reflecting both determination and caution. "I'm with you, but we've got to tread carefully. If they're going to lengths like disposing of bodies, they won't hesitate to target anyone who gets in their way. We need a smart approach to avoid putting ourselves or others at risk."

Adam looked visibly shaken, his complexion pale as he released a shaky breath. "In all my years of reporting, including the CRISPR series, I've never encountered anything like this," he confessed, his voice revealing a rare vulnerability. His eyes, wide with a blend of fear and determination, bore into theirs.

"We need to find more insiders, people like Cam," he suggested, trying to steady his trembling voice. "There must be others out there, equally frightened, who have inside knowledge. If we can reach them, maybe we can start to unravel this whole mess." His suggestion, fraught with both risk and bravery, resonated in the room.

Harper pondered the idea, her thoughts racing with the potential dangers and rewards. Adam's point was valid; more inside information could be crucial. Yet every new contact increased their exposure, and the risk of drawing CytoLife's attention was real and intimidating.

"Okay," she finally said, steeling herself for the path ahead. "We'll start looking for others who can help us. But we have to be incredibly cautious, not just for our own safety but for theirs as well."

Ethan nodded solemnly. "I'm still working on some leads, courtesy of our favorite gentleman hacker, Neon. I'd rather not divulge the details just yet, but I think we're getting closer to cracking this thing wide open."

"Alright," Harper said, locking eyes with Ethan, her expression a blend of gratitude and anxiety. "We're going to need all the help we can muster."

Ethan stood, his stance reflecting determination. "I'm on it," he assured, heading towards the door. "We'll keep each other posted on any new developments."

"Sounds good," Harper responded, her gaze following him as he left. She then turned back to Adam, feeling the enormity of the journey they were undertaking. There was danger ahead, but backing down wasn't an option.

Harper reached out, placing a reassuring hand on Adam's shoulder. "You've done incredible work," she told him, her voice infused with a blend of firmness and care. "We'll get through this together, but you need to look after yourself too, alright?"

Adam nodded, a tired but grateful smile crossing his face. "I appreciate that, Harper. I'll do my best." With those words, he stood and made his way out, his posture reflecting the heavy responsibility he carried.

Left alone, Harper briefly put her head in her hands. Her focus shifted to the here and now; Mama Dee and Deandra would be arriving soon, and she needed to be prepared, both mentally and emotionally, for whatever discussions lay ahead.

The scent of dinner wafted through Harper's kitchen as she bustled around, her hands expertly preparing a feast of Southern comfort food. Collard greens simmered on the stove, cornbread baked golden brown in the oven, and sweet tea chilled in the refrigerator. It was a meal designed to soothe and nourish, a balm for the raw wounds left by Judge Jackson's funeral.

When the doorbell rang, Harper wiped her hands on a dish towel and hurried to answer it. Mama Dee and Deandra stood on her doorstep, their faces drawn and weary from the strain of recent events.

"Harper, honey," Mama Dee greeted, her voice warm and grateful as she enveloped Harper in a tight hug. "It's so good to see you again."

"Likewise," Harper replied, stepping back to let them inside. "Come on in, y'all. I've got dinner just about ready."

As they settled around her dining table, the three women took solace in the familiar flavors of their shared Southern roots. They ate in companionable silence, each lost in her own thoughts.

"Harper, this meal is heavenly," Deandra said at last, breaking the silence. "I don't know how you do it."

"Thank you, Dee," Harper replied, smiling as she refilled their glasses with sweet tea. "It's just something I picked up watching Mama Dee."

"Well, I'm very proud of you, Harper," Mama Dee agreed, her eyes misty with emotion. "Isaac would be too, bless his heart."

Harper's chest tightened at the mention of the late judge, but she nodded, determined to keep her composure. "I hope so, Mama Dee. I truly do."

"Remember when Daddy would sneak me into his courtroom?" Deandra chuckled, dabbing at her mouth with a napkin. "I'd sit there all wide-eyed, watching him lay down the law."

Mama Dee smiled fondly, her eyes crinkling at the corners. "Oh, I remember that. He was so proud to show you off, Dee. And Harper, my goodness, he always said you had a fire in you, even back then."

Harper felt a bittersweet ache in her chest at the memories, but she managed a smile. "He certainly knew how to inspire us, didn't he? I'll never forget the day he let me hold his gavel. It felt like I was holding the power of justice in my hands."

"Isaac had a way of making everyone feel important," Mama Dee agreed, wiping away a tear. "We sure are going to miss him."

As the reminiscences continued, the weight of Judge Jackson's absence grew heavier, casting a solemn shadow over the meal.

"Harper, sugar, it's been on your heart for a while now," Mama Dee said, placing a hand on top of Harper's. "It's time you share with us what you've been keeping inside."

Harper paused, torn between maintaining the comforting warmth that had enveloped the table and confronting the inevitable truths that lay ahead. The shared laughter had been a welcome diversion from the chaos that had recently engulfed their lives. She locked eyes with Mama Dee, finding solace in the depth of strength and affection reflected there.

"Before Isaac passed away, you know he wrote me a letter," she said, her voice steady even as her heart fluttered anxiously. "I received it just before he died."

Mama Dee looked surprised, her eyes widening with curiosity. "You did? I had no idea he actually sent that letter. He was so upset that I just let him stew like I always did. Figured he needed time to work it out in his mind." She paused, recalling the conversation. "Is this what you mentioned you needed to discuss before the funeral, Harper?"

Deandra leaned in, her expression a blend of curiosity and concern. "What did it say, Harper?"

Harper nodded and hesitated for a moment, gathering her thoughts. Then she dove into the story, recounting the contents of the letter with precision and clarity.

"He admitted his involvement in the PenCore scheme," she said, her hands gripping the edge of the table. "He felt trapped, like he had no choice but to take part. It weighed heavily on him.

"But that's not all," Harper continued, her voice growing softer. "He explained how he got out of the scheme. He anonymously tipped off a journalist who wrote an article about PenCore. And he stopped taking the money."

The room seemed to grow still as Harper's words hung in the air, the enormity of Judge Jackson's actions sinking in. Mama Dee reached across the table to squeeze her hand, offering silent support.

Mama Dee's eyes sparkled with a blend of astonishment

and solemn pride. "I knew Isaac distanced himself from that bribery ugliness, Harper, but I never knew the how," she spoke softly, her voice threading through the silent room. "Discovering he reached out to a journalist in such a sly way? It's bitter and sweet all at once. I always knew him to be strong, but even now, he amazes me. There's a heavy cost to pay for choosing the righteous path sometimes, but, oh, how I love him for it."

"He said he was profoundly sorry for everything he'd done," Harper related, tears pricking at the corners of her eyes. "In his letter, he expressed how tormented he was by his actions and his gratitude for our friendship."

Mama Dee's eyes filled with tears as well, but she held Harper's gaze steadily. "He was a good man, through and through," she said, her voice thick with emotion. "Even in the end, he was trying to make things right."

Harper paused, a solemn look crossing her face. She realized the gravity of what she was about to disclose, knowing it would profoundly impact them, but it was essential they grasped the entire scope of the situation.

"Here's the thing," Harper began, her voice steady and eloquent as she shifted into attorney mode. "The PenCore scheme was only the beginning. When I took on Darrius Robinson's case, I started digging into PenCore's operations. What I discovered goes far beyond bribes and corruption."

Deandra leaned forward, her brow furrowed with concern as she listened intently to Harper's words. "Go on."

A thick silence hovered heavily in the room after Harper revealed the dark conspiracy bubbling beneath the surface of PenCore's actions. Harper's eyes flicked back and forth between Mama Dee and Deandra, both of whom wore expressions resembling a chaotic blend of shock, fear, and determination.

"Oh, sweet Jesus," Mama Dee breathed out, her eyes reflecting a storm of emotions, her hand instinctively grasping at the cross hanging around her neck. Her eyes searched Harper's, seeking clarity amidst this newfound revelation. "Harper, why in the world would they steal DNA like that? What could anyone gain from it?"

Deandra's eyes stayed locked on Harper, but her gaze seemed distant, lost in a haze of too much information. She tensed, her hands clasped tightly, visibly struggling with the aftershocks of Harper's revelations that reverberated through the room.

Harper tried to steady herself under the weight of their expectant gazes. "I wish I had all the answers, Mama Dee, but that's what I'm determined to find out. There are shadowy corners in this entire operation that I'm still trying to illuminate," she vowed, her voice steady, albeit showing the faintest cracks of emotional strain.

Deandra replied softly, "This is like something out of a dystopian novel... I can't believe it's really happening. But Harper, we stand with you. We'll get through this nightmare together."

Mama Dee's eyes flickered with confusion and shock, but a resolute spark ignited within them. She nodded deliberately, her fingers clasping her cross with renewed strength. "Yes, Harper. Whatever darkness you're confronting, remember you're not alone. We stand with you, ready to drag it into the light."

Harper, heartened by their unwavering support amidst the shock, nodded appreciatively. "Thank you, both of you. This won't be easy, but knowing I'm not alone in this gives me the strength to push forward.

"I've linked the company CytoLife to PenCore," she stated. "An insider claims they're analyzing the inmates' DNA for genetic markers."

Mama Dee shook her head, her eyes widening with shock. "Lord have mercy, child, I'm trying to wrap my old brain around all this," she said, her Southern drawl more pronounced in her confusion. "Can you break it down for me in simple terms?"

"Of course, Mama Dee," Harper replied, offering a reassuring smile before launching into a simplified explanation. "Every person's DNA is made up of unique combinations of genes. Certain patterns within these combinations are called genetic markers. Researchers can use these markers to study how genes influence our behaviors, health, and even our susceptibility to certain diseases or conditions."

She paused for a moment, allowing Mama Dee and Deandra to absorb the information, and then continued. "Based on what we learned—and some additional information gathered from an expert in molecular biology—we believe CytoLife may use these genetic markers to develop new ways of controlling people's behavior."

Deandra's face went from a contemplative frown to utter

shock, her mouth slightly agape. "CytoLife?" she pleaded, her voice trembling with disbelief. "The CytoLife that's hailed globally for their humanitarian efforts? That's been at the forefront of innovative research, vaccine campaigns, and providing medical aid in crises?

"I just can't believe it," Dee stammered, her voice uneven. "They're celebrated as worldwide heroes! How could they be mixed up in something so... so sinister?" With a tremble in her hands, she slumped back in her chair.

Harper's eyes lingered on Deandra's, a mirror reflecting the shock and tumult between them. She began, a measured steadiness in her voice, "Dee, I share your disbelief and horror."

She took her friend's hand, her voice soft but firm. "It's hard to believe, right? CytoLife, seen as global heroes, involved in something so evil." Her eyes flashed with both determination and fear.

"These whistleblower reports hint at a dark plot behind the scenes. We'll uncover it all and take a stand, even against those masquerading as saviors." Their hands clenched, sealing an unspoken promise amid the chaos.

Deandra's face paled at the implications, while Mama Dee's expression shifted from confusion to anger. "You mean they're playing God with these prisoners' lives?" Mama Dee asked, her voice trembling with poorly restrained fury.

"Unfortunately, that's what it seems like," Harper confirmed, her own anger simmering just below the surface. "And since we assume they're doing it without the inmates' knowledge or consent, it grossly violates their rights—not to mention a dangerous abuse of scientific power."

Harper could see the wheels turning in Mama Dee's and Deandra's minds. Much like she had, they were struggling to come to terms with this horrifying revelation.

"I just... I can't wrap my head around this," Dee admitted, her voice shaking slightly. "How can something like this be happening right under our noses?"

"Take a breath, sugar," Mama Dee said gently, placing a comforting hand on Deandra's arm. "Harper, is there more you need to say?"

Harper nodded, her throat tightening with emotion as she recalled her conversation with Adam. "When I spoke to my friend earlier, he was visibly shaken by what he'd learned from the whistleblower," she began, her voice cracking. "This person revealed something even more disturbing than the genetic research itself."

She took a deep breath, steeling herself for the impact of her next words. "He's seen bodies—human bodies—being taken into the depths of CytoLife's facility and disposed of in industrial furnaces."

"Oh Lord," Mama Dee exclaimed, her fingers tightening around the edge of the tablecloth.

"Are you saying they're killing these people?" Deandra asked haltingly.

"I can't be sure, but it's hard to imagine a legitimate reason for such grim disposal of bodies." Harper's fists tightened, the swell of anger within her threatening to overflow. "If they are behind these deaths, we're facing an evil far beyond what we imagined."

"Alright," Mama Dee said. "Then we need to find out the

truth—for Isaac, for those inmates, and for everyone who's been affected by this nightmare."

Harper noticed Deandra's eyes narrowing and her brows furrowing, a familiar look she recognized from their courtroom days. "Alright, Harper, let's dig deeper into this. What concrete evidence do we have? Do you have any documents or recordings?" Deandra asked.

"Nothing that would hold up in court," Harper admitted, rubbing her temples. "Everything is unofficial, off the record, or of questionable origin. We need solid proof if we're going to take down these monsters."

"Damn," Deandra muttered under her breath. "What about this whistleblower? Can they provide anything more substantial?"

"He's terrified for his life, Dee. He's already taking an enormous risk by talking to my friend at all. I don't want to push too hard." Harper sighed, feeling the weight of the situation bearing down on her shoulders.

Mama Dee's kind eyes clouded with disbelief, her voice trembling. "It's a nightmare, Harper. Isaac, always fighting for justice, is now trapped in this evil scheme. It doesn't sit right with me."

Harper held Mama Dee's hand firmly, her voice steady. "Mama Dee, in his letter, he swore he knew nothing about these medical experiments or the depths of PenCore's wrongdoings. He was honest, always. He might've known about some shady dealings, but he was in the dark about the true horror. He was manipulated like the rest of us."

After a poignant silence, Mama Dee's eyes welled up, but she held back her tears. "I want to believe that, Harper.

Deep in my soul, I know my Isaac was deceived by those he trusted."

"We'll find the truth, Mama Dee, for Isaac and all of us. We'll expose every secret." Harper vowed.

Deandra's voice was soft, beset with sorrow. "Daddy's legacy... It's tainted now."

"We can't change the past," Harper replied gently. "But we can reveal the truth and ensure justice. That's what your father would've wanted."

Mama Dee's eyes narrowed. "Isaac wanted the truth, regardless of how it impacted his legacy. The bribery troubled him enough. I can't imagine his torment if he knew what we suspect now."

Deandra's face was drawn. "It's hard to accept."

Mama Dee reached out, comforting her. "I know, sugar."

Harper steered the conversation with determination. "We need help, Dee. We could use your legal expertise."

Deandra hesitated, her eyes reflecting a whirl of emotions. "Harper, it's overwhelming. I'm new at the District Attorney's office. The logistics alone are daunting."

"We'll navigate it," Harper assured her. "Take your time, but think about joining our cause."

Mama Dee's voice held a fierce undertone as she met Harper's eyes. "You pursue those villains with all you've got, Harper. Make them answer for their deeds. Isaac's spirit is with you, cheering you on."

Harper nodded with appreciation. "Together, we'll pull back the shadows and ensure justice prevails. For Isaac, for all of us."

TWENTY

In a corner office at *The Standard*, Adam Burke stood before Ben's disorderly desk, his fingers drumming an anxious rhythm on a manila folder. It contained crucial discoveries for his latest article on CRISPR, revelations now sharpened by Cam's alarming disclosures.

"Ben, I think I've got something big here," Adam said, his voice hesitant but determined. The weight of his discovery hung heavy on his shoulders. "It's damning and... bold."

Adam observed Ben recline, the office chair's creak slicing through the silence. Ben's eyes, tempered by years of journalistic trials, regarded Adam with an interplay of worry and inquisitiveness. Ben, a pillar of journalistic integrity, recognized and respected Adam's sharp intellect, often guiding the enthusiastic reporter through the murky complexities of investigative journalism.

"Bold, you say?" Ben raised an eyebrow, his voice saturated

with wariness. "Alright, son, let me hear what you've got."

Adam tapped his fingers, revealing the unsettling truths concealed by CytoLife's respectable public image. Emotion wavered in his voice, reflecting his apprehension, but he persisted, understanding the gravity of these revelations.

"Adam," Ben interjected, his voice full of concern, "ensure your findings are solid. We can't publish such allegations without concrete proof."

Adam's stare was intense, bearing the weight of countless hours spent uncovering CytoLife's transgressions. "Ben, inside CytoLife, there are experiments that cross ethical lines, all masked by their public achievements."

Ben's curiosity piqued, he prompted, "Continue."

"They're not only aiming for innovation but also jeopardizing lives. There's evidence suggesting casualties due to their experiments." Adam's voice trembled as he conveyed his findings.

Ben's face tightened. "That's a serious allegation, Adam. Are your sources trustworthy?"

Taking a breath, Adam replied, "I've been approached by a whistleblower with substantial evidence. But they're scared, Ben."

Pausing, Ben advised, "Tread carefully. Verify every detail before proceeding."

"Ben, I know it sounds unbelievable, but I trust my source. This story has the potential to expose a hidden world of deceit and danger that people deserve to know about. It's our responsibility as journalists to bring this truth to light."

Adam noticed Ben's eyebrows drawing together as he studied him, clearly searching for any hint of exaggeration.

But all Adam felt was a deep-seated determination. Ben's voice softened. "Adam, you've always been relentless in chasing the truth. But you need to understand the gravity of this. CytoLife isn't just any biotech giant; they're revered by the public for their life-changing breakthroughs."

"And that's exactly why we can't expose them directly, not yet." A calculated calm was heavy in his voice. "What I'm proposing, Ben, is that we highlight the malevolence lurking in the biotech industry, touching on the illegal experiments, the unethical practices, but without naming CytoLife directly. We expose the shadow without casting it on them... for now."

Ben interlaced his fingers, eyes shifting towards the window. "This is a strategic game we're playing, Adam. A dangerous one at that."

Adam nodded. "I know, but it's a game we must play, Ben. The public deserves to know about the dangers that lurk behind the curtain of genetic advancements. But we'll be subtle, sowing seeds of doubt while we collect more concrete evidence against CytoLife."

Ben's eyes, meeting Adam's once again, flickered with a resigned agreement. "Alright, Adam, we'll run with it. But every detail, every insinuation, must be impeccably researched and verified. We'll walk this thin line together, but I need you to promise me we will proceed with the utmost caution."

The promise, indisputable and somber, hung in the air as Adam nodded. "Every step of the way, Ben. Every step of the way."

To Ethan, the dark web felt like a digital abyss, an underworld teeming with secrets and dangers. He had been trawling for information on CytoLife for hours, but had found nothing substantial yet. Frustration gnawed at him, and he knew it was time to call in a favor.

"Hey, Neon," Ethan said into his phone, trying to keep his voice steady. "It's Ethan Cook. I know it's been a while since we last spoke, but I need your help."

"Ah, Mr. Cook," Neon drawled, his Southern accent warming the line. "I remember you well. How can this humble hacker be of assistance to a fine gentleman such as yourself?" His voice carried a subtle flirtatious undertone. Ethan, stifling a grin, quickly shelved his amusement to refocus on the task at hand.

"Remember those documents we discussed? Well, I'm still looking into it, and I could use some help to navigate the dark web. I'm stuck." Ethan rubbed his temples, the weight of the investigation bearing down on him.

"Say no more, darling," Neon replied smoothly. "Consider me at your service."

With the gentle clicks of his keyboard providing a steady rhythm, he was connected to Neon over a secure line. A hacker with a penchant for mischief and a heart subtly tethered to a sense of justice, Neon provided Ethan with the digital keys to navigate through the intricacies of the dark web.

The atmosphere was tense, and Ethan's gaze was

unwavering, fixated on the maze of information and encrypted data flashing across his screen. Neon, unaware of the harrowing depth of CytoLife's experiments, navigated with an initially light, albeit focused, demeanor.

"I hope you've brought your digital spelunking gear, Ethan," Neon quipped, his voice mingling curiosity and a playful spirit through the secure channel. "This abyss looks deep and twisted."

A few keyboard strokes later, Ethan and Neon were immersed in a sea of stealth communications and secretive transactions, an underworld of encoded layers revealing shocking glimpses into uncharted territories of biotechnology.

In a carefully guarded anonymity, forums murmured about bio-hacking, DIY genetic modifications, and something ominously referred to as "The Merge." Ethan's fingers paused, hovering over the keys as he absorbed the snippets of dialogues, each more chilling than the last.

Neon, blissfully unaware of the dark reality Ethan was steeped in, navigated through encrypted barriers, occasionally letting out a satisfied chuckle at his digital mastery. "Look at them, thinking they're so clever with their cryptography," he mused.

But something shifted as they unearthed data fragments that spoke of undisclosed CRISPR applications, shrouded experiments, and whispers of biotech entities in unspoken alliances with shadow organizations. Threads of information began linking back to entities hidden behind the disguise of legitimate scientific research, and Neon's playful demeanor wilted, replaced by an uneasy seriousness.

Silence hung heavily in the digital space as Neon muttered, "Hellfire and damnation... what is this abyss we've plunged into, Ethan?"

Ethan's voice was low and purposeful through the secure line. "Something darker and more perilous than we imagined. This is no mere digital sin we've uncovered."

Unease was laced through Neon's response. "I was merrily aiding a dive into corporate secrecy, Ethan, not unveiling horrors of scientific dystopia."

"Listen, Neon, this isn't just another case. We're dealing with something serious, something dark. Harper's at the center of it all, trying to make sense of this tangled web. It's a nightmare, and it's getting worse by the day."

A momentary pause preceded Neon's response, the levity once present in his voice now a ghost of the past. "Get this to Harper, Ethan. She needs to see it. All of it. And whatever game y'all are playing against these Hellspawn, I hope to the digital gods it buries them."

Ethan, his body taut with tension, quietly thanked Neon and reassured him before ending the call. He paused, his fingers hovering over the keyboard, reflecting on the vastness of the secrets they had just begun to uncover and the ominous implications they held for everyone involved.

Ethan picked up his phone, his hands trembling slightly as he dialed Harper's number. When she answered, her voice was steady and confident, but he could hear the weariness lurking beneath the surface.

"Hey, it's Ethan," he began, trying to keep his own voice

from betraying his emotions. "I've been working with Neon, and we've uncovered some... disturbing things on the dark web."

"Go on," Harper prompted, her tone sharpening with concern.

"Biotech trading, unauthorized genetic materials, even tragic accidents from DIY gene editing," Ethan explained, his words tumbling out in a rush. "But that's not all, Harper. We've found data linking some of our firm's clients to these shadowy dealings. I don't know what it means, but it can't be good."

Harper sat in the familiar comfort of Sam Chapman's office, her gaze drifting across the warm glow of the afternoon sun filtering through the blinds. The muted sounds of office life buzzed softly outside the closed door. She fidgeted slightly, her hands clasped in her lap as she sat in the well-worn leather armchair, a legacy piece of the firm.

"Harper." Sam's voice was gentle, imbued with a comforting warmth as he leaned forward on his polished desk. "These past few months have been incredibly tough on you. Losing Judge Jackson and Darrius... I can only imagine what you're going through."

He paused, his eyes, reflecting years of wisdom, settled on her. "You're an exceptional attorney, Harper. Despite the hardships, remember, this firm, your colleagues, we're all here for you. We're eager to see you regain your footing."

Harper lifted her eyes, meeting his with a blend of gratitude and vulnerability. "Thank you, Sam," she said, her voice a soft echo of her usual firmness. "I appreciate that more than you know."

Sam nodded, his expression mixing satisfaction with concern. "Now, was there something specific you wanted to discuss?"

Harper took a moment, her intent wavering slightly. "Yes, there's something troubling I've stumbled upon," she began reluctantly. "It concerns some of our prominent clients and... connections that are rather disconcerting."

"Connections?" Sam's brow creased in confusion. "Can you elaborate?"

Taking a deep breath, Harper considered how much to reveal. "I'm still piecing it together, but there are undercurrents here that are unquestionably unsettling. I'm not sure yet what it means for us, for the firm."

Sam leaned back, his expression turning contemplative. "Harper, our clients come from all walks of life. It's our duty to represent them to the best of our abilities, regardless of our personal sentiments."

He gestured toward the shelves lined with legal tomes, symbols of their commitment to justice. "Think about the challenging cases you've handled, Harper. This is what we do."

"I understand that, Sam," Harper replied, her tone firm yet penetrated with unease. "But this feels different. It's not just about the clients; there's something bigger at play here."

A long silence followed as Sam processed her words, his

face a canvas of mixed emotions. Finally, he spoke. "Harper, you're a pillar of this firm. Whatever this is, let's tackle it together."

Harper's eyes softened, but her decision was clear. "I need to step away, Sam. I have to follow this through, and it's something I must do alone."

Sam's face registered shock, then understanding. "If that's what you need, Harper," he said, his voice heavy with unspoken emotion. "Know that this door is always open for you."

Harper stood, her heart heavy with the gravity of her choice. "Thank you, Sam," she said, her voice cracking. "For everything."

The silence in Sam's office was heavy with a mix of sadness and nostalgia. Sam, breaking the quiet, offered a hint of a smile. "Do you remember the Reynolds case? We worked all night and somehow ended up citing *The Godfather* in our brief," he reminisced, his eyes reflecting a mixture of amusement and fondness.

Harper's laughter, though touched with melancholy, was genuine as the memory resurfaced. "And that Christmas party," she added, her grin widening. "Your attempt to teach me the Charleston. I've never seen such commitment to dance steps."

Their laughter, echoing through the room, was a testament to the bond they had formed over the years. In that moment, it wasn't about legal battles or firm politics; it was about two friends recalling the lighter moments amidst the intensity of their profession.

Sam's expression grew more earnest as he spoke again, his tone imbued with deep emotion. "Harper, take whatever time you need. Know that you always have a place here. Whenever you're ready."

Harper nodded, feeling a surge of appreciation for the man who had been more than a boss, but a mentor and friend. "I can't thank you enough, Sam," she said, her voice brimming with gratitude. The decision to step away from the firm was daunting, yet Sam's unwavering support reinforced her commitment to pursue the path ahead.

Shortly after, Harper pinged Adam on the Beacon app. *"Can't discuss everything here, but we've found more evidence on the dark web: crypto transactions, black market genetics, DIY gene tinkering, and ties to established corporations. It's time, Adam. Go public with it."*

Adam immediately replied. *"Got it, Harper. Editor's on board. We're going live without naming names for now. Stay safe."*

Adam put the finishing touches on his article and prepared for any pushback from Ben or the newspaper. He even had a contingency plan: a version of the article ready to be anonymously leaked online by a friend if his work was suppressed. To his relief, however, the necessary permission arrived promptly, allowing him to publish his newest installment without delay.

BROKEN CODE

Bridging the Gap between Promise and Peril:
The Duality of Biotech Advancements
By Adam Burke, The Bluff City Standard

In our previous exploration of CRISPR's potential, we touched on the transformative power a single drop of blood now holds. The eradication of diseases that plagued humanity for centuries is no longer a distant dream, but an unfolding reality. Yet, as we stand on the brink of this new era, we are also confronted by the shadows that trail these luminous breakthroughs.

The biotech industry, a beacon of hope and innovation, often outpaces the regulatory frameworks designed to oversee it. This mismatch poses a quandary: how do we ensure that the tools meant to uplift humanity don't become instruments of division or, worse, control?

There have been whispers, unsettling murmurs of unauthorized experiments, clandestine trials, and the commodification of genetic traits. While the majority of firms tread the ethical line, the allure of power and profit in a loosely regulated environment raises alarming questions. What if the very tools designed to shape our future are wielded by those with hidden agendas?

Dr. Lysandra Cortez, a bioethicist, once remarked, "The promise of biotech is boundless, but so too is its potential for misuse. We must not be blinded by the marvels and forget to question the motives." As we delve deeper into this industry, it becomes evident that the line between savior and manipulator is perilously thin.

As we continue this investigative series, we urge our readers to remain discerning and vigilant. The biotech frontier is vast and holds the key to our future. But as we march forward, we must ensure the path we choose is one of equity, transparency, and ethics. And rest assured, in our upcoming pieces, we will be pulling back the veil further, daring to ask the questions many shy away from. Because the public has a right to know, and we will stop at nothing to ensure they do.

TWENTY ONE

Harper slipped into the leather booth of Brother Juniper's, a diner soaked in memories of late-night college cramming and early family breakfasts. Today, the atmosphere felt weighted with what remained unspoken.

A familiar voice called out, "Brass!" Harper looked up to see Deandra. Their embrace was tight, both of them still grappling with the aftershocks of Judge Jackson's funeral and the unsettling revelations about PenCore and CytoLife.

"Thanks for being here, Dee," Harper said, stepping back. The strain of Deandra's new job was apparent in her features. "I need to talk about something... something big."

Deandra, ever perceptive, slid into the booth, her demeanor sharpening. "What's going on, Brass?"

Harper met Deandra's stare, a look that had seen her at her best and her worst. "I'm thinking of leaving the firm. Maybe for good."

Deandra's surprise was noticeable. "But... why?"

Harper bit her lip, thinking of their last conversation about CytoLife. "I can't stand by with the CytoLife issue, Dee. It's gnawing at me."

A shadow crossed Deandra's face. "Harper, what are you planning?"

"I'm going to expose them," Harper replied, her voice resolute.

Deandra paused, weighing the implications. "How? Think about the jurisdictional hurdles, the potential charges, the logistics. We've been over this."

"I'm aware," Harper responded, her voice softer. "All those concerns? They're the reasons I can't sleep."

Harper could almost hear the wheels turning in Dee's mind, the weight of her new role at the DA's office clashing with their shared history and the legacy of her father, Judge Jackson.

Harper broke the silence. "I don't have all the answers yet, but I'm committed to unraveling the CytoLife scandal."

Deandra reached out, her fingers lightly touching Harper's. "Promise me you'll be careful."

"Dee, I need you on this. I can't pull it off alone."

"Harper, you're my best friend," Deandra responded, her eyes holding Harper's intently. "But tackling a global conglomerate? It's a dangerous path."

Harper's heart raced. "But, Dee, think about it. CytoLife's experiments, the way they dispose of bodies—it's horrifying. We can't turn a blind eye."

Harper leaned in closer. "You're my anchor, Dee. I trust

your judgment, your principles. We can bring their secrets to light."

Deandra hesitated, her voice shaky. "Everything you told me and Mama Dee... It's a lot to process. We're both still in shock."

Deandra took a deep breath, her eyes searching Harper's. "Harper, you know I'd back you in an instant," she began, her tone sincere. "But diving into this is like navigating treacherous waters. We're bound to face resistance, possibly even legal action. And the personal toll? It's immense. Just ensure you're prepared for every possible outcome. Be meticulous."

Harper nodded, her eyes unwavering. "That's why I need you, Dee. We can face this storm together."

She slid a folder towards Deandra. "Look at this," Harper blurted, her voice filled with urgency. "PenCore, right here in Memphis, is providing CytoLife with inmates' biological samples. No consent, no ethics. They're exploiting our own, Dee, and it's happening on our watch."

As Deandra scanned the documents, Harper continued, "This isn't just about work for me. It's personal. I've heard whispers linking CytoLife to some of the region's cancer centers. We'll tread lightly there, ensuring we're on solid ground before probing deeper. But with this PenCore evidence, we already have a strong starting point."

Harper's eyes pleaded with Deandra, seeking support. "We can change this, Dee. We need to expose the truth."

Deandra exhaled, her fingers grazing the files before her. Determination ignited in her eyes as she met Harper's gaze. "Of course I'm on board, Harper. This is abhorrent." A shadow crossed her face momentarily. "But we're dealing with more than just scandal. This could tarnish my father's legacy of justice. Despite that, he'd insist on uncovering the truth. We'll face it together, side by side."

Harper reached across the table, placing a supportive hand on Deandra's. "We'll see it through, Dee. We'll ensure justice for all involved."

"We need to act decisively and collaboratively. Involving the FDA's Office of Criminal Investigations could be a strategic move," Deandra remarked.

A wave of relief washed over Harper. "I'm glad you understand," she said, her voice filled with gratitude.

Deandra looked thoughtful. "Precision is key here. Every detail matters."

Harper met Deandra's gaze intently, probing for any uncertainty. "Have you read that recent exposé in *The Standard*?"

"Yes, I've gone through it. Piecing together what you've shared and the details from the article are overwhelming."

Harper leaned forward, emphasizing, "That article, while not naming names, is designed to awaken the public. It's just the beginning."

Deandra's eyebrows furrowed. "You're collaborating with a journalist? Harper, I need transparency. Who's in this with us?"

Harper spoke evenly. "Ethan Cook has been instrumental, but his ties to the firm complicate things. He introduced me to a journalist at *The Standard*, the one behind the article. That journalist was already investigating questionable genetic practices, and our investigations converged. He's our gateway to the whistleblower who first tipped us off."

Deandra, her lips curving into a smile, said, "This reminds me of our college advocacy days. Remember the late-night library campaign? You had me leading that sit-in!"

Both chuckled at the memory, eager to avoid the topic at hand. "All in the name of academia," Harper responded lightly.

Deandra's smile grew wider. "You've always been one to rally the troops. It feels like a familiar dance with you." The two women shared a moment, echoing in unison, "For the love of knowledge!" and laughed together.

Recalling past escapades, Harper grinned. "Remember our run-in with Prince Mongo at the pizzeria?"

Deandra burst into laughter. "Yes! We recognized him immediately, but our friend Jake was utterly baffled. He thought the guy was heading to some costume event."

Shaking her head, Harper commented, "Being from Memphis, we've seen our fair share of characters, but that was memorable!"

The air in the diner turned contemplative as Harper's mind wandered to an early case in their careers. Together, they had defended a man falsely charged with financial fraud. Their collaborative work had exposed the real culprit, securing justice in the end.

"Do you recall our first big case against that insurance giant? Those relentless nights, strategizing, finding the overlooked evidence, and eventually vindicating our client?

Our partnership was something else, Dee."

Deandra smiled. "That case was a defining moment for us. We were driven, and together, we were a force to be reckoned with."

Teasingly, Harper quipped, "Switching to the DA's side now? They must've realized they needed top-tier talent to stand a chance."

Amidst the camaraderie, the gravity of their current situation lingered in Harper's mind, gently nudging her back to the task at hand.

"We need to break this down," Harper urged.

"Alright," Deandra started with a composed tone. "If we're going to challenge CytoLife, our first step should be to look into any regulatory violations they might be involved in. Such breaches could offer us a point of leverage."

Harper nodded. Deandra's capacity to remain unflappable and strategic, even when confronted with such a grueling challenge, was something Harper truly respected.

"You have this innate ability to see the core of an issue, Dee."

Deandra offered a slight smile. "Brass, we've always been a formidable duo, always seeking the truth and championing justice. But I must admit," she hesitated, "I wonder about the repercussions. CytoLife has made significant advancements. If we expose them, what happens to those depending on their breakthroughs?"

Harper met her gaze. "It's not just about their accomplishments, Dee. If they're compromising ethics for these results, we need to question their other operations.

We owe it to the public to unveil the truth. They deserve transparency."

She continued, "Consider the potential lives saved if we halt their questionable actions. We can't let apprehensions deter us from pursuing the right course."

Deandra nodded thoughtfully. "Foremost, we must familiarize ourselves with the regulatory landscape of biotechnology and genetic engineering. The FDA oversees areas such as safety, ethical concerns, and investigative processes."

Harper absorbed Deandra's words, her thoughts consumed by the unsettling discoveries she'd unearthed. She was in awe of Deandra's ability to remain objective and methodical amidst such disturbing information.

"From the details you shared," Deandra picked up, "CytoLife could be contravening several federal guidelines. Unauthorized DNA utilization, inappropriate body disposal—these are grave violations. But we need tangible proof to move forward."

"Agreed. We have to conduct thorough research. It's imperative we maintain discretion. CytoLife can't get wind of our intent, or they might take measures to hide evidence."

"Exactly," Deandra agreed, pausing thoughtfully. "The FDA's Office of Criminal Investigations is designed for cases like ours. Though I've never worked with them before, I initiated contact after our last conversation."

Harper smiled, her expression a mix of admiration and gratitude for Deandra's proactive approach.

"Can we rely on them?" Trusting Deandra was one thing,

but involving an official body was a different ball game.

"Without a doubt," Deandra reassured. "Their primary goal is to unveil corruption and shield the public. Their expertise will be invaluable in building a robust case against CytoLife. I'll coordinate with my team to lay the groundwork for the Shelby County DA, and we'll liaise with the FDA. Given our current knowledge, I believe this is our best strategy."

A few days later, Deandra set up a video call with Agent Morgan Butler from the FDA's Office of Criminal Investigations. Harper, tense with anticipation, prepared to present her findings on CytoLife. She clung to the hope that building a solid case would offer the stability she sorely needed amid the chaos of her thoughts.

Agent Morgan Butler's face appeared on the screen, his features initially guarded, eyes assessing. The lines of his face hinted at countless cases tackled, many sleepless nights, and an unwavering commitment to his duty.

"Agent Butler," Deandra began with a nod. "Meet Harper Brasfield. She's come across intel on a company named CytoLife, which, if validated, will challenge even the most unflinching among us."

Harper unfolded her narrative. With each revelation, she observed the gradual change in Butler's disposition. From initial skepticism, his eyebrows knitted together in concentration, then occasionally lifted in disbelief and concern. Despite his vast experience, some details even caught him off-guard.

Throughout Harper's account, Deandra played an essential role, not just introducing the facts, but also emphasizing their credibility. She highlighted Harper's meticulous approach to her research, and her own growing conviction about the severity of the situation, based on the evidence presented.

A tense silence enveloped the room momentarily after Harper finished speaking, punctuated only by the heavy sighs from those on the call, each one feeling the weight of her words. After what felt like an eternity, Butler leaned forward, his eyes sharper, his voice carrying a mix of resolve and fury. "If half of what you've shared holds up, we're looking at one hell of a case. Consider me on board. We're going to get to the bottom of this CytoLife mess."

At CytoLife Dynamics, Lucas, standing tall and attentive by Rebecca's office door, couldn't help but steal glances at her as she worked behind her desk. The way her blonde hair cascaded over her shoulders, the furrow in her brow as she concentrated on the task before her—it all drew him in like a moth to a flame.

"Lucas," Rebecca said without looking up from her computer, snapping him back to reality. "How was your trip back home? I hope everything went well."

"Uh, yes, ma'am," Lucas replied, hesitating for a moment

as he considered how much to share. He settled on a half-truth. "The funeral was nice, and I got to see my sister."

He purposefully avoided mentioning his mother, Harper. The emotions were still too raw, too complex.

"Good, I'm glad you could spend some time with family," Rebecca said, finally looking up from her screen. Her eyes met his, and for a moment, Lucas felt his professionalism waver under her gaze.

"By the way," Rebecca continued, "there's a big meeting coming up soon here at CytoLife. I have a presentation to prepare, and I'll be busy for the next few days. I was wondering if you'd be open to working dinners together?"

Lucas felt a surge of excitement at the idea of meeting Rebecca beyond their work setting. However, he was acutely aware of the importance of keeping their relationship strictly professional. Their intellectually stimulating conversations had captivated him, and he replayed their discussions in his mind, valuing each interaction more than he cared to admit.

"Of course, Ms. Kent," he replied, his Southern manners shining through. "Whatever you need, just let me know."

"Great," she smiled, her eyes lighting up. "I appreciate it, Lucas. It's nice to have someone I can trust around here."

As she returned to her work, Lucas allowed a faint smile to touch his lips. He sensed the delicate balance between trust, loyalty, and love beginning to blur in his life. Yet how much this intricate dance of emotions would impact his future remained an elusive mystery.

That night, Lucas paused on the doorstep of Rebecca's stately residence, his heart thrumming with anticipation.

Recollections of past evening conversations at this very place brought a comforting warmth. He straightened his jacket, gave the door a confident knock, and waited.

"Come on in, Lucas," Rebecca called from within as she opened the door. She stood before him, radiant in a simple yet flattering dress that hugged her curves. Her hair flowed down her shoulders, perfectly outlining her porcelain features. The sight of her stirred an unfamiliar vulnerability in Lucas, as if he were seeing her for the first time.

"Evening, Ms. Kent," he said, forcing a professional tone. "I hope I'm not too early."

"Please, I've told you to call me Rebecca," she replied with a soft smile. "And you're right on time. Dinner's almost ready."

He followed her into the cozy, candlelit dining room, where an elegant table was set for two. The aroma of garlic and herbs wafted through the air, enveloping them in a comforting embrace.

"Take a seat. I just need to grab the food from the kitchen," Rebecca instructed, her voice lighter than usual.

"Sure thing, Rebecca," Lucas stumbled awkwardly, still struggling between their formal and informal roles.

As they sat down to eat, Rebecca became increasingly animated, discussing her preparations for the upcoming presentation. Between bites of savory chicken and roasted vegetables, she shared her passion for CytoLife's mission with a zeal that captivated Lucas.

"Lucas, there are a few things I wanted to run by you before the big day," she said. "I value your perspective, especially considering your background."

"Of course," he replied, feeling a surge of pride at her trust in him. "What do you have in mind?"

Rebecca shared her vision, her words rich with passion yet scant on specifics. She spoke of CytoLife's research in broad, sweeping terms, often emphasizing its world-altering potential without going into the granular details. She laid out her ideas, seeking his input on everything from security measures to the best way to present sensitive information. As they spoke, Lucas found himself drawn into her world, sharing her enthusiasm and commitment to CytoLife's success.

Beneath the surface, a persistent voice nagged at Lucas, hinting that CytoLife harbored secrets deeper than what was apparent. An intangible unease lurked in the shadows of the company, clashing with his growing fondness for Rebecca.

For the moment, he shelved these unsettling thoughts, immersing himself in their engaging conversation. As the evening progressed, he couldn't ignore the flirtatious glimmers in Rebecca's eyes. These sparks kindled a fire within him, challenging his willpower and threatening to override his caution.

"Thank you for tonight, Lucas," Rebecca said, her gaze lingering on him as they stood by the door. "I really appreciate your help."

"Anytime, Rebecca," he murmured. "It was my pleasure."

As Lucas stepped into the crisp night air, a weight descended upon him, signifying a boundary had been crossed—a line that might not be easily redrawn. His thoughts lingered on Rebecca, a mix of attraction and wariness. The path they trod was dangerous, yet it was this very danger that added an electrifying undercurrent to their interactions. His heart raced, not just from the potential risks, but from the exhilarating unknown that she represented.

Adam's pulse quickened as the notifications, reviews, and social media shares streamed in relentlessly. "Bridging the Gap between Promise and Peril: The Duality of Biotech Advancements" had transcended local buzz; it was making waves nationally. Top-tier news channels were spotlighting his piece, magnifying its influence. Whispers about his exposé echoed through the city, sparking intense discussions and drawing in scholars, bioethicists, and the general public.

Online chatter was rife with speculation about the corporations spearheading these innovations and the moral boundaries they might have overstepped. While CytoLife's name frequently surfaced, the discourse was divided: some hinted at deeper involvements, while others staunchly upheld its integrity. The ambiguity remained, but Adam had unmistakably unleashed something significant.

Ben's call broke his reverie.

"Adam, I knew when I greenlit this article that you'd be thorough and relentless, as always. But reading the final draft... it just hit me how profound this all is. CytoLife is a behemoth. Their influence, their breakthroughs are unparalleled."

"I'm aware, Ben. We talked about it, remember? That's why I've taken this route. Direct accusations could backfire without irrefutable evidence. So, I'm highlighting the larger issues, sowing seeds of skepticism. It discusses unauthorized testing, the potential for misuse, and ethical gray areas. It's a cry for openness and caution."

"And the insinuation about further investigation in subsequent pieces?"

"That," Adam replied, "is our coded message to CytoLife. A veiled warning. We're signaling that we're watching. That we have inklings."

Ben hesitated before responding, "This is a chess match, Adam. And it's a perilous one. Every move, every piece, every strategy has consequences."

"I realize that. But it's a match we must engage in. The public should be aware of the shadows behind genetic breakthroughs. By alluding to a deeper probe, we might coax some insiders to break their silence. We need more tangible proof against CytoLife."

Before Ben could reply, an email notification dimmed the atmosphere. An unidentified sender. A mysterious message. With a sense of foreboding, Adam clicked it open.

"Burke, shadows can be misleading, right? Beware, lest those close to you get entangled."

A rush of adrenaline surged through Adam. "Ben, I've just received a threatening email. It's disconcerting..."

Ben took a deep breath. "It might be just an intimidation ploy, Adam. Controversial topics draw all sorts of attention. But," he added with a tone of seriousness, "we shouldn't overlook it. The publication supports you fully. We'll investigate. Meanwhile, remain vigilant. Maybe maintain a subdued presence."

Adam's gratitude was transparent amidst his growing unease. "Thank you, Ben. I really appreciate it."

As the call ended, the weight of his choices bore down on Adam, intertwining the thrill of journalistic prowess with the lurking dangers of his pursuit.

TWENTY TWO

Lucas methodically moved through the conference room, his trained eyes sweeping over every corner, every shadow, ensuring the area was secure for Rebecca's upcoming presentation. The room was bathed in the soft glow of overhead chandeliers, and the rows of plush seats led to a large stage adorned with CytoLife banners.

Once satisfied, he approached Rebecca, who was reviewing her notes, a look of concentration etched on her face. "All clear," Lucas announced. "I'm going to step out for a bit. Call me if you need anything."

Rebecca looked up, a grateful smile touching her lips. "I'll be fine, Lucas. It's just a presentation. Nothing I haven't done a hundred times before."

Lucas hesitated, his protective instincts warring with his respect for her autonomy. "I'd feel better if I were closer, maybe near the stage. I want to keep a visual on you at all times."

Her smile grew warmer, more teasing. "Always the protector, huh? It's sweet, but this isn't some action movie, Lucas."

Lucas shifted uncomfortably. "It's just... it's my job to ensure your safety. I've seen unexpected things happen in the most controlled environments."

Rebecca paused, seeming to gauge his sincerity. "Alright. You can stand just outside the doors. You'll have a clear view of the entries and exits. Will that make you feel better?"

He nodded, appreciating the compromise. "Thank you, Rebecca. I just want to make sure everything goes smoothly."

She winked. "With you watching my back? I have no doubts."

Lucas took a deep breath, adjusting his posture as he stationed himself just outside the door. The lavish hallway was abuzz with activity, with prominent figures clad in high-end attire walking purposefully, engrossed in hushed conversations.

His focus was broken when a familiar figure emerged from the crowd. It was Rebecca, her confident demeanor in sharp contrast to the delicate dress she wore. On her left was the imposing figure of Thomas Baxter, his arm resting protectively on the small of her back. Lucas's heart constricted, remembering their brief, unsettling meeting. He didn't like seeing him so close to Rebecca. To her right was Felix, whose sharp features were all too recognizable.

As the trio approached, Lucas tried to piece together the

connection, but it all felt out of place. His surprise at seeing Baxter with Rebecca was clear, but he quickly reined in his emotions. The bond they shared, the subtle gestures, and the casual touch hinted at something deeper. But what?

His musings were cut short by Felix's cold, penetrating gaze. That unmistakable glare, one that he'd encountered before, seemed to pierce right through him. The message was clear: Stay in your lane. Without missing a beat, Lucas's training kicked in. His face turned to stone, every muscle in his body tensing as he resumed his vigil, every bit the soldier he was trained to be.

Under the moonlit sky, a procession of polished black cars glided toward the grand Evergreen Resort. Its majestic architecture, bathed in light, exuded wealth and power. The air buzzed with anticipation as a select group of influential figures converged for a secret meeting.

Lucas, stationed in a plush chair in the hallway, kept a vigilant eye on the conference room's entrances. His routine surveillance was interrupted by a crackle in his earpiece. Investigating, he found a door slightly ajar, its latch malfunctioning.

Peering through the narrow opening, he saw the illuminated stage and its occupants. Quickly, he discreetly adjusted his chair to align with the gap, gaining both a visual and an audio feed from inside, while remaining on guard.

From his covert spot, Lucas watched as Thomas Baxter took the stage, exuding a commanding presence. His silver hair shone in the light, and his piercing eyes held the audience captive. "Esteemed members of this consortium," Baxter began, his voice booming with authority. "You are part of a historic gathering."

The gravity in Baxter's voice signaled a significant revelation. He spoke of deep alliances and shared secrets, hinting at the power within the room. "Tonight, we reveal a breakthrough that will alter our understanding of humanity."

Then Rebecca Kent stepped into the spotlight, drawing Lucas's gaze. Bathed in soft light, she seemed ethereal. Lucas remembered seeing her earlier with Baxter, their interaction hinting at a bond that was more than just professional.

"Dr. Kent's groundbreaking research ushers in a new epoch for mankind," Baxter declared, his voice loaded with pride.

As Rebecca stepped up to present, Lucas subtly shifted for a clearer view through the door's gap. His heart beat a rapid tempo, anxiety and expectation intermingling. The upcoming revelations threatened to upend his perception of CytoLife and Rebecca's involvement, straining the delicate line he walked between duty and personal emotion.

He observed Rebecca with a complex blend of feelings. She addressed the world's most influential figures with poise and confidence. "Thank you, Mr. Baxter," she began, her voice steady and clear, betraying no sign of the moment's magnitude.

Taking center stage, Rebecca captivated the audience. "Ladies and gentlemen," she declared, "today, we redefine human nature."

She paused momentarily, adjusting her glasses. Lucas

noticed a faint sheen of sweat on her brow, the sole indicator of her internal pressure. Then, with a laser pointer in hand, she went into the core of her presentation. "The AGG1 gene paves the way to unprecedented human potential. Through examining DNA from individuals with unique behavioral traits, we've pinpointed a gene cluster—AGG1. It's a breakthrough in understanding and potentially moderating aggression." As Rebecca navigated through her slides, dense with intricate diagrams and data, Lucas hung on every word, absorbing the enormity of their discovery.

Rebecca's words about the AGG1 gene cluster captivated the audience. Lucas, from his hidden vantage point, felt the full weight of their implications. It was a staggering revelation, one that could fundamentally alter society.

Her next words echoed through the room with gravity. "Using CRISPR-Cas9, we can finely tune these AGG1 genes, gently steering human behavior," she declared, pausing to let the concept sink in. Her gaze swept over the audience, a silent challenge to any doubts. "This is about honing our innate potential, not erasing individuality."

Lucas watched the room react from his secluded spot. Whispers rippled through the audience, faces a mix of shock and calculation. Some were clearly in awe, while others seemed to be already calculating the potential benefits of such a genetic tool.

Rebecca's passion intensified as she outlined their grand vision. "Imagine a world with reduced violence, heightened empathy, and elevated human potential."

The mood in the room shifted to one of unambiguous

excitement. These powerful individuals were considering a monumental change in human evolution. Lucas admired Rebecca's intellect, yet he couldn't shake his unease about the ethical dimensions of such power.

A soft exclamation of "Extraordinary" emerged from a man in the crowd, his thoughtful expression suggesting he was envisioning the future reshaped by this advancement.

Lucas realized then the true depth of Rebecca's earlier caution. This presentation was more than a project reveal; it was the announcement of a revolutionary ambition. The enormity of the moment resonated within him, stirring a complex mix of admiration and apprehension about the impact of their research.

Baxter's voice filled the room, heightening the sense of anticipation. "We are on the cusp of an era-defining transformation," he declared, his voice a blend of confidence and vision. "Our goal is to nurture a world of unity, not domination. Imagine a society where strife is rare, and harmony is the norm, where every individual understands and values their place in the greater whole."

He paused, letting his ambitious vision settle among the audience. "This isn't about exerting control; it's about fostering a balanced and cohesive society."

Around the room, heads nodded in agreement, faces alight with interest. Baxter's compelling oratory skillfully painted a picture of an almost utopian future, smoothing over any lingering skepticism.

Hidden in his vantage point, Lucas was captivated, yet disturbed by the presentation. The idea of such sweeping influence over human nature was daunting. Despite the unease, he found himself drawn to the captivating promise of Baxter's vision. It was becoming clear that Baxter was more than a patron; he was the driving force behind CytoLife's audacious and possibly dangerous ambitions.

Lucas wrestled with mixed feelings. Rebecca spoke with the authority of a committed scientist, her confidence plain to see in every word. But the ethical quandaries of their project loomed large in his mind, casting a shadow over his admiration for her.

Rebecca's gaze, firm and almost defiant, swept over the audience. "Our trial subjects were meticulously chosen, adhering to strict guidelines. The results are promising, heralding a new frontier in behavioral science."

The audience's rapt attention was unmistakable as they absorbed the implications of her words. Lucas observed their expressions change; the realization that CytoLife's research had moved from theory to practice clearly struck them.

Baxter stepped up, reinforcing the narrative. "Our dedication to ethical research is paramount. We're leading not only in genetic innovation but also in setting new standards for responsible science." His words elicited nods of approval, emphasizing the responsible and pioneering nature of their work.

From his vantage point, Lucas watched as Baxter and Rebecca masterfully orchestrated their presentation. Their shared ambition was captivating, yet Lucas's sense of unease grew. The breadth of their project's impact loomed large, and he questioned whether they fully understood the consequences of unleashing such technology.

Baxter's voice, both inspiring and ominous, filled the room. "This technology promises a world where aggression is obsolete, where our lifespans are longer and healthier, united by peace and cooperation."

Rebecca's agreement was unwavering. "We stand at the dawn of an era where human potential aligns with the greater good."

Baxter concluded with a calming yet earnest tone. "Our aim is to elevate societal harmony and well-being. This isn't coercion; it's a step towards a more peaceful, cooperative world."

Lucas's heart pounded as the enormity of CytoLife's ambitions struck him. The idea of altering behavior on such a massive scale was as enthralling as it was chilling. He recognized the profound ethical questions shadowing their scientific breakthrough.

He fixated on the discussion about their drone delivery system, a critical element for the widespread deployment of their genetic modifications. This technology, he realized, was pivotal to their plan.

Baxter's voice carried a note of pride. "Our drone technology is more than a delivery system; it's the key to our global outreach. These drones can precisely target areas, from regions to neighborhoods, ensuring efficient distribution of our nanoparticles where they're needed most."

Lucas listened intently as Baxter expounded on the drones' technical prowess. The idea of these unmanned vehicles, discreetly releasing behavior-modifying particles into the atmosphere, was both revolutionary and unnerving. The potential for such technology to reshape society was immense, but so were the risks.

Rebecca's explanation of the drone technology added another layer of complexity. "Their design is such that they operate discreetly, almost unseen, making the distribution process smooth and unnoticed. This allows the public to unknowingly benefit from our advancements, without any disruption to their daily routines."

Lucas, listening intently, grappled with the ramifications. The ability to covertly influence behavior was a technological marvel, yet it teetered on the edge of ethical propriety. Questions of consent and the risk of misuse loomed large in his mind.

A mix of enthusiasm and cautious skepticism permeated the audience. Some attendees visibly wrestled with the moral implications, while others seemed captivated by the potential of such a pioneering technology.

A woman's cautious tone pierced the room. "This is extraordinary, but what about ethical limits? How can we ensure that such power isn't misused?"

Baxter's response was immediate, his expression serious. "The ethical dimensions are not lost on us. Our research and development have been conducted with the utmost care. We're dedicated to responsible, ethical use of this technology."

Rebecca interjected, reinforcing their stance. "We understand the gravity of this power. To that end, we're establishing an independent ethics board to oversee its implementation, guaranteeing our commitment to the highest moral standards."

From his hidden vantage point, Lucas's attention was riveted on the exchange. Rebecca's eloquent response to the question about potential risks showcased the thoroughness of their research. Her detailed explanation of the nanoparticles' targeted functionality highlighted the scientific sophistication underpinning their project.

A question from an attendee, clad in a tweed blazer and exuding an air of authority, about navigating regulatory hurdles elicited a sly grin from Baxter. His reply, laced with subtle shrewdness, hinted at the consortium's capability to sidestep typical regulatory barriers. Lucas noted the audience's knowing nods and soft chuckles, a clear acknowledgment of the influential networks at their disposal.

The conversation progressed, with audience members scrutinizing the ethical, logistical, and practical dimensions of the project. Lucas absorbed each exchange, his mind racing with the ramifications of such an innovative yet ethically fraught endeavor.

The meeting had laid bare not only the extent of CytoLife's ambitions, but also the vast web of power and influence supporting it. It deepened Lucas's apprehension about their path and its consequences.

Lucas, still concealed, focused as a question arose from the audience about the practicality and rationale behind using drones for nanoparticle distribution, challenging the need for such a method over traditional approaches.

Baxter, his eyes gleaming with fervor, was quick to answer. "Our drone program is more than an innovative delivery system; it symbolizes CytoLife's commitment to pioneering solutions. We've been at the forefront of global health, from vaccinations to DNA testing, but drones represent a quantum leap in our capabilities."

He elaborated with distinct pride. "Envision our drones stealthily crossing the skies, becoming a seamless part of everyday life. They're already familiar, thanks to their use in Baxter Global's surveillance operations. This familiarity is our strategic advantage. The public's acceptance of drones makes them the ideal vehicle for our nanoparticles—a subtle yet effective approach."

Baxter's pride was almost arresting as he highlighted the strategic ingenuity of his plan. "The true elegance of this method is its stealth and efficiency. We avoid panic and unwanted attention. Our drones will covertly deliver our innovative solutions, unnoticed by the very people benefiting from them."

For Lucas, each revelation compounded the scope of what he was witnessing. The blend of advanced technology and clever implementation unveiled a scenario where CytoLife's reach was vast and undetectable, woven into the fabric of everyday life.

An imposing gentleman from the front row rose, his presence commanding attention. "Mr. Baxter," he intoned, his voice resonating in the room. "How do you address the ethical implications of gene manipulation, particularly in terms of behavior?"

Baxter responded with an assertive tone, confidently outlining CytoLife's ethical framework. "Our goal is to elevate human capabilities, not restrict or undermine them. We're enhancing the human experience through this technology, embarking on a path of improvement and insight, rather than control."

Rebecca, maintaining her composure next to Baxter, contributed her insights. "Our objective is to understand and gently steer behavior, reducing harmful tendencies for societal betterment. Our vision is to create a more unified, peaceful world."

Lucas, from his hidden spot, digested their assertions with mixed feelings. The conviction in their voices was persuasive, yet it also sparked concerns about the breadth of their project's impact.

Another participant, a contemplative man, responded to their statements. "Your emphasis on ethical practices is reassuring, given the potentially revolutionary impact of this technology."

Baxter acknowledged the comment with a gracious nod. "With great innovation comes great responsibility. We're acutely conscious of our pioneering role and are dedicated to harnessing our discoveries for the betterment of humanity."

A note of skepticism permeated a woman's question from the crowd. "But by altering genetic predispositions, aren't we risking an infringement on free will?"

Baxter, with a diplomat's poise, answered with composed confidence. "Our focus is guidance, not dominance. We aim to soften the extremes of impulsive behavior, contributing to a society that is more reflective and harmonious."

Rebecca, turning towards the questioner, added her

perspective. "We're not looking to suppress individuality or control decisions. Our goal is to create a setting where more considerate and community-oriented choices are naturally more prevalent."

Lucas, hidden from view, felt his emotions stir, especially hearing Rebecca's words. He was caught in a conflict between the appeal of her vision and his reservations about the project's deeper consequences. Where did the distinction between guidance and control lie? And what was Rebecca's true position in this ethically grey area?

Baxter, with his inherent charisma, captivated the assembly with his engaging voice. "Imagine the human mind as a room filled with lights, each representing different behaviors and traits. Some lights highlight our best qualities, while others cast shadows on less favorable behaviors. Our work with the AGG1 gene is akin to installing a nuanced dimmer switch." He mimed turning a dial. "With this, we can gently dim negative traits, enhancing overall harmony in our collective psyche."

Lucas observed as the crowd absorbed Baxter's metaphor, a wave of agreement and thoughtful consideration moving through them. The vision Baxter articulated seemed to captivate many, their expressions a blend of intrigue and reflection.

His attention then shifted to Rebecca. She leaned forward, taking in the audience. "Our goal is to scientifically temper violent or overly aggressive behaviors," she articulated passionately. "This isn't about suppression; it's about offering a chance for a more balanced life to those struggling with these tendencies."

The audience was visibly enthralled by Rebecca's earnest delivery. Lucas, too, found himself momentarily caught up in her words, despite the undercurrent of doubt that persisted within him.

A query pierced the hushed room. "What about the downsides or unforeseen consequences, particularly for those without a specific gene marker?"

Rebecca took a moment to consider her response. "Our nanoparticles are designed to interact with a set of genes common to all, though varying in expression. It's not a matter of presence or absence, but of degree. If these genes or their variants are sparse, the nanoparticles simply remain inactive, posing no risk."

"Dr. Kent," inquired a man clad in a sleek suit. "What practical applications do you foresee for this technology?"

After a brief exchange of looks with Baxter, Rebecca answered.

"Picture a world where those prone to violence can access treatments to moderate their impulses," she started. "Through gene manipulation, we can provide relief for those battling their aggressive nature.

"But it's not limited to extreme cases," she added. "This technology can enhance therapies, education, and more, helping many lead calmer, more fulfilling lives.

"Ultimately," she concluded, her eyes sweeping the audience, "our aim is to forge a safer, more harmonious world. A world free from the constraints of destructive behavior, where human potential is fully realized."

An elegant woman, her sophistication marked by an unplaceable accent, stood and captured the room's attention. "Mr. Baxter," she inquired, her voice commanding yet inquisitive, "could you elaborate on the broader societal implications of this technology?"

Baxter's searching glance hushed the room. "Consider the possibilities," he began. "A dramatic decrease in violent crime, a chance for those with severe aggression disorders to lead balanced lives, and a shift in our prison systems towards true rehabilitation."

Rebecca broke in, her voice unwavering. "Beyond that, its applications could extend to therapy, corrections, and even education, mitigating disruptive behaviors to enhance learning environments."

Lucas's attention shifted as a tall man rose, his commanding gaze locking onto Baxter. The room hushed in anticipation.

"Mr. Baxter," he intoned, his voice rumbling like stones in a barrel, "as a long-standing supporter of CytoLife's humanitarian efforts, I'm keen to understand how this new direction aligns with the company's esteemed values."

Baxter's response was measured, his smile conveying both charm and assurance. "Thank you, Sir Reginald, for the insightful query. CytoLife has always endeavored to uplift humanity. Our initiatives, from clean water to education, have improved lives globally. This genetic venture is a natural progression of our mission."

He gestured gracefully as his voice filled with conviction. "Envision a world with reduced conflict, social disharmony, and resistance to authority. A world where people live in peaceful coexistence, respecting norms yet celebrating their individuality. Our goal isn't control. It's about fostering societal harmony."

Baxter paused, capturing the room's attention before concluding, "Our goal is a brighter, unified future. With the support of partners like you, we're on the brink of an era defined by global tranquility, in perfect alignment with CytoLife's values."

He added, his gaze sweeping the room, "This initiative resonates with not only CytoLife's ethos but also the collective vision of this consortium. Together, we're shaping a future where worldwide stability and progress are realities, not just aspirations."

Lucas observed the audience's reaction. Baxter's charisma seemed to alleviate any lingering doubts, with murmurs and nods indicating agreement.

As the atmosphere settled, Lucas noticed Baxter's discreet signal to Rebecca. She immediately perked up, her eyes shining even from a distance.

Rebecca, infused with pride, announced, "To add to our discussion, we're excited to share another aspect of our work: significant extension of human life." The room fell silent, all eyes intently on her. "Our research suggests the possibility of extending life expectancy to 160 years or more."

A buzz of astonished whispers filled the room, reaching Lucas in his hiding spot. The audience's varied reactions, ranging from skepticism to eager anticipation, were notable.

A voice of doubt cut through the murmurs. "Is such

longevity truly achievable?" inquired a skeptical attendee.

Baxter responded affirmatively, "Absolutely. Rebecca, would you elaborate on this?"

Rebecca stepped up, her excitement palpable. "Our team has identified key genes associated with aging. By targeting these, we've developed a treatment with the potential to significantly prolong life, surpassing historical limits."

Baxter, basking in the intrigue their announcement had stirred, opened the floor for questions. A woman near the front asked about the treatment's mechanics, wondering if it was a single intervention.

"An excellent question," Baxter said, turning the response over to Rebecca.

Rebecca dove into details. "It's a series of treatments, designed to work in harmony with the body's natural regenerative processes. We envision a continuous, evolving therapy to not only extend life but also enhance its quality."

Lucas, listening intently, pondered the implications. The prospect of extended life was alluring, yet he couldn't dismiss concerns about potential misuses and unforeseen complexities of such a groundbreaking development.

As Rebecca elaborated on the treatment, a wave of excitement rippled through the audience. Baxter interjected, enhancing her points, "We're not speculating here. Our approach combines CRISPR's gene-editing capabilities with cutting-edge stem cell therapies. These treatments, applied over time, are designed to rejuvenate the body from the cellular level."

He continued, "Our goal is to augment the body's natural

repair mechanisms, leading to substantially prolonged, healthy, and active lifespans."

A critical question then emerged from the crowd. "What are the possible side effects of living beyond 160 years?"

Baxter responded thoughtfully, "In any groundbreaking field, there are unknowns. Our extensive trials and rigorous testing are geared towards minimizing these risks." He paused, ensuring his message of careful optimism was clear. "We seek not just longer life, but a life filled with health and vitality."

Rebecca said, "Our vision goes beyond merely adding years. We're committed to enhancing the quality of life in those extra years. While our preliminary results are promising, continued research is crucial to fully understand and refine this treatment."

A man in the audience, his demeanor marked by seriousness, raised his hand. "What's the timeline for public availability, and what are we looking at in terms of cost?" he asked, his voice shaded with anticipation.

Rebecca addressed the query with confidence. "Currently, the project is in its early stages. Our priority is ensuring safety and efficacy. As we make progress, we'll look towards wider application. Be assured, making the treatment both affordable and accessible is a key part of our strategy."

The room hushed, contemplating the implications of her statement. After a moment, another attendee sought further clarity. "Can you elaborate on the specifics of the longevity treatment?"

Baxter responded, a clear blend of pride and enthusiasm

in his voice. "The procedure involves a sequence of gene therapies. We use CRISPR to target and modify genes associated with aging. This, combined with state-of-the-art stem cell treatments, is designed to rejuvenate cells and organs at a fundamental level."

Rebecca added, "Our findings so far are encouraging, but we're still exploring and understanding various aspects. That said, we believe the benefits of this treatment will far surpass any potential risks." Her delivery struck a fine balance between excitement for their progress and an awareness of the responsibility they bore.

A woman, her attire as stylish as her demeanor, raised a question, her voice rich with curiosity. "Assuming this longevity therapy becomes a reality, Mr. Baxter, who would you see as the initial beneficiaries?"

Baxter, composed and assured, replied, "Our first priority would be individuals who play pivotal roles in driving societal advancement—like the distinguished members of this consortium." He paused, letting the implication of his words sink in. "Starting with influential leaders ensures the continuity and stability of our common goals. Wider public availability will follow, but with careful oversight. The essence of extending life isn't just about longevity; it's about sustaining the core intellectual and leadership pillars of our society."

Rebecca, her voice both firm and engaging, added, "Launching such a groundbreaking treatment requires meticulous planning. We're considering the extensive societal, economic, and global effects. A gradual, methodical rollout is key to keeping societal balance."

Baxter, standing with Rebecca, glanced around the room. A hint of satisfaction flickered across his face as he mused, "Think of the prolonged contributions to humanity that could come from the extraordinary minds present here, with the gift of extra decades."

As the meeting concluded, Lucas silently slipped away, disappearing into the shadows. His mind buzzed with the enormity of what he'd heard, the implications of their words echoing in his thoughts.

The final applause echoed in the ornate conference room, a testament to the admiration for Baxter and Rebecca's work. As the audience dispersed into buzzing groups, Baxter stood at the center, a picture of composure and influence. His gaze swept the room, subtly assessing the potential in each face.

Approaching him was Mrs. Wallace, a force in the tech world, her mouth set into a firm line, her voice authoritative. "Baxter, that was revolutionary. This technology could redefine our era."

"Thank you, Mrs. Wallace," Baxter responded, his voice smooth and his demeanor confident. "We're on the brink of something extraordinary." His words lingered, inviting contemplation.

"Indeed," she said thoughtfully. "But caution is key. This technology could be seen as a threat by some."

"Agreed," Baxter nodded, his mind already strategizing.

"It's vital we guide its course."

Their conversation flowed, with Baxter subtly navigating the intricate dynamics of the consortium. He knew their support was crucial, and every word with Mrs. Wallace was a step in a delicate dance of influence.

"Rest assured. This breakthrough won't fall into the wrong hands."

"Good." A hint of a smile emerged. "Play this right, Baxter, and we might just change the world."

Baxter's triumph was interrupted as Mr. D'Souza, a finance titan, approached. The billionaire's bespoke suit and sharp gaze spoke of his calculating nature.

"Thomas," Mr. D'Souza greeted him with a firm handshake. "Your presentation hints at a world transformed. The potential for collaboration is significant."

"Thank you, Mr. D'Souza," Baxter acknowledged, a hint of pride in his smile. "CytoLife's advancements could reshape even finance. It's about finding the right partnerships."

"Wealth preservation gains new meaning with extended lifespans," Mr. D'Souza noted, eyeing Baxter thoughtfully. "I'll be watching your progress closely."

"Your interest is invaluable," Baxter kept his tone even. "With support like yours, we can make a profound impact."

After a brief nod, Mr. D'Souza blended back into the crowd.

Immediately, Lady Felicia, a figure of elegance, glided forward. Her every movement was a dance of nobility and poise, a silent ode to ancient legacies that seemed to flow through her veins.

"Mr. Baxter," she said, her voice a harmonious mix of grace and command. "Your vision could redefine legacy and lineage."

"Lady Felicia," Baxter greeted, aware of her clout. "Our work aims to preserve what matters most."

"Your research might keep our estates and titles in our families for generations," she pondered. "Your work on the AGG1 gene could alter society itself."

"It has that potential," Baxter agreed, excitement visible. "Together, we can shape a future that honors tradition."

"Then I await our collaboration," Lady Felicia said, offering her hand.

"Indeed, my lady," Baxter replied, accepting her hand, his ambition clear. "Together, we'll make history."

Cigar smoke twined around the crystal chandelier, casting a soft glow on the mahogany walls. Baxter basked in the room's charged atmosphere, where hushed whispers and knowing looks spoke volumes. The admiration and awe in the air were inescapable, and he reveled in it.

Dr. Wei approached with an extended hand. "Mr. Baxter, your work is groundbreaking. I wish you every success."

"Thank you, Dr. Wei," Baxter responded, his eyes burning with ambition. "Together, we're at the dawn of a new era."

As the last guests departed, the room's grandeur settled. The air, once buzzing with excitement, now lay calm, a silent testament to the monumental events that had unfolded.

In the grand hall's dim embrace, Felix Ross's words wove through the silence, hinting at unseen machinations among the elite gathering.

"Dr. Kent's strides with the AGG1 gene are... noteworthy," Felix remarked, his smile more a strategic maneuver than a genuine expression.

A woman with a sharp gaze and a voice laced with hidden schemes responded thoughtfully, "Indeed. And with Baxter as the face of philanthropy, CytoLife's reach is our ideal camouflage. We're strategically positioned."

In the dim light, a silhouette paused, his drink catching a brief sparkle as he mused, signaling a moment brimming with tactical insight. "The longevity treatment opens new, untapped possibilities. Its potential is vast."

A complex play of emotions flickered in Felix's eyes. "Our current alignment is advantageous, but caution is paramount. Our true goals must remain as hidden as they are ambitious."

Their nods transcended mere agreement, silently sealing their complicity in a larger, hidden agenda.

Pressed against the cold wall outside the conference room, Lucas's heart pounded relentlessly. The overheard presentation haunted him, igniting doubts about CytoLife. His chest tightened as he reminded himself his duty was to protect, not to judge.

Rebecca emerged, radiating triumph. Her joy clashed with his inner turmoil, highlighting a rift he couldn't ignore.

"You seem... distant." Rebecca's voice, laced with concern, cut through his thoughts.

"It's been a monumental evening," Lucas replied, skirting his own unease. "A lot to take in, huh?"

"It is just the beginning," Rebecca mused, her eyes fixed on him. "We should celebrate, don't you think?"

"Sure," Lucas agreed, torn between his reservations and her enthusiasm.

"How about my place? We can talk more there," she suggested, a subtle intrigue in her eyes.

"Sounds good," Lucas managed, concealing his mixed emotions.

At her home, Lucas admired the surroundings, their familiarity comforting yet conflicting. "Your home reflects you well, Rebecca," he noted, his voice imbued with Southern charm.

"Thanks," she replied, her cheeks coloring. "It's a reflection of constant change."

Returning with wine, their fingers brushed as she handed him a glass, sparking a tangible connection.

"To a memorable night," she toasted.

"To new beginnings," he echoed.

As they conversed, the tension of the evening gave way to laughter and shared stories, their bond deepening beyond the professional. When their lips met, it was a tender exploration of unspoken feelings, yet Lucas couldn't shake the undercurrent of his unsettling discoveries.

Their kiss deepened, overpowering his urge for truth with a wave of desire. Time blurred as they shared past experiences and future dreams, their connection intensifying.

But as dawn crept in and Rebecca slept, Lucas lay awake. The joy of the night had faded, replaced by the heavy realization of how entangled he'd become in CytoLife's intricate web.

Lucas lay awake, the room's shadows weaving an ominous tapestry on the ceiling. His feelings for Rebecca, deep and undeniable, now warred with the stark reality of his position at CytoLife. In crossing the line between personal and professional, he feared he had compromised more than just his job.

Moving silently across the room, he was drawn to the faint light seeping from her home office. The door stood slightly open, an unspoken invitation—or a test. "Forgive me, Rebecca," he pleaded, stepping into the dimly lit room.

Her computer screen glowed in the dark, illuminating the meticulously organized desk. Hesitation gripped him. Duty and loyalty battled within as he sat down, poised between two worlds.

With each file he opened, the horrifying truth of CytoLife's plan unfolded. Detailed protocols on AGG1 gene manipulation, charts of genetic targets, drone schematics, even obscured references to human trials and behavioral control lay starkly before him. The clinical coldness of the data was a sharp contrast to the horror it represented.

He ensured the computer looked undisturbed, feeling

the heavy weight of his discovery. His affection for Rebecca, once a beacon of light, now felt tainted with betrayal. How could she, with whom he'd shared such a deep connection, be part of something so monstrous? His heart ached with conflict, torn between his feelings for her and the chilling reality of her involvement.

Resolved but heavy-hearted, Lucas knew he had to act. Duty called him to step forward into a path clouded with uncertainty and danger.

TWENTY THREE

Harper's fingers tapped nervously on her desk, echoing her inner unrest. Across from her, Deandra sat poised, her calm exterior masking her doubts.

"Ready for this?" Deandra's voice was even, her posture relaxed yet alert.

"As ready as I can be," Harper replied, her focus on the computer screen. "This is our shot to unveil CytoLife's true colors."

The computer chimed with the incoming call. Clicking accept, they were greeted by the image of Agent Morgan Butler, his seasoned appearance marked by graying hair and piercing eyes. Harper straightened, feeling the gravity of the moment.

"Good evening," Agent Butler began, his expression a mix of wariness and interest. "I've reviewed your information on CytoLife. Some of it raises eyebrows, but much seems speculative. How reliable is your source?"

Harper paused for second, briefly closing her eyes. "A whistleblower passed this to Adam, a trusted associate. He had a geneticist confirm the details. It's secondhand, but Adam's judgment is sound."

Butler's eyebrow arched skeptically. "So, this is all based on hearsay?"

Undaunted, Harper continued, "Our initial probe into a bribery case led us to PenCore, owned by a shell company linked to CytoLife."

Butler folded his arms, skeptical. "CytoLife and Thomas Baxter are renowned for their medical breakthroughs and humanitarian work. It's difficult to see them involved in anything illicit. And your evidence? A single photo with Baxter?"

Harper persisted. "In that photo, Baxter is with Dr. Rebecca Kent and a man named Felix at a charity event. It might look circumstantial, but there's a pattern here. We can't ignore potential wrongdoing just because of CytoLife's public image."

With a determined look in her eyes, Harper leaned in. "In my research, I came across videos of Dr. Rebecca Kent discussing CRISPR. These interviews highlight CytoLife's role in genetic modification." She shared her screen, playing a clip of Rebecca speaking fervently about CRISPR's potential.

Agent Butler watched briefly, then raised an eyebrow. "Harper, all this seems to reinforce CytoLife's reputation as a leader in genetics. On the surface, they're exemplary. We need to separate their legitimate advances from any alleged misconduct. Take their cell-healing agent, for example; it's revolutionized recovery, especially in sports. It's a testament to their innovation."

He leaned back, adding, "I've scrutinized CytoLife's records—FDA dealings, clinical trials, certifications. Even their HIPAA and FTC compliance. They're impeccable. Any wrongdoing, if it exists, is skillfully buried." Pausing, he underscored the challenge. "Finding any misconduct in CytoLife will be painstaking."

After a moment of silence, he cautioned, "CytoLife is seen as a beacon in medical science. We need solid proof to challenge that. Do you understand my reluctance?"

Harper's determination commanded attention. "Butler," she began, her Southern accent saturated with tenacity. "I've faced giants in boardrooms and politics, men who underestimated me. I didn't come to you lightly. Something about CytoLife is off. I can feel it."

Leaning forward, her gaze didn't waver. "I trust my instincts. They've never failed me. I respect your skepticism, but I need you to trust that I wouldn't be here if I didn't believe there's more to CytoLife."

Butler was visibly taken aback by Harper's intensity. Her unwavering conviction was compelling and difficult to ignore.

Butler took a deep breath, before he said in a serious tone, "If we misstep, the repercussions could be severe. CytoLife is influential and well-resourced. A false move or hint of suspicion could backfire significantly."

Her voice steady, but emphatic, Harper interjected, "I

understand the risks. Yet, if our suspicions are valid, it's imperative the truth comes to light regardless of CytoLife's stature."

Leaning closer to the camera, Butler's hands clasped on his desk. "The FDA's Office of Criminal Investigations starts with a thorough assessment of all relevant data. This initial phase determines if there's enough basis to warrant deeper investigation." His gaze was cautious as he eyed Harper. "Your unconventional sources make this phase even more critical."

He elaborated, "If we move forward, we'll assemble a specialized team: genetic engineering specialists, laboratory analysts, field agents for undercover work, and possibly surveillance. Tracking a corporation like CytoLife is a formidable task."

Harper and Deandra shared a glance, silently acknowledging the enormity of what lay ahead. Their background was in law; participating in covert operations was a new frontier.

Butler's sigh was audible. "I'll send you some background on previous FDA investigations for reference. If we're doing this, it needs to be meticulous and by the book. Be prepared for a lengthy, intricate process. If CytoLife is hiding something, they'll make uncovering it exceedingly difficult."

A profound silence settled over the room, reflecting the weight of their imposing task. The air was thick with a mix of determination, apprehension, and a united belief in their cause.

Butler's face filled the webcam, his intensity hitting

Harper like a challenge. "We need irrefutable evidence. The whistleblower, anyone who can substantiate these claims, must step forward."

Harper and Deandra exchanged a silent, unflinching glance. Their unspoken agreement was clear: they were ready to confront CytoLife's formidable presence.

"We're on it," Deandra stated emphatically. "We'll leverage every resource to rally support."

Butler nodded approvingly. "I'm with you. But remember, discretion is key."

Harper spoke with growing clarity. "Our strategy is to discreetly gather intel on CytoLife, staying under their radar. We have to be meticulous."

Butler's voice was stern. "I'll coordinate with other agencies to ensure we're synchronized and not overstepping boundaries."

Deandra's expression turned inquisitive. "Legally, Morgan, how do we proceed?"

After a moment, Butler responded, "We present our findings to a judge. Convincing evidence will get us the authorization we need."

"Let's start with the whistleblower," Harper suggested, tapping her desk thoughtfully. "Their testimony could be pivotal."

"Agreed," Deandra said. "We need corroboration. This requires a deep dive."

Butler concurred. "Document everything. Our case against CytoLife must be bulletproof."

The conversation intensified, with Harper feeling a familiar surge of nerves but maintaining her focus. Now was not the time for doubt.

Butler concluded, "We'll collaborate with the right experts and consolidate our efforts. This is a joint operation, and stealth is our ally."

Harper nodded, her mind racing with the enormity of their task. This was their only chance.

"We'll move covertly, keeping CytoLife in the shadows," Butler continued. "Our goal is to gather irrefutable evidence and strike decisively before they're aware."

"Understood," Deandra responded, her voice unwavering. "And once we have substantial evidence?"

"That's when we intensify our efforts," Butler answered. "We'll initiate raids and inspections to surprise CytoLife, amass more evidence, and methodically dismantle their operation."

Harper's grip tightened under the table, fueled by anger and determination to reveal CytoLife's transgressions. The thought of bringing their deeds to light strengthened her resolve.

"We'll drag them to court and expose them publicly," Butler declared. "We'll implement measures to prevent any recurrence from CytoLife and ensure justice and compensation for the victims."

Harper's voice carried a newfound conviction. "Let's get to work. It's an overwhelming task, but together, we'll bring CytoLife down."

Deandra's eyes shone with shared determination, reflecting Harper's intensity. Butler nodded, his demeanor all business.

The call ended, leaving Harper and Deandra in

contemplative silence. Harper's eyes narrowed, sensing Deandra's matching dedication. The time for action had arrived. They prepared mentally for the formidable challenges ahead, their shared mission binding them in solidarity.

Harper entered the coffee shop, a familiar hub of past strategies and discussions. She immediately spotted Ethan and Deandra at a corner table, their easy rapport noticeable in their laughter and conversation. As she approached, Deandra beckoned her over with a smile.

"Hey, stranger," Ethan greeted warmly, rising to offer Harper a seat.

Once settled, Harper said, "Our meeting with Agent Butler was enlightening. He's scrutinized CytoLife's records, and everything seems impeccable on the surface."

Deandra's expression was skeptical. "That doesn't automatically clear them."

Ethan, ever the pragmatist, added, "It does suggest they're meticulous. We need to be sharper in our approach."

Harper sighed, a hint of guilt in her voice. "Ethan, with me on leave and you still at the firm, I hate to impose this on you."

Ethan chuckled. "Actually, I spoke with Sam. He's officially putting me on this case with you, full salary and everything."

Harper's eyes lit up. "Really? That's incredible. Sam's getting a thank-you cake."

Ethan's laughter filled the air. "He'd love that, especially if it's chocolate."

Harper, puzzled, looked at Ethan. "Why would Sam do this, though? It's generous, but unexpected."

Ethan's smile widened. "Harper, you sometimes miss how people see you. Sam's seen that determination in your eyes before. He might not know the details, but he knows you're onto something big. He trusts your instincts."

Harper's laughter joined Ethan's. "That instinct has gotten us into trouble more than once."

Ethan nodded, his expression shifting to seriousness. "But it's also gotten us out of trouble. Remember, you're still part of the firm. Its resources are at your disposal." Leaning in, his tone became focused. "So, what's the plan, Tacks?"

Harper, feeling a mix of responsibility and gratitude, nodded resolutely. "Let's peel back the layers of CytoLife and uncover what they're hiding."

TWENTY FOUR

Adam Burke gazed out the window, his mind occupied with CytoLife and the implications of CRISPR. A blend of exhilaration and apprehension coursed through him as he contemplated the potential of exposing the hidden truth.

His gaze drifted to a framed photograph on his desk: a memorable moment captured with Ben, his mentor and boss, during a celebrated awards night. The image seemed to echo Ben's ethos of journalistic integrity, a silent reminder of the standards they strived to maintain.

Adam picked up his phone, realizing he needed Ben's seasoned perspective. "Ben, you know I'm all in for the truth, no matter what. But this investigation... I'm starting to question if the cost will be worth it."

He envisioned Ben in his familiar, chaotic office, the epitome of a seasoned journalist, amidst piles of papers and perpetually half-empty coffee cups. As Adam spoke, he could almost picture Ben's contemplative demeanor.

Ben's voice, laden with years of journalistic wisdom, came through the phone. "Adam, journalism is a field fraught with risks. Yet our core mission is unwavering: to uncover the truth. Tread carefully, but don't let apprehension deter you."

Adam absorbed Ben's advice, feeling steadied by the mentorship that had always guided him. "Thanks, Ben. That means a lot."

Amidst the organized clutter of his home office, with papers, notepads, and books scattered in every available space, Adam immersed himself in the complex realm of CRISPR technology and CytoLife's covert activities. He wrestled with alarming concepts of genetic manipulation, unsettling rumors of mortality, and obscured intentions.

Scouring through the documents, Adam muttered in frustration, "Where did I put that report?" Standing up, he stretched, trying to ease the tension that had built up from hours of searching. Amid this labyrinth of information, he knew a crucial piece of the puzzle was hiding. Yet, finding it in such chaos was a demanding task, even more so with his inclination towards a somewhat disordered workspace.

Reorganizing his research with renewed focus, Adam remembered Ben's advice: follow every plausible lead, but proceed with care. He methodically sorted through the pile, driven by the seriousness of his quest and the potential risks involved.

A specific note caught his eye, reading, *DARPA—Anti-CRISPR Tech. Defense against gene editing? Breakthrough or peril?*

Memories of a past conference where this topic was discussed surfaced, its significance now striking him with full force.

Pondering, Adam glanced at the clock. Time was pressing on, but the urgency of the matter allowed no delays. He needed Meera, his geneticist friend from college, to help unravel this mystery.

Dialing Meera's number with a mix of apprehension and hope, Adam waited. Soon, her voice, always a blend of practicality and insight, answered. "Adam? What's up?"

"Meera, I've come across something potentially big," he started nervously. "It's about Anti-CRISPR tech from an old DARPA conference. I need your insight to decipher this."

There was a brief pause before she responded, "Okay, send me the details. Let's set up a Zoom call to go over it."

Soon after exchanging emails, Adam and Meera's faces filled their respective screens. Adam's expression was a mix of keen interest and uncertainty, while Meera exuded her usual composed and analytical demeanor.

Meera reviewed the notes briefly before sharing her insights. "Adam, CRISPR's precision in gene editing is groundbreaking. But a tool this potent necessitates safeguards. That's where Anti-CRISPR could play a role."

Adam, keen to understand, interjected, "So, it acts as a safety mechanism for CRISPR?"

Meera, methodical in her explanation, drew a basic diagram. "Imagine CRISPR as scissors cutting through a DNA strand. Anti-CRISPR could be akin to a safety cover for those scissors." She looked at Adam, gauging his grasp of the concept. "It's theorized to be a natural countermeasure, though there's much we still don't know."

Adam scribbled notes, mulling over her explanation. "Could it then serve as a defense against inappropriate gene alterations?"

Meera paused, clearly choosing her words carefully. "Potentially, yes. But we operate on hard evidence in science. We need more research to make definitive claims."

As the discussion about Anti-CRISPR's potential unfolded, Adam felt an increasing sense of urgency. Concerns about CytoLife's involvement and the conversation's security surfaced. "Meera, is our chat secure?"

Meera's reply was reassuring and confident. "Our communication is encrypted, Adam. I trust in our security measures."

Adam paused, taking in her assurance, then nodded. "Okay, let's proceed."

As Meera elucidated the complexities of Anti-CRISPR, Adam traced the detailed diagram on his screen. "So, if DARPA's exploring this, they're likely viewing it as a defense against harmful gene edits, correct?"

"Exactly," Meera concurred. "Consider a situation where a CRISPR-altered organism is weaponized. Anti-CRISPR could act as a neutralizer, countering such threats."

Adam felt a shiver at the thought—battling invisible, genetic dangers seemed almost otherworldly.

Meera, however, tempered her explanation with a note of caution. "But we must be mindful that any technology can be misappropriated. Anti-CRISPR isn't solely defensive; it could also hinder beneficial genetic modifications. It's about finding equilibrium."

Sipping her coffee, she added, "Let's get into the practicalities of using Anti-CRISPR for defense."

She held up a finger. "First, if a malicious CRISPR entity is released, we could deploy Anti-CRISPR genes in a compatible host to counter it."

"Like a counter-agent?" Adam interjected.

"Precisely," Meera smiled. "Second, for specific threats, such as a modified virus in humans, targeted Anti-CRISPR therapy could be developed, introducing inhibitors directly into the body."

Her expression grew serious. "However, implementing Anti-CRISPR on a large scale presents challenges: precision, speed, and potential side effects must all be carefully considered."

"So, it's a promising avenue, but fraught with complexities," Adam summarized.

Meera nodded in agreement. "Exactly. With thorough research, Anti-CRISPR could become a crucial safeguard against CRISPR misuse."

Adam leaned forward, curious. "Have there been practical applications of this, Meera?"

Meera's gaze became intense. "Controlled lab experiments, yes, as discussed in scientific papers and at conferences." She hesitated. "But extrapolating that to real-world scenarios is another story."

She continued thoughtfully, "DARPA often operates in the shadows. Their advancements might be more developed than publicly known. We only catch glimpses; the full picture remains behind closed doors."

Adam, sensing the layers of secrecy, pressed further. "Have actual trials been attempted?"

Meera exhaled slowly. "Trials have occurred, but the specifics are limited. Some showed promise, while others encountered unforeseen complications."

Adam's voice carried a hint of urgency. "Can you elaborate on those challenges?"

Meera's expression clouded with concern. "There were whispers about unexpected genetic repercussions in the initial trials. It's a stark reminder that technologies like these need to be approached with extreme care. Their potential is vast, but so are their risks."

Adam tapped his fingers, a visible sign of his anxiety. Meera, perceptive to his tension, leaned closer, her eyes intent. "Adam, remember, DARPA is always pushing boundaries, often hidden from public view. Unearthing specific details about their Anti-CRISPR developments is no small feat."

Adam's features tightened with frustration. "So, we're navigating in the dark?"

"Not entirely in the dark. While DARPA's work is secretive, it's not necessarily nefarious. We need to be cautious in distinguishing between hypothesis and hyperbole."

"This is overwhelming, Meera."

Her gaze met his, warm and understanding. "Take a step back when needed, Adam," Meera advised, her tone reassuring. "In your work, it's easy to get caught up in theories and speculation. Remember, clarity comes when you're levelheaded."

Adam managed a weary smile, appreciative of her support. "Thanks, Meera. Sometimes it's tough to see the forest for the trees," he acknowledged. "And your willingness to assist, should I need it, means a lot."

"Always here to help," Meera assured with a supportive nod. "Just don't forget to surface for air occasionally. Don't let the what-ifs consume you. I'm here to offer support when you need it."

As Lucas drove onto CytoLife's premises, his mind was a whirlpool of disturbing revelations and his deepening connection with Rebecca. The clash between his burgeoning feelings and the duty to act on his discoveries weighed heavily on him.

He parked his armored Range Rover and saw Rebecca approaching, her hair catching the soft sunlight. Despite their growing intimacy, her demeanor remained impeccably professional as she joined him in the car.

"You're quiet today, Lucas," she observed, adjusting her lab coat.

"Just thinking," he replied, his tone guarded, still wrestling with his internal turmoil. The drive was wordless, each lost in thought.

Approaching the lab, a decision crystallized in Lucas's mind. He had to reveal CytoLife's secrets, no matter the personal cost.

Rebecca broke the silence as they parked. "I'll be in the

lab all day. Just pick me up when I'm finished. I'll text you," she said, preparing to leave the car.

"Sure thing," Lucas responded, feeling a sense of relief at the prospect of some time alone to contemplate his next steps.

They walked towards CytoLife, their routine familiar yet strained under the current circumstances. Lucas, courteous as ever, assisted Rebecca with her belongings, his actions belying the internal conflict he faced.

As they neared the entrance, Lucas subtly brushed against her, discreetly pocketing her access badge. Their fleeting touch spoke volumes, a silent communication between them.

"Stay safe," she murmured, their shoulders brushing briefly.

"You too," he replied, holding the door open for her as she stepped into the lab, unaware of the badge now in his possession.

Leaning against a wall, Lucas allowed himself a moment of solitude. The turmoil of emotions—guilt, fear, and determination—surged within him. The thought of betraying Rebecca, whom he was growing closer to, pained him. Yet the haunting details of the presentation and the incriminating information he had found compelled him to act.

Lucas spent most of the day secluded in the security booth, painstakingly trying to connect the dots. Craving fresh air and a clearer mind, he stepped out for a walk. Since the unsettling presentation, he had been toying with a bold idea. He strode through the corridors, his steps deliberate yet casual, heading towards an area rarely frequented.

Approaching a door he had once seen Felix exit, Lucas felt a surge of apprehension mixed with purpose. He hesitated, grappling with the moral implications of his actions. Was he about to cross a line?

Taking a deep breath, Lucas used Rebecca's badge on the security panel. A discreet chime signaled success, and the door unlocked with a soft click. Emboldened, he pushed the door open, revealing a dimly lit passageway. He moved slowly, peering into rooms, until he found a storage area.

The room felt starkly different from the rest of the facility, filled with towering shelves burdened with documents and boxes. The enormity of information was daunting. Lucas wondered if the key to CytoLife's secrets lay within this room.

A musty smell hung in the air, hinting at the room's infrequent use. This sparked a flicker of hope in Lucas; perhaps this was where CytoLife's hidden agendas lay buried. He meticulously sifted through the materials, searching for any mention of CRISPR or the AGG1 initiative.

File after file, his hope waned—each document seemed irrelevant or outdated. The constant threat of being discovered loomed over him, driving him to work swiftly yet cautiously.

"Come on," he begged in frustration. But then, amidst a pile of papers, he uncovered a stash of hard drives, each labeled with a date. Hidden deliberately, they could be exactly what he was looking for.

Adrenaline surged through Lucas as he carefully packed the drives into a discarded bag, aware that time was not on his side. Just as he zipped up the bag, the sound of footsteps approached, growing louder by the second.

Heart pounding, Lucas ducked behind a shelf, just a moment before the door creaked open. The sound of footsteps filled the room, and Lucas held his breath, hoping against hope to remain unseen.

Lucas discreetly watched through a narrow opening as a shadowy figure moved through the storage room. The person's face was shrouded in dimness, making identification impossible. Lucas tried to discern who it might be, but all he could see was an indistinct silhouette.

He stayed motionless, silently hoping to go undetected by the figure. Tension filled the air until the intruder finally departed, leaving behind an unsettling silence. Only when Lucas was sure he was alone did he let out a controlled breath, his heart still pounding.

He thought to himself, "I can't risk being caught again." The stakes were high. Accessing the data on the hard drives without alerting anyone at CytoLife would be a treacherous task. A single misstep here could have dire repercussions.

Lucas stepped out of the storage room, his eyes quickly scanning for anything that might help him access the drives discreetly. He spotted a workstation nearby, cluttered with various cables and adapters—just what he needed. Swiftly, he collected them and tucked them into his bag alongside the hard drives.

With each step, Lucas felt the weight of the crucial task ahead. The drives in his possession held the potential to reveal CytoLife's unethical activities, a realization that fueled his courage. Despite the risks, this sense of purpose spurred him on, ready to confront whatever challenges lay ahead.

Exiting CytoLife's facility, the night air was a refreshing change from the lab's stifling environment. The contents of his bag, much like the Rosetta Stone had been to ancient texts, held the promise to decode and lay bare CytoLife's most closely guarded secrets.

The buzz of his phone abruptly interrupted Lucas's train of thought. It was a text from Rebecca.

Finishing up. Ready to pick me up?

He muttered a curse. Time was slipping away.

Be there shortly.

Setting off towards his SUV, he tossed the bag onto the passenger seat. He drove quickly to his cottage, each moment critical. Once inside, he hastily hid the bag in a makeshift compartment at the bottom of his closet, vowing to examine its contents later.

With the evidence secured, Lucas rushed back to CytoLife. Rebecca climbed into the car, her smile betraying no hint of the drama that had just unfolded.

"Hey," she greeted him with a quick kiss. "You seem a bit rushed. Everything okay?"

"Yeah, just some home stuff," Lucas lied, masking his anxiety with a feigned smile. "Nothing major."

Rebecca eyed him curiously. "I was thinking maybe we could hang out tonight, like last time?"

Lucas's heart ached at the suggestion. His desire to be with her clashed with the burden of the secrets he'd just unearthed. "Actually, I've got a task from Felix tonight," he said, trying to sound nonchalant.

Disappointment flickered across Rebecca's face, but she didn't press him. Instead, she gave his hand a reassuring squeeze. "I understand. Work first," she said softly. "But if things are getting too complicated between us, we can keep it professional at the office."

"Thanks, Rebecca," Lucas responded, touched by her understanding. "It's not you. It's just... complex."

She chuckled softly. "When is it not? Just talk to me when you're ready, okay?"

"Will do," he promised, reluctantly releasing her hand. Watching her exit the SUV, Lucas felt a surge of conflict between his deepening feelings for her and the damning secrets he held.

As he started to pull away, he muttered to himself, "This is going to be a rough ride."

Rebecca suddenly turned back towards the SUV, catching Lucas off-guard. His heart pounded as he quickly put down the window. In a hurried move, he had slipped her badge into the seat, intending it to appear accidentally dropped. A swift glance confirmed it was too conspicuous. As Rebecca approached, Lucas grabbed the badge, pretending to have just found it. "Looks like you dropped this," he said, offering it to her.

But Rebecca's focus was elsewhere. Her eyes, intense and searching, met his. "Lucas," she began softly, her voice filled with emotion, "you need to know how much you mean to me."

Lucas was momentarily lost for words. "Rebecca, I—"

His response was cut short by her impassioned kiss, their emotions surging like a storm.

In their embrace, a shift occurred. Rebecca's usual caution melted away, revealing vulnerability and openness. For a moment, the weight of their secrets faded, replaced by the thrill of genuine connection.

Wordlessly, they made their way into her house, ascending the stairs to her bedroom in silent understanding.

Later, as they lay together, Lucas held Rebecca close, savoring the intimacy. The thought of leaving her in such a candid state pained him, yet the urgency of the hard drives beckoned.

"Rebecca," he said gently, "I have to go. Felix's assignment can't wait."

She nodded. Her voice was soft but resigned. "I get it. But please, let's talk about us soon."

"I promise," Lucas assured, his gaze meeting hers. With a final, lingering kiss, he reluctantly extricated himself from her embrace.

Stepping out into the night, Lucas's mind was a whirlwind of conflicting emotions. The drive back to his cottage felt like a journey through a dream, torn between the potential revelations on the hard drives and his deepening feelings for Rebecca.

Upon returning to his cottage, Lucas wasted no time. He hastily emptied the bag, sorting through the cables and adapters. Fingers hurried and slightly agitated, he attempted to connect the first hard drive to his air-gapped laptop, but the screen remained stubbornly blank, heightening his frustration.

"Come on," he urged under his breath, swapping out another cable. Finally, the computer whirred to life, revealing the contents of the drive as if teasing him for his impatience. A sense of relief and renewed focus washed over him.

The computer screen was soon cluttered with files, each one more unsettling than the last. Harrowing images of prisoners, strapped to gurneys with complex machinery encircling their heads, filled the display. Accompanying reports detailed invasive brain experiments, their subjects ranging from catatonic to violently agitated. One video clip was particularly disturbing: a test subject, in a frenzy, assaulted a staff member, necessitating multiple people to subdue him. The report ended grimly, noting the subject's termination for facility safety.

"God," Lucas murmured, his hands hovering over the keyboard, shaking. "What have they been doing?"

He scrolled through more files, discovering documents on the disposal of failed subjects. References to an incinerator appeared repeatedly, a macabre testament to the fate of these unfortunate individuals.

"Jesus Christ," he declared, rubbing his face in disbelief. "This can't be real."

As he dug deeper, a series of emails between Rebecca and Baxter surfaced. Their exchanges were clinically focused on manipulating aggression through gene therapy, discussing risks and outcomes. Amid these dispassionate emails, one detail stood out starkly—a casual reference by Rebecca to Baxter as "Papa."

"Son of a bitch..." Lucas gasped, a sense of betrayal washing over him.

He sank back in his chair, overwhelmed by the enormity of his discovery. Only hours before, he had been enveloped in Rebecca's warmth, lost in her apparent vulnerability. Now, that intimacy was tainted by the stark reality of her involvement in these heinous experiments.

"Dammit, Rebecca," he choked out, his voice laden with a mix of sorrow and disillusionment. "Why?"

Lucas, torn between anger and disbelief, contemplated a direct confrontation with Rebecca. He wanted answers, wanted to salvage any fragment of trust that might still linger. But a voice of caution echoed within him, urging a more prudent approach. He needed a comprehensive understanding before acting.

"Alright," he muttered to himself, his determination hardening. "I need to play this smart."

He spent the entire night combing through the accessible files on the hard drive, seeking any information that could shed light on the project's full extent and how to expose it. As dawn's first light crept through his window, Lucas knew he couldn't keep this to himself any longer.

"Rebecca," he sighed, staring at her photo on his phone. "There has to be more to this than what I'm seeing."

The room, lit only by the glow of the computer screen, felt more confining than ever. The weight of his discoveries made each breath feel heavier, and the incriminating emails on the screen were a constant reminder of the grim reality he faced.

"Come on," he urged himself, mustering the courage to make the call. Taking a deep breath, Lucas dialed the number, his heart pounding. He paced the room, bracing for the conversation ahead, contemplating the possible outcomes and their implications.

The phone rang persistently, unanswered, increasing Lucas's anxiety. Finally, it connected, but the voice that greeted him wasn't Rebecca's.

"Lucas?" came the voice, unexpectedly familiar.

"Mom," he responded, his voice riddled with hesitation. "We need to talk."

TWENTY FIVE

Harper's voice, mixed with a hint of surprise, came through the phone. "Lucas?"

"We need to talk," Lucas started. "Things at work are getting... complex. I feel a bit lost."

Harper's concern was noticeable, yet cautious, as if navigating around old scars. "What's happening, Lucas?"

He hesitated, regretting his impulsive call. "It's complicated. Maybe I shouldn't have called."

There was a brief silence; then Harper's voice softened. "Lucas, regardless of our past, I've always wanted the best for you. If you're struggling with something, I'm here."

Lucas bit his lip, appreciating their slowly mending relationship. "Thanks, Mom. It's just some tough decisions at work."

Harper paused thoughtfully. "Life is about tough choices. Remember, integrity and loyalty are important, but so is your gut feeling. And no NDA overrides your conscience."

Lucas felt the sincerity in her words, the years of strained relations, and the effort she was making now. "Thanks, Mom. That means a lot."

Harper's voice warmed with a mixture of nostalgia and present care. "No matter what, Lucas, I'm proud of who you are. We may have our differences, but you're my son."

A lump formed in Lucas's throat. "Thank you," he replied.

Ending the call, Lucas felt a tentative sense of connection, a bridge slowly reforming between them.

The next morning, filled with a mix of determination and apprehension, Lucas grabbed his jacket. "Felix," he said, pausing briefly. "I need a few personal days. I'll be back later this week."

Felix looked up, mildly surprised. "Everything alright?"

Lucas nodded, maintaining a semblance of normalcy. "Yeah, just need to sort some things out." He left quickly, avoiding further questions.

Outside, Lucas texted Rebecca. *Taking a few days for family stuff. Will explain later. Take care.*

As he pocketed his phone, guilt surged through him. Hiding the truth from Rebecca, after their closeness, was painful. But the revelations he'd uncovered demanded discretion.

Walking towards the high-speed rail station, Lucas felt the weight of his decision. He tried to steady his racing heart. Each step was a step into uncertainty, yet driven by a firm conviction that he was on the right path, despite the personal costs involved.

Adam stood against a pillar at the rural Georgia high-speed rail station, watching passengers disembark. His eyes sharpened as he noticed a man moving through the crowd, his stride purposeful yet discreet, his face familiar but not immediately recognizable.

As the man neared, Adam extended his hand. "You must be...?"

"John," the man replied, his voice measured, masking his true identity.

"John, it is," Adam acknowledged with a slight nod. "Let's talk somewhere more secluded."

Their handshake was brief, yet conveyed a mutual understanding of the gravity of their meeting. John's calm demeanor carried an underlying tension.

Walking together, Adam pondered the circumstances that had driven "John" to contact him, curious about the extent of CytoLife's wrongdoings.

"The voice distorter on the call was quite the touch," Adam said, trying to lighten the mood.

John offered a brief chuckle. "Needed to be careful."

"Now that we're here," Adam pressed, "why all the secrecy?"

John paused, choosing his words. "Your articles, especially on CRISPR, caught my attention. You're onto something, but it's deeper than you think."

Adam leaned in, sensing the seriousness. "Where do you fit in with CytoLife?"

John hesitated. "I'm more involved with them than I'd prefer. What's going on there... it's complex, not just black and white. And there are people I care about caught in the middle."

Adam's reporter instincts were piqued. "Someone you're connected to at CytoLife?"

John looked down briefly, revealing his inner conflict. "Yes," he admitted. "But she may be as unwitting a participant as any."

The scope of the story dawned on Adam, along with the risks involved. "We need to bring CytoLife's actions to light, John. But we'll do it carefully, ensuring innocents aren't caught in the crossfire."

A faint look of relief appeared in John's eyes. "That's all I ask."

Adam studied "John" closely, feeling the magnitude of their conversation. "I'm working with a sharp attorney," he began, his fingers idly circling his coffee cup. "They call her Brass. She's insightful and thoroughly invested in uncovering CytoLife's secrets."

John's reaction was telling; a brief hitch in his breath and a flicker of recognition in his eyes betrayed his composure. "Brass?" he repeated, his attempt at nonchalance betrayed by a slight strain in his voice.

Adam, oblivious to the potential connection, continued, "She's driven, determined to expose the truth. It's almost personal for her."

John managed a measured response. "She sounds like someone worth meeting."

Adam took John's reaction as a reflection of the topic's intensity. "Together, you two could be a formidable force against CytoLife."

Later that evening, Adam paced his hotel room, replaying the conversation. There was an unspoken layer to John's responses, a hidden depth he couldn't quite grasp. He picked up his phone and dialed Harper.

Harper answered quickly, her tone crisp. "What's going on, Adam?"

"I met another whistleblower," Adam began. "He's different. He's seen presentations, found hard drives—significant stuff."

Harper was immediately attentive. "Any name? How's he tied to all this?"

Adam hesitated. "He goes by John. But there's more to him; his knowledge is too precise. He might be on the inside."

There was a pause on Harper's end. "Gather all you can. Let's meet. And Adam, be cautious."

Adam nodded to himself. "He's ready to talk. We'll coordinate a meeting."

The next morning, Adam sent a secure message to John. *Need to meet again. Someone else will join—another key player. Tomorrow at noon?*

Same place? John replied.

Yep. Adam confirmed, already planning the rendezvous with Harper, keeping her identity a surprise for now, an extra card up his sleeve.

The early morning light cast a warm glow over the quaint café just outside Macon, Georgia. As Lucas hesitated at the entrance, his eyes were drawn to Harper's familiar silhouette inside. A whirlwind of memories, some filled with warmth, others with pain, swirled within him.

The café felt suddenly constricted, and for a moment, Lucas considered turning back. But Harper's intense expression, a complex tapestry of astonishment, concern, and unspoken questions, held him in place. Compelled by their shared past, Lucas moved towards the table, sitting across from her with a heavy heart.

"You," he began, his voice laced with accusation, directed at Adam, "didn't say she'd be here."

Harper's voice carried a blend of warmth and trepidation as she addressed him. "Hello, Lucas, my son."

Adam's expression shifted from confusion to realization as the significance of Harper's words sank in. The connection between Harper and Lucas suddenly became clear.

The air thickened with tension as Adam faltered, the weight of this revelation undeniable. "Harper, Lucas, I had no clue about your connection. I swear."

Harper's eyes welled up with tears, each a reflection of the emotions she had long suppressed. "Lucas, why didn't you tell me?" Her voice cracked, laden with hurt and hidden truths.

Lucas struggled with the weight of their shared history and his recent decisions. "I thought I could handle it alone. I thought it was better, given everything between us."

A moment of vulnerability passed between mother and son, Harper's eyes softening. "I sensed something was off in our last conversation," she murmured regretfully. Tentatively, she reached across the table, her fingers lightly touching Lucas's hand.

Adam interjected, seeking to explain. "Lucas reached out after reading my articles. I had no idea he was your son, Harper. This whole investigation has been a maze of surprises."

In the charged silence that followed, Harper and Lucas remained lost in their thoughts, each grappling with the magnitude of the situation and the emotions it unearthed.

Ethan, until now silent, shifted in his chair, his steady gaze meeting Lucas's. Their past was a patchwork of brief interactions and distant acknowledgments, mostly in Harper's presence. Yet beyond the formalities, there was an unspoken camaraderie, a mutual understanding that came from shared experiences and the weight of their military badges.

Ethan, his hand extended, revealed lines that spoke of years and experiences. "Lucas, weren't you the young soldier from Memphis who made headlines a few years back?"

Lucas, slightly taken aback by the recognition, accepted the handshake, noting the seasoned strength in Ethan's grip. "That was me, sir. I enlisted shortly after your tenure. I've heard quite a bit about your service."

A blend of nostalgia and pride briefly crossed Ethan's face. "The days in uniform, eh? I may have laid some groundwork, but it was your generation that really made its mark. I remember hearing about the bravery of soldiers in places like Kandahar."

With a respectful nod, Lucas acknowledged the compliment. "Your legacy was well known among us, Ethan. It was an honor to follow a path you helped carve."

Their exchange was brief but significant, a mutual understanding shared in silence, forged in the crucible of military service.

Adam and Harper watched this interaction, sensing a temporary easing of the room's tension. In the midst of uncertainty, there was a comforting familiarity in common experiences.

Harper's eyes were gentle yet firm as she addressed Lucas. "This business with CytoLife, Lucas... do you comprehend the full scale of their operations?"

Lucas's response was measured, heavy with implication. "I've started to piece it together. It's more intricate than I initially thought."

The momentary silence that followed was charged, underscoring the complexity of their intertwined histories and the challenging path ahead.

Finally, Harper spoke, her voice filled with purpose. "Then let's uncomplicate it. Together."

Lucas raised his eyes to meet Harper's. In that moment, they transcended their roles as mother and son, uniting as allies in a cause far greater than their personal history.

The tension in the room was almost tangible, an amalgam of unresolved feelings, lingering distrust, and piecemeal information. But the time had come to connect the dots.

Lucas's voice wavered slightly, betraying a hint of trepidation. "I was brought in by Felix Ross for Rebecca Kent's security. Initially, I saw it as just another assignment." He paused, collecting his thoughts. "However, the more I got to know Rebecca and immersed myself in CytoLife's world, things started to unravel."

Harper's expression remained stoic, but her eyes revealed her growing concern. "Continue," she urged.

Meeting her gaze, Lucas's tenacity was beyond question. "I've interacted with Thomas Baxter. Not long ago, I uncovered that he's actually Rebecca's father. They've been keeping it under wraps."

Harper visibly tensed, surprise etching her features. "That's unexpected," she said, her composure briefly slipping. "Why would they conceal such a connection?"

Ethan, analytical as ever, added thoughtfully, "Secrets like that, especially within a family, often hint at deeper, more complex schemes. It suggests they're involved in something they don't want exposed."

Adam leaned forward, his reporter's instincts fully engaged. "Secrets about Baxter and Rebecca, and now this gene project? Why keep all this under wraps?"

Lucas shook his head, his expression one of confusion and concern. "I don't have all the answers. But what I overheard by accident about the AGGI gene, nanoparticles, and some drone delivery system... it was staggering."

Harper's expression morphed into a blend of anger and disbelief. "Wait, Lucas," she interjected sharply. "Baxter's hidden relationship with Rebecca, a covert genetic program, drones... You're saying you just stumbled onto all this?"

She exhaled, attempting to compose herself. "We need the full story, Lucas. Start from the top and don't leave anything out."

Lucas sat straighter, visibly shifting into a mode familiar to Harper—the disciplined soldier ready to report. "I happened to be near Rebecca and Baxter during one of their high-level discussions," he began, recalling the events. "Due to a technical glitch, I could overhear their presentation through their mics, and a partially open door gave me a line of sight. What I saw and heard... that's why I reached out."

He paused, gathering his thoughts. "They talked about AGGI genes, linked to aggressive behaviors. They've developed a method to influence these genes. But it's not about suppression or control; they're framing it as enhancing human potential."

Adam absorbed the details, his journalistic mind racing, while Ethan's expression turned contemplative, deep in thought.

Lucas continued, his voice firm but troubled. "Baxter was almost evangelical about their work. He described their approach as a dimmer switch for the human psyche, claiming they could adjust these genes to curb or eliminate negative behaviors. He portrayed it as a beacon of hope for those struggling with their own volatile nature."

Meeting Harper's intense gaze, Lucas added, "Throughout the presentation, Baxter kept emphasizing 'the betterment of humanity.' He spoke about refining human traits, unlocking the best versions of ourselves."

A heavy silence enveloped the group as they absorbed the implications of what Lucas described. Ethan was the first to voice his concern. "They're essentially playing God, deciding who should be aggressive and who shouldn't?"

Adam, incredulous, interjected, "This sounds like it's straight out of a dystopian novel. Are we saying it's actually happening?"

Harper's expression hardened as she turned to Lucas. "This dimmer switch... who gets to control it? How do they determine the limits?"

Lucas's expression grew somber, his eyes locked with Harper's. "There's more," he said gravely. "During the presentation, there was an undercurrent of... anticipation. The audience wasn't just surprised; they seemed prepared for what Baxter was unveiling."

He leaned in, his voice dropping. "I sensed readiness among them, as if they were expecting a significant breakthrough and were willing to accept it without questioning the consequences."

Lucas hesitated. The solemnity of his observations weighed on him. "The casualness with which they discussed altering human nature... it was chilling. There was no moral deliberation, just a cold acceptance."

Ethan leaned back, his expression thoughtful and concerned. "The potential ramifications of such technology... If it falls into the wrong hands, or if it's already in them, we're looking at a situation with unprecedented implications."

Harper's fingers tapped rhythmically on the table, a

visible sign of her legal mind at work. "We need to dig deeper into these elites and their involvement." Then, clenching her fist, anger knotted her voice. "Baxter, the supposed humanitarian, isn't just involved—he's orchestrating the entire operation."

Ethan added, "I've been examining BluePulse Technologies' drone equipment. It's state-of-the-art, far beyond simple surveillance capabilities. What exactly it's designed for, though, remains unclear."

Lucas nodded at Ethan, conveying the gravity of his findings. "Baxter spoke of using drones in the presentation. And later," he paused, choosing his words carefully, "I stumbled upon classified documents. They're planning to use drones to disperse nanoparticles, targeting the AGGI genes. People will inhale them without any clue."

Ethan's expression turned steely. "That's a level of behavioral manipulation beyond comprehension."

Adam, caught in the moment, added his journalistic perspective. "A covert operation to alter the very core of humanity."

Harper shook her head, her voice quivering with a mix of fear and anger. "They're playing with the fundamental aspects of human identity."

Ethan's brow furrowed as he contemplated the potential complications. "What about individuals without the AGG1 gene, or those who might react unpredictably to these nanoparticles?"

Lucas massaged the bridge of his nose, recalling the details of the presentation. "They explained that AGG1 gene expression varies among individuals, like it's on a spectrum. It was quite technical. The gist was that these nanoparticles are designed to be activated only in the presence of the AGG1 gene. If the gene expression isn't at certain levels, the nanoparticles are supposed to remain inert. During the presentation, they emphasized their commitment to safety and ethics, claiming the technology would be used responsibly."

Harper clenched her pen, her expression a mix of skepticism and concern. "It sounds insidious," she said, locking eyes with Lucas. "Despite their claims of safety and ethical use, this feels like an alarming misuse of power veiled as a breakthrough."

"That's not the full extent of it," Lucas added, regaining the group's focus with a grave tone. "Baxter unveiled another component in the presentation—a so-called longevity therapy that borders on the dystopian."

Ethan's interest piqued, he asked, "Longevity therapy?"

Lucas confirmed with a nod. "Yes, they're claiming the potential to significantly extend human lifespans, perhaps beyond 160 years, using a blend of CRISPR and advanced stem cell treatments."

Harper's eyes widened, skepticism undeniable. "I suppose this so-called miracle therapy isn't intended for the general public?"

Lucas's expression hardened. "That's correct. Baxter implied that the initial beneficiaries would be an exclusive group, those *elites* present at the meeting. The therapy will be offered selectively, only to individuals they consider worthy of such longevity."

Ethan whistled softly. "They're not just manipulating behaviors; they're now promising prolonged life. It's like they're assuming the role of gods."

Adam shook his head in disbelief. "Creating a privileged class with extended lifespans... This could upend societal structures as we know them."

Harper, her expression shifting to one of intense scrutiny, pressed Lucas for more details. "Even with such technology, bypassing government regulations, the FDA, and the ethical barriers... how are they planning to do it?"

Lucas, appearing both weary and burdened, replied, "Baxter touched on that during the presentation. He mentioned it almost casually, as though regulatory hurdles were a minor inconvenience. He claimed they have the necessary influence in key places to ensure their project moves forward without obstructions."

Ethan clenched his jaw. "That level of confidence implies deep connections, possibly even moles within important institutions."

Adam contributed, his tone reflective of his reporting instincts. "Or maybe they have leverage over influential figures."

Lucas elaborated. "Baxter's every word was laced with absolute certainty. It's clear they've been meticulously orchestrating this for quite some time."

Harper leaned back, wearily massaging her temples. "It's staggering to think this all started from a simple prison kickback scheme. To go from exploiting inmate allocations for bribes to... orchestrating a plan of this magnitude. It's almost inconceivable."

Lucas's voice was laden with a mix of grief and disbelief. "I wish I could erase what I've seen, Mom. After overhearing that presentation, I couldn't just sit back. I did some digging and found hard drives and videos that I'm certain show prisoners. They were in labs, subjected to what looked like open brain surgeries. The aftermath... some went completely catatonic, while others turned unpredictably aggressive and violent."

The color drained from his face, his usual composure giving way to visible distress. "I've seen combat, faced direct threats, and witnessed friends in peril. But this... this was an entirely different kind of horror. The sheer inhumanity of it. They treated these people like lab rats, disposable after experimentation."

Harper's expression froze as she absorbed his words, her eyes becoming a turbulent storm of anger and pain. In the silence that followed, her gaze intensely focused on Lucas, conveying more than words ever could.

Adam leaned in, his expression grave. "This corroborates what Cam uncovered about unexplained casualties."

Ethan, offering a supportive hand on Lucas's shoulder, straightened up with a resolute look. "Lucas, we need to document everything you discovered. Walk us through the details of what you found and how you came across it."

Lucas steeled himself for the recount. "I couldn't just ignore what I overheard in that presentation. I found an opening one evening and took the chance to investigate.

I managed to access an unattended computer, and later, I discovered a storage room. There, hidden away, was a collection of hard drives. They were clearly meant to be concealed. Not all of them worked, but the ones I could access were filled with incriminating evidence and countless dark secrets."

Ethan's seasoned intelligence background was inarguable as he considered Lucas's account. "Operational security is critical, Lucas. How sure are you that you weren't detected, or that you didn't leave a trail?"

Meeting Ethan's gaze, Lucas's response was firm and assured. "I neutralized the security cameras in that area temporarily. I also made sure to erase any digital footprints from my access. The hard drives? They're not at my cottage anymore. I've hidden them in a secure location. I've been diligent in checking my company vehicle and surroundings for surveillance. I know the signs, and I've made sure to cover my tracks thoroughly."

Ethan acknowledged Lucas's precautions with a nod. "That's meticulous work. We need to maintain that level of caution."

Ethan leaned forward, his hands clasped tightly, a look of concern crossed on his face. "With assistance from an expert in cyber-intelligence known as Neon, I've been navigating the dark web's depths. The findings are more disturbing than I anticipated."

Adam and Harper exchanged a glance, bracing themselves for what was to come.

"There's a sprawling black market in biotech," Ethan

started, his voice dripping with disgust. "Genetic materials are being traded like commodies, unauthorized and unregulated." He paused, his face contorted with revulsion. "But it goes beyond mere trading. There are reports of amateur gene editing leading to catastrophic outcomes. Some pursue self-improvement, but many end up suffering dire effects out of naïve curiosity."

The gravity of Ethan's words visibly unsettled Lucas.

Harper's brow furrowed. "Individuals experimenting with gene editing on their own? The risks are unimaginable."

Ethan nodded gravely. "It's a dangerous game. And it's not just hobbyists. There are hints, whispers really, of established entities operating in these shadows. They're bypassing legal boundaries and pushing their agendas in secrecy."

Adam interjected, "So, what we're seeing with CytoLife might be just the tip of the iceberg?"

Ethan nodded slowly. "Precisely. CytoLife may just be one part of a much larger and darker puzzle."

Harper, adopting her assertive courtroom demeanor, updated the group. "Deandra has been actively working on the legal front. She's coordinating with the DA and connected me with Agent Butler from the FDA's Office of Criminal Investigations. Initially, he seemed skeptical about our findings, but his reactions hinted at deeper concerns. There was a certain unease in his eyes that suggests he's taking our information seriously."

Intrigued, Adam leaned in. "What's his current stance?"

Harper explained, "He's in a delicate position. The FDA needs solid evidence to act, especially for a case of this magnitude. And Butler is understandably cautious about the potential repercussions."

Lucas asked, "Does he think there might be corruption within the FDA itself?"

Harper pursed her lips. "He didn't say it outright, but his cautious approach implies as much. Deandra will manage our communication with him to ensure confidentiality until we're ready for a full disclosure."

Ethan, deep in thought, remarked, "If the evidence in those hard drives is as compelling as it sounds..."

Harper quickly agreed. "Exactly. The hard drives, those videos, the evidence of unethical experiments—they could be pivotal. Presenting this to Butler might not only convince him to join us, but also expedite the FDA's response."

Lucas cautioned, "We need to be careful. If there are insiders, we can't afford to reveal our hand prematurely."

Adam then asked, "Do you know a CytoLife employee named Cam?"

Lucas hesitated. "I have limited access within CytoLife. It's possible our paths haven't crossed."

Adam's expression grew concerned. "We need to find Cam. It's crucial."

"I'll see what I can find out discreetly," Lucas assured, pausing briefly. "Is Cam his actual name?"

"I'm not entirely sure." Adam continued, his voice carrying a mix of excitement and concern. "My latest piece on CRISPR is generating more attention than I anticipated." He displayed his news site on his phone, showcasing the flurry of comments, shares, and reactions to his article on the contentious gene editing technology.

"See, while I didn't specify any company in the article, it seems the online community is connecting the dots themselves. There are a lot of mentions of CytoLife."

He paused, letting the significance of his words sink in. His eyes held a dual expression of journalistic satisfaction and apprehension about the potential consequences.

"I've been careful," Adam quickly added, noting Harper's worried look. "But there's a clear public outcry for transparency. People are curious and concerned about what's happening behind these scientific advancements."

Ethan said, "Getting the public's attention is crucial. We need their awareness and scrutiny on this matter."

Harper released a deep breath. "It's a precarious situation. Public engagement is beneficial, but it also means CytoLife might start feeling the heat, and their reactions could become less predictable."

Lucas interjected, "When pushed into a corner, they might react more aggressively."

With a determined expression, Adam surveyed the table. "We've set things in motion. We have to see it through, whatever the response from CytoLife."

Lucas leaned back, absorbing the gravity of their undertaking. The scale of the conspiracy was overwhelming, but a sense of hope stirred within him. He was no longer isolated in this fight; their collective strength bolstered his resolve.

His thoughts briefly drifted to Rebecca, a tangle of emotions clouding his mind. He wrestled with his feelings for her, but he knew those personal battles would have to wait. Right now, there was a larger fight at hand, and he needed to focus on the task ahead.

Harper straightened, her presence commanding the room's attention, embodying both a mother's protectiveness and an attorney's sharp acumen. The atmosphere seemed to pulse with her resolve, signaling her pivotal role in guiding their efforts.

"Let's be clear on our strategy," she began, her tone both warm and assertive. "Adam, your article has started to turn the heat up on CytoLife. Another follow-up could intensify the public's scrutiny. That pressure is invaluable.

"Ethan, your exploration of the dark web is uncovering vital secrets. Keep digging; we need every shred of information you can find."

She then turned to Lucas, her gaze softening slightly, mixing professional urgency with maternal concern. "Lucas, as our inside source, your insights are crucial. Stay alert and gather whatever evidence and intelligence you can. We need to anticipate CytoLife's maneuvers."

Her expression sharpened. "Communication is key. We'll coordinate through the secure app Beacon. Everything—updates, information, plans—must be shared there. We can't afford any leaks."

Harper's determination was unmistakable. "I'll spearhead the legal aspect. With Deandra's DA connections and my upcoming discussions with Agent Butler from the FDA, we'll craft an airtight case against CytoLife."

Her eyes swept across the group. "We're up against a

formidable opponent, but we have the resolve to withstand this storm. We're not just facing a crisis; we're fighting for what's right. Is that clear?"

The group's atmosphere intensified as they focused on their strategy. Suddenly, Lucas's phone buzzed, drawing all eyes to him. He checked the message—an alert from CytoLife's security system.

The attached video showed a blurred view from a lab camera. Staff were frantically dismantling equipment, packing boxes, and seemingly deleting data.

Lucas, analyzing the footage, said, "They might be accelerating their timeline. This is one of the labs I have access to..."

Adam, catching the implication, added, "They might know someone's onto them."

Harper said, "If they're hastening their plans or trying to destroy evidence, we don't have the luxury of time."

Ethan, his hand clenched in a fist, concluded, "And if they erase their tracks, proving their guilt could become nearly impossible."

Ethan's eyes narrowed sharply as he caught sight of Lucas's phone. "Is that phone issued by your company? They could track it!" Noticing Lucas's alarmed look, Ethan moderated his tone. "Okay, it's a slipup, but we can manage this. Get a Faraday bag immediately to block any tracking signals."

Ethan's experience was apparent in his decisive advice. "We have to assume your cover might be blown. Be on high alert—"

Lucas's cheeks flushed with embarrassment. "I understand. I'm always on a swivel. I told Felix I needed time off for personal reasons, so it shouldn't raise suspicions. But you're right," he quickly conceded. "I'll pick up a Faraday bag right away. Thanks for the heads-up."

He paused, a grim realization setting in. "I'm always on the lookout for external threats. Now, I have to be just as vigilant about internal dangers."

The room grew charged with a sense of immediacy and peril. Every moment was critical, and the risk had intensified.

Lucas closed his eyes briefly, coming to terms with the situation. "This is deeper than I ever imagined, isn't it?"

Harper reached out, placing a reassuring hand on his. "We're all in this together, Lucas. Together, we have a fighting chance."

TWENTY SIX

Lucas entered his cottage at the Evergreen Resort, where its once-soothing charm now clashed with the turmoil inside him. After thoroughly checking for bugs, the familiar scents of pine and cedar seemed oppressive, and the playful shadows from the fireplace appeared menacing, mirroring his troubled thoughts.

Staring out at the dense woods, he felt like a mere piece in a twisted game. The act he kept up at CytoLife was becoming unbearable. As he reflected on his colleagues' faces, he wondered who among them was aware of the company's true nature and who were, like him, unwittingly entangled in deception.

Rebecca haunted his mind. Concealing the grim reality from her was becoming agonizing. Each smile and hushed word of comfort increasingly felt like a betrayal, and he could sense the concern in her eyes, her perception of him shifting day by day.

Resolved, Lucas put on his jacket and made his way to the secret spot in the forest where he had hidden the drives. His heart pounded as he approached, knowing any disturbance could be catastrophic.

After a careful search, he found the well-hidden spot undisturbed, the drives safe. Reassured for the moment, he recognized the perilous path he was on, but the need to reveal the truth overshadowed the dangers.

Back in his cottage, the gentle crackling of the fireplace offering scant comfort, Lucas mulled over his discussion with Adam about finding Cam. The name now weighed heavily on him. How could he discreetly search without arousing suspicion?

Drawing a deep breath, Lucas steeled himself. His best chance lay in the security logs—a risky endeavor, but it might lead to Cam or a clue about him. He planned his investigation for nightfall when the risk of detection would be minimized.

Closing his eyes briefly, he hoped his decision was the right one. With each step more perilous than the last, retreating was no longer an option. The stakes were too great, and he was in too deep to turn back now.

Adam briskly walked into *The Bluff City Standard*'s office in downtown Memphis, buoyed by the recent developments. The alliance formed with Harper's group, and Lucas's inside information from CytoLife had injected a new vigor into his steps.

Eager to share the news, Adam knocked and entered Ben's office without hesitation. "Ben, things are coming together. We have an insider at CytoLife, and the revelations are serious!"

Ben looked up, his eyes betraying a hint of concern that didn't escape Adam's notice. Adam, impassioned, continued, "You've always taught me to chase every lead, to uncover the truth. This could change everything."

However, Ben's response was unexpectedly guarded, his hands fidgeting with papers on his desk. "Adam," he started, avoiding direct eye contact, "in light of the sensitive nature around CRISPR and gene editing, perhaps we should consider a more... balanced approach in our reporting."

Adam's enthusiasm faltered, replaced by a blend of surprise and suspicion. "Balanced? Are you suggesting we soften our stance on CytoLife?"

There was a noticeable fracture in Ben's usually steady demeanor. "Not exactly praise, but... we should at least include their perspective for fairness."

A chilling realization dawned on Adam. "Ben, you're being influenced by them, aren't you? This isn't about editorial balance. It's their reach... it's more extensive than I imagined."

Feeling a profound sense of betrayal, Adam's voice was laced with disappointment. "I thought I knew you, Ben."

Ben hesitated to respond, but Adam had already turned, leaving the office with a firm click of the door.

Stepping out of Ben's office, Adam was struck by a sobering clarity: the scope of the battle against CytoLife was far greater, and the adversaries were more deeply entrenched than he had ever anticipated.

The late afternoon sun cast a warm, golden glow through the windows of Harper's home office. The once-cozy retreat had been transformed into a bustling war room. It was now a hive of activity, with charts, documents, and evidence adorning the walls and covering the desk. A large whiteboard stood prominently, mapping out their complex strategy.

Deandra stepped in, her eyes scanning the room in awe. "Harper, you've turned this place into a command center."

Harper, leaning against her desk, managed a weary but determined smile. "It's a lot, Dee. We've got a long road ahead." She hesitated, then added, "There's something else. It's Lucas. He's working for CytoLife. He's in deep."

Deandra's expression shifted from surprise to concern. "Lucas? Your boy? In the heart of that beast?"

"Yes," Harper confirmed, her voice laced with a complex blend of maternal worry and a strategist's resolve. "You know the job he took in DC? He's providing security for Rebecca Kent, right at the core of CytoLife. He's got firsthand insights and... evidence."

Deandra's Southern twang thickened with emotion. "Lord, Harper, that's brave, but so dangerous. Does he realize the kind of hornet's nest he's stirring?"

Harper nodded. "He does, and he's ready to face it. He's already uncovered things we couldn't have imagined."

Deandra's face softened with empathy. "I've loved that boy since he was in short pants running around Mama's kitchen. I can't even begin to imagine the worry eating at you, Harper."

Harper sighed, her eyes revealing the depth of her internal struggle. "Lucas reached out to Adam initially as an anonymous source. He's seen firsthand the horrors CytoLife is capable of. It's more than just corporate greed; it's... it's monstrous."

A mix of shock and realization dawned on Deandra's face. "So, this is personal for him too. And for you."

Harper's gaze briefly flitted down, then back at Deandra with a flicker of vulnerability. "When he took the job, we weren't on the best terms. Now, I can't help but feel if I had been there more... maybe he wouldn't be in this mess."

Deandra placed a reassuring hand on Harper's arm. "We all have our paths, Harper. What matters is how we walk them now."

Harper straightened, refocusing on the task at hand. "We've got to get those drives to Agent Butler. It's not just about CytoLife anymore; it's about protecting Lucas and stopping whatever nightmare they're planning."

A determined fire lit up Deandra's eyes. "We'll get it done, Harper. We're in this together."

Harper's home office, now a nucleus of their resistance against CytoLife, was a hive of activity. She and Ethan were absorbed in analyzing CytoLife's latest PR offensive. The screen displayed a montage of emotional testimonials and celebrity endorsements, each crafting a narrative of hope and miracle cures.

"They're masters at this game," Harper observed, a hint of grudging respect in her tone as she watched a mother with her child, both beaming with gratitude towards CytoLife. "They're weaving a story so powerful it overshadows the truth."

Ethan, his eyes fixed on the screen, nodded. "It's a classic tactic. Drown out the dissenting voices with a flood of positive imagery. Makes our job tougher."

Harper switched to a clip of CytoLife's glittering event, a who's who of the elite. "They've got the media, the influencers, even the politicians in their pocket. It's like they're untouchable."

Ethan leaned closer, scrutinizing the screen. "But it's all surface. Their 'data' lacks real substance, just enough to dazzle and distract."

Harper smirked. "Exactly. They're controlling the narrative, Ethan. Every testimonial, every event is a calculated move to rebuild their image."

An interview with a CytoLife executive came on, subtly casting aspersions on their critics. "They're playing dirty," Harper remarked, her voice full of frustration. "They're not just defending themselves; they're going on the offensive, undermining us without directly engaging."

Ethan watched as a well-known actor praised CytoLife for saving a family member. "It's a different battlefield," he said, his expression grave. "They're using emotional leverage, making it personal for the public."

Harper paused a video of a beloved actress crediting CytoLife for her rejuvenated health. "They've turned this into a cultural narrative. But we can't let that deter us. We have to stay focused on the truth."

Ethan's eyes met Harper's. "We'll keep digging, Harper. The truth is out there, and we'll find it, no matter how deep we have to go."

One particular morning, in the bustling war room at Harper's, a tense silence hung in the air. Harper and Ethan watched as Adam anxiously scrolled through his phone. "Cam's gone dark," Adam finally said, a trace of worry in his voice. "He's always been methodical in his communication. This sudden radio silence isn't normal."

Harper, her brows furrowed in concern, questioned, "Has Lucas seen him around CytoLife?"

Before Adam could respond, he quickly sent a Beacon message to Lucas, seeking any new information. The response was almost immediate, but its brevity and tone were unusual.

`Heads-up, landscape changing.`

Ethan stopped typing, a look of unease crossing his face.

"That's it? Lucas is usually more forthcoming."

Adam's expression was one of growing unease. "Something's off. Cam's silence and now this cryptic message from Lucas…"

Harper leaned back in her chair, her mind racing. "We need to be extra cautious now. Every move is critical." She glanced at Ethan, her voice firm, "If we don't hear anything concrete from Lucas in the next 24 hours, we need more information. Press him, Ethan."

The call from Sam shattered the silence. Harper exchanged a few brief words before concluding the conversation.

Harper remained still for a moment, staring at the phone in her hand. Sam's words echoed in her mind, amplifying the sense of danger and the enormity of what they were up against. She had always known CytoLife was a formidable opponent, but Sam's cautious tone and veiled warnings indicated a threat level beyond her initial estimations.

As she looked out the window, the twinkling lights of the city seemed less vibrant, overshadowed by a cloud of foreboding. Sam's concern, while unsettling, was a stark reminder of the risks they were taking.

Shaking off the unease, Harper refocused on the task at hand. She knew there was no turning back. The stakes were too high, and the truth was too important to be silenced. With renewed courage, she turned back to her desk, her mind already strategizing their next move.

The war room, once a place of solace, had transformed into a command center where every decision carried the weight of potential consequences. Yet, amidst the tension, there was a thread of unyielding determination.

Harper knew the journey ahead would be fraught with challenges, but she also knew they were not in this fight alone. They had a team of dedicated, capable individuals, each driven by a shared commitment to expose CytoLife's malevolent schemes.

Days melted into one another, casting long shadows over the evidence-laden war room. The team gathered around the table, their faces etched with concern and determination. Harper, with thinly concealed fatigue, poured a strong cup of coffee, setting the tone for the day's crucial discussion.

"You're right. There are whispers, doubts," Harper began, acknowledging the unspoken tension in the room. "CytoLife's PR machine is in overdrive. Their testimonials, their events... they're swaying public opinion, creating a narrative that's hard to counter."

Ethan's background was clear in his analytical approach. "Their tactics are sophisticated. They're not just defending themselves; they're reshaping the narrative, turning potential critics into supporters."

Adam rubbed his forehead, a hint of frustration in his tone. "It's affecting us too. My recent article on CRISPR drew attention, but CytoLife's response has been swift and powerful. They're leveraging their success stories, casting doubts on our motives. Even my editor is pushing for a balanced view."

Deandra continued, her voice tight with anxiety, "The DA's office is feeling the pressure too. Politics is a shifting sand, and right now, the tide's in CytoLife's favor. Some are beginning to question the validity of our claims."

Harper's determination was unwavering. "We knew this wouldn't be easy. CytoLife's reach is far and deep. But remember, we have solid evidence, and we're on the side of truth. We can't let their smokescreen distract us from our goal."

The group nodded in agreement. Ethan spoke up, "We need to stay focused, keep digging. Our strength lies not just in what we find, but in how we use it. We'll adapt our strategy to their moves."

A determined look came over Adam's eyes as his reporter's instincts kicked into gear. "We've uncovered a story that needs to be told, no matter how much they try to bury it. We'll keep pushing, exposing every piece of evidence we have."

Harper's eyes swept across her team, her voice firm and commanding, fueled by a boost of renewed determination. "We're up against a giant, but we have the truth on our side. We'll stick to our plan, keep gathering evidence, and build a case that's irrefutable."

A momentary surge of unity filled the room. Yet as it lingered, Harper's eyes caught a faint shimmer from a tiny lens hidden in the corner. Her heart raced...

"Shut Up. Now," she ordered, singling out the device. The room fell eerily silent, and for a moment, comprehension eluded everyone. Ethan was the first to react, quickly moving to see what had captured Harper's attention.

Ethan inspected it. "It's a micro-surveillance cam. This is high-end gear." With the practiced precision of a seasoned soldier on a critical operation, Ethan wordlessly signaled for everyone to evacuate the house.

In the car, racing towards Ethan's safe house, the team's shared shock slowly morphed into a cold, focused energy. Adam's worried tone broke the silence. "If they've bugged Harper's place, they could have reached any of us. We need to assume we're all compromised."

Harper, her hands tightly gripping the steering wheel, nodded grimly. "We've underestimated their reach. This is more than just corporate espionage; this is a full-scale war."

Ethan, seated beside her, his eyes scanning their surroundings for any sign of being followed, added, "We'll do a full sweep at my place. Check for bugs, make sure it's secure. Then we plan our next move."

As they pulled into a nondescript location, a sense of urgency permeated the air. Ethan's safe house was a fortress of privacy, a nondescript building that betrayed none of its high-security features.

Inside, they gathered in a sparsely furnished room, the air thick with the seriousness of their predicament. Ethan's demeanor was all business as he produced bug detectors and began a thorough sweep of the area.

Deandra, her face reflecting the gravity of their situation, spoke up. "We need to think about protection, not just for ourselves, but for those close to us. If CytoLife's willing to go this far..."

Adam chimed in, his journalist instincts at the forefront. "We can't let this intimidate us into silence. If anything, this proves how crucial it is to expose them."

Harper, now seated at a plain table, her gaze fierce, began strategizing. "We go on the offensive. We use their tactics against them. We leak what we know, bit by bit. Let the public and the press do some digging for us."

Ethan nodded in agreement. "I'll reach out to my contacts, see if we can get some off-the-record help. We're going to need all the allies we can get."

Harper slapped her palm on the table, a rare show of raw frustration. "They're not just erasing doubt. They're erasing us, our credibility. They want to make us look like conspiracy theorists, clutching at straws."

Ethan began pacing. "It's not just about the facts. It's the psychological impact. They're sending a clear message: we're in their sights, and they're steps ahead."

Deandra, her voice full of worry, added, "Harper, this is bigger than we thought. They've infiltrated deeper than any of us realized. What if they've compromised someone close to us?"

The suggestion hung heavily in the room, the unspoken fear that they could no longer trust anyone outside their inner circle.

Harper responded, "Then we tighten our circle. We double-check everyone's background, even those we've known for years. No more assumptions, no more blind trust."

Adam, leaning against the wall, his expression grim, said, "I need to reach out to my contacts in the media. Get ahead of this. If they're manipulating the narrative, we need to counter it, fast."

Ethan halted his pacing, turning to Harper. "I'll make contact with my sources in the intelligence community. We need to find out how deep this goes. And we need to do it now."

Harper, her eyes scanning the group, declared, "We're in the eye of the storm. But we're not backing down. We fight smarter, harder. We're the only ones standing between CytoLife and their unchecked power."

The team nodded in agreement. The atmosphere crackled with a newfound determination. They had been pushed, threatened, and tested. But rather than breaking, they had only grown more fixated on their mission to expose the truth.

Deandra broke the tense silence. "We're facing a betrayal from within. Someone managed to infiltrate your space, Harper."

Ethan's expression mirrored inner turmoil, his voice hesitant but laden with meaning. "It's hard to consider, but we can't ignore any possibility. Lucas is heavily involved with CytoLife. Could he have been unknowingly manipulated into a pawn?"

Before Harper could speak, Deandra intervened, her tone a blend of certainty and incredulity. "Betrayal by Lucas? That boy's integrity was undeniable even when he was just a child."

Harper, with a mother's fierce belief, affirmed her stance. "Lucas is on our side. His actions and risks speak louder than any baseless suspicions."

The group shared a look, acknowledging the delicacy of their situation while doubt lingered in the air.

Ethan, his demeanor marked by a mix of resolution and urgency, addressed the group. "From this point onward, we can't leave anything to chance. Our conversations, planning, everything goes through the Beacon app. It's our most secure line. No emails, no leaving files out, nothing that can be intercepted or compromised."

Harper nodded. "Ethan's right. We agreed to use Beacon, but got lax. That mistake has cost us. Now Beacon is our only line—fully encrypted, off the grid. No more slipups. We also didn't anticipate a camera planted in my home."

Adam, looking a bit more reassured, asserted, "I'll make sure all my sources funnel their information through Beacon too. No more face-to-face unless it's absolutely necessary."

Ethan's tone grew more assertive. "From now on, no sensitive discussions in our homes or offices. After those sweeps, still assume they're compromised. We'll only talk here, in this secure location. I acquired this space some time ago under an LLC for different reasons, but it's discreet and defensible."

The team collectively acknowledged the gravity of the situation. Harper, seeing the renewed focus in everyone's eyes, felt a spark of hope amidst the uncertainty. "This setback won't stop us," she declared. "We adapt, we strengthen our defenses, and we continue the fight. Together."

TWENTY SEVEN

Ethan paced the shadow-filled expanse of his makeshift office, a labyrinth of desks and tech gear. The anticipation of meeting Neon, the hacker known only through cryptic digital exchanges, hung in the air. This face-to-face encounter was an uncharted territory for both.

As Neon slipped through the door, his hair—a riot of vibrant luminescence—played with the dim light, casting an aura of mystery. His attire, a seamless blend of corporate sharpness and street-style rebellion, intrigued Ethan. The man was an enigma, wrapped in a tailored suit and neon sneakers.

"Ethan?" Neon's voice, saturated with a playful drawl, broke the silence. "A real pleasure to finally put a face to the name."

Ethan's handshake was firm, his response light with an undertone of curiosity. "Neon, you're quite the surprise."

A knowing chuckle escaped Neon. "Isn't that the fun part? Oh, and just so you know, I took a few detours to shake off any tails. Can't be too careful, right?"

Ethan, amused and impressed by Neon's theatrics, motioned towards a chair. "Your flair for the dramatic might just be what we need."

Settling into the chair, Neon's eyes briefly danced around the room, an unspoken assessment. "Then let's get to the heart of it, shall we?"

Ethan placed the surveillance camera from Harper's home on the desk, an unspoken question hanging between them. Neon's fingers grazed the device, his eyes meeting Ethan's with a hint of flirtatious challenge. "High-end tech for high-end problems. I see you don't play games, Ethan."

Ethan's laugh was genuine, mixed with an air of camaraderie. "Playing it safe isn't my style, especially with what's on the line."

As they dug into the heart of the matter, the room seemed to shrink, drawing their worlds closer. Ethan found himself unexpectedly at ease with Neon.

Ethan watched Neon's fingers move with practiced ease over the contours of the surveillance camera, like a pianist acquainting himself with a new keyboard. "This isn't your ordinary spy gadget," Neon mused, his attention never wavering from the device. "It's got a brain and a memory. If luck's on our side, it might've snagged some footage for us."

Leaning forward, Ethan's expression mirrored his growing interest. "Can you crack into it?"

Neon's gaze flicked up, a spark of mischief in his eyes.

"Ethan, I've unraveled tougher puzzles before my morning coffee." His lips curled into a familiar smirk. "Trust me, if there's a secret in this little gizmo, I'll unearth it."

"And if you find footage of our elusive installer...?"

With a nod, Neon set the camera down, producing a sleek toolkit from his bag. "Then we're one step closer to unraveling this mystery. No promises, but let's just say I like our odds."

As Neon's hands deftly navigated the camera's intricacies, Ethan found himself absorbed not just in the task at hand, but also in the hacker's methodical brilliance. In the seriousness of their mission, Ethan recognized an invaluable ally in Neon. "Let's get to the bottom of this," he said, his voice carrying a note of camaraderie and shared purpose.

Under Ethan's watchful eye, Neon orchestrated a symphony of technology. His fingers flew over the keyboard as he connected the camera to his laptop, an intricate dance of cords and connectors. The screen came alive with a flurry of code, cascading down like a digital waterfall—a display of Neon's deft skills and the task's complexity.

"Encryption," Neon muttered, half to himself, as he navigated through the digital maze. "Tricky, but familiar territory."

Ethan felt each second stretch into an eternity, his anticipation building. Then, with a flourish of keystrokes, Neon broke through. "There we go," he announced, his focus unwavering from the screen. A video window blinked open.

The footage unraveled the muted scene of Harper's home office, a sight that twisted Ethan's gut with unease. A shadowed figure moved into view, back turned, setting up the camera with practiced haste.

As the figure turned, adjusting the lens, Ethan's heart slammed against his ribs. The face on the screen was a jarring revelation, the last person he could have ever suspected.

Catching Ethan's stricken expression, Neon's voice softened. "Hey," he said, breaking the heavy silence. "You good?"

Ethan's response was a momentary battle between shock and composure. "Yeah," he managed, his voice a tremor of disbelief. "It's just... I didn't see this coming. At all." He let the sentence hang, the full weight of his thoughts unspoken.

With a nod of solidarity, Neon's hands hovered over the keyboard. "Should I save this? It could be crucial."

Still reeling yet cognizant of the importance of their find, Ethan gave a firm nod. "Yes, save it. This changes everything."

Lucas's instincts, honed from his days in uniform, instantly picked up the undercurrents of danger as he stepped into Felix's lavishly appointed office. Despite the grandeur, an oppressive atmosphere hung heavily in the air.

Felix paced deliberately around Lucas, reminiscent of a general inspecting his troops. "Lucas," he began, his voice heavy with authority, "your position guarding Rebecca is one of deep trust. And then, of course, there are those... additional tasks you handle for me." His eyes, dark and penetrating, emphasized his point.

Lucas held Felix's intense gaze, responding with controlled evenness. "I am fully aware of my responsibilities, Felix."

Felix drew closer, his voice a menacing whisper, "Then you know that any slipup isn't just a mistake—it's a betrayal. We're tied by a soldier's oath, a trust that should be unbreakable. Is your loyalty absolute?"

Under Felix's scrutinizing gaze, Lucas fought to keep his composure. "Loyalty is a two-way street," Felix continued, his voice carrying a veiled threat. "Show your dedication to CytoLife, to Rebecca, and especially to me. Fall short, and the fallout will be much more serious than losing your job."

Felix's sinister words resonated with a chilling clarity for Lucas. He had been careful to maintain a routine appearance, limiting personal interactions and focusing solely on professional matters. All while keeping a vigilant watch for any signs of exposure. But now, every conversation with Felix, always an imposing figure, was fraught with unspoken dangers. Lucas chose not to confront Felix about his growing suspicions. Staying off Felix's radar was crucial for his surreptitious operation.

In the half-lit expanse of the CytoLife lab, Rebecca paused her meticulous work at the microscope. She approached Lucas with a calculated grace, each step narrowing the space between them, charging the air with an electric tension. As her fingers grazed his palm, a deliberate yet delicate gesture, she spoke, her voice a blend of concern and conviction. "Lucas, do you truly grasp the magnitude of our recent breakthroughs? The world outside these walls isn't ready."

A cold unease coiled in Lucas's gut, the burden of his concealed knowledge pressing heavily upon him. "The pace is dizzying, Rebecca. Yet there's so much you've kept from me. What aren't you telling me?"

Her laugh, light but layered, did little to ease the intensity of her gaze. "Discovery thrives on its secrets, Lucas. Not everything can be revealed prematurely. We are at the cusp of a new era."

Lucas, standing in the shadowed confines of their shared endeavor, couldn't shake off the magnetic pull she exerted on him, heightened now as she drew closer, her proximity a silent challenge.

Her words were a hushed murmur, her breath a whisper against his skin. "I sense a shift in you. What's on your mind, Lucas?"

The conflict within Lucas was glaring. Caught between his deepening feelings for her and the unsettling doubts about their work, he faltered. "It's not just the project that troubles me, Rebecca. It's us... the unspoken truths."

Her touch lingered on his face, gentle yet probing, as her eyes sought the depths of his soul. "Every journey is fraught with uncertainties. But in our purpose, and in us, I have faith."

The tension hung heavy as Lucas wrestled with his inner chaos. What were her true motives in bringing him here? Was this a trial, or something more sinister? The advanced lab surroundings mirrored their complex dance of trust and deception.

Cornered, Lucas ventured a question. "Why bring me here today, Rebecca?"

Her smile held a mysterious edge, her tone mixed with hidden meaning. "Perhaps I was curious about your insights."

Before he could delve deeper, she shifted focus. "You were stationed outside during the presentation. Did you hear anything? Any impressions?"

Lucas hesitated, wary of a trap. "Bits and pieces. Your work, it's ethically challenging. Have you weighed the consequences?"

Leaning in, her eyes intense, she countered, "We are on the brink of a revolution, Lucas. The suffering we could alleviate, the transformations we could pioneer..."

Her eyes connected with his, seeking honesty beyond the surface. "I don't doubt its potential," he replied softly. "But at what cost?"

Rebecca's expression became a complex mosaic of emotion and uncertainty. "Progress always carries its risks. Yet the prospect of a brighter tomorrow, that's a cause worth championing."

As Lucas absorbed her words, the haunting images he had secretly unearthed flickered unbidden in his mind—harrowing scenes of their experiments, too grim to ever erase fully. They lurked in the shadows of his thoughts, a stark reminder of the chilling reality behind their quest.

Rebecca's passion, though seemingly genuine, now tangled with these spectral echoes of what he'd seen. Could her fervor mask something more ominous, or was she too blinded by Baxter's vision? The line between groundbreaking and nightmarish was blurring, leaving Lucas adrift in a sea of moral ambiguity.

He was left in a whirlwind of doubt and conviction, the boundaries between trust and betrayal increasingly blurred. Her fervor seemed authentic, but could it be a guise? What secrets lay beneath the surface?

In Ethan's downtown Memphis office, a hub of evidence and leads, a surprising twist had them reeling.

Ethan, his composure uncharacteristically rattled, met Harper and Deandra with a grave expression. "There's something important," he started, avoiding Harper's piercing gaze. "I had to bend the rules for some intel."

He sighed, the burden of his actions apparent. "Harper, remember Neon? We met here. He's an enigma—part punk rocker, part Southern gentleman. His style is as contrasting as his manner. It's bizarre working with him, but the man's a genius in his field."

Harper's lips twitched into a smile. "Ah, Neon. A bundle of contradictions, yet incredibly skilled. What did you find out with him?"

Ethan got to the point. "The camera in your house. It's Melanie," he revealed carefully. "She's feeding information to CytoLife."

Harper blanched. "Melanie? My assistant? But why?"

"They're paying for her father's medical expenses," Ethan explained. "CytoLife's using any leverage they can."

Harper's voice trembled with a dawning realization. "Could they know about... about Lucas?"

Ethan responded softly, his tone grave, "We're up against a formidable opponent in CytoLife. Their reach is unmatched. Plus, it's likely they knew who you were from the start. Probably dug deep during Lucas's background check before offering him the job. We have to assume they're always one step ahead."

Harper's voice was heavy with self-reproach. "I should've seen this. She had complete access to my life."

Deandra interjected, her voice filled with disbelief, "Melanie seemed so dedicated to you."

Ethan, with a note of regret, said, "Betrayal always hurts the most from those closest to us."

Deandra added, "We can't blame ourselves. This shows how far CytoLife will go."

Harper, shaken, struggled with the betrayal. "How could I have missed the signs?"

Ethan offered a consoling hand. "It's not your fault, Harper. Trusting others is part of being human." His voice, though comforting, lacked its usual assurance.

Deandra, pragmatic as ever, suggested, "We need to focus on what to do next."

Harper agreed. "We're exposed. And they're exploiting it."

Ethan added, trying to offer a semblance of reassurance, "Based on the timeline of when you started using your home office more frequently, I'd say the camera was planted recently. It means the amount of information they gathered could be somewhat limited. It's not much, but it's something to keep in mind."

The group nodded, taking a moment to absorb this small silver lining in the midst of their turmoil. It was a reminder that while they were vulnerable, they weren't entirely defenseless.

Lucas sat engulfed in the silence of his cottage, a stark contrast to the inner turmoil raging like a tempest within. Felix's enigmatic threats loomed large in his mind, a haunting echo that stirred a relentless unrest. Compounded by his recent, tension-filled encounter with Rebecca, his thoughts were a battleground, torn between duty and doubt.

His mind wandered, sifting through a mosaic of memories dominated by Harper's pervasive presence. He remembered her as a figure often silhouetted against the backdrop of ambition and occasional solitude with a glass of liquor. The void left by her frequent absences was a wound that never fully healed. Anger and bitterness had been his armor, a shield erected over years to guard his vulnerable heart.

Yet, beneath that shell of resilience, he acknowledged an undeniable truth: Harper, despite her flaws, had been a constant in his chaotic existence. She was more than a beacon; she was like a lighthouse, intermittently illuminating the turbulent waters of his life. Now, as he found himself adrift in the storm conjured by CytoLife, Lucas wrestled with the choice: should he reach out to Harper for guidance, or navigate these perilous waters alone?

The sudden buzz of his phone jolted him from his reverie. Harper's name illuminated the screen, stirring a whirlwind of emotions. He paused, his heart skipping a beat, before decisively pressing the mute button and placing the phone face-down. Lost in a sea of thoughts, he chose solitude over connection. For now.

Harper's heart plummeted with each unanswered ring of Lucas's phone, her third attempt fading into the void. The unease in her stomach deepened, a tangible weight with every silent vibration. She checked the Beacon app again: no updates, no sign of acknowledgment from him.

Gathering with her team, she saw her own worry reflected in their faces. "Something's not right," she said, her voice laced with a heavy dread. "Lucas never just disappears. This is out of character for him."

Deandra extended a comforting hand, her touch light on Harper's arm. "He's in deep with CytoLife, Harper. The strain of maintaining that pretense... it's immense. But we can't lose focus on what we're here to do."

Harper nodded, the conflict between her maternal instincts and her professional duty a turbulent storm within. "I just hope he's safe. We need to remain united, more than ever, if we're going to succeed."

As the screen flickered to life, OCI Agent Morgan Butler's face emerged from the shadows, stress etched in the lines around his eyes and forehead. The subdued lighting accentuated his grave expression.

Deandra leaned towards the screen. Her tone professional yet warm, she said, "Agent Butler, it's good to see you. We're diving into the binder you sent. There's an update we need to discuss—"

Morgan interrupted, his voice low and strained, "Harper, Deandra, there's a change in my assignment. I've been removed from the CytoLife case. They're citing conflicts of interest, among other bureaucratic reasons." He paused. His lower lip caught between his teeth—a tell Harper picked up on.

Harper's heart raced, her instinct as a seasoned attorney kicking in. "Morgan, that's absurd! You've been integral to this investigation. They can't just pull you out like this!"

Deandra, steady yet insistent, added, "There's been significant progress since our last update. Surely there's a way to challenge this decision."

Morgan sighed, a picture of resignation. "It's complicated. We're up against more than just procedural hurdles."

Harper was undeterred. "We have concrete evidence, Morgan. This goes beyond speculation. We've got tangible proof linking them to illegal acts."

A flicker of curiosity passed through Morgan's eyes at the mention of "evidence," momentarily piercing his guarded mask. But it vanished as quickly as it came. "I don't doubt you," he replied softly. "But I'm constrained by the decisions of those above me."

Deandra's tone softened, but carried an unwavering conviction. "Then guide us to someone who can act on this evidence, Morgan. If you're sidelined, point us to someone who isn't."

Morgan looked visibly conflicted, torn between duty and helplessness. "I wish I could offer more assistance. Just... be cautious," he advised, a note of genuine concern in his voice.

With a final, regretful look, Morgan ended the call. The screen blanked out, leaving Harper and Deandra enveloped in a heavy silence, the enormity of their challenge more apparent than ever.

Thomas Baxter's study within the Estates at Evergreen Resort was the very definition of luxury, a direct reflection of his achievements. Dark mahogany shelves, heavy with first editions and rare manuscripts, adorned the walls, encircling an imposing oak desk at the room's heart. A fireplace cast a warm, flickering glow, enhancing the opulence, while outside, autumn leaves danced a silent ballet in the gardens, visible through the expansive French windows.

Standing amidst this grandeur, Baxter, the epitome of self-assured success, was impeccably dressed in a Savile Row suit. He absently swirled whiskey in a crystal glass, surrounded by a carefully curated collection of art and awards from his ventures in the environmental and biotech industries. The study, with its luxurious trappings and symbols of success, mirrored the man himself—accomplished, confident, and deeply influential.

Felix entered, his controlled bearing contrasting sharply with the surrounding opulence. His steps were measured, his expression focused. "The negative press is mounting," he reported, a hint of concern in his voice. "Our public image is starting to crack."

Baxter, smirking, played with the whiskey in his glass. "Negative press? That's always fleeting. The public's memory is short. It will pass."

Felix's eyes narrowed. "We're already taking action. Heartwarming stories about CytoLife, positive testimonials, charity events—a campaign to reshape our image."

Baxter chuckled as his fingers traced the edge of a silver letter opener. "You sound confident, Felix. But let's not forget who's the visionary here. I see the larger picture."

Felix maintained his stoic demeanor, but allowed a hint of pride to show. "I'm steering our response. But we can't afford to underestimate this challenge."

Baxter's confidence was unshaken. "You're here for your precision, Felix. But remember, I'm the one who dreams big." He gestured around the room. "Ensure any *nuisances* are handled."

Felix's jaw tightened, betraying a flash of irritation, quickly masked by composure. "Immediate threats are under control. However, we need to accelerate our plans. Start the protocols we discussed."

Baxter paused, his gaze drifting to the window. "Is it worth it, Felix?" he asked, a rare note of doubt in his voice.

The question caught Felix off-guard. "Our ambitions are world-changing," he asserted, regaining his confidence. "This is merely a temporary obstacle."

Baxter nodded, the mask of invulnerability back in place. "Proceed as you think best."

As Felix left the room, the weight of their conversation lingered, a silent acknowledgment of the daunting path ahead.

In the hushed calm of his own study, Felix reclined in his leather chair, enveloped in deep thought. The only sound was the rhythmic ticking of an antique clock echoing through the room.

To Felix, the future he envisioned for CytoLife was clear and unchallenged, far surpassing the company's current ambitions. While others were preoccupied with short-term issues, his sights were set on long-term dominance. He prided himself on his ability to foresee and orchestrate events, a skill honed through years of strategic planning.

Felix was aware of Lucas's connection to Harper from the outset, having ensured a thorough background check before bringing him onboard. However, what he hadn't anticipated was Harper's central role in the efforts to probe into CytoLife's affairs. This unexpected twist, while intriguing, did not significantly shake Felix's confidence in his ability to control the situation. In his view, they were simply nuisances, lacking the real power or knowledge to disrupt CytoLife's plans.

He also regarded Lucas as a manageable element, one that could be controlled and contained within the scope of their operations. The true endeavors, shrouded deep within the labs, remained concealed from Lucas. Rebecca understood that maintaining this veil of secrecy was crucial.

The relationship developing between Lucas and Rebecca was something Felix noted with interest. He saw it as a potential advantage, a means to further secure Lucas's loyalty. Felix believed in leveraging personal connections to strengthen professional ties, confident in his ability to manipulate these dynamics to his favor.

Felix was convinced that the current challenges were manageable. The strategy to accelerate their timeline, in his opinion, would keep any potential threats off balance. In his eyes, Harper and her allies, no matter how persistent, were ultimately outmatched by CytoLife's resources and his strategic acumen.

Resolute in his decision, Felix leaned back, his mind already plotting the next moves in what he saw as a grand chess game. To him, the path forward was clear, and he was ready to navigate any minor turbulence that came his way.

The makeshift office in Memphis was a hive of activity, computers humming and papers strewn across tables. Harper noticed Deandra moving with an uncharacteristic heaviness that morning.

She gestured for Deandra to sit, pouring her a cup of black coffee. They sat in silence for a moment, Deandra cradling the warm mug, her thoughts seemingly far away.

Breaking the silence, Dee spoke up, "We've hit a blockade. Those subpoenas for PenCore and the local medical units? They're being stalled at every turn. Their lawyers are outmaneuvering us."

Harper let out a slow breath. "They're not just defending. They're actively working to derail us."

Deandra's tone grew heavier. "It's more than just legal hurdles. I've got word from the Capitol. Some senator is questioning our case's validity, calling it a waste of taxpayers' money. They're playing the political card now."

Harper's expression hardened. "This is a calculated move. They're leveraging political influence, not just legal tactics."

Deandra's frustration was transparent. "And there's more. A new bill, disguised as bioethics reform, is being fast-tracked. It's designed to protect companies like CytoLife from investigations like ours. They're framing it as protecting medical advancements."

A heavy stillness fell over them. Harper then reached out, grasping Dee's hand tightly. "Dee, we knew this battle wouldn't be easy. They have resources, yes, and they're scared. That's why they're fighting back so hard."

Deandra locked eyes with Harper, a blend of anger and obstinacy in her gaze. "So, what's our next move?"

Harper's voice was steady, despite the uncertainty. "They're using every tool at their disposal, and it's unsettling. But these are desperate moves."

Deandra's eyes searched Harper's. "Harper, does this mean..."

Harper cut in. "It means we're in a tough spot. But their aggressive response? It's the reaction of an entity caught off-guard."

Deandra's voice trembled slightly. "But what if our efforts, our pursuit of the truth, aren't enough against their power?"

Harper paused, her resolve unwavering. "I don't have all the answers, Dee. But we must believe that ultimately, the truth will prevail. It has to."

TWENTY EIGHT

In the relative safety of her living room, post-Ethan's thorough sweep, Harper tried to unwind with a glass of wine. The past days had been a relentless series of legal battles and frustrating obstructions. Emotionally spent, her usual resilience gave way to a creeping despair. She allowed herself to sink into the depths of her defeats, reflecting on the sacrifices and burnt bridges her pursuit of justice had demanded.

As she was engulfed in self-reflection, a sudden buzz from her phone jolted her. It was a call from Charlotte's school, a call Harper felt meant trouble.

The vice principal's voice was calm, yet filled with concern. "Mr. Fairbanks suggested we contact you since he's away. Ms. Brasfield, an anonymous package was delivered for Charlotte today. We felt it was urgent to inform you, given what was inside."

Heart racing, Harper hurried to the school. There, she was handed a small, plain box. Inside were brass bullet casings, twisted and gleaming ominously, with a note chilling in its implication. "See how easily brass can be bent? Everything has its breaking point."

Arriving at Rob's house in Midtown, Harper found Charlotte, her young face etched with worry, the usual teenage nonchalance shattered. "Mom, why would someone send this to me?" she asked, her voice quivering with fear and anger.

Harper paused, the reality of her professional life colliding with the regret of her past choices. "I don't know, sweetheart," she said soothingly, enveloping Charlotte in a protective hug. "But I promise you, I'm going to find out."

Harper took a moment to compose herself before dialing Rob's number. She needed to explain things carefully to prevent unnecessary panic. The phone rang, and soon Rob's voice came through, full of worry. "Harper? What's happened?"

"Rob," Harper started, her voice steady, "there was an incident involving Charlotte today. It's been handled, and she's safe with me now."

A sharp intake of breath from Rob signaled his mix of relief and concern. "What kind of incident?"

Choosing to spare him the alarming details, Harper offered a measured overview. She stressed the precautionary measures already in place and underscored the need for Charlotte to feel secure amidst the turmoil.

"She should be with me," Rob insisted, his paternal

instincts clear in his voice.

Harper, drawing on her experience in delicate negotiations, responded with calm assurance. "I understand your concern, Rob. But given the current circumstances, she's safer with me. My place has tighter security, and I can keep a close watch. It would be disruptive for you to come back to Memphis right now."

A pause hung in the air as Rob processed this. Finally, he exhaled, a sign of reluctant acceptance. "Alright, Harper. Just... keep her safe, please."

"I promise," Harper affirmed, her voice imbued with determination. She had managed to assuage Rob's immediate worries, but she was acutely aware of the complex challenges looming ahead. For Charlotte, she was ready to confront whatever came their way.

The atmosphere in Harper's house grew increasingly tense over the next few days. One chilly evening, Harper and Charlotte sat facing each other at the dining table, an uncomfortable silence stretching between them.

Charlotte, her face partly obscured by her bangs, listlessly pushed her food around her plate. Harper braced herself for a difficult conversation. "Charlotte, I know this has been tough..."

Charlotte's response was sharp, thick with the edge of teenage sarcasm. "You think? Mom, this isn't some small hassle. Someone sent a threat to me to get at you!"

"I understand you're scared," Harper began, but Charlotte cut her off.

"Do you really? Sometimes it seems like your job, these...

missions, they matter more to you than being a mom."

The words struck Harper like a blow. This confrontation was more than just about the recent threat; it was a culmination of long-held feelings. "Charlotte, I've made mistakes. But everything I do, I do it for a better future for you. I love you so much."

Tears welled in Charlotte's eyes, but she held them back. "I just wish you'd prioritize us over your work." With that, she left the table, leaving Harper alone with her thoughts and their uneaten dinner.

In the following days, a strained detachment lingered in the house. Then, one evening, Charlotte paused at the doorway, a troubled look in her eyes. "Mom, there's a man. I've seen him near school. He's always at a distance, but I feel like he's watching me."

"What did he look like? Did anyone else see him?" Harper immediately began cross-examining a frozen Charlotte.

A wave of cold fear washed over Harper, but she regained her composure for Charlotte's sake. She gently took Charlotte's hands. "I'm sorry you're caught up in this. This is my battle, not yours," Harper said, her voice thick with emotion. "I promise you, we will get through this. I'll keep you safe."

Charlotte's eyes brimmed with tears. "I just want things to be normal again."

Harper embraced her tightly. "Me too, sweetie. But for now, I'm here to shield you. We won't let them intimidate or harm us."

Harper's purpose solidified. Her fight had spilled over

into her daughter's life, and she couldn't allow that to continue. It was time to consider serious security measures—a decision she had hoped to avoid. The stakes were higher than ever, and she was determined to protect Charlotte at all costs.

Late into the night, a spark of inspiration ignited in Harper's mind. It was a long shot, a gamble, but with dwindling options and the weight of inaction pressing down on her, she knew it was a risk worth taking.

With a sense of newfound purpose, Harper uploaded a photo from the charity ball featuring Baxter, Felix, and Rebecca into a reverse image search engine. The digital gears of the system hummed, processing her query. Soon enough, a flood of links cascaded onto her screen. The most striking result was from a high-profile society magazine, boasting an extensive feature on the Evergreen Charity Ball. Harper clicked the link, her screen filling with photographs of the crème de la crème, but it was Thomas Baxter who dominated the narrative.

The article detailed the ball's purpose—raising funds to restore historic art landmarks across Europe. Scrolling through the page, Harper's attention was snagged by a section titled *The Baxter Collections*. It chronicled Baxter's vast and impressive art collection, spanning from the Renaissance to contemporary pieces. One specific quote from Baxter stood out. "I pride myself on my discerning eye for art. There's one elusive piece that I've longed for years to find. It would be the pinnacle of my collection."

As Harper connected the dots, a strategic plan began to take shape in her mind. This insight into Baxter's passion for art, his pursuit of a particular piece, could be the key to gaining access to his closely guarded inner circle.

The high-speed rail, located at the South Main Street train station in downtown Memphis, a sleek marvel of modern engineering, glowed under the ambient city lights. Its engines hummed softly, heralding the onset of its journey. As Harper boarded, her steps echoed a mix of apprehension and firm resolve. Outside, the scenery transformed into a blur, melding with a stream of memories: Charlotte's innocent gaze, the late-night strategy sessions with her team, and the relentless challenges that had tested her spirit.

Each memory was like a piece in the elaborate mosaic of her life's journey, each piece reinforcing her tenacity. The thought of failing Charlotte, or herself, was unfathomable. Yet a shadow of doubt crept in, centered around Lucas. Their intertwined past, woven like a complex tapestry of trust and discord, hovered in her mind.

Would this trip to the Evergreen result in an encounter with Lucas? And if so, would he stand with her or against her? Harper pushed these questions to the back of her mind, choosing to deal with them when the moment arrived. For now, her focus was on the Evergreen and the mysteries it held.

As the sleek train sped on, one name echoed in Harper's mind more than any other: Thomas Baxter. At the center of this convoluted web of deceit, he seemed to be the mastermind. Harper's legal background had always guided her to approach matters with meticulous strategy, but this mission was different. It was fueled by a deep-rooted sense of justice, transcending beyond her professional obligations. She viewed this journey as an opportunity to confront the architect of this grand scheme, to look into Baxter's eyes and discern his true motives.

Four hours passed before Harper arrived at the rail station near Capitol Hill in Washington DC. She stood up, straightening her collar, preparing to disembark. Exiting the train, Harper immediately found herself in a blaze of bright signs, pointing to various destinations. She quickly spotted the directions for the rental car counter.

Harper nervously cleared her throat while she filled out the paperwork, requesting a standard sedan. The 90-minute drive from DC through rural Virginia to the Evergreen Resort was a mix of calm and underlying tension. The steady hum of her rental car's tires on the smooth highway provided a rhythm to her thoughts, interspersed with views of dense forests that eventually opened up to reveal the resort's grandeur.

The Evergreen Resort was a showcase of luxury: manicured lawns, elegant fountains, and the elite of society indulging in its splendor. Yet beneath this veneer of opulence, Harper was acutely aware of the gravity of her mission. The prospect of facing Baxter, the linchpin in a tangled web of deceit, grew more daunting by the moment.

She handed her keys to the valet with a composed demeanor, took a deep breath to center herself, and straightened her glasses. Her suit, chosen for its tailored precision, was part of her armor today. She had to convincingly play the part of an experienced art dealer. The hurried study of art history and *The Baxter Collections* on the train ride had to bear fruit. Equipped with the crucial information Neon had unearthed from the dark web, Harper was ready to execute her bold plan.

As she strode through the opulent lobby, the staff's polite nods and smiles greeted her. The resort's elegance was overwhelming, every element crafted to impress. Harper moved with calculated confidence, her steps purposeful.

Reaching one of the resort's upscale bars near the art gallery, Harper ordered a drink. She allowed herself a moment to reflect. Was this plan too audacious, too risky? The nagging doubt began to creep in. Just then, her grip on her art portfolio loosened, and papers tumbled out, scattering across the floor in a disarray that mirrored her fleeting uncertainty.

As Harper bent to retrieve her papers, a voice, smooth and confident, offered assistance. "Let me help you with that."

Looking up, Harper's pulse quickened. Standing before her was Thomas Baxter, embodying an air of urbane danger. He was dressed impeccably in a suit that spoke of wealth and precision. His smile was easy, charming, yet there was a shadow in his eyes, a hint of something calculating and unseen.

With a practiced grace, he stooped to gather her papers,

his movements deft and sure. His fingers brushed against hers briefly, sending an unexpected jolt through her. "No need to worry," he said softly, his voice a rich blend of sophistication and warmth, yet with an undertone that hinted at something more enigmatic.

Guiding her gently by the elbow, he led her to a nearby table. "Take a moment. Then perhaps you'd like to visit the gallery across the hall. There are some exquisite pieces there."

Seated across from Baxter, Harper momentarily lost her bearings. His cologne, understated yet distinctive, seemed to envelop the space around them. She was momentarily taken aback by the stark contradiction of the man before her. His polished, courtly exterior, and composed presence conflicted with his capacity for dark deeds. Yet she quickly marshaled her inner strength, meeting his gaze with a purpose that belied her turbulent emotions.

"Thank you, Mr. Baxter." Her smile was a veneer masking her heightened pulse. Every word and gesture was crucial in navigating this high-stakes dance.

Baxter, with an effortless command of the conversation, inquired, "And to whom do I owe the pleasure of this encounter?"

"Tinley Satterfield," Harper responded, her smile a subtle play of light and shadow. "It's an honor, Mr. Baxter."

He appraised her, his eyes sharp and probing. "An art enthusiast, I gather?"

As if on cue, a server glided to their table, a silent embodiment of the resort's elegance. He deftly placed Baxter's preferred scotch and a glass of wine for Harper on the table, his movements a whisper of efficiency that scarcely interrupted their conversation.

"Among other interests," Harper replied, her tone laced with irony. She picked up the glass of wine with a steady hand, taking a sip without breaking eye contact with Baxter. "The way art intertwines with the machinations of corporations like CytoLife is quite the spectacle. A dance of intrigue and illusion, akin to your company's recent ballet in the public eye."

A fleeting glint of iciness passed through Baxter's usually warm eyes. "Art, like news, is open to interpretation, Ms. Satterfield. We simply present the narrative."

Harper leaned back; her gaze unwavering. "Yet sometimes, narratives obscure more than they reveal. The true stories, those with living, breathing victims, are often glossed over and repainted to suit the narrative."

Baxter, unflappable, countered, "Every story, every canvas, has its blemishes. We strive to showcase the most compelling aspects. The rest are mere details."

"Except those *details* are people's lives," Harper shot back, her voice resolute. "To those caught in the crossfire, it's not just a narrative. It's their lived reality."

Baxter's expression was a study in enigmatic calm. "Progress demands bold decisions, some more drastic than others."

"And when those decisions harm innocents? Put children in harm's way?" Harper pressed, her tone sharp.

He sighed, feigning regret. "In the tapestry of progress, some threads will fray, sadly. It's an unfortunate yet necessary part of the larger pattern."

Harper leaned in closer, her eyes ablaze with intensity. "But it's through the fraying of those threads that truths are revealed. And there are those of us committed to ensuring every thread, every life, is seen and honored."

Their intense exchange was suddenly interrupted by Felix's entrance, which cast a chill over the room. As Felix's figure emerged, Harper recognized him instantly from the photo, and her blood ran cold. His presence was akin to a dark cloud, his gaze sharp and unnerving as it settled on them.

Baxter, with a casual lift of his glass, greeted Felix, though Harper noted a trace of tension in his posture. Despite Baxter's composed exterior, Felix's arrival introduced an element of unpredictability, an undercurrent even Baxter seemed wary of.

As Felix approached, Harper resisted the instinct to recoil. She remained outwardly composed, fully aware that any display of fear would only play into their hands. The dangerous air that Felix exuded was substantial, a silent yet unmistakable threat.

Baxter, attempting to ease the palpable tension, invited, "Felix, join us. Ms. Satterfield and I were just indulging in a thought-provoking discussion. It's always beneficial to hear diverse perspectives, wouldn't you agree?"

Baxter's tone, casually dismissive, didn't escape Harper's notice. Yet she held onto a glimmer of hope, seeing Felix's arrival as a potential pivot point in her strategy. She reminded herself that in every challenge lay hidden an opportunity.

Felix fixed Harper with a piercing gaze, his expression inscrutable. "Ms. Satterfield," he said, his voice carrying a mix of intrigue and authority. "I've heard of your interest in the art world. It's an unexpected pleasure to meet you."

Maintaining her composure, Harper replied, "I was just wrapping up with Mr. Baxter. Your presence here is quite the surprise."

Felix's smile was thin, more a show of control than amusement. "It seems our plans have changed. Shall we continue this conversation in a more private setting?" His gesture towards the exit was polite but unmistakably a directive.

Standing, Harper felt a surge of defiance tempered with caution. This unplanned turn, led by Felix, was a risky deviation from her intentions. She glanced briefly at Baxter, seeking any indication of what this new development might mean.

Baxter, with a hint of playful condescension, raised his glass to her. "Ms. Satterfield, you've brought a refreshing intrigue to an otherwise mundane evening. I trust Felix will find your perspectives as fascinating as I have."

Though his words bordered on patronizing, Harper detected an undertone of respect, perhaps even a trace of genuine curiosity. As she followed Felix, her mind was alert, preparing for the unforeseen challenges ahead. She had entered Felix's arena now, where the game was different, and every move mattered more than ever.

The journey through the Evergreen Resort's opulent halls felt like an odyssey to Harper. The lavish décor, from the intricate chandeliers to the soft strains of music, contrasted sharply with the growing knot of apprehension in her stomach. Her footsteps on the marble floor echoed, a foreboding soundtrack to their silent procession. Felix, tall and imposing, walked ahead with purposeful strides, casting a long shadow in his wake, and remained stoically silent.

Arriving at a nondescript door, Felix's thumb on the scanner was the key to a hidden world. The door slid open, revealing an office that starkly contradicted the resort's grandeur. Here, luxury melded with functionality—a study in controlled power. Dark wooden furniture and elongated shadows dominated the room, while a large window offered a commanding view of the resort's lush grounds.

Felix gestured for Harper to enter; his stance was unyielding. Despite her instincts screaming for caution, Harper stepped inside, her determination overriding her fear. She wasn't about to retreat now, not after coming this far.

She settled into one of the leather chairs facing the polished desk. Time seemed to stretch, each second amplifying her racing heartbeat as she waited in solitude.

When Felix finally entered, his demeanor was an embodiment of austere authority. He took a slow, deliberate walk around the desk, his eye never leaving Harper. "Ms. Satterfield," he said, his voice deliberately drawing out her assumed name, laden with a knowing undertone. "Or perhaps there's a more fitting name I should use?"

Harper's pulse quickened, Felix's veiled threat resonating with an ominous clarity.

"You've certainly made an impression," Felix remarked, a wry note in his voice. He leaned forward, his hands planted rigidly on the desk, his gaze icy and unyielding. "I prize discretion, Ms. Satterfield. Just as I imagine you value the safety of your loved ones."

Harper's mind raced, piecing together his implications. "What are you suggesting?"

His smirk was devoid of warmth. "Merely that you appreciate the gravity of your actions. The world is an intricate tapestry, and occasionally, threads can become... entwined. It would be unfortunate if you, or someone close to you, were ensnared."

A wave of cold realization washed over Harper. She'd anticipated a confrontation, but Felix's blatant threat was jarring. She needed to regain her balance.

Felix reclined, fingers steepled, appraising Harper. The silence was heavy, accentuating the tension enveloping them.

"People like you," he continued, his voice smooth but ominous, "believe they can disrupt the established order. It's commendable in a way. Naïve, but commendable."

Harper fought to keep her composure. "Your threats won't deter me."

Felix's chuckle was soft, yet it carried an undercurrent of cold authority. "Ms. Satterfield, your efforts, while admirable, are ultimately inconsequential in the grand scheme of CytoLife's ambitions. But make no mistake," his voice hardened ever so slightly, "should you become an impediment, rest assured, I won't hesitate to address the situation."

Harper's eyes darted around the room, searching for any clue, any advantage. She noticed an open dossier on Felix's desk, marked with a peculiar emblem—a spiral with three branches. Without being able to discern the details, she memorized the symbol, sensing its potential significance.

"You may leave now," Felix said dismissively. "But remember, while you're out there playing detective, we remain steps ahead. It would be wise to keep that in mind."

Harper left the office, Felix's haunting laughter trailing her. The encounter had revealed the depth of the waters she was treading. She had evaded his immediate grasp, but the true challenge still lay ahead.

Back in Memphis, Harper sat in her living room, her thoughts swirling in the aftermath of her encounter. Baxter's untouchable demeanor and Felix's unsettling words echoed in her mind, fueling a frustration she was reluctant to acknowledge. A fool's errand, she thought bitterly. The days slipped by, each passing hour finding Harper increasingly immobilized by doubt and uncertainty. What had she been thinking, challenging forces so formidable?

The door groaned softly as it opened, and Dee entered, her brow furrowed in concern at the scene before her. "Harper? Why's Charlotte over at Mama's place?"

Harper looked up, her face pale and worn. Tears had left their mark on her cheeks, and her voice wavered as she spoke. "Someone sent... sent bent bullet casings to Charlotte's school with a note."

Dee's worry escalated to alarm. "Excuse me? Bullet casings?! What did the note say?"

Fighting back tears, Harper repeated the chilling words, "'See how easily brass can be bent? Everything has its breaking point.'"

The color drained from Dee's face. "Have you told the police about this?"

"The school might've," Harper murmured. "But, Dee, there's something else..."

Dee leaned in, her eyes sharp with urgency. "Tell me everything, Harper. Right now."

Harper drew in a shaky breath and confessed, "I went to the Evergreen Resort, pretended to be an art expert, and I met Baxter. I thought I could somehow confront him about CytoLife."

Dee's face shifted rapidly from disbelief to shock, and then to clear frustration. "You did what? Confronted Thomas Baxter? By yourself? Without telling me, or Ethan, or anyone? Harper, that's reckless!"

"I thought I was in control, Dee," Harper's voice cracked under the weight of her admission. "I thought I could outmaneuver him."

Dee's disbelief was evident, her voice escalating. "Harper, that's insane! You can't just go up against someone like Baxter on a whim. This isn't a game. It's dangerous!"

Harper's gaze fell, shame and regret washing over her.

Dee's expression suddenly changed to one of concern. "Wait, Harper," she interjected urgently. "What about Lucas? Did you see him there? Is he alright?"

Harper slowly shook her head, the worry distinct in her eyes. "No, I didn't see him. I've tried contacting him, but there's been no response. It's like he's just... disappeared."

Dee's frustration with Harper was apparent, yet it couldn't mask her genuine concern. "You should have been more careful, Harp. If they've targeted Charlotte, Lucas could be next. And God knows who else."

Harper hesitated, her fingers nervously twisting the fabric of her sweatshirt. "There's more, Dee," she said, her voice crumbling. "At the Evergreen, after my encounter with Baxter, I was approached by Felix."

"Felix? The guy you mentioned before?" Dee's eyebrows furrowed with worry.

Nodding, Harper's eyes brimmed with tears. "He took me to his office. We had a... conversation. He knew I wasn't really an art dealer. Dee, he made it clear that... we're all in danger if I don't back down."

Dee's eyes grew wide, a mix of shock and disbelief. "Sweet mercy, Harper! What were you thinking?"

Harper covered her face, her voice muffled by sobs. "I thought I could handle it, Dee. I thought I could stand up to them, but it's all just... it's too much."

Dee stepped in, her arm wrapping around Harper in a comforting embrace. "Harp, rushing in like that without a plan... But what's done is done. We need to think about what's next."

Harper raised tear-stained eyes. "I'm sorry, Dee. I just... I had to try."

Dee locked eyes with Harper, her voice unwavering and comforting. "I know. But we're better when we work together. You, me, Ethan—we've always been a team. We'll figure this out, together. We always do."

Harper drew in a deep, shuddering breath, striving for composure. "Dee, Felix... he said something. It's been haunting me ever since I left the Evergreen."

Dee's gaze was intent, focused on Harper. "What did he say?"

Harper drew in a deep, shuddering breath, trying to steady herself. "He didn't say it outright, but it's like... CytoLife's plans are already unstoppable. Standing against them now feels futile, like trying to stop a freight train with a feather."

Her voice was a whisper, laden with worry. "He highlighted their power, their resources. Seeing what they've already done, I can't help but fear he's right. And Lucas... his safety is in jeopardy. It feels like we're trapped in their shadow."

Dee squeezed Harper's shoulder, offering a semblance of comfort. "Harper, Lucas is well-trained for high-risk situations. We have to have faith in his abilities, and in our own strength as a team."

Her face set in a look of determination. "These people, they rely on fear and intimidation. But remember, even the strongest adversaries have their weaknesses. We just need to find and exploit theirs."

Harper looked up, her eyes red from tears. "But how, Dee? Where do we start?"

Dee nodded energetically, taking a moment to gather her thoughts. "The same way we always do—together. We'll regroup, strategize, and never give in. We're not done yet."

TWENTY NINE

Lucas sank into the well-worn leather chair of the security room, his mind a battleground of conflicting loyalties and emerging emotions. The array of LED screens displayed live footage from around the building. Yet his thoughts were captivated by flashes of Rebecca—their stolen glances and the brief touches had deepened his inner conflict.

More than matters of the heart troubled him. The weight of secrets hung heavy: his mother's covert mission entrusted to him, Felix's sharpening suspicions, and the pressing task assigned by Adam to track down someone named "Cam."

The soft hum of computers filled the room, punctuating the tense silence. Lucas's fingers moved rapidly over the keyboard, sifting through the logs for any trace of 'Cam'—Cameron, Camille, Camila...

Suddenly, his attention snapped to one of the screens. A live feed caught Felix walking briskly through a sterile corridor, but it was the figure following him that sent Lucas's pulse racing—Harper, his mother.

His heart hammered in his chest. *What the hell is she doing here?* A surge of panic tightened his throat. He frantically switched between camera feeds, desperate for a better view into Felix's office, but the angle he needed was elusive. And now, to his dismay, Felix seemed to be heading straight for the security station.

Lucas's mind raced, trying to make sense of the baffling situation unfolding before him. Lost in his thoughts, he was abruptly pulled back to reality by the creaking of the security room door. Standing in the doorway was Felix, his presence even more imposing at close range.

"Just checking in," Felix said, his nonchalant demeanor failing to calm Lucas's growing unease.

Lucas mustered a steady voice. "Everything's under control here." Felix's piercing gaze lingered a moment too long before he finally nodded and left. Lucas's eyes remained glued to the camera feed, tracking Felix back to his office, where Harper waited. Time seemed to crawl until Harper finally emerged, her pale, strained expression wrenching Lucas's heart. He wanted to go to her, to comfort her, but the risk was immense.

Footsteps suddenly interrupted his tangled thoughts of guilt and regret. Rebecca appeared, further stirring the turmoil within him. As he braced himself to greet her, a young man walked out behind her. "Take care, Cameron," Rebecca said casually.

The name struck Lucas like lightning. This was the 'Cam'

Adam had mentioned. Emotions surged within him—love, guilt, duty. At that moment, Lucas knew it was time to act.

Forcing herself out of bed, Harper tried to shake off the weight of her recent failures. She drove in silence to Ethan's, seeking the comfort of camaraderie in these troubled times.

As she opened the door to their makeshift office, the scene inside was a tableau of dedication and distress. Deandra hunched over a pile of notes, her concentration etched into her furrowed brow. Ethan stood by the window, bathed in a soft light that accentuated his contemplative stance. Adam, unable to stay still, paced the room, his fingers tapping rhythmically on the papers in his hand.

The air was thick with tension, a tangible reflection of their collective frustration and the lingering uncertainty that cloaked their efforts.

Ethan's voice cut through the unease. "Every setback, every obstacle... it's like we're being told to just pack it in."

Deandra let out a weary sigh, her posture sagging. "You're not wrong. We're hitting dead ends at every turn."

Settling into a chair, Harper nodded in agreement, the weight of her own fears heavy in her voice. "I feel it too. But we can't afford to give up."

Harper's gaze swept across the room before settling on the worn carpet at her feet. Gathering her composure, she looked up, determination shining in her eyes. "There's something I haven't told you all."

Ethan, who usually exuded energy, leaned forward, his expression subdued as he sensed the gravity of Harper's words. Deandra looked up, her eyes intently searching Harper's face, while Adam stopped pacing, his expression a mix of concern and curiosity.

"I made a move against Baxter at the Evergreen," Harper confessed, the weight of her decision discernable in her voice. "I posed as an art consultant to get close."

Adam's eyes went wide. "Harper, you—"

But she interrupted him, her tone urgent. "We know CytoLife's roots are there, and Baxter's fortress-like grip on it. I thought I could uncover something valuable. But Felix... he confronted me, and he didn't mince words about CytoLife's reach."

Deandra remained outwardly calm, but Adam's shock was unmistakable, his face paling. Ethan, however, remained composed, absorbing the news with a steady gaze fixed on Harper.

After a moment, Ethan spoke, his voice a mix of concern and understanding. "That was a huge risk, Harper. But we're all feeling the pressure. What matters is we're in this together. We'll find a way forward."

Harper hesitated for a moment, then looked directly at Deandra, who gave a slight, reassuring nod. The air in the room grew heavier, laden with unspoken worry. "Going to the Evergreen wasn't a rash decision," Harper revealed, her voice unsteady. "Someone targeted Charlotte. They sent her bent bullet casings and a threatening message."

Adam's shock was pronounced, his eyes widening in

disbelief. However, it was Ethan's reaction that drew Harper's focus. The normally composed man tensed, his features hardening, a reminder of his past. "Bullet casings?" he asked sharply.

Deandra interjected, her voice steady, "The note read, 'See how easily brass can be bent? Everything has its breaking point.'"

"Damn it, Harper," Adam muttered, ruffling his hair in distress. "This is spiraling into territory we hadn't anticipated."

Ethan, ever the tactician, leaned forward, his mind clearly formulating plans. "Harper, have you contacted the police? What measures are in place at your home? Charlotte's safety is paramount, as is yours—"

Harper raised her hand, signaling for calm. "I've taken steps, Ethan. Charlotte's safe with Mama Dee, and you know she's vigilant. The school's also been informed. They're increasing security for Charlotte."

She inhaled sharply, her gaze meeting Ethan's. "I get the risks. This was a grim reminder. But I can't let fear paralyze us. We need proactive steps, a solid plan. It's time for us to act decisively."

Ethan's eyes lingered on Harper, as if gauging the depth of her conviction. After a moment, he gave a slow nod. "Alright, Tacks. It's time we shift gears. We'll devise a new strategy, one that puts us on the offensive. No more waiting and reacting."

Harper said, "Exactly. It's our move now."

Before the momentum could wane, Adam cut in, an edge

of excitement in his voice. "Hold up, everyone. We might be onto something."

Adam shifted, his fingers tapping against the stack of notes he held. "I came across these old notes from a tech summit I attended on Anti-CRISPR technology. Back then, it was all a bit over my head—the technical jargon, the presenters' deliberate vagueness. It was new, cloaked in military secrecy. But in our current situation, these notes might just be the breakthrough we need."

Pausing, he glanced at his papers, his usual restlessness morphing into focused intensity. "DARPA—the Defense Advanced Research Projects Agency. They're the brains behind some of the most groundbreaking military tech. A contact of mine, Professor Meera Kapur from UT, mentioned DARPA's work on Anti-CRISPR tech. It's complex stuff, requiring precise execution, and so far, it's been confined to lab experiments. But if we could leverage it..."

Harper focused squarely on Adam. "Are you saying this could be our way to counter CytoLife's actions?"

Adam hesitated, weighing his words. "Meera mentioned some of the trials were promising, but there were... complications. Talks of unintended genetic side effects."

Deandra's expression mirrored her concern. "Complications? That sounds risky."

Ethan joined in, his tone pragmatic. "Risky, maybe, but it's a new angle. Something we haven't explored yet."

Her voice full of curiosity, Harper asked, "Adam, why are we only hearing about this now?"

Shifting uncomfortably, Adam clasped his hands

together, his face marked with regret.

"It never seemed relevant before. Meera said DARPA keeps a tight lid on their projects. There's a lot of guesswork about their capabilities. Even if they have something that could help us, getting access to it is another story."

Deandra paused thoughtfully. "So we're looking at a long shot."

Adam's nod was resigned but hopeful. "A long shot, yes. But one we didn't have until now."

A newfound sense of cautious optimism replaced the despair that had previously filled the room. Despite the uncertainty and the slim chances of military cooperation, they now had a direction, a lead worth following.

Ethan's expression reflected his intrigue, balancing the obvious risks with the potential breakthrough. As Adam elaborated on the technical aspects, Harper's Beacon app vibrated on her desk, Lucas's name flashing across the screen.

She answered without hesitation, switching to speakerphone. "Lucas?"

His voice, clear and urgent, cut through the tension in the room. "Mom, I've identified Cam. I can get him to you. Head to the Evergreen. Find a secluded place nearby. There should be plenty of short-term rentals available off-season. Send me the address."

The room erupted with questions, each voice overlapping in a burst of excitement and urgency. Lucas's message, coupled with the looming threats they faced, instilled a fresh determination in them all. They were united in purpose, ready to seize this unexpected opportunity.

The rhythmic hum of the high-speed rail underscored the team's silence as they settled into their compartments. Harper gazed out the window, her thoughts a whirlwind as cityscapes gave way to rolling countryside. Ethan, with determined focus, reviewed their gathered intelligence. Adam, ever the journalist, jotted down notes about their journey. Deandra, typically composed, frequently glanced at Harper, her expression reflecting the weight of their undertaking.

As they disembarked in Washington DC, the team was mentally prepped for the task ahead. Amidst the bustling crowd, they navigated their way to a car rental service. Ethan, assuming the role of leader, adeptly guided them through the city's labyrinth and onto the highways leading to the Appalachian Mountains.

The transition from urban chaos to the serene mountain landscape was dramatic. Trees towered overhead, their leaves rustling as if sharing secrets, and the distant mountains stood as silent, majestic guardians.

Within two hours, they reached a secluded farmhouse, its white walls a stark contrast against the lush greenery. The property, ensconced in dense woods, offered a sense of isolation and security. A driveway snaked towards the house and a nearby barn, the air filled with the fresh, earthy scent of wilderness.

Harper, unloading their gear, looked around approvingly. "This is perfect. Secluded, but close enough to the Evergreen.

We can plan our next steps here."

They wasted no time in transforming one of the larger rooms into their makeshift headquarters. A sturdy wooden table, once a centerpiece of rustic charm, now served as their strategic hub. It was covered with an array of tech gadgets, maps detailing the layout of the Evergreen Resort, and stacks of crucial documents. Adam and Deandra busied themselves with affixing photos and pieces of intelligence to the walls, while Harper and Ethan organized their digital resources.

By the time evening rolled around, the room had shed its homely vibe, morphing into a nerve center bristling with technology. Cables crisscrossed the wooden floor, and a projector cast sharp images of maps and data across one wall, turning it into a canvas of their battle plans.

As the darkness of night enveloped the farmhouse, Harper surveyed her team—a group of steadfast friends and allies, all driven by a common goal. A deep conviction filled her voice as she addressed them. "This is where we turn the tide. It's time to take them down."

The soft patter of rain against the windowpanes provided a gentle backdrop to the evening's work. Inside, the hum of computers and subdued discussions between Adam and Ethan filled the room. Deandra was absorbed in analyzing a satellite image of the Evergreen Resort.

Abruptly, the sound of tires crunching on gravel cut through the night, halting their activities. Adam edged towards the window, trying to identify the unexpected visitor.

Before he could report, the rhythmic knocking at the farmhouse door punctuated the tense atmosphere.

With her heart pounding, Harper approached the door, an instinctual certainty about who it was. She carefully opened it to reveal Lucas, drenched from the rain and slightly out of breath.

Their eyes met in a moment laden with unspoken emotions. "Lucas..." Harper's voice was barely audible as she stepped forward.

Lucas closed the gap, enveloping her in a reassuring embrace. For a moment, the weight of recent events seemed to dissolve.

"I was worried sick," Harper sniffed, her voice muffled against his shoulder.

Lucas gently stepped back, his eyes reflecting a mix of regret and relief. "I'm sorry, Mom. Things got... complicated."

Their moment was interrupted as Ethan approached, a cautious relief on his face. "Good to have you with us," he said, patting Lucas on the back. Deandra and Adam looked on, their expressions a blend of surprise and understanding.

Lucas nodded. His voice carrying a sense of immediacy, he said, "There's a lot we need to cover. I've located Cam. We need to come up with a plan, and we need to do it quickly."

THIRTY

Lucas, now dry, surveyed the room, his eyes reflecting a blend of appreciation and concern. "Quite the setup you've got here," he observed, his voice filled with admiration yet underscored by apprehension.

Ethan responded with a hint of terseness, "It's what we need to stay ahead."

Lucas's focus, however, remained on Harper. Taking a deep breath, he addressed her directly. "I saw you, Mom. On the security feed, with Felix. Why didn't you tell me?"

A shadow of guilt crossed Harper's face as she averted his gaze. "I was trying to protect you," she regretfully admitted. "I thought I could confront Baxter, make him see reason. But he just brushed me off like I was nothing."

Lucas's expression turned to one of concern, his stance protective. "What happened in Felix's office, Mom? The cameras didn't show everything."

Harper swallowed hard, her eyes meeting Lucas's. "Felix was... different. Threatening. He said their plans were too far along to stop. He made it clear they'd go to extremes to keep us out of the way."

Lucas was a tumult of emotions—fear, anger, and anxiety intertwining. "That fits with what I've experienced. Felix cornered me, issued veiled threats, and seemed intent on ensuring my compliance at CytoLife. It's like I was being coerced into a dark pact. Felix is an enigma, Mom. He's a shifting shadow, hard to pin down."

Tears threatened to spill from Harper's eyes. "I'm sorry, Lucas. I was trying to help, but maybe I've only complicated things."

Lucas stepped closer. "Remember, we're in this together. They're trying to break us apart, to undermine our strength. But we won't let them. We have to keep pushing forward."

The room fell silent as unspoken emotions hovered in the air. Harper's voice became a hushed murmur. "There's more I haven't told you. Charlotte received a package at school— bent bullet casings with a note."

She described the unsettling contents and the ominous message. Shock ran through Lucas as the reality dawned on him.

The group absorbed the news in a heavy silence, each person clearly grappling with the escalating threat. Deandra and Adam shared a glance of concern, while Ethan's expression was restrained anger.

Lucas finally spoke, his voice strained with emotion. "I wish I'd known earlier, Mom."

Harper's eyes welled up as she looked at him. "I thought I was protecting everyone. But I see now how serious this is."

She reached out, placing a hand on Lucas's arm. "Charlotte's safe with Mama Dee."

Lucas let out a slow breath, a nod acknowledging Harper's words. "If anyone can keep her safe, it's Mama Dee."

He then enveloped Harper in a comforting embrace. "We'll get through this," he promised, his arms tight around her. "Together."

Resolute nods and affirming looks passed between the team members. The stakes had never been clearer, and their determination had never been stronger.

Harper drew back slightly, her expression lined with worry. "Lucas, you've been elusive, always dancing around details. Why is that?"

Lucas shifted, revealing his discomfort. "There are two reasons, Mom. First, I'm constantly worried I'll be discovered. Every message I send, every step I take, could be the one that exposes me." He paused, his jaw clenching. "And second, I've been trying to shield Rebecca."

Shock flashed across Harper's face. "Rebecca? You mean Dr. Rebecca Kent, the scientist in Baxter's inner circle? The one driving this CRISPR nightmare? You're protecting her?" Her voice conveyed a tumult of disbelief and confusion, reigniting an age-old tension between them.

Lucas's voice wavered as he replied, "Yes, Mom. But it's not as straightforward as it seems. I think there's more to her story, and she could be a crucial ally."

Ethan interjected, his tone a calming influence in the

escalating tension. "Let's take a step back. Our priority is to get a clear picture and develop a strategy. Lucas, your perspective is crucial. And Harper, we need to align our approach based on this new information."

Lucas, appreciative of the chance to explain, explained his complex interactions with Rebecca. "She's wholly committed to CytoLife's mission. For Rebecca, this isn't just cutting-edge science—it's a calling. She sees CRISPR as a tool to propel humanity into a new era, a sort of golden age."

Lost in thought, he recounted their in-depth discussions. "She talks about this grand vision, this overarching purpose. Any setbacks are just temporary obstacles in her eyes, minor compared to the scientific strides they're making. Anyone who challenges her perspective is just a short-sighted obstructionist, blind to the future she imagines."

Lucas spoke with both respect and concern, pausing briefly to compose his thoughts. "But as much as I recognize her brilliance, I can't ignore the inherent dangers. The real-life implications and the risks involved. They seem to be just footnotes to her grand plan."

Harper's expression softened. "Lucas," she said gently, her voice firm yet caring. "Your empathy, your ability to see the good in people, it's part of what makes you special. But sometimes, the world is more complex than we'd like. I hate that you're entangled in this situation."

Adam locked eyes with Lucas, his straight-backed posture exhibiting urgency. "Lucas, has Rebecca ever mentioned anything about countermeasures to CRISPR, like Anti-CRISPR technologies?"

Caught off-guard by the sudden pivot in their discussion, Lucas furrowed his brow, searching his memories. "She alluded to it once, talking about efforts to offset CRISPR misuse. But the specifics were beyond my grasp."

"But did she give any details? Any leads on where this research might be happening?" Adam prodded, his reporter's curiosity in full swing.

Lucas shook his head, his response thoughtful. "Nothing concrete. She mentioned there were teams working on counter-strategies, but no details."

Adam's expression intensified. "What about DARPA? Did she ever mention them?"

A flicker of recognition crossed Lucas's face. "No, she didn't. But, you know, I have a contact at DARPA. A friend from my Army days. We still keep in touch."

Adam's face lit up with excitement. "That could be a breakthrough. A real lead."

Harper and Deandra exchanged knowing looks at the possibility of a new avenue opening up in their quest.

Lucas's tone shifted, becoming more somber. "The hard drives I mentioned before, the ones with evidence against CytoLife, they're still secure. There could be mentions of DARPA or Anti-CRISPR tech on them. I didn't dive deep, partly because I had trouble accessing some files, and partly because what I did see was... absolutely disturbing."

Adam's eyes widened in realization, and even Ethan emitted a low, impressed whistle. Harper's face lit up with a glimmer of hope, sensing a crucial turning point in their investigation.

Ethan's demeanor instantly turned focused and decisive. "We need those drives, Lucas. As soon as possible."

Lucas nodded, his expression mirroring Ethan's resolve. "Let's get them. They're not far."

A short drive later, Lucas and Ethan exited the vehicle, Lucas immediately scanning for any signs of movement. He gestured towards the darkness, his tone clipped and factual. "Drives are that way; let's move," he directed, the precision in his voice unmistakable.

Without a word, Ethan fell into step with Lucas, matching his pace as if on instinct. Together, they moved swiftly, a testament to their common history. They located the hidden drives in the forest with practiced efficiency and retraced their steps to the farmhouse in less than thirty minutes, Lucas feeling a cautious confidence in their stealth.

The farmhouse door swung open, and Ethan and Lucas entered, carefully carrying a box between them. They placed it on the rustic wooden table, and Lucas gingerly opened the lid, revealing an array of hard drives, their metallic surfaces catching the light.

As Lucas locked eyes with Harper, her expression revealed deeper concerns, but he quickly redirected his attention to the contents of the box.

Without a moment's hesitation, Ethan began unpacking a variety of cables and connectors, along with a high-speed laptop. "Time to dive in and see what we're dealing with," he announced, his hands efficiently setting up the first drive.

The rest of the team crowded around the table in anticipation. Each hard drive was a potential key, a piece of the intricate puzzle they were trying to solve. The air was thick with the sense of urgency; every discovery, every piece of information they could unearth from these drives could be crucial in their fight against CytoLife.

Ethan's hands danced across the keyboard, swiftly navigating a maze of files and folders. He paused at a video file that Lucas hadn't highlighted and opened it. The footage that played was disturbingly different from anything they'd seen before.

"This is new," Ethan murmured, his focus unbroken as the scene unfolded onscreen.

The video depicted a sterile, clinical laboratory, similar yet distinct from the ones Lucas had mentioned. The harrowing images of human experimentation were stark, the anguish on the subjects' faces painfully clear.

Lucas gasped. Alarm clear in his voice, he said, "I've never seen this footage."

The group watched intently as the footage continued, revealing more than it was meant to. A figure entered the frame, seemingly unaware that the recording was still ongoing.

It was Felix, his face partially shrouded in shadows. "Excellent progress," he said to someone off-camera. Then, Baxter's unmistakable voice filled the room, though he remained unseen.

"Secure this footage, Felix. We cannot risk exposure," Baxter's voice commanded authoritatively.

A sardonic smile played on Felix's lips. "This will never see the light of day," he assured.

The group exchanged glances, recognizing the irony that the supposed secure footage was now in their hands.

Baxter's voice continued, distant and calculating. "Proceed with the next phase. Our objectives are close at hand."

The video captured a brief, silent exchange between Felix and the off-screen Baxter, filled with an unspoken agreement. Then, abruptly, the footage ended.

The room fell into a reflective silence, the screen's sudden darkness mirroring their somber mood. The implications of what they had just witnessed hung heavy in the air.

Harper's voice cut through the heavy silence. "That's Baxter, no doubt about it. We can't see him, but his voice is incriminating." Her tone was hopeful but cautious. "This changes our entire approach."

Ethan's gaze intensified. "This is more than evidence; it's concrete proof. It could expose CytoLife's true colors to the world."

Deandra, nodding in agreement, added, "We need to get this out there. It's about justice, not just legally but in the court of public opinion."

Adam, piecing things together, turned to Lucas. "Lucas, earlier you mentioned you found someone named Cam. Do you have more information on him?"

Lucas took a moment, then shared, "He's Cameron Roberts. He works in the lab with Rebecca."

Harper's eyes lit up with urgency. "Can we meet him? Every ally counts in this fight."

Lucas shifted his weight from one foot to the other. "I'll

try to reach out to him tomorrow. I'll head back to my cottage tonight and maintain the usual routine."

Harper stepped closer, her hand resting reassuringly on his shoulder. "Be careful, Lucas. We've seen their ruthlessness. Remember, you're doing this for the right reasons."

A determined look crossed his face. "I know, Mom. I'll stay vigilant."

The team shared a collective nod of understanding. "We'll regroup once you've made contact with Cameron," Ethan said, echoing the sentiment.

With a resolute nod to his allies, Lucas left to continue his delicate balancing act, a key player in the intricate chess game unfolding.

Lucas lay awake that night, the sinister images from the hard drives replaying in his mind. A shower did little to clear the lingering unease, but duty called the next day. He drove to Rebecca's place, their routine unbroken despite the turmoil beneath the surface.

As he pulled up, memories of their last intimate encounter—deep conversations, tentative touches, a budding passion—flooded his thoughts. Rebecca emerged, bathed in the soft glow of the morning sun, her appearance stirring the familiar chemistry between them.

"Morning, Lucas," she greeted him, her voice gentle, a faint smile touching her lips.

His response came out strained, "Morning, Rebecca."

Their drive to CytoLife was marked by a tense undercurrent. Lucas kept his eyes on the road, acutely aware of Rebecca's presence next to him. The landscape outside contrasted sharply with the complex emotions swirling within the car.

Rebecca broke the silence with a note of caution. "Things are shifting at the lab, Lucas. You might notice some changes today."

He shot her a quick glance, trying to read between the lines. "The security's been tighter lately. Is everything okay?"

She exhaled softly, her fingers idly playing with her briefcase. "Just extra precautions. Our work demands it."

Lucas pondered her words. Was she hinting at something more? The line between their personal connection and their professional roles was growing increasingly blurred.

As they approached CytoLife, Rebecca turned to him, her eyes reflecting a mix of concern and connection. "Today could be tough, Lucas. Just remember, we're in this together."

His heartbeat quickened at her words. "Always, Rebecca," he affirmed, a sense of solidarity strengthening amidst the uncertainty.

Haunted by the harrowing images he had seen, Lucas struggled to reconcile his feelings for Rebecca with the knowledge of her involvement in such disturbing research. The dissonance was agonizing, casting a shadow over every moment he spent with her.

The atmosphere at CytoLife was tense, an undercurrent of apprehension permeating the air as soon as they stepped inside. Employees spoke in subdued tones, their eyes darting around nervously. Despite his efforts to appear untroubled, Lucas couldn't ignore the increased security measures.

While escorting Rebecca, he overheard fragments of conversations about "new protocols" and "security breaches," hinting at the company's internal chaos. Lucas kept a low profile throughout the day, masking his inner conflict with a veneer of professionalism.

Leaving CytoLife later, Lucas noticed Cameron exiting the lab. His trained instincts took over as he discreetly observed Cameron's movements. The man seemed cautious, almost wary, as he headed to his car.

Dropping Rebecca off and ensuring she was safely inside, Lucas doubled back to the CytoLife parking lot. There, he found Cameron still in his car. Approaching furtively, Lucas tapped on the window, which Cameron lowered with a hesitant motion.

Facing Cameron, Lucas's voice was steady but charged with urgency. "Cam," he said, "we need to talk."

The drive back to the farmhouse was a silent journey marked by underlying tension. Cam, visibly unsettled, frequently cast anxious glances at Lucas. In stark contrast, Lucas exuded a calm, almost disconcerting focus, his eyes fixed ahead, embodying the precision and control honed through his training.

Upon entering the farmhouse, Cam hesitated at the doorway, scanning the room with a mix of curiosity and apprehension. Adam, recognizing the moment's significance, approached with an open, welcoming gesture.

"Cam, right? I'm Adam. We've been in touch, but it's good to finally meet you in person," he said, his voice conveying both warmth and a sense of camaraderie.

Cam's tension eased marginally at the familiar name, and he managed a small, acknowledging nod. His eyes, still nervously surveying the room, eventually rested on Lucas, seeking some reassurance in the midst of unfamiliar faces.

Lucas gestured for Cam to sit down and dove straight into an exhaustive account of their findings and efforts. The room fell into a hushed stillness as Lucas outlined their dire circumstances.

Once Lucas concluded, the revelation's impact lingered heavily. Cam, visibly shaken, absorbed the details in stunned silence. After a tense pause, he spoke, his voice unsteady. "Oh thank God, I thought you were going to do something to me. What you've described... it's worse than I feared. But I have something important too."

The atmosphere in the room grew taut with anticipation as Cam, hands slightly quivering, pulled out a small thumb drive. His expression was grave, his eyes reflecting a turmoil of emotions. "I took this from their main server," he said, his voice trembling. "I had my suspicions, needed proof."

Ethan, ever vigilant, quickly took the thumb drive. "First, we have to ensure this is safe to use," he asserted, his tone steady and commanding.

He connected the drive to a secure, air-gapped laptop set up for this purpose. As he opened the files, the screen filled with a trove of data: diagrams, confidential notes, and detailed plans. Among them were blueprints of CytoLife's underground bunker, revealing schematics for a massive drone deployment project, likely to disseminate their gene-editing technology.

The documents revealed a chilling picture: satellite facilities dotted across the United States, each integrated with CytoLife's central operations, primed for a synchronized release. Plans for a future global expansion underscored the enormity of their intentions.

Lucas, processing the gravity of the information, spoke up. "This isn't just a local threat," he said, his tone loaded with concern. "They're planning a worldwide operation, beginning right here."

Cam, his eyes conveying a mix of fear and relief, turned towards Lucas. "I thought you were coming after me on Felix's orders," he confessed. "I feared the worst. I can't tell you how relieved I am to be wrong."

Harper, ever the empathetic presence, gently placed a hand on Cam's shoulder. "You've shown remarkable bravery, Cam," she said softly. "Stepping forward when it would have been easier to stay quiet."

Cam looked away briefly, grappling with his emotions, before meeting Harper's face. The strain of carrying such a heavy secret was visible in his eyes.

Harper continued, her voice steady yet compassionate, "What made you decide to come forward now, Cam? What was the turning point for you?"

Cam trembled, his voice wavering slightly. "Talking to

Adam, carrying this secret... it's been overwhelming," he admitted. "The scale of what's happening at CytoLife, the implications... it was too much. The guilt was unbearable."

He let out a weary sigh, his posture deflating. "Every day, seeing the dark reality behind their plans, feeling complicit in my silence... I had to act before it was too late." His voice faltered, his eyes glistening with unshed tears. "I needed to hold on to the hope that there's still good worth fighting for in this world."

Cam's eyes met Lucas's, conveying a sense of desperate urgency. "Lately, I've been working more closely with Rebecca. I could feel the tension rising each day. The lab's atmosphere changed, became more hurried and anxious. Sections were closed off, and there was an inescapable sense of something big about to happen."

He paused, then continued in a strained voice. "I was terrified they'd destroy critical evidence, or it would be lost forever. I saved some hard drives that I was ordered to dispose of. I wanted to retrieve them earlier, but there was never a safe moment. I just couldn't let them cover up their tracks. It was too important. That's why I reached out. We have to stop them."

Harper shook her head, her mind racing with the implications. "This gives us a much clearer view of their operations. Our next step is to devise a plan, and we need to act quickly."

The next morning, Lucas reached out to Max, his old Army friend now at DARPA. Their friendship, forged in the intensity of deployment, had remained strong despite their diverging career paths. Max's expertise in advanced technology had made him an invaluable asset at DARPA.

To ensure confidentiality, Lucas used GhostComm, an encrypted messaging app created by a team member, which they had relied on during their service. The app was a trusted tool in their arsenal, offering a secure line of communication.

Opening GhostComm, Lucas sent a coded message to Max. "Long time, Max. Remember the desert ops under starry skies? Need your help on a new mission. Could use that DARPA insight. Secure chat?"

A quick reply from Max appeared. "Ready when you are. GhostComm video channel in 10. Stay safe."

Lucas signaled to Ethan, needing his expertise for a secure setup. Together, they prepared a laptop in the basement, ensuring a hardline connection for added security.

When they activated GhostComm, Max's face appeared on the screen, his features bearing the marks of time, but still familiar. The ensuing conversation would be critical to unraveling CytoLife's sinister plans.

The rapid camaraderie that formed between Lucas, Ethan, and Max was a testament to the bonds formed under the pressures of combat, now rekindled in their united front against CytoLife.

"Max," Lucas started, his voice heavy with urgency. "CytoLife's escalated beyond anything we imagined. Their experiments have moved out of the lab."

He took a moment to gather his thoughts, then detailed the alarming situation. "They've identified something called the AGG1 gene. Their intention is to disperse nanoparticles globally, starting with drone deployments from hidden bunkers across the US. It's beyond gene-editing—we're talking behavior modification on a massive scale."

Max's expression turned to one of shock. "They're playing with the fundamental elements of human nature. This is beyond ethical boundaries," he said, disbelief coloring his tone.

Ethan added his perspective. "Their setup is advanced, Max. And they're gearing up to launch this operation imminently."

Max leaned back, his face reflecting the weight of their words. "CytoLife's been on our watchlist. We've picked up on irregularities, but there's a difference between suspicion and actionable intelligence. The bureaucracy, the need for undeniable proof... it complicates matters." He gave a rueful chuckle. "But what you've shared today might be the key piece we've needed. It corroborates some of our gravest concerns."

His expression turned serious. "However, moving against them, especially on this scale, it's not straightforward. The amount of red tape, the demand for concrete evidence... it's a minefield. But Lucas, what you've brought to light today... it's significant. It might be just what we need to cut through the fog."

Max let out a slow whistle, his eyes meeting Lucas's. "Always in the thick of it, huh? Your boots have a knack for finding the proverbial pile."

Lucas leaned closer, his expression etched with deep concern. "We're running out of time, Max. We need to act fast. Cut through the bureaucracy."

Max nodded solemnly. "Understood. We've been working on a defense against rogue gene-editing technologies. One key development is an Anti-CRISPR agent. It's designed to neutralize these kinds of nanoparticles, effectively disabling them."

Lucas, grasping for any advantage, inquired about the specifics. "I'm no scientist, Max, but CytoLife's using this AGG1 gene. How much do you need to know to counteract it? What's our margin for error here?"

Max replied with a sense of urgency. "Any details you have on their research could be crucial. Without it, we're looking at a general countermeasure. It's like an antibiotic—not always precise, but can be broadly effective. It's uncharted territory for us. Send over whatever you have, Lucas. The more specific our knowledge, the better our chances."

Ethan, concerned about the practicalities, asked, "And the effectiveness of this agent?"

Max's face conveyed both assurance and realism. "In a controlled environment it's highly effective. But in a real-world scenario, with so many variables at play? It's our best option, but there are no guarantees."

Lucas's eyes flickered with a mix of apprehension and

willpower. "We'll take any advantage we can get, Max. What else is on the table?"

Max's voice took on a more serious tone. "We're developing drone countermeasures. DEWs—Directed Energy Weapons. Essentially high-powered lasers, and advanced jamming technology. But remember, these are localized solutions, not global fixes. And officially, some of this tech doesn't exist."

Ethan, ever the tactician, said, "So if we can get close to one of these bunkers—"

"We could neutralize their drones before they even launch," Max interjected, finishing Ethan's thought.

Lucas met Max's gaze. The weight of their task was clear in his expression. "It's a high-stakes gamble, Max."

Max's smile was mixed with a grim determination. "When has that ever stopped us? *De oppresso liber*, right? It's what we do."

A silent understanding passed between them, a bond forged in the crucible of service.

Max's demeanor grew solemn. "Listen, Lucas, Ethan, there are others here at DARPA who are willing to push the envelope. They understand the stakes. I'll handle the bureaucratic side, but let's be clear—I'll be in the crosshairs once this is over. But in situations like these, I'm a firm believer in action first, forgiveness later. Especially given the magnitude of CytoLife's plans."

Ethan nodded. "We've got our work cut out for us."

Lucas echoed the sentiment. "We always do. Get us what you can, Max. We'll take care of the rest."

Max offered a mock salute, a moment of levity amid the

tension. "Understood. And guys, keep your heads down out there."

Lucas chuckled in response. "Wouldn't have it any other way."

The channel went dark, leaving the room momentarily silent. The gravity of their situation hung in the air, but so did a renewed sense of determination. They had a plan now. It was time to execute it.

THIRTY ONE

The farmhouse's dimly lit corner had been transformed into a makeshift recording studio. A small table with a laptop and two facing chairs were surrounded by advanced cameras and microphones, their indicator lights blinking quietly in the semi-darkness.

Adam, with the meticulousness of a seasoned journalist, adjusted the camera angles. He was determined to keep Cam's identity protected. "You're in good hands, Cam," he reassured, noticing the anxiety in Cam's eyes. "Our setup will obscure your face and alter your voice. You'll remain anonymous."

Cam looked uneasily between the high-tech equipment and the room's exit, the reality of his upcoming confession weighing heavily on him. "I never imagined I'd be in a situation like this," he murmured.

Deandra, her notes organized and pen in hand, exuded

calm and confidence. "We understand it's overwhelming, Cam. But your insights are crucial. The more detailed your account, the stronger our case against CytoLife." Her voice carried the perfect balance of authority and compassion, a testament to her experience in guiding witnesses through critical testimonies.

Cam met Deandra's gaze, a mix of resolve and apprehension in his eyes. "I know it's important. It's just a lot to process."

Deandra kept her voice reassuring. "Your testimony could be the key to exposing CytoLife's wrongdoing. Stay focused on the facts. Let them speak for themselves."

Adam finished his final checks and looked up. "We're all set," he announced, a serious expression etched on his face, reflecting the significance of what they were about to undertake.

Cam took a deep breath, gathering his courage, and nodded towards the camera. "Okay. Let's do this."

The steady hum of the SUV's engine offered a soothing background to Harper's racing thoughts. She glanced at Lucas, noticing the firm grip of his hands on the wheel, the veins standing out against his skin. The dashboard lights cast a soft illumination on his face, accentuating his resolute expression.

Harper marveled at their journey, both physical and emotional. From a strained mother-son relationship to allies in a grueling crusade, their paths had merged in unexpected ways, forging a bond more profound than ever.

Lucas, feeling Harper's stare, turned to her with a faint smile. "Funny, isn't it?" he said, his voice suffused with newfound warmth. "A few months back, I couldn't have pictured us together like this, on a mission... facing such odds."

Harper let out a light, tremulous laugh. "I never saw this coming either. I let my work overshadow my time with you and Charlotte. The guilt... it's been a heavy burden. But now, in these extraordinary circumstances, we're here, united, making a stand. Together."

Lucas's hold on the steering wheel tightened briefly. "Having you here, Mom, it means a lot. It's not the reunion I imagined, but there's no one else I'd rather have at my side in this moment."

Emotion welled up in Harper's eyes. "Lucas, my belief in you has never wavered, though I struggled to express it. And I've got a lot to make up for, with Charlotte especially. But if there's a silver lining to this chaos, it's that it brought us back together."

He nodded, a deep breath escaping. "What we're about to face won't be easy. But with you here, I feel like we can take on anything."

Harper reached out, placing her hand atop his. "Together, we'll face whatever comes our way."

Hidden behind a grove of trees, Ethan surveyed the dark landscape, contrasting sharply with the distant lights emanating from CytoLife's compound. Beside him, a three-man ops team from DARPA meticulously prepped their gear, their movements precise and practiced in the tense air.

The crackle of his earpiece broke the silence. Max's voice came through with a low, steady urgency. "Ethan, we're treading into uncharted waters here. If we pull this off, it's going to be one hell of a debrief, to say the least. So much for a dull exit. But it's necessary. Operation Helix Breaker is a go."

Ethan replied, his voice calm yet purposeful. "Appreciate the backup, Max. Lucas is off-grid for now, but he's with us in spirit. We'll kick it into gear once he's back in the loop."

"Good to hear," Max responded. "Our teams are positioned nationwide, targeting each of CytoLife's bunkers, thanks to the intel from Lucas. We need to hit them simultaneously. Any delay could compromise the entire operation."

Ethan visualized a mental map, each point representing a crucial target. "Copy that. We're poised and ready on our end."

Max continued, "The moment those drones lift off, that's your cue. Remember, the DEW's range is limited. You need to be close enough for effective deployment."

"Understood, moving in as soon as we see them," Ethan affirmed.

Max's voice, crisp and focused, came through again. "Our tech team's gearing up for a cyber assault on CytoLife's network. It's untested in the field and off the record, but we're going all in. Once we neutralize their ground assets, we'll unleash the Anti-CRISPR agent. And Ethan," there was a brief pause, tinged with concern, "stay sharp out there."

As Lucas steered the SUV into CytoLife's driveway, the stark exterior of the compound loomed ahead. Both he and Harper could sense the heightened alertness that pervaded the area, an undercurrent of urgency perceptible in the air.

Parking the vehicle, they exited in unison, their movements reflecting the close rapport they had developed in recent days. Approaching the entrance, two security guards intercepted them, their expressions stoic and unreadable.

Lucas felt a slight tension rise within him. "I have authorized access," he stated, trying to project a confidence he didn't fully feel.

One guard, imposing in stature, regarded Lucas skeptically. "Your visit wasn't communicated to us," he challenged.

As Lucas searched for a response, Rebecca appeared. Her quick glance at Harper betrayed a moment of surprise, but she quickly regained her composure.

"Lucas is here under my authorization," Rebecca interjected, her tone leaving no room for argument. "He's part of my personal security detail today." She paused, her eyes questioning Lucas silently about Harper's presence.

Lucas met her gaze. "And Harper is with me," he said,

hoping his tone conveyed the necessity of her acceptance.

Rebecca gave a brief nod, though curiosity lingered in her eyes. "Follow me, please," she said, leading them briskly into CytoLife's interior.

Walking beside Harper, Lucas felt a reassuring solidarity in her presence. They were stepping into the lion's den, facing what could be their most critical challenge yet. United, they prepared to confront whatever awaited them inside CytoLife.

In the sterile conference room, under the glare of cold lights, Harper watched as Lucas, maintaining his composure, initiated the conversation.

"This is Harper," he said, gesturing to her. "My mother."

Rebecca's carefully maintained poise wavered. "Your mother?" she repeated, her voice a blend of confusion and sudden apprehension. She then turned to Lucas with a questioning look. "Lucas, why the silence this morning? What's happening here?"

Her eyes flicked between Harper and Lucas, a hint of unease in her expression. "With the lab on high alert, it's peculiar timing for family introductions."

Lucas held her gaze, his voice steady. "Rebecca, there's something you need to know. You're Thomas Baxter's daughter, correct?"

Rebecca's momentary hesitation gave way to a calm acceptance. "Yes, I use my mother's maiden name. It was important for me to establish my career independently, free from my father's influence."

Harper's tone, filled with indignation, asked, "And what exactly are those achievements, Rebecca? Playing God with human lives? Altering the essence of who we are?"

The tension in the room intensified as Rebecca assessed Harper. "Mrs. Fairbanks—"

"It's Brasfield," Harper corrected sharply, her voice painted with sarcasm. "But you can call me Brass."

Rebecca, unflustered, continued. "The world is on the brink of a transformative era, Brass. Our work at CytoLife is pioneering a new future for humanity."

Harper opened her mouth to retort, but a subtle signal from Lucas made her reconsider. Instead, she remained silent, her gaze fixed intently on Rebecca.

Lucas's hands clenched into fists, the weight of their shared past pressing down on him. "Rebecca, it's not just about shaping the future. It's about how we shape it. With compassion, with understanding, or with cold-hearted manipulation?"

Rebecca's voice trembled, her veneer of composure beginning to crack. "You don't understand, Lucas. The world is changing, and if we don't take control, someone else will. I refuse to be at the mercy of those who don't share our vision."

Lucas's gaze pierced into Rebecca. "Is this truly your vision, Rebecca? Or just a reflection of your father's twisted ambitions? I've seen what CytoLife is planning. It's monstrous. Your father isn't just seeking progress; he's aiming for dominance at the cost of countless innocent lives."

Rebecca paled, the weight of his words pressing down on her. "Lucas, you're misunderstanding—"

But Lucas cut her off, his voice rising with intensity. "I've seen the experiments, the test subjects, the communities he's willing to sacrifice for his *greater good*. How can you justify continuing this? How can you be a part of this nightmare he's creating?"

Rebecca faltered, the stark reality of her father's actions hitting home. "I... I thought he was doing it for the right reasons. I believed in the potential for a better world."

Lucas's expression softened slightly. "Rebecca, potential built on suffering and manipulation isn't a future worth striving for. You have to see that."

Rebecca squared her shoulders and met Lucas's gaze. "Lucas, each test subject gave their consent. They knew what they were getting into."

Lucas stared at her in disbelief. "Consent? You're using that to rationalize the inhumane treatment of these people? Do you even hear yourself?"

Rebecca's voice grew firm, her conviction clear. "Lucas, these were individuals abandoned by society, labeled as throwaways. We gave them a second chance when no one else would."

Lucas's face contorted with anguish. "Rebecca, that doesn't justify the means. You can't play God, deciding who's redeemable and who's not. It's not our place."

Harper stepped forward, her expression grave. "What about the ones who didn't survive, Rebecca? The ones who paid the ultimate price for your *second chance*? I still hear their screams in my nightmares."

Rebecca's face paled further, tears glistening in her eyes. She opened her mouth to speak, but no words came out. The weight of Harper's revelation, paired with Lucas's accusations, left her speechless and visibly shaken.

Tears welled in Lucas's eyes. "I loved you, Rebecca. I thought you were different. But now I see you're just like your father."

Rebecca hesitated, her resolve visibly wavering. "It doesn't have to be this way," she said faintly.

The tension in the room reached its peak when the doors slammed open forcefully. Felix Ross, flanked by armed guards, strode in. The cold, gleaming guns were pointed directly at Lucas and Harper. The atmosphere in the room instantly shifted, filled with an intense sense of danger and urgency.

"Enough of this," Felix declared, his voice dripping with authority. "You two will come with us. Now."

Lucas and Harper stiffened, instinctively raising their hands in surrender. As the guards moved closer, Lucas's eyes met Rebecca's. A torrent of raw emotion, shared history, and the heavy weight of the moment passed between them in a heart-wrenching glance. Rebecca's eyes brimmed with tears, mirroring the sadness in Lucas's expression.

Without another word, the guards began to escort Lucas and Harper out of the room. Felix led the way, leaving Rebecca behind, trembling in a whirlwind of emotion.

The chilling grip of the guards' hands on Harper's arms was nothing compared to the cold dread settling in her chest. As she and Lucas were led down the sterile, echoing corridor, her thoughts raced. Every step felt heavy, weighted down by the realization of just how deeply they were caught in Felix's clutches.

The door to Felix's office loomed ahead, a stark reminder of the power he wielded. The guards ushered them inside, then took their positions outside, leaving the trio alone in the room.

Felix, relishing his role, took his time. He slowly walked around his massive wooden desk, his fingers trailing over its surface. He paused, his gaze settling on Harper, then shifting to Lucas. His expression was eerily calm, a stark contrast to the turmoil raging inside Harper.

Felix's eyes slid from Lucas to Harper, his smirk unmistakable. "Harper," he began, his voice layered with a dangerous edge. "Or should I address you as Ms. Satterfield? How naïve do you take me for? Or is it Brass now?" He scoffed. "Soft yet tough? More like malleable and easily shattered. Much like spent bullet casings. I did warn you, didn't I? That your antics would drag those you care about into a whirlwind of regret. And here we are, with Lucas caught in the crossfire. And you, right beside him. How... unexpected."

Harper's stomach churned. She refused to let Felix see how much his words affected her. But the subtle shift in Lucas, the tightening of his jaw, betrayed his own unease.

Felix reached into a drawer, pulling out a handful of brass bullet casings. He let them slide between his fingers, their metallic clink echoing in the room as he played with them absentmindedly, a gleam in his eye.

"You see, Harper," he began, allowing a casing to roll down to the tip of his finger before catching it with a swift movement. "These remind me of you. Shiny on the outside, empty on the inside." He paused, letting the weight of his words sink in. "Did you honestly think I wouldn't piece it together? That Harper Brasfield, the mastermind in Memphis with her ragtag team, is also Lucas's dear mother?"

He leaned in closer, his voice dropping to a dangerous whisper. "You've been a thorn in my side for too long, Harper. And while your latest stunt was... entertaining, it changes nothing. You're playing a dangerous game. And the stakes? They're higher than you can imagine."

Lucas clenched his fists, his anger unmistakable. But Felix only smirked wider, clearly enjoying the tension he was creating. "You should've stayed out of this, Harper. For both your sakes."

Harper retorted, "We've unveiled the truth. In fact, the entire chilling revelation was broadcasted just moments ago."

Felix scoffed, rolling his eyes. "The masked whistleblower video? And that melodramatic article from your journalist friend? Please. They're nothing more than sensationalist noise. The public will forget in a week."

Felix chuckled, a dark, hollow sound. "Truth? My dear, in this world, truth is malleable. While you were busy playing detective, I had my team counter every smear with positive PR. With Baxter's name and influence, it was all too easy. A few backroom deals, some well-placed threats, and the scales tipped back in our favor. And just like before, we'll mount another PR offensive to handle this latest hiccup."

Lucas's voice was icy. "You won't get away with this, Felix."

Felix's smirk grew wider, more menacing. "Oh, Lucas.

Always so naïve. This is bigger than CytoLife, bigger than any of us. There are forces at play here that you can't even begin to comprehend."

The weight of Felix's gaze was almost tangible as he stared down at Harper and Lucas. "You think this is a game?" he asked, his voice low and dangerous. "I've been in places and done things you can't even imagine. Baxter has a vision, and I ensure it becomes reality. You and your little rebellion are just a minor inconvenience."

Lucas stepped forward, angry fists clenched. "We won't be silenced, Felix. Not by you, not by Baxter."

Felix's laugh was cold and devoid of humor. "You don't get it, do you? You're out of your depth. You're up against forces you can't comprehend."

Harper's voice was steely. "We're not afraid of you or your boss."

Felix's menacing eyes glinted. "You should be."

He straightened, the faintest hint of a sneer playing on his lips. "You two are but specks in the vast expanse of our influence. Do you really believe your efforts, your little plots and rallies, can even begin to dent the empire we've built?"

Harper's eyes flashed defiantly, but she remained silent, letting Felix continue his tirade.

"We control every lever of power," he boasted, gesturing expansively. "There isn't an opinion we can't sway, nor an outcome we can't guarantee. While you've been playing at revolution, we've been pulling the strings, and orchestrating a new world order."

Lucas struggled to contain his anger. "You can't control everyone, Felix."

Felix chuckled, the sound chilling in its dismissiveness. "Oh, Lucas. It's cute that you think that. Our plan is already set in motion, irrevocably changing the course of history. In the grand scheme of things, you and Harper? Insignificant."

Harper reached into her bag, producing a sleek hard drive. Holding it up for Felix to see, her expression was unflinching and defiant. "This is my insurance," she declared forcibly. "If anything happens to us, its contents will be released publicly."

She continued, her voice unwavering, "This drive contains footage from one of your secret labs. It didn't just capture the experiment, but also your celebration afterward. You and Baxter, gleeful about your success, discussing your plans." Harper's stare was piercing as she locked eyes with Felix. "This isn't just damning evidence; it's concrete proof of your involvement."

Harper noticed a brief flicker of concern on Felix's face when he saw the hard drive, a model Cam had identified as CytoLife's. He quickly masked it, but the momentary lapse was telling. "That drive is insignificant. It proves nothing," Felix retorted, though Harper noted the slight quiver in his voice.

Her smirk grew, sensing his discomfort. "Are you sure you want to gamble CytoLife's future on that assumption?"

Felix's eyes flitted around the room, clearly assessing Harper's fortitude. "You're playing a high-stakes game, Harper," he cautioned, his voice dripping with menace.

She met his challenge head-on. "Am I? Or am I simply evening the odds?"

Felix leaned forward, his hands flat on the desk. "Harper,

think about what you're doing. Give me that drive and we can find a mutually beneficial resolution," he suggested, but his voice betrayed a hint of desperation.

Harper's eyebrow arched in skepticism. "What assurances can you give me?" she asked, her tone indicating she wasn't easily swayed.

Felix's demeanor shifted to one of calculated calm. "Your family's safety, for starters. No more threats, no more uncertainties. Think of Lucas," he urged, his voice smooth but insistent.

Harper's gaze remained steadfast as she looked toward Lucas. "I am thinking of him. That's exactly why I'm here. But safety alone isn't enough. What concrete guarantees can you offer?"

Felix paused, considering the implications of his next words. "Complete financial security for you and Lucas," he began, then added after a moment. "And my personal commitment that you will be left undisturbed."

Harper met Felix's gaze head-on. "You think I'm playing games, Felix. But this is about fighting for justice," she stated firmly. "However, I know when to be pragmatic. You want the drive? It's yours. But my family's safety and Lucas's financial future are nonnegotiable." She left the specifics unsaid, allowing the implication to resonate in the air. Clasping her hands tightly, her defiance was indisputable. "We accept your offer, but be warned—we are as watchful as you are."

In their moment of silent understanding, Harper could sense the high-stakes game they were both playing. She had no intention of honoring her end of the deal, and she strongly suspected Felix felt the same way. Yet this exchange of veiled threats and calculated promises was a necessary step in their complex dance. For Harper, securing even a fleeting advantage, no matter how transient, brought a sense of bitter satisfaction.

Nodding, Felix swiftly made a call, issuing concise instructions. "Consider this an initial gesture of goodwill," he said, smirking, hinting at more benefits for their cooperation. "But remember, this hinges on your ongoing compliance."

Harper's eyes stayed locked on Felix, her face a mask of icy determination. "We have an agreement, Felix. I'll be holding you to it." She added, her voice steely, "But don't think for a second that this is over. Trust is the last thing you should expect from me."

Internally, Harper's emotions were a whirlwind of apprehension and anticipation, but she maintained her composure. Felix's slight shift in behavior had not gone unnoticed; the hard drive had clearly unnerved him.

"You may think you've won a small victory with that drive," Felix retorted, a venomous edge to his voice. "But don't fool yourself. Our plans are far bigger than you can comprehend, and they're proceeding as intended." His eyes narrowed menacingly. "My advice? Go back to your lives, try to salvage what you can. But remember this: our eyes will always be on you."

With a dismissive wave of his hand, Felix signaled the guards. The office door swung open, and the guards stepped in, their stance and expression indicating that Harper and Lucas were to be escorted out immediately.

As the new Toyota SUV pulled away from the CytoLife complex, the silence in the car was stark. Replacing the Range Rover Lucas had been using, this SUV held not just their personal belongings, but also a duffel bag filled with cash and an envelope with the vehicle's title. Lucas and Harper rode in silence, each absorbed in their own thoughts about the intense encounter they had just survived.

Harper's mind was a whirlwind of emotions, but she resisted the urge to discuss the painful encounter with Rebecca. There would be time for that later.

After a few minutes of driving, Harper finally exhaled a long sigh of relief, breaking the silence. Lucas glanced at her, a hint of a smile playing on his lips. "Well, that went exactly as we planned," he said with a touch of irony.

Lucas's grin broadened, a spark of triumph in his eyes. "I'll admit, I had my doubts for a moment there. But Felix played right into our hands." He looked over at Harper, a glint of shared strategy in his eyes. "That DARPA listening device we slipped onto the drive is a stroke of brilliance. Even if Felix tries to dispose of it, it will still transmit every word. It's undetectable, and it's our ace in the hole. The moment he makes the call to deploy the drones, we'll be ready."

Harper nodded, a sense of achievement growing inside her. "Now, we move to the next stage of our plan," she said, her voice filled with tense anticipation. "It's time to end this."

Lucas's fingers worked deftly on his phone, unlocking the layers of security. Once inside, he initiated the secure communication line with a focused intensity.

"Ethan, it's Lucas. We're set on our end. The device is in place," he spoke softly, but with a clear sense of urgency.

Ethan's voice crackled through, steady and reassuring. "Good work. We now have direct access to Felix's inner sanctum. We're one step ahead."

Lucas nodded, though Ethan couldn't see it. "The tech is active. We're ready to monitor every move inside CytoLife. They won't even know we're there."

"Ready when you are," Ethan confirmed, his voice conveying a mix of excitement and determination.

Closing the call, Lucas looked at Harper. Her adrenaline rush and determination was mirrored in his face. This was it—their strategic upper hand.

Lucas said, "Now, we wait and watch. We've got them right where we want them."

Outside the farmhouse, in the dense underbrush, Ethan lay concealed, his body tense. The ground was cold and damp beneath him, a stark contrast to the cutting-edge tech surrounding him. The DARPA team, in position, had their equipment trained on the skies, ready to counter the incoming threat from CytoLife.

Felix's command echoed through his earpiece. "Activate the Nemesis Protocol."

On cue, the forest's tranquility was shattered by the buzzing of drones. Ethan, peering through the foliage, saw them whizzing overhead, their metallic bodies glinting in the fading light. They moved with a precision that was almost inhuman.

Suddenly, a blinding flash from one of the DARPA devices sent several drones spiraling down, crashing into the underbrush. However, others persisted, maneuvering deftly around the countermeasures.

The team rapidly recalibrated their equipment, trying to regain control. Despite the chaos, they maintained focus, their eyes fixed on the screens that displayed the battlefield in the skies.

Ethan keyed his secure line to Max. "Max, it's Ethan. The drones are out. We need the Anti-CRISPR now."

Max's voice was calm but urgent. "Understood, Ethan. Launching countermeasures now."

In the forest, DARPA's counteraction began. Specially equipped drones carrying the Anti-CRISPR solution soared into the sky, their mission to intercept and neutralize CytoLife's harmful agents.

Back at the farmhouse, every eye was glued to the monitor. Harper leaned closer to the screen, her heart racing. "It's happening," she announced, the weight of their actions settling heavily upon her. They were in a race against time, and every second mattered.

Ethan's return to the farmhouse was met with anxious faces. The group gathered around, their expressions a mix of hope and apprehension. As he walked in, the weight of the mission seemed to follow him, settling heavily in the room.

Lucas and Harper exchanged a look of shared concern, their recent encounter with Rebecca and Felix still fresh in their minds. Before Lucas could go over their meeting, Ethan's voice cut through the tense atmosphere.

"Felix ordered the drone release," Ethan reported, his voice carrying the weight of their grim reality. "We intercepted the command almost immediately after you two left."

Harper's expression turned to one of shock. "So quickly?"

Ethan nodded solemnly, his gaze sweeping over the group. "The ops team managed to down some drones, but it's too early to gauge the full extent of our success. This night might stretch longer than we anticipated."

Ethan, holding a tablet, continued, "We're in constant contact with Max. The Anti-CRISPR deployment has begun." He raised the tablet, showing a live feed of the operation. The screen displayed an intricate dance of digital warfare, where the harmful agents from CytoLife met their match against DARPA's countermeasures.

Deandra leaned in, her voice hushed. "Is it effective?"

Ethan shrugged, a hint of uncertainty in his eyes. "It's working, at least partially. But remember, we're in uncharted waters with this technology."

Lucas exhaled a heavy breath, his shoulders dropping slightly. "We owe Max and his team a lot. They've given us a fighting chance."

The group huddled around the tablet, watching as the

digital representation of their efforts unfolded in real time. A cautious optimism began to fill the room, tempered by the knowledge that their battle against CytoLife was far from over.

Baxter stood before the large window in his study, his back to Felix as he gazed out over the sprawling estate. The tension in the room was clear as Felix spoke urgently into the phone.

"Our entire operation hinged on those drones going undetected. This was supposed to be a clean launch!" Felix's voice was strained with frustration.

On the other end, the contact from the Department of Defense was clearly on edge. "Felix, this was unexpected. The tech that took out your drones... it wasn't even on our radar. It's like nothing we've seen before."

Felix slammed his hand on the desk. "You assured us our tech was untraceable, that there'd be no interference!"

There was a moment of silence on the line before the contact responded, "We're doing everything we can to figure out where this countermeasure came from. Someone has access to resources we didn't account for."

Baxter turned slowly, his eyes cold and calculating. "Your assurances mean nothing now. You've compromised a key part of my plan. I expect this to be rectified. Immediately."

The voice on the line was apologetic. "We're on it, Mr. Baxter. I assure you we'll find out how this happened."

Baxter's voice was icy as he issued a warning. "See that

you do. Failures are not something I tolerate. Fix this, or you'll find yourself in a position you won't envy."

Hanging up the phone, Felix looked at Baxter, uncertainty flickering in his eyes.

Baxter's expression was unreadable as he contemplated their next move. "We adapt. We always have. This is but a minor setback. The game is far from over, Felix."

Baxter shifted his gaze from the encrypted phone to Felix, his cold blue eyes piercing. "Felix," he said, each word heavy with disappointment, "you promised a flawless operation. Explain."

Felix, unflinching, met his gaze. "Sir, the laser tech was off our radar. We couldn't predict this interference."

Baxter's voice took a mocking edge. "I'm painfully aware, after our recent... debacle. What's the status? Now."

Felix pushed through the sting of rebuke. "Some drones broke through, dispersing the nanoparticles. It's not a complete failure."

Baxter raised an eyebrow. "And the opposing drones that appeared? I have teams reverse-engineering them. Their payload, Felix?"

Felix felt the gravity of the moment. "Likely a countermeasure, neutralizing our CRISPR tech and the gene-editing potential of our nanoparticles."

Baxter's voice dripped with sarcasm. "With our influence, you'd think we'd anticipate this. Time to redefine *prepared*."

His nostrils flared, but Felix interjected, "Remember, Thomas, we're already injecting AGG1 gene therapy globally. This drone issue is just a hiccup. Our control remains intact."

Tension hung heavy. Baxter nodded slowly. "Fine. But handle any more disruptions. We can't afford missteps now."

Felix nodded with feigned calm. "A minor hiccup, nothing more. We will prevail."

Leaning in, Baxter's presence was icy. "And about the leaked video and article. They're spreading fast, exposing us."

Felix's jaw clenched. "We're handling it."

Baxter's laugh was humorless. "Handling it? It seems your handling only multiplies our problems. The drones, now this PR disaster. The world's glimpsing our operations."

Felix inhaled sharply. "The video won't derail us. We'll contain the fallout."

Baxter's eyes narrowed. "You better. We can't let carelessness ruin our vision. I want results, not excuses."

Rebecca's fingers flew across the keys, securing the last critical files to a covert encrypted cloud, known only to a select few. The progress bar filled steadily, mirroring the rhythm of her racing heart. When the upload finished, she paused to collect herself, then activated a protocol to erase and destroy any traces on her system.

Thoughts of Lucas intruded, their deep connection and the ache of their recent separation. She longed to explain her choices, but time was relentless.

Refocusing, Rebecca connected the DataDissolver to her computer. It glowed blue and sparked, rendering her machine useless.

With a heavy heart, she packed her essentials, leaving behind her sanctuary and Lucas, their paths now veiled in secrets.

Outside, a sleek black sedan awaited. Her father greeted her with a look of understanding.

"Rebecca," he said softly, embracing her. In his arms, she found a momentary solace, her mind still entwined with thoughts of Lucas.

"This isn't the end, Papa," she said, her voice a blend of determination and sadness. "Our mission is more vital than ever."

Baxter's eyes reflected wisdom and steadfastness. "We've overcome challenges before, Rebecca. Our allies are powerful; they're with us."

She nodded, caught in a whirlwind of emotions. "Where now? Switzerland? Iceland? France?"

He smiled, a hint of nostalgia in his eyes. "We have options. We always do."

THIRTY TWO

In Felix's sprawling office, the disorder amplified the suffocating feel. His normally pristine desk was buried under legal documents, each stamped with seals and emblems from US institutions. Screens around him flashed unrelenting, scathing headlines, all zeroing in on CytoLife's controversial activities.

Outside, a relentless media swarm jostled for position, eager for the latest on CytoLife's predicament. Felix, always a master strategist, now faced an unprecedented challenge.

To many, this seemed CytoLife's unraveling. But to Felix, it was a mere blip in a grander plan, one even Baxter couldn't fully grasp. The consortium, with its immense resources and influence, was playing a far deeper game.

His phone buzzed. An anonymous message: *Stay the course*. Its brevity belied its significance. He was a key piece in a larger puzzle.

Felix tapped his desk rhythmically. Public inquiries and scrutiny were inevitable, but he knew true power lay in the shadows. The consortium was ready to reshape the narrative.

The phone's shrill ring pierced the tense air. *Private Caller* flashed on the display.

Felix answered with a simple command. "Speak."

A cold, calculated voice replied, "Do what's necessary. Endure this. We're aiming higher."

A slight smile touched Felix's lips. "Understood."

As the call ended, Felix felt a resurgence of determination. The world might view this as CytoLife's end, but for Felix, it was a new beginning. The landscape had shifted, yet the players remained, each biding their time for the next strategic move.

In the buzzing room, Baxter's elite team engaged in intense deliberation. A young, renowned PR specialist leaned forward, capturing their attention. "Mr. Baxter, distancing yourself from certain CytoLife figures might be wise now."

The suggestion hung heavily in the air, the implication clear. All eyes turned to Baxter.

Before he could respond, a legal counsel added, "It's common for CEOs of major corporations like CytoLife to miss internal details. Blaming Felix could be our best play."

A seasoned PR strategist declared, "We can craft a narrative of betrayal, portraying Felix's actions as a deception. Public sympathy often favors a redemption story."

Baxter's eyes narrowed, considering the gamble of sacrificing Felix. Their shared history was intricate, but survival was paramount.

He spoke carefully. "I've always aimed for the greater good. If Felix acted against our principles, he should answer for it. But," he paused, choosing his words, "that's our fallback. First, let's explore ways to rebuild my image."

His team nodded, jotting notes and brainstorming. Ideas flew: an interview with a renowned journalist focusing on Baxter's philanthropy and Baxter Global's successes. A series of articles highlighting CytoLife's positive impacts. Maybe a hefty donation to a genetic research ethics foundation.

Determination filled the room. They were preparing for a public opinion battle. Baxter, resolute and backed by brilliant minds, was ready to engage.

In a lavish room atop a towering skyscraper, the atmosphere was charged. The consortium members, indifferent to the sprawling cityscape through the vast windows, were engrossed in their urgent discussion.

An elegant woman with keen eyes broke the silence. "The CytoLife issue is regrettable, but manageable. We've overcome greater challenges."

The man at the table's head, his presence imposing, agreed. "It's a minor disruption in our broader plan. We'll adapt."

Another, scrolling through a digital dossier, mused,

"Baxter at CytoLife may have overreached. Should we reconsider his future role?"

The woman's lips twitched slightly. "Baxter's vision is in line with ours, but his execution is faltering. Reevaluation may be necessary."

The elder member paused thoughtfully. "What about the other one, the shadow player?"

A younger, confident member responded, "He remains effective and loyal. However, he too requires direction."

An unspoken accord filled the room. The consortium, a hidden hand in global affairs, remained steadfast. The recent turbulence only reinforced their determination.

The elder, with decisive authority, declared, "CytoLife is but one step in our ascent. We move forward, with or without Baxter. We're ready to shape the world's new direction."

The setting sun cast a golden glow over Memphis. The enticing scent of barbecue filled the air, luring both locals and tourists to the city's renowned eateries. Lucas had picked the Rendezvous for its familiarity—a place grounding even the most significant discussions.

Seated in a booth, Lucas watched Max attack a slab of ribs, barbecue sauce smearing his face. "Damn, Lucas," Max said, mouth full, "this is incredible. Southern hospitality at its best."

Ethan chuckled, his tone light. "Well, if there's one thing we do right in the South, it's food. Consider it a small gesture of our big hospitality."

Lucas's gaze rested on Max. The risks Max had taken deserved more than this simple gratitude, yet for now, this meal would suffice.

As they explored the issues, Max, now serious, wiped his hands. "We did our best against CytoLife. But there's no surefire way to know if we stopped them all."

Lucas pondered the dilemma. "Even if we took down most of the drones, CytoLife's influence is pervasive—clinics, campaigns. Direct outreach might've been happening all along."

Ethan's voice carried a note of frustration. "We're grappling with shadows. Every victory seems fleeting."

Lucas broke the tension, putting words to their shared concern. "We're left with a pile of questions and no clear answers," he remarked, his expression troubled. "The situation's taken on a life of its own, and the debates out there? They're just angry noise now."

Max took a deliberate sip of his drink, then spoke up. "Yeah, and there's the DARPA initiative—Safe Genes. It's like everyone's just realizing the power of gene editing, and now the government wants to play watchdog. But the way they're going about it, it's like handing them a loaded weapon and hoping they don't accidentally pull the trigger. It's dicey either way, man."

Lucas felt the weight of their dilemma as the clamor of the restaurant faded into the background. "So, taking on CytoLife might've just traded one devil for another, huh? More oversight?"

Max's nod was heavy. "Feels like it. It's walking a tightrope. I got my wrist slapped pretty good, but with the brass looking at bigger targets, I'm left hanging. Where this leads, for the likes of me, is anyone's guess."

The meal ended in thoughtful silence. Leaving the Rendezvous, its sign softly illuminating the sidewalk, Lucas felt the enormity of their struggle and the challenges ahead.

In the shadowy office of *The Bluff City Standard*, Adam Burke felt his stomach twist into knots. Across from him, Ben Mitchell, the experienced editor-in-chief and Adam's mentor, sat behind his aged oak desk, etched with the marks of a long journalism career.

Adam broke the tense silence, his words laden with gravity. "The story's out, Ben. It's exposed CytoLife's tampering with AGG1 genes, their brazen attempt to alter human behavior. Allegedly for the greater good, but it's caused an uproar. The whistleblowers... their accounts have torn away the façade of CytoLife's so-called harmonization."

Ben raised his eyes, his expression a blend of pride and concern. "Your work is exemplary, Adam. You've revealed their hidden agenda to manipulate humanity at its core. This isn't just making headlines; it's sparked official inquiries. Governments are stepping in, and CytoLife is shut down. I regret the paper's initial hesitation. Got caught up in corporate politics."

Adam's voice was weary. "But at what cost? It's chaos out

there. The public is enraged, pundits are polarizing the issue, and the government... they're playing their own game."

He paused, his voice shaded with a mix of anger and helplessness. "And Thomas Baxter, he's being raked over the coals, but I can't shake the feeling he'll come out of this untouched."

Ben leaned forward, his determination carved into his features. "Power can deflect many things. But your story, Adam, it's more than journalism. It's a light in the darkness. Thomas Baxter might evade the fallout for now, but the public's gaze is relentless and unforgiving."

Adam sighed. "I just hope it makes a difference."

Ben's hand fell reassuringly on the article. "You've ignited a critical flame, Adam. And sometimes, that's all it takes to start a fire. Brace yourself for the backlash, though."

Adam nodded, feeling a sense of purpose inspired by Ben's guidance. "Thanks, Ben. I'm prepared for what comes next."

Their story, now in the public domain, did more than expose CytoLife's misconduct. It stood as a testament to the bravery of those who broke the silence. In that moment, with Ben, Adam wasn't just reporting news. He was upholding the enduring power of truth.

In the tranquil room, the soft chime of Lucas's new phone was a sharp contrast to his turbulent thoughts. This phone, bought recently as a shield from the past and a safeguard for the future, was known only to a select few.

His pulse quickened when he saw the sender's name: *Rebecca.*

Hesitating briefly, Lucas opened the message.

Lucas, I know you're surprised to hear from me, especially here. Trust me, I found a way. I've been thinking—a lot—about us. About everything.

A lump formed in Lucas's throat. Memories of their last, pain-laden conversation flooded back—the confusion in Rebecca's eyes, the growing gulf between them, the choices she made that seemed so alien to the woman he was coming to love.

He replied, his fingers unsteady.

Rebecca, I didn't think I'd hear from you again. After all that's happened... What do you mean?

Her response was swift.

I wish I could tell you everything, make it all clear. But it's too risky. For both of us. Just know that.

Staring at the screen, Lucas felt a storm of emotions. The unspoken truths and the vast distance between them were palpable. Yet her reaching out, defying the risks, sparked a faint hope. Maybe she wasn't entirely lost to Baxter's influence.

He typed back, weighing each word.

Rebecca, whatever you're entangled in, remember who you are. I'm here if you ever need to talk or need help.

He watched the screen as the typing indicator flickered, then stopped. Time stretched on, but no further message arrived. The silence was loud, leaving Lucas with unanswered questions and a heart burdened with longing and unresolved hope.

The Elmwood Cemetery was a haven of serenity, with leaves rustling softly in the breeze. Ancient trees towered above, their branches casting dappled shadows across the gravestones. Harper walked along the grassy path, Dee accompanying her in warmhearted solidarity. They approached a newly laid gravesite, where a polished tombstone sparkled in the sunlight.

Mama Dee stood there, the epitome of elegance and sorrow in her mourning attire. Her eyes, shimmering with both pride and grief, were fixed on the tombstone of her beloved Isaac. Harper felt a tightness in her throat, profoundly touched by the scene.

Charlotte and Lucas were already there, offering their respects in subdued murmurs. Harper exchanged a warm smile with them as she drew closer.

Mama Dee cleared her throat, capturing everyone's attention. "Isaac might have complained about all this," she said, her voice wavering, "especially this grand tombstone. He always claimed he was just a simple man."

Dee chuckled. "That he was. Always fussing over the little things."

Harper smiled, a tender memory surfacing. "I remember

his rants about the courthouse coffee. He called it *an abomination to all java beans.*"

Their laughter briefly lightened the solemn air.

Mama Dee, dabbing at her eyes, added, "Yet for all his grumbling, Isaac's heart was full of love. I've been so proud of him. Always. Complications and all."

Harper spoke gently. "He was a beacon of hope, a guide for so many."

Mama Dee motioned towards the tombstone. "Harper, would you read it out loud?"

Stepping forward, Harper's eyes traced the graceful inscription:

Isaac Ambrose Jackson
Sunrise: August 12, 1949
Sunset: September 18, 2023
A guiding light in the darkest times.

A reflective silence enveloped the group, embracing the profound meaning of the words.

Mama Dee, her voice thick with emotion, continued, "Isaac's light reached so many—the lost, the broken, those warmed by his wisdom. He touched countless lives."

Harper, eyes moist, added, "In his light, we all found growth. He shone the brightest, and because of him, we flourished."

The breeze seemed to carry their sentiments, whispering through the trees, as they stood united in their mourning and gratitude for a man whose legacy was imprinted on their hearts.

EPILOGUE

A year later.

In the golden light of her new office in Memphis, Harper Brasfield reflected on her journey. Facing unthinkable evils and nearly losing everything had steered her to this moment. As she gazed at the Brasfield Law & Advocacy logo, it represented not just a new venture, but a stand against the darkness that had almost engulfed her life.

Harper recognized the need for a vigilant watchdog in the legal landscape, particularly after the societal upheaval brought about by unchecked technological advancements. Her firm would be a bulwark, ensuring legal frameworks evolved alongside rapidly changing technologies, protecting rights in a world still reeling and reorienting itself after recent events.

She intentionally steered clear of the news. Its constant, frustrating intensity hit too close to home, echoing the very events she had lived through. Instead, she focused her energy on driving meaningful change through her firm while nurturing the bonds with her family, each aspect equally vital in the fabric of her life.

In the warm glow of her office, Harper wrestled with a lingering question: despite their new beginning, were they truly free from the shadows of the past, or did unseen threats still lurk? As the world continued to grapple with the fallout from the CytoLife scandal, Felix Ross, a once-menacing figure in their ordeal, had vanished into thin air. His mysterious disappearance, amid the turmoil, left a trail of unease and unanswered questions.

Her thoughts drifted to Lucas. His recent demeanor, a mix of withdrawal and openness, was enigmatic. His travels—were they an escape from hidden demons, or a journey towards understanding himself? Harper, now more introspective, held back. She chose to respect the delicate threads of their rekindling relationship, her maternal instincts discreetly alert beneath the surface.

Her phone buzzed, interrupting her thoughts. The caller ID read *Charlotte*.

"Charlie," Harper answered cautiously, the wounds from their past struggles still fresh in her mind.

"Hey, Mom," came the slightly hesitant reply. "I heard about the new firm. Brasfield Law & Advocacy. It's quite the name."

Harper's voice softened a touch. "Thank you. It's a big step, and I'm hoping to make a difference."

There was a slight pause before Charlie ventured, "I've got a break next week. How about dinner? That new rooftop place downtown?"

The invitation surprised Harper, but she welcomed it. "I'd like that. It's been a while since we've caught up."

Charlie's voice held a hint of maturity. "It has. And, well, there's something I want to discuss regarding my pre-law courses."

Harper raised an eyebrow, intrigued. "Alright then, looking forward to hearing about it."

The call ended on a note of tentative optimism, a bridge slowly mending between mother and daughter.

Ethan Cook paused at the entrance of the refurbished warehouse office, taking in the transformation. The space, once a cluttered shell, now buzzed as the sleek, tech-driven hub of *CookCyber Solutions*. Servers hummed in the background, and state-of-the-art technology sparkled around him, a testament to his newfound expertise in the digital world.

However, as he stepped inside, a flicker of unease followed him. The widely exposed CytoLife scandal had left him wary of the limitations of governmental oversight in the aftermath of such an audacious genetic manipulation attempt. His forays into the dark web, particularly those uncovering CytoLife, had unveiled the murky depths of technological progress.

His eyes briefly rested on a server light, blinking rhythmically—a subtle reminder of the veiled threat he'd received following his investigations. The message, encoded and layered, was a clear indicator that his actions had stirred attention in hidden corners.

Shaking off these thoughts, Ethan moved toward his desk. And yet the feeling of looming danger persisted, casting a shadow of uncertainty over his future. He pondered the world's next steps and the potential unseen threats that might emerge from his past digital escapades.

"Late again, Mr. Investigator?" Neon's voice, woven with playful mischief, echoed in the room. Surrounded by a labyrinth of wires, he sat in stark contrast to his surroundings, his spiky hair and neon sneakers juxtaposed with an elegant three-piece suit.

Ethan responded with a chuckle. "You'd think a Southern gentleman would be more patient."

Neon, feigning shock, stood up, straightening his jacket. "Patience is a virtue, but so is keeping you on your toes, Ethan. The digital world doesn't pause."

Despite Neon's playful demeanor, Ethan had come to deeply respect the hacker. Underneath the flamboyant exterior lay a razor-sharp intellect and a commitment to ethical hacking. Their partnership was an intriguing contrast: Ethan's down-to-earth pragmatism meshed with Neon's unpredictable brilliance.

Leaning against a table, Ethan mused, "You know, Neon, you were an enigma when we first met. A hacker with a gentleman's charm and a rebel's spirit."

Neon flashed a wink. "Life's too dull in just one box, Ethan. But I'm glad we teamed up. We're quite the duo."

Ethan nodded, acknowledging their unique synergy. "Together, we're making waves, challenging the norms."

In that shared moment, they recognized the strength of their bond. In the intricate world of technology, they stood united, ready to face its challenges with a blend of integrity and skill.

Dee picked up her phone and dialed a number she knew by heart. "Hello, Mrs. Evans, it's Deandra Jackson. I wanted to talk to you about The Daylight Foundation."

"Deandra! A career with the District Attorney's office, and now you're starting a foundation too? You're truly leaving an imprint," Mrs. Evans responded with enthusiasm.

As Mrs. Evans continued with her praise, Deandra's thoughts were clouded by the omnipresent CytoLife scandal. It dominated news headlines, congressional hearings, and public discourse, with fervent calls for justice and accountability. Amidst this maelstrom, Deandra felt a growing apprehension. It seemed only a matter of time before the investigative tide would reach her father's doorstep, threatening to tarnish the revered legacy of Judge Jackson.

"Thank you, Mrs. Evans," Deandra said, her voice a careful blend of gratitude and hidden anxiety. "The foundation is very close to my heart. It's inspired by something my father often emphasized—the importance of making the most of our *daylight*, especially during challenging times."

Mrs. Evans's laughter was warm. "Your father's wisdom

has certainly found a home in you. He'd be proud of how you've carried his lessons forward."

Deandra, motivated by a deep sense of purpose, outlined her vision. "The Daylight Foundation is committed to education and legal aid. We aim to empower and uplift those in need, ensuring that everyone has the opportunity to make their daylight matter."

Mrs. Evans responded with admiration in her voice. "Your dedication is truly commendable, Deandra. How can I assist with this admirable endeavor?"

Deandra's smile masked her internal turmoil. "Your support would mean everything. Let's work together to give everyone their chance in the sun."

Adam sat in the stillness of his old office at *The Bluff City Standard*, surrounded by the relics of the story that had altered the course of his career. The papers from his exposé on CytoLife lay scattered, a testament to the chaos that had ensued.

The aftermath of the scandal continued to reverberate—congressional debates, the Safe Genes Initiative, and the relentless media coverage weighed heavily on him. Stepping away from the daily grind, Adam was channeling his efforts into a memoir, chronicling the tumultuous journey of uncovering the gene-editing controversy.

As the door creaked open, Ben Mitchell appeared, his expression a mix of nostalgia and understanding. "Quiet in here, huh? Never thought I'd see Adam Burke away from the action." A wry smile curved his lips.

Adam chuckled softly. "The action hasn't stopped, Ben. It's just shifted. Everywhere I turn, there's talk of the congressional hearings, the Safe Genes Initiative... the whole landscape's changing."

Ben leaned against the doorframe, his tone serious. "And in the middle of that storm, there's still so much left unsaid, so many questions unanswered. Your voice, your insight into these debates—it's crucial, Adam."

Adam nodded, his gaze thoughtful. "That's why I'm writing this memoir, Ben. To make sense of it all, and maybe, to prepare for what's next."

Ben's eyes met Adam's, conveying a deep respect. "Well, just know this—whatever you uncover next, whatever paths you tread, you'll always have a home here to share those truths."

Adam's response was a mixture of gratitude and determination. "Thanks, Ben. I might just take you up on that. There's a lot more to this story, and I intend to stay on its trail."

As Ben retreated from the doorway, leaving Adam in his contemplative solitude, the air was filled with an unspoken acknowledgment that this was not an end, but a prelude to deeper investigations and revelations yet to come.

Across the cobblestone streets of Paris, Lucas Fairbanks sat at a wrought-iron table outside a quaint French café. The aroma of freshly baked croissants mingled with the air as he sipped his coffee, deep in thought. The heavy burden of CytoLife's money, once a constant reminder of secrets and betrayals, had lessened. He had found peace in redirecting a significant portion of that wealth to The Daylight Foundation, a cause dear to his family's heart.

Setting his cup down, the gentle hum of surrounding conversations was briefly interrupted by the rhythmic click-clack of heels on stone. He looked up, squinting against the afternoon sun, to see a familiar silhouette approaching. The unmistakable grace in her steps, the distinct tilt of her head— it all felt so known, yet distant. Could it truly be Rebecca, the enigmatic figure intertwined with his past? A slight smile curled the corners of Lucas's lips, a blend of surprise and anticipation. As the woman drew nearer, the world around them seemed to blur, and for a fleeting moment, everything else faded into insignificance.

DIVE INTO THE NEXT CHAPTER OF THE HELIX CHRONICLES!

Are you ready to follow Harper and Lucas beyond the streets of Memphis to a global stage in *Echoes of Control: The Final Stand*? The stakes are higher than ever as they navigate the perilous waters of genetic manipulation—a journey that pushes the boundaries of human freedom and the future of evolution itself.

Continue the thrilling saga!

www.monicachase.com/echoespreview

PERSONAL JOURNEY

"When did you start writing?" Someone asked me not too long ago. I laughed before answering because, in truth, I've been at it forever—just not always in the ways you'd expect. This book is me stepping into the light, after years of hiding behind different masks. It's been quite the ride, filled with ups and downs. I've faced off against cancer and reconnected with a family member in the most unexpected way.

Through all of this, my family's been there—pushing me forward, sometimes with a nudge, other times with a full-on shove. But always, they've been my anchor, keeping me from drifting too far from who I am and what I dream of doing. This book? It's more than just a story; it's bits and pieces of me, a nod to the wild, wonderful web of connections we're all part of. It dives into themes that have touched my life, the kind of stuff that makes us all tick.

TO THOSE WHO WALKED THIS PATH WITH ME

To everyone who caught glimpses of the writer in me, even when I was busy doubting myself or sidestepping my own abilities, your faith in me was like a nudge in the right direction. It helped me find my way through the maze, always reminding me of where I really needed to be.

To my dad, always the steady hand and the voice of reason, who told me, "Listen to your mama—she's usually right." Dad, you've been my real-life roadmap, always helping me navigate through the confusing bits of life.

To my mom, who's all courage and love, and has this amazing knack for spotting the truth in a sea of fibs. You've taught me that being brave doesn't mean you're not scared; it means you go for it anyway, even when you are.

To my bonus dad, who's always been kind and sharp as a tack. I can always count on you for a good laugh or the perfect piece of advice when I need it most. I'm so thankful for your wisdom and your wit in my life.

To my siblings, looks like we've finally settled the favorite debate. (Just kidding—though, let's be honest, you all know it's me.)

To my husband, you've been the rock I didn't even know I needed until we started this journey together. Through every late-night writing session, fueled by endless cups of coffee, you've kept me grounded. Turns out, love and chocolate are the best combo ever.

To my son, who teaches me new depths of courage every day and proves that students can indeed surpass their teachers. You fill me with pride.

To my daughter, joy personified and my heart in human form. The magic you bring to my life is indescribable.

To my son-in-law, thank you for being the source of my daughter's happiness, for being a wonderful father, and for your genuinely kind soul.

To my granddaughter, our little fearless wonder, your brilliance dazzles us all. I have so many stories waiting just for you.

And to the team at Paper Raven Books, your belief in this story has been unwavering. For every step we've taken together, my gratitude knows no bounds.

MEMPHIS, SCIENCE, AND THE SPACE BETWEEN

My roots are deep in Memphis soil, a city of soul and stories. Harper Brasfield's journey is a love letter to this place, its grit and grace a canvas for our tale.

The heart of this novel beats with the rhythm of CRISPR's promise and peril. It's a reflection of my fascination with the threads of destiny we might one day weave or unravel with our own hands.

A NOTE ON IMAGINATION AND REALITY

As you wander through these pages, you'll find traces of the Memphis I call home and leaps into the realms of what could be. If you come across a high-speed rail to DC, know it's a flight of fancy my mother wishes into existence. Any creative liberties taken are mine alone—a blend of memory, hope, and the whims of storytelling.

ENGAGING WITH THE FUTURE

My hope is that this story stirs your curiosity about the science that shapes our tomorrow and the ethical landscapes we navigate. It's an invitation to ponder, to dream, and to question.

CONNECT WITH ME

This conversation doesn't end here. Find me at:

MONICACHASE.COM

and join the dialogue on social media (@themonicachase).
Your insights, your laughter, and your dreams
are the sparks that keep the story alive.

www.ingramcontent.com/pod-product-compliance
Lightning Source LLC
Chambersburg PA
CBHW061854310726
48972CB00004B/1026